GHOSTS & GAMBLERS

Enter the world of romantic intrigue from the Prince of Storytellers. E. Phillips Oppenheim published over 150 books in his lifetime, and here we present one of his very rare romantic thrillers from 1896, *The Modern Prometheus*, coupled with another collection of previously unreprinted stories and autobiographical pieces, including six stories featuring gentleman adventurer, Andrew Thesholm.

The Modern Prometheus is the story of two struggling artists, Francis and Marcia, thrown together by desperation and poverty in a Chelsea boardinghouse. After being forced to give up hope, Francis burns his manuscript, sells the last of his possessions and strikes out for the colonies. He cannot take Marcia and leaves her behind as he vows to find either riches or death. Ten years later, Francis returns as Sir Francis Kernham, fabulously wealthy and famous throughout England. He searches everywhere for Marcia, fearful of what she may have become, only to discover by chance that she is now Princess of Hohenmahn. Will they now find love and happiness together, or has time and truth forged bonds of a different sort?

The Reluctant Gambler gives us a new Oppenheim hero, the rakish and wealthy Andrew Tresholm. In these six never-before-reprinted stories, we see this curiously brave and moral adventurer mixing himself up in the problems of friends and acquaintances as he gambles on himself and others to overcome their personal tragedies.

We also offer 12 stories published in various newspapers from 1896 to 1916 but which have never before been collected into book format—stories of espionage, romance, adventure, and comedy—including a speech to his alma mater which rounds out the collection. All this plus editor Daniel Paul Morrison's latest, and certainly his most definitive, bibliography of the many and varied works of E. Phillips Oppenheim, an absolute boon to collectors.

E. PHILLIPS OPPENHEIM (1866 – 1946)

GHOSTS & GAMBLERS
The Further Uncollected Stories of E. Phillips Oppenheim

■ ■ ■

Includes THE MODERN PROMETHEUS

■ ■ ■

Introduction by Daniel Paul Morrison

Stark House Press • Eureka California

GHOSTS & GAMBLERS: THE FURTHER UNCOLLECTED STORIES
OF E. PHILLIPS OPPENHEIM

Published by Stark House Press
1315 H Street
Eureka, CA 95501, USA
griffinskye3@sbcglobal.net
www.starkhousepress.com

The Modern Prometheus originally published by Unwin, London, 1896, and by
Neely, New York, 1897. Various stories appeared originally in *Cosmopolitan,
The Sketch, Windsor Magazine, Boston Daily Globe, The Strand, Good Housekeeping,
Redbook* and *New York Times Book Review* (full credits at end of book).

"E. Phillips Oppenheim and the Love of Books in the Digital Age"
copyright © 2014 Daniel Paul Morrison.
Cover illustration by C. E. Brock.

ISBN: 1-933586-56-7
ISBN-13: 978-1-933586-56-4

Cover design and layout by Mark Shepard SHEPGRAPHICS.COM
Proofreading by Rick Ollerman

*The publisher would like to dedicate this labor of love to the memory of Gerry de la Ree,
the small press publisher and book dealer who first introduced us to the works of
E. Phillips Oppenheim in the 1960s.*

First Stark House Press Edition: July 2014

Table of Contents

For John Calvin Morrison, my favorite son.

E. Phillips Oppenheim and the Love of Books in the Digital Age

by Daniel Paul Morrison

The book in your hands is a labor of love.

You will love reading this collection of Oppenheim stories; tales of espionage, mystery, romance, and supernatural thrills.

I loved digging for these stories in the book stacks and microfilm reading rooms of big city libraries.

And the folks at Stark House Press love publishing forgotten gems of old school fiction.

Most likely, you're reading this book because you're a fan of genre fiction—mystery, fantasy, science fiction.

Stark House Press has carved a niche for itself in the publishing world, resurrecting worthwhile titles of neglected authors. They also bring to print fresh voices that continue old school traditions.

And all their work is a labor of love—no one's getting rich.

But here's the tough question: Is there room for the love of books in this digital age? Is there a place for a specialty publisher like Stark House Press lovingly turning out, hand-picked, hand-crafted gems?

The digital age has changed the world of books: how we read them, how we buy them, and how we make them.

One-quarter of new books sold last year were e-books. While paper and ink will never disappear completely, more and more books are nothing but ones and zeros in digital code.

Nearly half of all new books sold last year were sold online. The brick-and-mortar store that offers a chance to browse and be surprised is an endangered breed. And the neighborhood used bookstore, where out-of-print authors like E. Phillips Oppenheim lurk, is fading fast.

Finally, the digital revolution also is changing how books are created. Google Books vacuums up public-domain titles by the thousands. They feed the books into an optical character recognition (OCR) gizmo that transforms scanned pages into readable and searchable text.

And bunches of companies will sell you one-off prints of those scanned books. Or they will sell you an e-book based on those scans. Go to Amazon or Abebooks and search for E. Phillips Oppenheim. You'll be deluged by print-on-demand and e-books titles—all of them garbage.

Here's the ugly truth about machine-made books and e-books: they are jam-packed with typographical errors. An eight-percent OCR error rate is considered good these days. Some of the errors, you can figure out. But lots of times, you have no clue what the original text might have said. And the worst case is when you don't even know that there is an error, because the wrong reading still makes sense in normal English; it's just not what the author wrote.

Think of it: would you buy a book from a legitimate publisher that has dozens of errors on every page? That's exactly what these OCR reprint publishers are cranking out these days. And it's robbery, if you ask me. They're robbing readers of their hard-earned money and they're robbing authors of an honest presentation of their original work.

That's where the book in your hand is different.

This book began with me haunting libraries in Philadelphia and New York City, looking for old Oppenheim stories that never made it into book form. By the 1920s, Oppenheim had published hundreds of stories in magazines and newspapers. Most were collected into books during his life. But a few gems got lost in the shuffle.

As I turned up a lost Oppenheim yarn in a newspaper like *The Boston Daily Globe* or a popular monthly like *Windsor Magazine,* I took a clean photocopy of the story for my files. Sometimes the original publication was not so clear—keep in mind we're dealing with century-old newspapers and magazines—and then I would have to find a second copy, just to double check.

After I gathered a large group of stories, I culled the duds and began to transcribe the winners by hand—no OCR used to make this book—every word typed in, checked and double-checked against the originals.

What you're holding is a hand-made book. Like I said, it's a labor of love. And I hope you love what you read.

What's Inside?

So here's a rundown on what's inside.

The Modern Prometheus. This volume opens with the hard-to-find novella by Oppenheim, *The Modern Prometheus.* It's a rare book—second only to *The Amazing Judgment.*

While this novella strikes many familiar Oppenheim themes—mistaken identity, romance, overcoming dismal poverty to win great wealth—what surprises me about this book is that it's really about sex.

Oppenheim loved to write about romance. Even his detective novels have plenty of romance. But he was always rather bashful in writing about sex. The hanky-panky happens off scene and nothing illicit is ever condoned.

But *The Modern Prometheus* is different. In this book, the key to the drama—in addition to the struggle for wealth and power—is a single act of illicit sex. And I'm not talking about a fleeting kiss on a balcony. I'm talking about a brazen rendezvous at a posh hotel. The main characters of this novella just rent a room and "do it," as we say. That seems tame to us these days but in 1898, when this work was published, such shenanigans would land you in jail.

In addition to the illicit sex, this work has a harder edge and a more cynical attitude than most of Oppenheim's later novels. Oppenheim was a wildly successful writer, in part, because he learned to give his readers what they wanted—diverting thrills nicely resolved in a happy ending.

But in *The Modern Prometheus,* we see Oppenheim in an earlier, rawer incarnation. In this story, the characters get what they are looking for, but when they get it, it doesn't look so pretty. Published when he was 30 years old, *The Modern Prometheus* reveals a young novelist in search of his mature voice.

The Reluctant Gambler. Andrew Tresholm is the protagonist in six terrific stories that seem like one-half of a would-be Oppenheim bestseller. Rakish, wealthy, brave and incongruously moral, Tresholm amuses himself by getting mixed up in other people's problems and doing them a good turn.

The Reluctant Gambler—the title's ours, not Oppenheim's—is an appealing collection of stories, not unlike Oppenheim's *Mr. Laxworthy's Adventures* or *The Amazing Partnership.* Oppenheim published 37 short story collections, most of which center on a single character or group of characters. Typically, these volumes had 10 or 12 stories and it seems like these stories about Andrew Tresholm were on their way to becoming another hardcover collection.

What prevented Oppenheim from finishing another six Tresholm stories I've never been able to find out. Whatever the case, these stories are among my favorites.

An Oppenheim Sampler. In the twenty-year period between 1896 and 1916, Oppenheim was busy establishing his reputation as a writer. Espionage, detection, adventure, mystery, romance, supernatural—Oppenheim wrote it all.

And here you'll find a dozen doozies.

"Darton's Great Picture" and "The Reformation of Circe" are ambitious stories, both originally published with the fitting subtitle, "A Novel in a

Nutshell." Curiously, the characters in "Darton's Great Picture" show up again in "Darton's Successor," a story collected in *Those Other Days,* and "A Sprig of Heather," a story in *For the Queen.*

A pair of espionage stories, "The Little Grey Lady" and "The Two Ambassadors," pit the young Ronald Stourton, a junior Foreign Service officer, against his charming black-sheep uncle-in-law, a freelance spy and master of disguise.

Oppenheim sold lots of books to women, but early in his career, he also catered to men and boys. Three he-man action-adventure stories appear in this collection: "The Lord of Crersa," "One Shall be Taken," and "A Strange Conspiracy."

As he matured, Oppenheim's writing acquired a sense of humor. "The Girl from Manchester," "The Storming of Eve," "A Lesson for Mr. Cutts," and "And Mr. Baggs was only Twenty-Three!" are all romantic comedies with a dash of detection and adventure and a heap of social commentary.

Finally, "The Road to Liberty" takes up a theme often presented by Oppenheim: a poor, but noble continental girl rescued from difficult circumstances by a wealthy, adventuresome Brit. Love, for Oppenheim, is always the reward for noble deeds.

Autobiographical Pieces. In addition to his endless stream of fiction, Oppenheim wrote lots of nonfiction articles for both newspapers and magazines. "My Books and Myself" appeared in the *New York Times Book Review* and is a handy self-description of his writing methods circa 1922. His American publisher, Little, Brown, issued a reprint of the piece.

Oppenheim's "Address to the Boys of Wyggeston School" is a 1926 commencement speech given by the so-so scholar returned to his alma mater as a conquering hero in the literary game.

E. Phillips Oppenheim in the Digital Age

Literature is created by genius but it's transmitted and distributed by ever-changing technologies.

Oppenheim rose to public prominence during the golden age of popular, fiction-based magazines like *The Strand* and *Collier's.* These cheap entertainers showed up monthly or weekly on newsstands and in mailboxes, bringing the English-speaking world a steady diet of fresh stories.

Radio came along in the 1920s and began to compete with magazines as the go-to source for entertaining fiction. In response, British paperback Oppenheim books carried the slogan, "Switch off the wireless—it's an Oppenheim!"

Movies also appeared in the 1920s and offered fresh thrills each week. Oppenheim sent many of his stories to Hollywood, though he never wrote scripts himself. Oppenheim's 1920 novel, *The Great Impersonation,* made it to the big screen three times in three decades.

And, of course, Oppenheim sold millions of books: hardcovers and paperbacks, short-story collections and novels. In the United States, Little, Brown was his publisher for decades, while in the United Kingdom, Hodder and Stoughton was his mainstay.

We now live in the digital age and it remains to be seen how Oppenheim fares during these times. Not a single Oppenheim title is still in print by the original publishers, but many of his early works are passing into the public domain and are enjoying a second life.

Will the careless use of OCR technology lead to a sloppy degrading of Oppenheim's work? Or will specialty publishers like Stark House Press— people who are in the business because they love the stories—continue to care for and curate Oppenheim's literary legacy?

The answer is in your hands.

Willow Grove, Pennsylvania
October 2013

THE MODERN PROMETHEUS

Chapter 1

A man, stalwart, tall, distinguished, slowly descended the steps of the Metropole Hotel, and turned his face westward. The doorkeeper, who had bowed low at his exit, raised his whistle to his lips.

"Hansom, sir?"

The man shook his head.

"No, thanks! I prefer to walk!" he said, shortly.

His clothes were perfectly correct, and his carriage was commanding, but amongst Londoners it is always easy enough to mark the stranger. His cheeks were bronzed with the heat of a tropical sun, and his bushy black beard, carefully trimmed though it was, suggested at once the colonial. As he walked slowly up Northumberland Avenue, he glanced frequently around him. Once or twice he made a brief inquiry of a policeman. Yet he had the air of one who revisits a locality perfectly familiar to him at some time or other during his life.

The month was May, and the sky was blue, dotted here and there with fragments of fleecy broken clouds. The waters in the fountains at Trafalgar Square glittered like little specks of molten silver in the clear sunlight. The air was soft and warm. At every corner women were selling great bunches of yellow primroses and fragrant violets. One, more energetic than the rest, planted herself in his way, holding out a bunch of the purple blossoms so that their sweetness forced itself upon him.

"Sweet violets, sir? Only tuppence a bunch! 'Ave a bunch? 'Ave a buttonhole, sir?"

He stopped short and stood in the middle of the pavement while she fastened them deftly in the buttonhole of his immaculate frock coat. When she had finished he dropped something in her palm, at which she started, and, being by chance honest, called after him. He only waved his hand.

"It is quite right," he said. "I have not smelt English violets for ten years. You are welcome."

His eyebrows contracted slightly at her shrill volley of excited thanks, and he passed on a little more rapidly. The girl, with the instincts of her class, tested the little piece of gold between her white teeth. There was no doubt about it. It was perfectly good. She commenced to discuss her good fortune volubly with her fellow-sellers until a neighbouring policeman separated and moved them on.

Meanwhile the man to whom the perfume of English violets had seemed so sweet a thing passed along Pall Mall and into Piccadilly. Here his leisurely walk became a saunter. Everything he saw seemed to interest him. He looked into the faces of the passers-by as though they were the faces of a people from whom he had drifted apart, and with whom he found it no ordinary pleasure to be once more in touch. The shops, too, attracted him, especially the art and picture shops, before every one of which he lingered. London was full—full of the keen, throbbing vitality of her best season, and the whirl and bustle of it all seemed to possess a distinct and curious fascination for him. He was evidently only an onlooker at present, yet in his strangeness there was no touch of gaucherie. He moved like a man accustomed to rule and to be obeyed. Even in the thoroughfare, whose pavements are pressed every day during certain halcyon months by the footsteps of the most distinguished-looking men in Europe, his presence attracted some attention. He had the air of being somebody. His face, with its clean-cut features, its firm mouth and dark bright eyes, was the face of a ruler. Even the deep bronze of his cheeks was, in its way, becoming. A good many people wondered who he was.

With perfect unconsciousness of sundry turned heads, he pursued his leisurely way, until he came to a standstill before the massive front of one of the great clubs. He asked a question of a passer-by, and slowly mounted the broad steps. The glass doors flew open before him. He came to a standstill upon the marble and mosaic tiles of a luxurious circular hall. An elderly man in quiet livery came forward in answer to his interrogative glance around. He produced a letter and a card from his pocket.

"Is the secretary of the club, Colonel Welland, in?" he inquired.

The steward shook his head.

"He is not in at present, sir. We expect him here about four o'clock today. Can I give him any message, sir?"

"You can give him this note and card. I will call again, perhaps this afternoon, or to-morrow."

He was turning away when the man glanced at the card. An instant change took place in his manner. Before he had been quietly civil, now he was deeply respectful. The alteration was subtle but significant.

"I beg your pardon, sir. I have special instructions about you in case you should arrive during Colonel Welland's absence. He desired me to say that he would have called upon you, but you did not mention your hotel."

"It is of no consequence."

"Colonel Welland sent me out to make inquiries, sir, but I could not find you. You are a visiting member here for as long as you choose, sir. Will you allow me to show you over the club?"

The visitor took off his hat.

"I am very much obliged to Colonel Welland," he remarked. "I may as well have some lunch here then. I won't trouble you to show me over just now. Another time will do."

"Just as you please, sir," the steward answered. "The luncheon room is this way, if you will be so good as to follow me, sir."

The steward opened a door leading into a room of magnificent proportions and appointments, where several men were lunching at small tables. If he had expected the newcomer to be impressed, he was disappointed. He glanced around and made his way to a round table near a window.

"By the by, are there any letters for me?" he inquired of the steward, who still lingered by his side.

The man smiled.

"I believe so, sir," he answered, and disappeared. In a few minutes he was back again, staggering beneath the weight of a huge paper-basket. The newcomer laid down his knife and fork and looked at its contents aghast.

"Do you mean to say that all that lot is for me?" he exclaimed, with knitted brows. "There must be some mistake."

The steward bowed and thought not.

"There is another basket which holds as many again, sir," he announced, with the ghost of a polite smile still upon his lips. "I could not have carried it in myself. The bottom would have come out."

The man sat back in his chair with his hands stuck in his waistcoat pocket and looked up from the basket to the steward's face. Evidently he was speaking the truth, and as to this mass of correspondence being intended for him, there could be no doubt about it. Francis Kernham, Esq., was staring up at him from a hundred different envelopes in a hundred different handwritings—envelopes square and long, perfumed and commercial, type-written, and traced in the most delicate of feminine characters. A good many men and women in very different stations of life seemed to have something to say to Mr. Francis Kernham.

"I do not understand it," he said, simply. "I do not know half a dozen people in London."

The man smiled openly.

"Possibly not, sir; but all London knows you, sir," he remarked.

"Ridiculous! And how the deuce did all London know that I was coming to the Wanderer's Club?" the newcomer protested.

"Three or four of the society papers have announced the fact, sir," the man answered. "It was in the *World* last week. The next morning we had over a hundred letters for you. You will find that quite half of them are begging letters and circulars, sir."

"And the remainder?"

"The remainder are probably invitations, sir."

"But I told you just now that I did not know any one in London."

The steward smiled again, a gentle, deprecating smile.

"That makes no difference at all, sir. You are famous. If you have only just arrived, perhaps you have not seen the papers lately. There has been a good deal written about you, sir, the last few days."

Mr. Francis Kernham leaned forward and recommenced his lunch. Evidently this was a phase of his home-coming which presented itself to him now for the first time.

"Take them away," he said, shortly; "they interfere with my appetite. I will arrange for a secretary, or something."

The steward withdrew with his burden, and the man who had become famous continued his lunch. It was a meal almost severely simple, but with his cheese he ordered a pint of the best Burgundy upon the wine list. He remained for some time sipping it and gazing meditatively out of the window. At last he rose, paid his bill, and walked slowly out into the streets again.

Almost opposite was Hyde Park Corner, already alive with a brilliant stream of the fashionable world. But he turned away from the park, and set his face southwards. This time he asked no questions. He found his way as though by instinct. A change had come over him. He walked no longer as a stranger, sauntering along the highways of a great city, fairly curious, master of his time, indifferent as to his destination. The alertness of his wandering gaze, and the good-humoured smile upon his curving lips, had alike vanished. He walked now like a man dwelling in the past, yet having a fixed destination to which his feet bore him only too slowly. The lines of his face had relaxed. His soft, bright eyes had become the eyes of a dreamer. He had turned the key of a chamber in his thoughts across the portals of which the dust of many years lay thick and undisturbed. A storehouse of old memories had escaped from long confinement; they were thronging around him, they glided along by his side through the crowded streets, they whispered in his ear, caught at his heartstrings, and floated before his eyes. Ah, well! the hand of repression had lain heavy upon him all these years. It was lifted now. Of his own free will he was yielding himself up a willing victim to memories poignant enough still and touched with an inimitable sadness. Yet this was one of the luxuries which he had promised himself at the very crown of his success.

He came to a standstill before a dark, gloomy house in the purlieus of Chelsea. His feet had led him there unerringly, without hesitation or uncertainty. He looked up at the windows. The old legend was still on hand, "Apartments to let." He stretched out his hand and rang the bell.

A girl with a pale sallow face and untidy gown answered it. He looked at her searchingly. She, at any rate, was not familiar.

"Does Mrs. Seely live here still?" he asked.

The girl shook her head.

"Never heard of her. Is she a lodger?"

"She used to let the apartments here," he answered. "It was a long time ago. I daresay that she has left now."

"I guess so," the girl answered. "We've lived here seven years. Our name's Patchett. Did you wish for apartments?" she asked, doubtfully. His appearance was not quite the appearance of a man seeking lodgings in the back streets of Chelsea.

"If you have the room I want, I might take it—for a short time," he answered.

Her face brightened.

"The first floor is all to let," she said briskly. "Won't you step in and look at it?"

He accepted her invitation, and the door was closed. But he did not follower her into the front room.

"It is a room upstairs that I wanted to see," he explained.

"Upstairs! The best rooms are all down here."

"It is not the best rooms I want," he answered. "It is a small room upon the fourth floor."

The girl's face fell.

"The fourth floor! Why there isn't a room fit for you there, sir!" she exclaimed. "They're mostly attics—tiny little holes!"

"I know that they are not large," he persisted; "but there is a room there which I am particularly anxious to take if it is unoccupied. I can show it to you if you will come upstairs with me. I am not particular about the price of it. You can charge me as much for it as the first floor, if you like!" he added, noticing her fallen face.

She seemed puzzled, but became more cheerful.

"Oh, they're mostly empty," she said, leading the way to the stairs. "Letting rooms is just starvation now. There's all the cheap new flats to stop you from letting your best rooms, and the others don't pay anyhow. I can't see what folks see in flats," she added, disconsolately. "I think they're beastly!"

He followed her in silence. He was sound in wind and limb, but his heart was beating fast when they reached the fourth floor. He led the way to a room at the end of the passage, and touched the handle.

"This is the one," he said. "Is it empty?"

She nodded, and threw open the door.

"You can have it for fifteen shillings a week," she declared, boldly trebling the price.

He pressed some money into her hand.

"I will take it for a month," he said. "Here is the rent in advance. I will go in and sit down if you will be so good as to leave me for a few minutes."

Three pounds! Her fingers closed upon the money. What a stroke of luck! A dull, brick-red streak of colour stained her cheek. Some latent spirit of covetousness was awakened by the sight of the gold.

"There is no bed in the room, you know," she said, looking around. "That will be extra if we put one in."

"Thank you. I shall not sleep here," he answered.

She left him then. He crossed the threshold and shut the door after her. Standing quite motionless just inside the room he listened to her retreating footsteps. When they had died away, when he was sure that he was absolutely alone, he looked around him.

It was the same room. A particular crack in the falling paper running zigzag to the panel, a risen rafter in the uneven floor, a hole in the threadbare carpet where a cinder had dropped—some one of these things brought back, with a vividness which thrilled him through and through, the whole procession of heart-shattering memories. He sank into the hard horsehair easy-chair and sat there with drooped head, a figure curiously at variance with his shabby surroundings. The little drama of years ago rose up before his eyes. A bridge was thrown over to the past. The life-labours of the man seemed but as the dreaming of a dream.

Chapter 2

She was leaning back in that self-same chair, her eyes half closed, and her shabby little jacket thrown back. Her hat lay on the table where she had thrown it, while her ringless hands met clasped together behind her head in a tumbled mass of silky black hair. Neither the pallor of her cheeks nor the frowning contractions of her eyebrows, or the dejection of her posture, seemed to have any power to detract from a beauty at once singular and comprehensive. Something cruelly like starvation had laid its hand upon her wan features. Her cheeks were a trifle hollow. Her eyes were unnaturally bright and large. Her lips lacked the fresh ruddiness of youth. Yet of her beauty there could be no doubt.

A man came to her out of the shadows of the ill-lit room—a young man with dark fiery eyes and pale-lined forehead. She looked up at him listlessly.

"I did not hear you come in," she remarked.

"I was here waiting for you," he answered. "I have been here for an hour."

"If you have been doing nothing for so long you might have come and met me."

"I wish I had. You are tired tonight, Marcia. It is a horrid walk from the Strand."

"Everything is horrid. Life is horrid. Death, I suppose, would be horrid too, or I would try it," she murmured wearily.

He came over to her and she saw his face more clearly in the dim candlelight. There were black lines under his eyes. If he had been a woman you would have said that he had been weeping. She looked at him and sat up in her chair.

"You have heard from those people?"

He clenched his teeth, but a little moan found its way out.

"Ay, it is there, you see."

He pointed to a brown paper parcel lying in the distant corner upon the floor. Her dim eyes followed his shaking finger.

"There lies the letter." He pointed to a pile of white ashes upon the grate. "It was like all the rest. Damn them!"

She nodded softly. Her eyes, as they rested upon him, spoke of pity. They spoke, too, of other things. An inscrutable look had come into her face.

He commenced to walk restlessly up and down the narrow confines of the room. His eyebrows were drawn close together. He seemed to be interested in the pattern of the threadbare carpet.

"It came back soon after you left," he began. "Since then I have been thinking—I have been thinking many things."

"Yes," she murmured. "Tell me about them."

"I have been a dreamer," he said, slowly, "and my dreaming has been the dreaming of a fool. I have been following the old will-o'-the-wisp, like the veriest yokel who ever came up from the provinces to pick up gold in the streets of London. I have dreamed of fame and honour, of winning a share of the beautiful things of the world, of turning my back for ever upon the misery of these days—the grinding, sordid misery of empty pockets and an aching heart. And it has been all a fool's dream."

"Not quite that," she sighed. "You have done a little. You have had some encouragement. You have had promises."

He stopped and faced her now. A spot of colour flared in his sunken cheeks. His eyes were on fire.

"It has been a fool's dream," he repeated, fiercely. "I have wasted my days and my nights. I have spent the labour of my hands and the labour of my brain in vain. I have promises," he cried, a strain of infinite bitterness rising into his words. "What then? What do they mean? Years of strenuous toil, of semi-starvation, of physical suffering, of mental anguish, and then—what then? A place amongst the third-rate scribblers of the day, perhaps a provincial editorship, a villa at Tooting, a migration from the attics of starvation to the suburbanism of genteel poverty. Not for me! A pest upon such promises. If the world can pay me no better for my work than that, it can go to—the flames."

He stooped and flung the brown paper parcel onto the smouldering fire. She half rose as though to check him, but he snatched up the poker and held the package down until the curling flames arose from underneath it and around. A red glow lit up his stooping face. Decidedly he was very handsome. For the first time she saw in his features a suggestion of that subtlest and hardest to define of all the qualities which make men dear to women—power. She sighed and smoothed her ruffled hair.

He stood up only when the manuscript had become a mass of smouldering grey ashes. It seemed to himself that he was holding himself more upright. There was a new glow in his eyes, a new curl to his lips. The white ashes, which a draught of wind from down the chimney sent floating into the room, were like the disintegrated atoms of his old life. Henceforth they marked an era to him.

"Do you mean—that you will write—no more?" she asked, half fearfully.

"No more!" he answered, firmly, and to her listening ears there was more of triumph than regret in his tone. "I have wasted two years of my life. To-night I start afresh. To-night, Marcia—to-night, we must say—farewell!"

It was like the loosening of an anchor to her. She was sad, unaccountably sad.

"What are you going to do?" she whispered.

He laughed.

"Do! I am going to join the vulgar hustling throng of those who rule the world—I am going to seek and find gold! Oh, it is all very well to rail at wealth, and the barbarisms of wealth, to write philosophy in a sumptuous library with a golden pen, to preach religion in a lawn surplice, to prate of the ethics of content with a well-filled bank-book in your pocket. It is all sham and humbug! There is only one philosophy and one religion, in this country at any rate, and that is *gold*. I must have it! I will have it!"

His eyes flashed fires at her through the semi-darkness. She listened to him, fascinated, with bated breath.

"I used to dream of art," he cried. "What can art give to a starving man? What can it do but look down from the skies, and mock at him? Grant that I am an artist, that I have a desire for, and a keen appreciation of, the beautiful. I am the more miserable for it. I am more miserable than the dullest clerk who bends his back over a city desk, and sees no further into life than the pages of his ledger. I have no money. I am forced to eat coarse food, and loathe it. The luxuries of clean service, of glass and flowers, and seemly dress are all beyond me. I must spend my days within these hideous walls, where everything I look at is unlovely and stultifying. What can art do for me but deepen my miseries? True, I can go to the National Gallery amongst the great pictures, and lose myself for a little while if I can find a corner where the British sightseer is not munching sandwiches, or the Kensington schoolgirls giggling—and what then? I must come back here! My little dream of beauty is over. The darkness is greater than ever. It is the same with books, the same with that fascinating scribbling." He pointed to the pulp of paper upon the fire. "A few hours' escape only makes return the more miserable. I have done with it! I am young! I am strong! I am passionate! I will taste life or die! I am not content to find happiness in dreams, or to borrow fleeting glimpses of it through other people's spectacles. And in the world there is but one royal road—wealth—which I have not but will have; and the capacity for life, which I have. I will fill my own cup, and my own hands shall hold it to my lips! I will do this or I will die!"

She leaned towards him, her hands clasped, her eyes bright. His excitement was infectious. A spark had thrilled her.

"It is true, what you say!" she cried. "Life without power is misery—misery deeper than ever for us who thirst for beautiful things. You will fight for wealth. You will join in the battle, and you will win! You are a man and you can do it. But what of me? I, too, loathe and shrink from poverty. I, too, desire to live. What of me? What can I do?"

He looked at her with a sudden intentness. Her's was a problem indeed—harder to solve than his, deeper and swept with many strange currents.

"You are prompt in solving your own fate," she cried. "Solve mine! I am a woman without friends, without any particular talent, until to-night a minor actress at a minor theatre, with no hope of advancement, perfectly conscious of my own limitations. I have been cursed with education, and nature has chosen to instil into me a desire for the beautiful. What am I to do with it? I am a woman and I have been delicately bred. I have all a woman's love of soft clothes, and fine linen, of dainty surroundings, of educated companionship, of freedom from the grosser cares of life! I have been earning twenty shillings a week, and living—here! To-night I am dismissed. Our play is a failure, and it has been withdrawn. Our manager is bankrupt. I do not know where to turn, even if I would, for another engagement. What can I do? What hope is there for me? You and I have drifted together here, and we have been friends for a little while. Give me your advice. Let me hear how my position sounds to some one else besides myself!"

She rose suddenly from her chair, and swept across the room to his side. He turned and looked at her. In the half-lights the outline of her superbly graceful figure was softened—its angularities were toned down, the suppleness remained. Even the shabbiness of her gown was invisible. Her pale cheeks only served to heighten the beauty of her soft, dark eyes. He looked out into the lamp-lit streets and away into the darkness.

"You are beautiful," he said, coldly.

She caught the restraint in his tone, and she was grateful for it. She laid her white, ringless fingers upon his arm. A quiver passed through his frame. She was so close to him that her warm breath fell upon his cheek.

"Yes, I have that," she answered, softly. "It is my one marketable commodity. It is the one key which could open the gate into the promised land. You have your sex and your strength—and I have my beauty. But, now tell me, how am I to use it? I am nearly twenty years old. I have been on the stage two or three years—quite sufficient to tell me that I am no use there! To-night has settled that finally. And yet—no one has offered—to marry me. There is no one who seems inclined to. I have been honoured with—other offers. There seem plenty of men who want a mistress—but not a wife. No! no! Don't interrupt me! You are a novelist, or rather you were until a few hours ago. Look upon this as simply a situation—a psychological problem. Here am I dowerless and poverty-stricken, save for two gifts alone—my beauty and my honour. Frankly I cannot live this life any longer. I am half starved now, and from to-night I shall be penniless. Now, what shall I do? Mind, I do not pretend to be a moral woman at all. It is true that I have lived for years alone, and that I have refused all offers. That has been simply a matter of self-respect. If a man came to-night, this moment, for whom I could care, I would go to him. My destiny has never given me the chance of choosing between right and wrong. I should not hesitate a moment. I should go to him without a single qualm. But to become the tool of one of those creatures who come with gold in their hands to tempt—oh, it is hideous!—vile! vile! vile! I should loathe myself. I should feel that I had sunk to their level, that I had become a beast. To think of it even—and I have thought of it—is a nightmare. Yet, what am I to do? I have never seen one man for whom I cared a straw. Perhaps I have not the gift of caring. Perhaps I shall never love any man. Then what am I to do?"

He kept his face turned from her. His voice trembled.

"The lives of such as you and I are hard to shape," he said. "You ask me a riddle. All that I can say must sound like mockery."

"I have been patient," she went on. "I have lived here"—she waved her hand around the room—"for three dreary years. Who can say that I have not been patient? I have waited until my heart is growing old, and sometimes I feel that if I do not escape from it, I must die! To-night, when I received my dismissal, I was glad. At any rate, the crisis had come. Francis"—he felt her hand tighten upon his arm. Unwillingly he suffered himself to be drawn a little closer to her—"Francis, will you take me with you? I care not how. I am not afraid of any hardship. If you are going into a new country—well, I can work. We can be good comrades. It will not be any hindrance to you. Save me, Francis! If you leave me here alone—my God! don't you see that I must—I must—"

He held out his hands. Her sentence died away.

"Marcia, I cannot!" he cried, vehemently. "I am going into a new world. I am going where you could not go. I am going to work as you could not work. For many years I shall not want to look into a woman's face. You are the only thing that I have to regret in life—but we must part. I am bound for a wild, rough country, where other men have carved their way into future by the strength of their arms and the power of their will. And I shall follow in their footsteps. I shall do the same. But it would be no land for you, Marcia."

Her warm cheeks touched his. Her arms were around his neck.

"I would work, Francis. Do not fear that I cannot work because my hands are soft and you have known me indolent."

He set his teeth, and almost roughly unyoked her arms.

"You would be a hindrance to me every moment," he cried, harshly. "Where I am going no woman could follow. If she did it would be death to the man who brought her—and worse than death to her. No, I must have no drawbacks. I am going to start life free. We must part!"

She left his side abruptly. He remained gazing out of the window. The dark clouds away westward were lightening with a faint lurid glow rising up from the centre of pleasure-seeking London. He watched it, fascinated. It was the one side of London he loved, of the joys he thirsted for. Wealth— wealth that was power, that could bring him freedom for ever from sordid cares and hideous surroundings. That was what he craved. That was what he would have; and behind him, in the shadow of the room, a woman sat gazing into the trembling fire, with sad, dull eyes, bidding farewell to the fragments of her past life; a tragic figure indeed: the type of those things at which men mock to-day and sorrow to-morrow. But he never glanced behind. What was passing in her bosom was hidden from him. Between them was a wall of darkness. He was young, and eager, and selfish; his foot planted firmly upon the threshold of his destiny, his strenuous eyes fixed upon the future. He was young, and eager, and selfish—and he was a man.

Chapter 3

The curtain had fallen. It was the end of the first scene in this little drama of reminiscence. The man rose from his uncomfortable seat and walked slowly around the room. At the blindless window he paused and gazed out into the gathering twilight with slow, lingering eyes. The past seemed suddenly to have been brought into marvellous proximity to the present. The effort of recollection had been complete. He could not believe that since that May evening, when he had stood on the same spot with swelling heart, a decade of years had fallen, lives had been lived and lost, others besides himself had measured will with ambition—some to fall, some, like him, to rise. In the grim, uncertain light, he almost fancied that those white arms were once again outstretched towards him, that once more the cry of her despair was in his ears. Often he had fancied that he could hear it, ringing across the grey ocean, throbbing through the dense forests which lay between him and the seaboard, wailing in the light winds which blew down the mountain-side. But in those days of enthralling work, when great schemes throve beneath his hands, and the destinies of a great new country seemed gradually to be gathered in under his control, they had never troubled him for long. Now it was different. That cry of his for wealth and power which had rang out so bitterly from within those shabby walls, had been answered a thousandfold. All and more than he had dreamed of had been accomplished. The world had listened to him. He stood in a position altogether unique and wonderful. And now, when the struggle was over, when the tension was relaxed and the pressure had fallen away, the romance of those early days was blossoming out afresh. A nightmare of conscience had suddenly laid hold of him. He looked back upon that night, and the joy of his triumphs paled. He had kept his word, he had won his battle. And she—

He tore himself from the room, and, putting the key in his pocket, walked slowly back to his hotel through the darkening streets. The men whom he passed on the way he regarded with indifference, but into every woman's face he glanced with a sort of wistful earnestness. Somewhere in the bosom of the great city she doubtless was, but where—how? He shrank from all such thoughts. Certain words of hers seemed fixed into his memory. Every now and then he thought of them, and shuddered.

Once or twice he wandered out of his way, and it was late when he reached his hotel. Dinner was already proceeding in the brilliantly-lit salon, and little groups of people, men in evening dress, and women in soft white opera cloaks, stood about in the hall sipping coffee and waiting for their carriages. He walked past them unnoticing, and took a letter from his bureau with his key. In the lift he tore it open. It was from the man on whom he had called earlier in the day.

"Wanderers' Club,
"Piccadilly,
"*May 7th.*

"Welcome to England, my dear Kernham. You were not expected until the 10th. London will be taken by surprise. Whatever engagements you may have, put them off, and dine here with me at eight o'clock. A very distinguished person is coming in later in hope of meeting you. Be sure that you do not fail!

"Yours,
"Mortimer Welland."

He threw the note on one side, and changed his clothes, assisted by a quiet, dark-faced servant, who had answered his ring. With his cloak upon his arm, he scribbled a few lines to Colonel Welland.

"Dear Colonel Welland,—I have to dine—with an old friend. It is an engagement of long standing. If I am not detained I will call upon you about twelve o'clock.
"Yours,
"Francis Kernham."

He addressed the note, and handed it to the servant. Then he walked slowly downstairs, and stood upon the steps.

"The Genoa Restaurant is still in existence, I suppose?" he said to the door-keeper.

"The Genoa, sir? Certainly," the man replied. "Shall I call you a hansom?"

Kernham buttoned his coat and lighted a cigarette. "No, thanks. It is not far. I don't care about driving."

He walked slowly through the streets, now thronged with men and women wending their way theatre-wards, and still he kept up that curious watch of his. Once or twice he half-stopped and glanced anxiously at a veiled face, or into eyes which sought his with significant readiness, and at such times a sharp pain shot to his heart, followed by a sense of inexpressible thankfulness. When he reached the restaurant he gave a little sigh of relief.

Apparently the Genoa still maintained its rank. Outside a little string of carriages were waiting, and directly he passed the portals his coat and hat were taken from him by a footman in knee breeches and powdered hair. He made his way to the famous oak dining-room, and stood for a moment looking in upon the brilliant scene. An attendant came up to him.

"I am afraid that you will have to wait a short time, sir," he said, "unless you care for one of the smaller dining-rooms. Every table here and on the balcony is engaged to-night."

"I ordered table No. 34 for to-night by wire from Southampton," Kernham answered. "My name is Kernham—Mr. Francis Kernham."

The man bowed low. "It is quite right, sir," he said. "This way, if you please."

It was a very familiar way, though he had only been in the room once before in his life. Kernham followed him to a distant corner, where, upon a small, round table, was a card bearing his name, and the magic word "Engaged." He sat down and drew a long breath.

No waiter came to him for a minute or two, and he had time to collect himself. In a wild country, where men carried often their lives in their hands, and no one could be sure of seeing the morrow's sun, he had been spoken of and written of as a man of iron nerve, of never-failing *sangfroid* and presence of mind. Yet from his corner he looked out upon the gay roomful of men and women with dimmed eyes, and a heart beating more tremulously than it had ever done in the presence of death, or when, between the hours of dawn and noon, working with torn shirt, and half-naked beneath a boiling sun, he had drawn from the earth, a spade in one hand and a revolver in the other, a great fortune. A sudden memory of that day, the crowd of envious, scowling faces, himself knee-deep in a trench of rocky sand, parted his lips as he glanced around him. It was odd to think that he was living in the same world. Rose-shaded electric lights were burning in dainty lamps on every table, flashing out from the dark oak walls upon the jewelled hair and white shoulders of beautiful women, shining upon the silver and glass, and upon the soft banks of perfumed flowers. The hum of pleasant conversation, varied with little trills of feminine laughter, filled the air. Waiters moved noiselessly over the thick Oriental carpet. There was no rattling of plates, no disturbing sounds; everything was noiseless, deft, perfect. It was just the same as he remembered it. There was no change. Ten years ago on a May evening he had looked out upon just such a scene as this, only the most beautiful woman in the room sat in that empty chair, with her dark eyes flashing unutterable things upon him over the scarlet flowers at her bosom, and a faint tinge of colour in her cheeks.

A waiter came to him, and he wrote out his dishes, choosing them with a mechanical effort of memory, and selecting his wine at random. They brought him his food, and he ate like the others, and drank. But she was there, his guest had come. He heard the soft swish of her skirts as she sank into her chair, her strange little laugh as their eyes met. He saw her cloak fall away from her white shoulders on to the back of the chair, and that marvellous colour steal into her cheeks as the wine, strange to both of them, glided through her veins, and the heat of the room increased. The sweet caress of her voice was in his ears. She looked at him and spoke.

Chapter 4

Her glass was raised to her lips. The wine was foaming to the rim.

"To our farewell, and your future," she murmured. "Drink with me, Francis."

"To the future, yes," he answered; "but to our farewell, no."

"Yet, to-night—we part—for ever."

He looked away from her, and swept an angry glance around the room.

"I could curse these people for their laughter and their happiness and their money," he said. "I am almost sorry we came. What a ghastly farce it is!"

She laughed at him gaily.

"Don't say that, Francis! It was a brilliant idea to spend our last night like this. Let us eat and drink and be merry, for to-morrow we die. Isn't it fascinating to think of? I would not be without the memory of to-night for anything in the world."

He filled his glass and drank, looking at her with growing admiration. She became conscious under his keen scrutiny.

"You mustn't look at me like that," she laughed. "Is there anything particularly wrong with my toilette. Of course my gown is very old-fashioned, but it was a good one once, and I have done my hair well, haven't I? You haven't paid me a single compliment, sir."

"You are the most beautiful woman here—the most beautiful in London," he declared. "Every one looks at you. You know it. You have tried to make yourself beautiful to-night. Was it to madden me, I wonder?"

She laughed softly. Her eyes spoke to him across the tiny table. He set his teeth.

"My beauty, you know, is to be my stock-in-trade."

He writhed in his chair under the sting of her calm words. His eyes were flashing dark lightning out upon the little groups of well-bred, *insouciant* men, and the gay, smiling women. What a mockery the festivity was! He looked back at her, and the ethical horror of this great, black gulf loomed at her very feet made his heart feel sick and his blood run cold.

"Not that!" he whispered. "Not that! God! I cannot bear to think of it."

She was suddenly grave. She bent towards him.

"Will you take me with you, then?"

"Marcia, how can I?" he answered hoarsely. "I have not enough money for our passages."

"You have yours, and I can sell enough for my own," she went on, eagerly. "Take me, Francis! Won't you save me?"

His moment of indecision had passed away. The thing was altogether out of the question. He shook his head doggedly.

"I must have a free hand when I get there, and I must go alone."

She shrugged her white shoulders, white as alabaster against that band of black velvet. Her sudden gravity was gone. The brilliant smile of a few minutes ago played once more upon her lips.

"It is settled, then," she said, lightly. "Don't look so tragical, my dear

Francis. I will not tease you any more. Let us keep to our compact. Let us forget that to-morrow exists. Nothing makes me want to be rich so much as cookery like this. The salad is perfect. I wonder how— Why, it is Lord Mallingford!"

She held out her fingers, and flashed a smile of welcome at the newcomer, a tall young man, who had been passing down the room. He dropped his eyeglass in surprise, and came to a standstill before her.

"Miss Goring, by all that is wonderful!" he exclaimed. "Why, I—I thought that you never came out," he added, with a glance at her companion and a shade of reproach in his tone.

"You mean because I would not come out with you," she remarked. "Ah well, my acquaintance with you was very slight, wasn't it, when you first asked me. Do you come here often?"

"Pretty well," he answered. "The supper they give you is awfully good, but it's just a little out of the way. I have never seen you here before."

"I have never been here before. Everything must have a beginning, you know, and an ending. This promises to be both in my case."

He moved on with a bow, and a careless glance at Francis Kernham. He recognized him at once as the good-looking boy who generally met Marcia at the stage door and took her home. Probably a brother or relation of some sort, he imagined. With Francis the recognition was mutual, and he was boiling with rage.

"Confounded ass!" he muttered under his teeth. "I wonder you could speak to him, Marcia, after the way you used to snub him coming out of the theatre. Didn't you tell me once that he had been rude to you, and you hated him?"

"In future," she said, "I shall hate all men. I shall probably have cause to."

He rose from his chair. The perspiration was standing out upon his forehead.

"Come out upon the balcony," he said. "This room is stifling. I can't breathe."

They strolled outside, and leaned against the stone parapet. The murmur of voices seemed suddenly to fade away into a far distant sound. The red tips of cigarettes burning like glowworms here and there upon the balcony alone reminded them that the solitude was peopled. A faint breeze was rustling in the pine-trees. As yet there was no moon, and the stars gave no light. She leaned over with her eyes fixed upon the river.

"It is the end, then," she said, softly, without looking at him. "It is all over."

He tried to answer her, but he could not. His throat was thick with sobs.

"Light a cigarette," she whispered. "You look too much in earnest. People will notice."

He obeyed her in silence. It was a relief to be doing something. He struck a match and smoked.

"Are you going back to Chelsea?" she asked.

He shook his head. "No. My things are all at Waterloo. I shall find a bed somewhere for the night. To-morrow I go to Southampton."

"They will think that we have left together," she remarked.

He stopped smoking, and looked at her. Her face was turned away. He could only see the outline of her delicate profile gleaming white through the darkness.

"Do you mean that you are not going there?" he asked.

There was a full minute's silence. A burst of laughter floated out from the room. A man seated close to them struck a match. By its fitful light Francis saw his face. It was Lord Mallingford, and he was watching them closely. Then she answered him.

"No, I am not going back."

"And—to-night?"

"I do not know. I have not decided. It is for fate to decide."

He trembled from head to foot, as though some one had struck him a blow in a vital part. He tried to look at her, but she kept her face averted. Another wave of distant laughter came floating out from the long dining-room. Then there was silence. He could hear his heart beat against his side.

"Marcia!"

She raised her eyes and looked into his. There was a scarlet flush upon her cheeks. She looked away almost immediately. The hand which played with the fastening of her cloak shook.

"Come," he whispered.

She followed him back into the room. He paid the bill, and walked out through a different entrance. They were in the hotel.

She stood beside a tall palm tree whilst he went into the office. People who passed by looked at her curiously. Her cloak and her dinner gown were simple and a little old-fashioned, and she had not a single jewel upon her person, but her beauty was paramount and extraordinary. The colour in her face kept coming and going. Her eyes were soft and brilliant. She held herself like a queen.

He came back to her and whispered in her ear.

"Tell me where to send for some of your things."

There was a writing-table in the centre of the marble hall. She moved towards it, and, taking up a pen, wrote a few lines with unfaltering hand. He passed them on to a commissionaire. For a moment they were alone.

"Marcia," he whispered, "you have no regret? You are perfectly sure?"

Her eyes dropped before his, but he caught their light for a moment, and he did not doubt.

"None. Why should I? Don't you know that I love you?"

He stepped across the hall and rang the bell for the lift.

□ □ □ □

There was a sudden commotion in the brilliantly lit room. A man who had been sitting alone at a small table had suddenly dropped his glass with a low, moaning cry. The wine in a little river was running across the table. The man was leaning back in his chair, as pale as death.

"Shall I fetch a doctor, sir?" whispered the waiter in his ear.

The man opened his eyes and set his teeth hard.

"I am not ill, only a little faint," he said. "Give me your arm. I want fresh air. I will get out on to the balcony."

He rose up slowly, and disappeared through the broad, open window, leaning upon the waiter's arm. Conversation was renewed at once. The incident was forgotten. A man had felt a little faint. That was all. And outside, on the balcony, the man was leaning over the parapet with half-closed eyes, and a pain at his heart like death. It was the end of the second scene in the little drama of his memory, the second and the last.

Chapter 5

"That," said a great painter to a girl who stood by his side, "is success— the heart and core of success. You and I, Miss Fanshawe, are only upon the borderland."

They were standing together in a recess looking out upon Lady Widnerton's drawing-room. She raised her eyes and looked steadily at the man towards whom her companion had inclined his head. She looked at him searchingly and with curiosity, for she knew by the world's report that the painter's words were true.

"It is the head of a conqueror," she said, thoughtfully. "I should like to paint him."

The man by her side smiled.

"That is how we all feel," he said; "but it is useless. He will not sit to any of us. He declined an offer from the President only the other day. I should not like to be sure, Miss Fanshawe—it is a good deal to say of any one now-a-days—but so far as my judgment goes, the man is honest. He is entirely without vanity."

"A man, and without vanity," she murmured. "Is that really possible?"

"I am almost convinced that it is so—in this case," he continued. "He has made a great name, and he carries his honours with dignity and with modesty. I daresay that you saw his baronetcy gazetted last night. I know for a fact that he refused a peerage, and was very averse to accepting a title of any sort."

His companion nodded. As a matter of fact she had not been listening. She had scarcely removed her eyes from the man whom they were discussing.

"He has an interesting face," she remarked, "especially for a successful man!"

"Why the addendum?" he asked. "Isn't success generally interesting?"
She shook her head.

"No! Success so often means content, and content is absolutely fatal. It is different with this man. He has one trait in common with all the men who have done great things since the days of Moses. There is a German word which nearly expresses it. I cannot transcribe it."

"You mean—"

"I mean that he is unhappy. He has been disappointed, or he is nursing a vain desire. Perhaps he has still greater ambitions than he has been able to gratify. One cannot tell. But he is not satisfied. He is very far from being contented. My sex will find him charming. He has just that air of languor freed from affectation which they love, only in his case I should say that it was heart languor—heart weariness."

"You know him so well that you must know him better," the painter remarked, smiling. "I will present him to you. We must be quick, though, or he will be gone. He never stays anywhere longer than a few minutes."

They crossed the room, and by an opportune turn came face to face with Kernham. A slanting ray of sunlight, which had somehow eluded the holland blinds and the closely drawn venetians, touched the girl's head as they came to a standstill, and a few loose threads of hair, escaped from underneath her hat, shone like threads of gold. Kernham, on whose lips the words of farewell were already framed, stopped short in his progress towards the door. He held out his hand to the painter with more than his usual cordiality.

"I did not know that you were here, Treganon," he said. "I was just going."

He glanced at the girl who stood between them. Treganon hastened to utter a few words of introduction. Kernham heard her name with more than ordinary interest.

"You are an artist too, Miss Fanshawe, are you not?" he asked, after the customary formalities had passed between them.

"I think that I may venture to call myself one—in a very small way," she answered, smiling.

He seemed more interested than the simple fact warranted. Following a half-unconscious movement of his, they detached themselves from the little group by which he had been surrounded, and moved a few steps apart. The slightly wearied air which they had both remarked upon some few moments ago had vanished. The lines of his mouth no longer drooped, his eyes were keen and bright.

"There is a picture—no, not a picture, a study—of a woman's head in the New Gallery," he said, turning to the girl. "It is signed A. H. Fanshawe. I wonder, is it yours?"

"I have several small things there," she replied, "and one is a head, I believe."

"Can you tell me, was it sketched from life?"

"No doubt."

"From a model?"

She considered for a moment or two.

"I really am not quite sure," she said. "I had several heads there a few weeks ago, and I transferred some to a smaller exhibition. I could tell, of course, if I saw it, but I am afraid that I did not give my instructions as to the transferring very clearly, and I could not say which have been removed. I am going to see for my own satisfaction though, and if you like I can let you know."

"You are very good indeed. I shall consider it a special favour," Kernham declared, warmly. "And will you forgive me for asking, is it for sale? If so, I should be happy to become a purchaser."

The girl laughed, her head thrown slightly back, and her white teeth gleaming for a moment. It was a musical little trill, but perfectly natural.

"For sale! Of course it is! Do you think that I am an amateur? I can assure you that I paint for my daily bread. If only the price were not in the gallery book, I should double it. We always do for millionaires, you know, and you are a millionaire, aren't you?"

"Whatever the price is, it is mine if you will do me the honour to sell it to me," he said. "The fact is that something in the pose, or in the face itself—I am not sure which—reminds me of some one whom I once knew, whose present whereabouts I am most anxious to discover."

A shade fell upon the girl's face. She felt unaccountably disappointed. After all, then, his interest in the picture was bounded by the fact that it reminded him of a woman he had known. She knew something of the lives of most of her models—certainly of the two or three who were old enough for him to have met before he left England. Was he like that? She looked at him and sighed. He had seemed different.

"I shall be passing Regent Street very shortly," she said. "I will look in then, and see if I can recall the study."

"We were going there now, were we not?" Mr. Treganon interposed.

"Why should not Sir Francis Kernham walk down with us? You can let him know on the spot then."

Kernham waited for her reply with a quiet deference which pleased her.

"Certainly, if you care to," she said, turning to him. "I can tell you the price of the picture at the same time."

"A most admirable suggestion," he declared.

Chapter 6

They passed from the somewhat faint atmosphere of green tea and roses and Bond Street perfumery, into the light, open space of the sunlit square. Kernham raised his hat for a moment, and drew a deep breath of relief.

"I wonder why we, any of us, go to afternoon receptions—especially on fine afternoons!" he exclaimed.

"Flaccidity of the moral caliber," Mr. Treganon suggested, "resulting in a want of firmness to stay away."

"A desire to see what other women are wearing," Miss Fanshawe remarked, looking down at her own perfectly made gown. "But as for you men, what you go for I cannot imagine."

"Neither can I," Kernham assented fervently.

They both laughed. No one cared about driving, so Kernham sent his carriage away. They walked together towards Regent Street, a noticeable trio; the artist with his white, curly hair and beard and grey frock coat, and Adela Fanshawe, tall, pale, distinguished, with large, earnest eyes and toilette elegant indeed, but stamped with an individuality which triumphed easily over fashion where it did not coalesce with it. Kernham, who walked by her side, was of another type, of another world. Yet, in a sense, he harmonised.

They talked on the way, almost continuously. Kernham, his old habit of self-restraint strong upon him, effectually concealed his impatience to reach their destination. She asked him a question or two concerning the country of which he had been in effect the ruler and organiser and he answered her readily. What he said was interesting; presently, stimulated by her sympathetic appreciation and unusual knowledge of the subject, it became fascinating. When they reached the New Gallery, one, if not two, of the little party had forgotten their destination. It was Treganon who brought them to a standstill. The girl drew a quick breath, and looked at the man.

"That was life!" she said, suddenly. "And to think that you were content to come to this, to the puppet show of the world."

His dark eyes flashed out upon her. Something in them seemed to have leaped into life at the sting of her words. Her eyes fell before his. The man was masterful.

"Ten years is a lifetime there," he said, quietly. "I have made more money than I can ever spend, more money than I know what to do with. I have made the way a little easier for those who follow me. Life may be tame here, but I need rest."

And the girl laughed. Once more, she stepped across the pavement, the sunlight smote her hair into red-gold and fire.

"There is life here too to be tasted," she said. "A psychologist would tell you that the human drama of Regent Street is deeper and more subtle than the drama of life and death on the banks of the Gold river."

"We fight for our lives there every day," he said, grimly.

"And we for our souls every hour, here," she answered, with a little quiver in her tone. "We are blocking the way. Let us go in."

Neither of them missed Treganon when he stopped to speak to some friends in the doorway. Kernham was suddenly conscious of a new interest in the girl who walked by his side. The environment of her fashionable attire, the faint perfume of her clothes, the drooping lace of her parasol, the faultless fit of her grey Suéde gloves, the soft, clinging folds of her gown, and the gentle swish of silk and lace as she moved—his consciousness of these things faded away. He looked into her eyes, at the curve of her lips, and like a flash he seemed to be brought once more into touch with that wilder, freer life from which he had so lately passed. Here was a woman who was no puppet, a woman of flesh and blood, a woman who was born to live. His heart gave a quick leap. The memory of that moment became an era to him. He was never altogether able to escape from it.

They had mounted to the gallery side by side, and he had led the way to the furthermost corner. A yard or two from the end he paused. A woman was standing before the little group of pictures towards which he was bound. The girl, who was a little in front, turned round. Her face had cleared. A smile was parting her lips.

"How odd!" she exclaimed. "That is the head you meant, is it not? I ought to have remembered. It is just a study for a portrait I was to have painted, and curiously enough my subject is here looking at it."

At the sound of her voice the woman turned round. She was tall and superbly handsome. Her toilette was perfect, and her carriage was the carriage of a queen. She smiled and greeted the girl with gentle patronage.

"Pray do not think me vain," she said. "I had no idea that the head was here until I looked for your things in the catalogue. I am only sorry now that I cannot stay in England for the rest. It is admirably flattering."

"I am glad you think so," Adela answered, quietly. "I have just sold it."

The woman frowned. "Sold it! I hope not," she said. "I see that you have ten guineas upon it. I am quite willing to give you fifty."

"And although I shall deeply regret depriving any one else of its possession, I am bound to remind Miss Fanshawe that I have the first offer, and I am willing to give a thousand," Kernham interposed, with a note of irritation in his voice.

The woman turned her head for the first time, and looked towards him. The man looked at the woman. Then his fingers locked like steel into the bannisters by his side. A light like the dawn broke across her face. She took half a step towards him and stopped. With a magnificent effort she stood quite still. The sound of his drawn breath passing between his clenched teeth choked back a cry. There was no one else in the corner. It was all over in a second, and it was between those three. The girl was bewildered, but in a sense she understood. She knew that a little drama of emotion and repression was played out before her eyes in those few seconds. The woman was as pale as death, and the man, whose bravery had become the household word of a nation, was white and shaken.

"You will let me present Sir Francis Kernham to you, Princess," Adela said, gravely. "Sir Francis Kernham—the Princess of Hohenmahn."

The man and the woman looked into each other's eyes. He read her bidding, and he was silent.

"The name has been made very familiar," she said, with a brilliant smile. "I think that I must be the last woman in London to bid you welcome home, Sir Francis. We have been on the Continent for a month or two—one always misses something."

He bowed over her outstretched hand. Adela turned away, ostensibly to find Mr. Treganon.

"Not now," she whispered. "Come to me to-morrow at four. You will find my house—Park Lane. Ah! Mr. Treganon, how do you do? I saw your sister in Rome, and she gave me a message for you. Will you see me to my carriage? and I will tell you all about it."

She swept past them with a gracious smile. The man and the girl were left alone.

"It is something like her, is it not?" the girl remarked, looking at the head. "Yes, I should say that the likeness is good."

"There is a certain resemblance," he admitted.

She looked after him.

"After all, I think that you will agree with me, some day," she said quietly. "There is plenty of dramatic interest in life, even in this humdrum capital. The puppet show is fair, and the men and women are wooden enough to look at. But if one stirs the water a little one finds out."

"If one stirs the water a little," he repeated, slowly. "Yes."

Chapter 7

"Life," the princess said, with her eyes fixed upon the green swaying branches of the trees in the park, "is a matter of volition. We have proved it."

"Yet, after all, it is a burdensome matter," the man answered. "We accomplish our desires, and then we are forced to pause. We have our will, and we do not know what to do with it."

Her dark eyes gleamed softly at him through the golden twilight.

"That is only a momentary feeling," she said, "an interlude. To a man who has conquered as you have conquered, all things are possible."

He looked into her face and sighed.

"Ten years ago," she continued, "I was a third-rate actress without an engagement, on the threshold of despair. You were penniless and disheartened. We lived in miserable lodging in a miserable street. There seemed to be no future for either of us. To-day you are one of the world's conquerors, you are more talked about than any man in England, you have wealth, rank, fame, and honour. And I— I—"

"You are a princess," he said, gravely.

"Yes, I am a princess," she repeated. "Since you came I have been wondering. Is it fancy, or are you disappointed to find me—like this?"

"It is not disappointment," he answered. "To find you as you are is a relief so great that I could not hope to make you understand how I feel about it. It is immeasurable. Yet you must remember that I am ignorant of many things."

"That is true. To you I must seem an adventuress. Do not shake your head. It is true. Yet tell me this. Which was the best? To have thrown myself on the mercy of the world, which has no mercy, to have sunk lower and lower and lower, to have given my body mortgage upon my soul—oh, I may as well say it—to have become the stained puppet of debauchery, or to have lied a little, and schemed a little for this? Which is the greater degradation, I wonder?"

"There can be no question about that," he declared. "I can answer it from my own sensations. Since I returned and found the money which I had sent untouched, my advertisement unanswered, I have suffered, God only knows what I have not suffered! Last night I felt that a load had passed away."

"You thought of me, then," she said, gently. "I am glad of that!"

"For ten years from the day I left to the day I landed again in England the only thoughts I had of any woman were of you. I want to be honest. Listen. When, that morning I awoke and found you gone without a word of farewell, with only that little strip of orange ribbon for a memory, I was glad. I was drunk with my desire to fight the world. Your flight seemed to me to relieve me of all responsibility concerning you. Later on it came back. Later on I suffered terribly. Whilst the fever of my struggle was upon me the thing remained in the background. Directly it was over it came back. When I returned to London the first visit I made was to that house in Chelsea. I stood in your old room, and the passion seemed born again. The past seemed to rise up, and my own black selfishness was there, plain, clear, ugly. From that moment until yesterday I have known no peace. And now—"

"And now?" she repeated, softly.

"I feel as though the cloud had passed away."

"Tell me," she said, "is that all you feel?"

He looked out of the high window across the darkening park. The perfume of spring flowers floated into the room from the heavily laden boxes. He was conscious that her eyes were following him.

"What am I to say to you?" he answered in a low tone. "I came home with the feeling that you belonged to me, that your future was my future, and my fortune yours. But all that is changed. You do not need my help. You are not free."

"It may alter events," she said, calmly. "It can not alter sensations. Do you want me to think that it was a sense of responsibility only which troubled you, that for me—the woman—you cared no longer. There was a time when you loved me, surely?"

"I do not understand," he said. "Would you have me love you still?"

"There was never a woman in the world," she murmured, "who parted with a man's love without regret."

He turned towards her, so close that a wave of her silky hair touched his cheek, filling him with half-forgotten memories. He took her hand. She did not draw it away. Her eyes were soft and dim.

"Do you mean that I am to claim you even now?" he said, softly. "I want to do what is right between you and me. In the sight of God you belong to me, and to no other man. But there is your husband. What of him?"

She withdrew her hand. The quiver upon her lips had ceased; her face was clouded. Instinctively he felt that he had blundered.

"You are right to remind me of him," she said, quietly. "So far as he is concerned, this is the position. When he pressed me to marry him, I told him—of you. I told him the exact truth, but I added a lie. I said that you were dead. And, knowing all, but believing that you were dead, he still persisted, and I married him."

"And if he knew that I was alive?"

"He would probably insist on a separation," she said, coolly. "He is not so much in love with me as he was. There is a dancing girl at one of the halls—I forget her name—but they say that he has taken her to Paris. It is very likely. He is old enough and foolish enough."

Kernham was silent for a moment or two.

"I feel like a stranger in a strange world," he said, in a low tone. "It seems to me that there have been many changes here during the ten years of my exile."

"It is true," she answered. "There is a little less hypocrisy and a little more freedom. Women are not quite the slaves they were. It is bad enough as it is!"

"Marriage, I presume, is still in vogue?" he inquired with bland satire.

"Marriage is an incident," she answered. "Love alone makes epochs, and of love there is very little left in the world. You come from your great new country, almost a stranger, into the shallows and whirlpools of our more complex life. I wonder how it seems to you. I wonder—"

A carriage laden with luggage drew up below. A man descended and entered the house. The princess leaned forward, and her face darkened. Kernham, who watched it, was troubled. She was looking downwards with curling lip.

"It is the prince—my husband," she remarked. "He is home several days earlier than I expected. Probably Suzette—I think it is Suzette—was not amiable. You will have the opportunity of making his acquaintance. In small matters he is most punctilious. He will pay his respects to me before he goes to his room."

Kernham half rose. "Would you rather I went away?" he suggested.

She motioned him back again.

"By no means. Sooner or later you would have to meet him. Much better now."

There was a knock at the door. A footman entered.

"His Highness the Prince has returned," he announced, bowing. "Is your Highness receiving?"

She half closed her eyes.

"Certainly."

The prince followed close behind. Kernham rose from his chair as he approached. The princess languidly held out her hand, but scarcely turned her head.

"Back again already?" she remarked. "Was Paris dull?"

He took her hand and held it to his lips. He was short of stature, grey, and smooth-shaven. For the rest there was little to be seen of him. From head to foot he was enveloped in a huge fur coat.

"Paris," he said, bowing over her hand, "is never dull. I, on the contrary, am never anything else, when—"

"When you are not with me, of course," she concluded abruptly. "How charmingly you say those things! Don't you see that I am not alone? Let me present you to my husband, Sir Francis. Maurice, this is Sir Francis Kernham—the Prince of Hohenmahn."

The two men bowed.

"My wife is fortunate in having made the acquaintance of so distinguished a man," the prince remarked with cold cordiality. "One hears much of Sir Francis Kernham nowadays. Are you home for long?"

"For good, I hope," Kernham answered. "I have no present intention of going back again. My work is over."

The prince bowed again as he turned on his heel.

"In that case I trust to have the pleasure of seeing more of you, Sir Francis," he remarked. "Are you dining at home to-day?" he added, turning to the princess.

"I have not the least idea," she answered. "Let your man ask Celeste. She knows. I am sure I do not."

"I will inquire," the prince said. "If you are not I can easily go to my club."

The door was closed again. They were alone.

"I was going to ask you to stay and dine with me whether I had any engagement or not," she said. "Perhaps it is better not. Perhaps you would not have thought it discreet?"

He stood up and looked down at her. There was a very stern look in his face.

"I have not deserved that," he said. "I do not understand you. You have talked to me in riddles. You have shown me an enigma, and you have withheld the key. Forgive me if I am blunt. As you say, life and morals have become a little complex here. I am not in touch with either. Listen. You have married that man. In a sense you have given yourself to him. Yet you belonged to me first. Who has the better claim to you—your husband or I? Choose for yourself, and for your own happiness. If you are content to stay with him—well, stay, and I will remain the most devoted of your friends. If you are not content to stay with him, put on your things, and come away with me now—this moment. I will take you to whatever country of the world you like. As for laws, I can buy them. I will buy you your divorce if you care for it. I cannot make you a princess, but anything else that the world has to offer I can give you. Will you come?"

She leaned back in her chair and laughed—a slow, rippling laugh.

"Oh, you are delightful!" she exclaimed. "This is the sort of wooing women love. Only persevere and you will be adored. Now, go away, please."

"Then you do not choose to come?" he persisted, unmoved. "You choose to stay! You consider yourself bound!"

"To no man on earth," she replied quickly. "Now you must please go away. Come and see me to-morrow—no, not to-morrow. I shall be away. Come on Friday. I may have something to say to you then."

He held her white fingers for a moment; she offered him the hand which the prince had not touched, and he looked into her eyes. After all she was not mocking him. A tear was trembling on her eyelid. She brushed it away proudly.

"Whatever you decide I—shall be content," he said simply.

She walked slowly to her room and locked the door. In an hour she opened it to her maid. Her cheeks were flushed, her eyeballs burned, her crumpled hair fell about her forehead. But what had passed in that hour she alone knew.

Chapter 8

She was leaning from an open window looking across a wilderness of housetops. The street below was uninspiring and dreary; opposite were the mews from a row of larger houses; away beyond slate roofs and chimney tops of every conceivable shape and pattern. But the girl was high up, on the sixth story of a block of small flats, and bounding the wilderness of suburbanism. She could catch faint glimpses of the spring sunshine upon the green trees of the park, melting away in the distance to a canopy of soft blue sky. So she leaned there, watching with half-closed eyes and listless manner. The light was good and there was plenty for her to do. Only the will was wanting. She leaned out of the window and watched the sunshine.

"Adela, come back to your work!" a shrill voice cried from the interior of the room. "You are unsettling when you moon about, and gaze, and dream, in the daytime too with such a light. Come and work before I too am made lazy!"

Adela turned from the window and walked slowly back to her easel, but she did not take up her brush. The girl who had addressed her, dark, keen-eyed, untidy, stopped painting and watched her for a moment or two unnoticed.

"Adela," she said, in a softened tone, "what is the matter with you these last few days? You are distrait. You do no work. Are you planning a new picture, or are you not well, dear?"

Adela took up her brush and yawned.

"I am well, but lazy, little one!" she declared. "A trifle low-spirited, perhaps. You see the conception of my work is finished now. It is all execution, mostly mechanical, and it becomes a little monotonous. Everything is monotonous. I wonder that any one lives long enough to do anything. It really does not seem worth while!"

The other girl looked across at her with wide-open eyes.

"Pshaw! what rubbish you do talk!" she exclaimed. "This is the result of going out into fashionable society, I suppose. And you are a worker, too! I should be ashamed to talk such vapid twaddle. Fancy if the men and women who have done great things in the world had encouraged such morbidness—your hero Kernham, for instance!"

Adela looked up quickly. There was a faint flush on her pale cheeks.

"My hero!" she repeated, sharply. "What do you mean, child? He is nothing to me!"

The keen black eyes sought hers and fixed them. Adela commenced to work again. The other girl leaned back upon her stool.

"Well, I never!" she exclaimed. "You are cranky to-day. I've called him your hero heaps of times, and you haven't stopped me. Haven't you read about him in the papers, and praised him and compared him with all these town men who saunter through life yawning and making vapid epigrams? Why, I was beginning to get almost tired of him."

"Oh, he is different, of course," Adela admitted, without looking up. "He may be a hero. I daresay he is. Only don't call him my hero."

The other girl smiled. The corners of her mouth twitched maliciously.

"Oh, very well. By the by, I was going to ask you. You have been out so much lately. I wonder if you have met him?"

Adela bent a little closer over her work.

"Yes," she said, indifferently. "I met him at Lady Widnerton's a fortnight ago. Mr. Treganon introduced me. He has bought my head at the New Gallery, I believe. Since you seem so curious about him," Adela continued, painting steadily on without change of countenance, "you may be interested to know that I saw him yesterday at the Clawsons', Tuesday at the Montagues', Monday at the New Arts Club, Friday in the park, and—oh, a few more times."

The girl laid down her brush, and her lips gathered themselves slowly together. It was not ladylike, but she certainly whistled.

"And you never told me one word!" she exclaimed. "Are you disappointed in him, then?"

Adela threw down her brush.

"Oh, don't tease me, child!" she cried. "Don't you see that I am in a vile temper? And don't ask me any more questions about Sir Francis Kernham. He is not a nice man. I do not want to see him, or hear him spoken of again! I want—oh, God! what do I want?"

She stood up in the middle of the room, her arms raised, her head thrown back. Her plain black gown buttoned close up to the throat, showed every line of her slim but perfectly graceful figure. Her hair, bronze and copper-coloured in the shadows, waved around her face and forehead like dull gold. Her eyes were suddenly flashing, her lips parted, her delicate nostrils quivering. The other girl, being an artist, forgot for a moment to wonder. She looked at her in admiration.

"I cannot tell, Adela," she said. "You have so much. You have fame. The critics are talking about you. You sell your pictures. The future is all bright before you. I cannot tell what it is that you do want!"

"Nor I, nor any one!" Adela cried with a sudden passionate outburst. "Only I know that I hate everything! My pictures sell, you say; the critics are talking of me. Well, that is good. Painting is good, but it is not life. Art is great, but it is not life. You and I who spend our days painting a little, walking a little, visiting and drinking tea—good God! we do not live. We do not know what life is. There are women whom anything seems to content. I am not one of them. I do not know what life is, but it is not this; it is not a little mild fame; it is not made or marred by a critic's word; it is not a succession of tea-parties blended with the occasional dissipation of talking to a young man with a turn-down collar and a green tic. Oh! I am so sick of it all—sick to death of our humdrum spinsterhood. I do not know what life is, but I want it—I want it!"

The other girl sighed. "Is it any man in particular?" she asked, quietly.

Adela walked to the window and back again.

"Oh, I don't care!" she cried, recklessly. "You won't make me simper and blush. Why shouldn't we be honest sometimes? I suppose I do want to care for some one. I daresay every girl feels the same now and then, if only she had the pluck to say so. I used not to. You know that. I used to talk a lot of rubbish at Girton about a woman's career, and her independence, and all the rest of it. It's a pack of lies! Woman has no career—alone. The world isn't made for her. She isn't made for the world. To talk of a girl's career may do for mawkish schoolgirls and ignorant children. A woman finds out that there is something else. This isn't life. I want to live, to take deep draughts of life, to feel it bubbling in my veins and burning in my heart. I have passion, I have emotion. I am weary of having them stirred at second hand by Bernhardt on the stage, and Patti, and the fire of poetry. I want to live poetry for myself. There! It may sound immodest, child, but at any rate it's honest. Don't look so frightened."

The other girl left her work and came over to Adela. She threw her arms around her neck.

"You do frighten me, Adela. You are so strong and so daring. When you love it will be the love that men have died for, and I am afraid—I am afraid of whom it may be—of where it may lead you."

"You are afraid that I am not orthodox, child," she said, laughing. "Perhaps I am not. You are afraid that if I were tempted I might dare to make my own laws and abide by them. Very likely I might. I cannot tell. But you see there is nothing to fear yet. There is nobody who cares for me. As yet the sky is clear. There is no mischief brooding."

The other girl sighed. "One cannot tell. I have never seen you like this. Something has happened the last few days. I am sure of it. You have been ever so odd and snappy. You have done no work. You have done nothing but read and dream, and you have been horribly restless. Tell me, dear—is it that man?"

Adela laughed gaily.

"You are afraid that the seed has been sown, then, little one!" she cried, mockingly. "You are waiting for the harvest!"

There was a knock at the door. It was opened almost immediately. A man, tall, dark, debonair, came slowly across the threshold, hat in hand. When he bowed his lips parted in a faint smile. The perfume of the violets in his faultless frock-coat seemed to fill the bare little room.

Chapter 9

For once Adela was not entirely mistress of herself. The man's advent was so entirely unexpected and yet so congruous with what had been passing between the two girls. She stood in the centre of the room, with a scarlet flush in her cheeks mounting slowly almost to the temples, and the other girl, who had never seen her friend blush, stood by her side, looking from one to the other with only half-comprehending eyes.

The man showed no embarrassment. He was simply a little perplexed.

"I am not quite sure whether I ought to have come up here," he said. "These flats are a mystery to me. I wanted to see you, and Treganon gave me your address. He said that you were at home on Wednesdays so I came. I asked the commissionaire for your studio, and he said, 'sixth floor,' and vanished. So I came up. Ought I to have waited anywhere?"

He spoke slowly, and it flashed into Adela's mind that he was making his explanation all the longer, that she might have time to recover herself. The idea stimulated her.

"Under the circumstances you couldn't very well do anything else," she said, laughing. "It is true that we receive on Wednesdays, but it is from two until four, and our proper studio is on the third floor. This is just a workshop where we indulge in dishabille, and don't, as a rule, see anybody!"

"I am exceedingly sorry," he said, gravely. "You will allow me—"

"Oh, since you are here you needn't go away. Kate, this is Sir Francis Kernham. Sir Francis Kernham—Miss Kate Mayne."

He noticed her for the first time, and bowed. She inclined her head and went on with her work.

"You have a very good light here," he remarked, looking around. "May I see what you are doing?"

Adela threw a cloth over her easel.

"Certainly not. The work we have for exhibition we keep down stairs. Miss Mayne may have something to show you," she added, with a touch of malice.

The girl looked up from her canvas for a moment.

"Certainly not," she declared, coldly. "I do not show my unfinished work to any one."

He laughed good-humouredly and remained perfectly at his ease.

"I must say that you are neither of you very encouraging to a pictureless man, whose chief desire in life is to become a patron of the arts. I did not understand that this was an amateur studio."

"An amateur studio!" Adela exclaimed indignantly. "What an insult!"

"May I be permitted to remark that you brought it upon yourselves," he said, with suave good humour. "I tell my friend Treganon that I want to buy some pictures, and ask him how to set about it. He tells me to avoid the dealers, and visit the studios. I obey him, and here I am!"

"If you wish to see our work it is downstairs," the other girl remarked, calmly. "You will find us there any Wednesday between two and four."

"I regret to see," he said, looking at his watch, "that it is now half past five. Perhaps, as I am a stranger though, Miss Fanshawe will pardon my being a little late, and take me downstairs?"

Adela laughed and took a latch-key from the shelf.

"You are very persistent," she said, "and a little rash. However, we are not going to turn away a buyer. Won't you come, Kate?"

The girl shook her head, "No, thanks. There is no need for both of us to go. You can show Sir Francis Kernham anything of mine he wishes to see."

Adela nodded and left the room followed by Kernham. They went down several flights of stairs, and she unlocked a door.

"I suppose," she remarked, "that you really came about that study?"

He shook his head.

"I took that home a week ago. The princess admitted that I had a prior claim."

"Then you came only to buy pictures?"

"I came without any definite purpose at all, except to see you," he said, slowly. "I am afraid that I have got into the bad habit of expecting to have my own way always. You were not in the park and I wanted to see you. Treganon, whom I met there, told me that it was your 'at home' day. So I came straight on here. The picture-buying came to me as an inspiration, when I found that my visit needed an explanation. Is your friend always so amiable?"

Adela smiled. She had meant to be angry, but, somehow, it was not easy.

His manner was so natural, and he was so obviously in earnest.

"Kate is an odd girl," she remarked. "Won't you sit down?"

"Thanks, since I am here I should like to look at the pictures," he said. "I really want a few."

The room they were in was half studio, half drawing-room. A score or so of pictures were hanging on the walls and distributed on easels. Sir Francis looked at them carefully one by one, with his pocket-book in his hand. Now and then he made a few remarks; several he passed at once after a casual glance. When he had finished he had thirteen entries.

"I like your odd little friend's work better, a great deal, than I expected to," he said, frankly. "Those two little landscapes, the 'Apple Orchard' and the 'Moorland Scene,' are charming. Next to your 'Girl's Head,' I prefer them to anything here. Have you nothing else to show me?"

"Nothing. Haven't you seen enough?"

"I heard something of a picture of yours in last year's Academy. Was it sold, or is it among those I have looked at?"

She hesitated. "No."

"Then may I see it?"

She pointed to a picture with its face to the wall.

"Will you help me turn it round?" she said.

Together they dragged it out, and placed it where the light was best. He retreated a few steps and stood looking at it. For several minutes he was silent. Then he spoke without looking away from the picture.

"What did you call it?" he asked in a low tone.

"I call it 'Despair,'" she answered.

He remained silent, his eyes fixed upon the central figure in the painting. A man's face, scarred, lined, aged, yet in a sense redeemed by the high forehead, piercing eyes, and a certain nobility of pose, looked out at him from a background of lurid, misty twilight. His feet were on a mountain-top. Above him was nothing but clouds and space. Below, dimly seen through wreaths of mountain mist, was a little phantasmagoria obviously allegorical. The path by which he had climbed was faintly denoted, and from its sides the white arms and passionate faces of golden-haired women were stretched upward towards that dark, lone figure, whose averted eyes swept the clouds. There was a palace from which he had come, a crown cast away in his haste, men stricken low lying by the wayside, a wasted world of triumphs seemed to lie forgotten behind him. And with his back to these things, yet with their undying marks written into the lines of his face, the man's fierce eyes still unquenched, seemed to look out into the open spaces by which he was surrounded, with a fire wholly unresigned, yet full of the most ineffable and absolute despair. To Kernham, that steadfast, half-scornful gaze seemed almost like a challenge. He stood in the centre of the room with folded arms, handsome, dark, determined, his eyes riveted upon that branded face, and as he gazed his cheeks paled, the corners of his firm mouth came together in rigid lines, a flash of answering fire seemed to be kindled in his own passionate eyes. Yet his heart was chilled. The man was mocking him. He, too, had triumphed. Him, too, the world of rest and pleasure, in one long, sweet chorus many-tongued and thrilling, was whispering into her embrace. Yet, it had come already. Like the first dim premonitions of a dread disease, he had felt it stir within him—that horrible heart-hunger, that strange shadow of depression thrown before—sure token of the eternal despair which the eyes of that man in the picture were flashing out upon him.

And the woman who stood looking into his face read his thoughts, and felt a sudden, deep remorse. The critics had spoken of her work as irreligious, pagan, a product of lassitude and pessimism. The memory of their words came back to her now, and cut her like a knife. If a fervent wish could have done it, she would have rent the canvas before his eyes. She moved closer to his side. Her warm breath fell upon his cold cheek. The low cadence of her voice was like a sudden, sweet music cleaving the darkness.

"You are not afraid of that," she cried, softly—"not you! That can only come to men whose hearts have been gnawed and eaten up with sin. For all others sorrows pass! For all others there is hope!"

A flash of sunlight came darting zigzag into the room. The face of the man in the picture was blurred and lost. Kernham looked away into the face of the girl who bent towards him.

□ □ □ □

The world of mild conventions and social masks seemed suddenly to have rolled away from beneath their feet. At a single step they had passed into vivid and sympathetic communion. And for that girl there came in that same second the crown of her desires. She lived—lived with every fibre of her being. The world went quivering around her with a strange new music. Her face caught a sudden light and held it. He looked at her and wondered.

"It is my fear," he said, in a low tone; "sometimes I feel that it may be my fate. Sometimes I seem to feel it moving on towards me. I am like that man! I have spent all my ambitions."

"There are other things—besides ambitions," she murmured.

"There are other things for other men," he answered. "They will not come to me."

"You cannot tell. Time is young yet with you. You have only just entered upon your second life. Oh, if I were a man! if I were you I would not suffer such thoughts to come to me. You have youth and wealth and fame. Life is full of possibilities."

He pointed silently to the picture. "He, too, had youth and wealth and fame. Yet he became—that! And he was no sensualist. It was not that you meant!"

She threw a cloth over the canvas.

"Do you want to make me sorry that I showed it to you?" she said softly. "Can't you see his greatest suffering? It is loneliness."

"And who is more lonely than I?" he exclaimed bitterly.

"You need not be lonely," she answered. "The world which rings with your praises will find you many friends."

"Parasites and hypocrites!" he cried, scornfully. "It is the same world at which I looked from a garret window ten years ago, unknown and friendless. I was very near starvation then, and the world was quite content to let me starve. I think the seeds of what you call my morbidness were sown in those days. Poverty is a bitter taskmaster!"

She sighed. "I, too, know what it is," she said, wistfully. "I was poor once, but I owe the world no grudge for that."

He looked at her in admiration. Before he had not thought of her as beautiful. He was bewildered by this new light in her face, and the magic of her soft, wonderful eyes raised so frankly to his.

"Ah, if I had known you then!" he exclaimed. "We might have been friends now."

"Is it too late? There is the future."

His hands clasped upon hers. She yielded them without reserve.

"It is more than I deserve, more than I have a right to," he said, and he forgot to release her hands.

When she drew them gently away, he watched them pass out of his keeping regretfully. They were ringless, white, and soft, not by any means small, but delicate and shapely. Their touch had given him a peculiar pleasure.

"I am going to exercise my rights at once," she said, briskly, moving a little way from him, and keeping her face in the shadows. "Give me your pocketbook, please."

He handed it over to her. She looked at the list of pictures he had written in, and drew her pencil through half of them.

"You must be content with these, please," she said. "The others are not worth your buying. I have left Miss Mayne's two landscapes and four others—and I have charged you full prices."

"The prices are ridiculous," he said; "but there is one other picture here which I must have."

He lifted the edge of the cloth which hung over it. She shook her head resolutely.

"I would rather not sell you that one," she said; "not as it is now, at any rate."

"I want it," he declared, firmly. "I want it if for nothing else, as a memento of to-day."

She swept the cloth away, and looked at it for a moment or two.

"Well, you shall have it," she said, "but not just now. I must alter it a little."

"As you will, so long as I have it," he answered. "Do you know that you have done me good already? I am feeling less despondent. After all, there must be things in the world which gratify."

"Try and keep in that faith," she said, gently; "and good-bye. You must really go away. You have been here more than an hour."

She took leave of him with a certain curious shyness, utterly strange to her, and when he had gone she sat for some time in the room alone. Somehow she shrank from facing the other girl and her questions. And he walked home through the crowded streets with a faint smile upon his lips, and a new buoyancy in his spirits—a buoyancy which lasted until he reached his rooms, and found upon his table a letter with a coronet, addressed to him in a handwriting rapidly becoming familiar. He opened it quickly, and read—

"Why did you not call this afternoon? I had something to say to you, and waited in for an hour. Come to-morrow without fail. By the by, where were you? You were not in the park. I shall be at the Opera to-night, and at the Marchioness of Downshire's afterwards. Perhaps we may come across one another."

The note fluttered out of his fingers and into the fire. He watched it burn into white ashes. If only men could dispose of their past like that.

Chapter 10

Adela threw down her brush. She was pale, and there were dark rims under her eyes.

"I have a headache, and I cannot work!" she cried. "Come, we have not had a holiday for a long time. Let us walk in the Park. I have a new gown, and I want to wear it before it becomes old-fashioned. It is already a week old."

The other girl rose, with a half-regretful glance at her work.

"As you will, Adela," she said. "The sun is hot in here, and you do not look fit to work. Only remember that I have no new gown, and I am very shabby. Fortunately no one will look at me while I am with you."

"Nonsense, child! Your magenta looks very well indeed. Don't try and put me off. Kensington Gardens will not do for me this afternoon. I want the real thing. I am going to play at being a woman of fashion."

They set off together, walking slowly towards Hyde Park Corner. Adela's pallor soon vanished. The new gown was a success. Even when they joined the ranks of the promenaders near the Corner she was still a distinguished figure in the little crowd. Her friend looked at her once or twice admiringly.

"Poor dowdy little me!" she exclaimed, gaily. "How dainty and cool you look! It is quite the prettiest dress in the park, but it must have cost you an awful lot of money."

Adela smiled. "Well, I don't often spend much money on dress," she remarked. "This one was a little expensive, of course. I am glad that it is a success. Let us rest for a moment or two. There are two chairs just by you."

They sat down. It was a little late in the season, but the park was still without any signs of thinning. The girls amused themselves by singling out their friends and acquaintances. Suddenly there was a rattle of a coach close to the railing. Adela looked up, and the colour faded beneath her veil. Sir Francis Kernham was driving, and by his side was the Princess of Hohenmahn.

His team was going well, and as he passed he glanced down the walk. Something in Adela's pose seemed to attract him. He looked again, and raised his hat. The coach was past in a second, with a whirl of yellow wheels and a cloud of dust. The girls were silent. Kate looked after it with a frown upon her forehead. She had watched her friend, and her heart was very sore. This was the cause, then, of Adela's pallor and headache. She felt inclined to cry. The pity of it was so great.

A voice from behind broke the silence.

"There goes the luckiest fellow in Europe," a man drawled. "Thirty-five years old, a millionaire, famous, and that most mysterious of all things— the fashion. All the women rave about him."

"Married?" inquired his friend tersely.

"No. The society papers are doing their best to arrange it for him every week, but I haven't heard anything definite. I should say myself that he was not a marrying man—a fact which I should think must cause the Prince of Hohenmahn some anxiety at times."

"The princess and he are a good deal talked about, are they not?"

Kate rose with an indistinct remark about the heat.

"Let us walk on and have some tea somewhere," she suggested.

But Adela sat still and shook her head.

"I am tired," she said. "I prefer to rest. We will go presently."

The man's voice reached them again from behind.

"The princess is the very last woman in the world whom one would have suspected of indiscretion. For years people used to call her the proudest woman in London. She was literally without a single admirer, and now this man comes along, and, 'pon my word, it looks like a case of *Veni, Vidi, Vici!* I happen to know that the prince is awfully savage. Serve him right! He's a wretched bad lot himself, and she must know all about it. All the same, I should think it likely that there'll be a big burst up there before long. I—hush! Here he is—and alone too!"

Adela looked up and found him standing before her, hat in hand. She greeted him with a word of surprise.

"I thought that I saw you drive by just now," she remarked, calmly.

"I did go by, and I saw you," he answered. "I have left my coach at the corner. I wanted to come and speak with you. Will you walk a few yards?"

Adela looked toward her companion.

"Do you mind?" she said.

The girl shook her head. Adela rose, and they walked slowly down the broad path. The colour had come back to her cheeks. She was carrying herself well, and her eyes were very bright.

"It is three weeks and a day since I saw you," he commenced.

"How strange that you should remember," she answered, fingering the lace of her parasol for a moment. "The princess is a very handsome woman."

He looked at her in some surprise at the apparent irrelevancy of her remark. Then a light seemed to break in upon him. He frowned, and just then his face was not a pleasant one to look upon.

"You have been hearing things—gossip, I suppose, about her," he said. "I know that women love to talk it. I did not fancy that you would be a willing listener."

"As it happens, I was an unwilling listener," she replied. "I am sorry I mentioned her name. Consider my remark unspoken, if you please."

"I have wanted to come and see you," he said. "I have wanted for three weeks and a day."

She raised her eyebrows. There was the faintest possible curl upon her lips, a shade of mocking sympathy in her tone.

"Dear me! Have you had so many engagements? How wearisome it must be to find one's self a man of fashion and a celebrity! I am sorry."

He looked away. She glanced at him, and her heart sank. He was looking white and ill. There was a change in him already.

"It has not been that—exactly," he said, after a moment's hesitation. "In fact, my engagements have had nothing at all to do with it. There has been something else."

At least he was sincere. Woman-like, she forgot herself and her wistful waiting.

"You do not look well," she said, kindly. "I hope you have not been imbibing any more morbid fancies."

He laughed shortly.

"You are persuaded that they are morbid. Well, I don't know. I don't want to talk about it now. When may I come and see you?"

"Exactly whenever you choose," she answered, smiling. "Forgive me if I was disagreeable just now. Frankly, I expected you to come before. I have been expecting you every day for three weeks and a day, and when you did not come I was disappointed. You know we were to be friends."

"At least, do not imagine that I have not thought of that," he said, earnestly. "If I have kept away it has been at my own expense. I have had fancies. Some day I may be able to laugh at them, and then I will tell you. May I come to-morrow?"

"I shall be at home all day," she answered. "Come about four, and I will give you some tea. Here is Mr. Treganon, and I want to speak to him. Do you mind if we turn back?"

He assented silently. She walked between the two men, talking mostly to Mr. Treganon, but every now and then appealing to Kernham. Her little friend was walking slowly a few yards in front of them with some friends. When the little group came together they were in the shadow of a coach. The prince looked down from the box seat with an air of relief.

"Here, Kernham!" he called out, "come and drive your own horses, for God's sake! Your wheeler's got a mouth like a brick. I wouldn't have the holding in of such a team if you were to give them to me."

Kernham made his adieu, without any particular hurry, and clambered up the side of the coach. The princess, who was looking a little bored, glanced down at the group through her gold lorgnettes, and bowed to Adela languidly.

"That little artist girl looks quite good style," she remarked to Kernham, as he took up the reins. "By the by, didn't I see you talking to her?"

"Probably. I have been talking to her," Kernham answered, shaking out the reins.

The princess gently closed her eyeglasses, and looked down with uplifted eyebrows. After all, the girl had very little presence. Her figure was too thin, and her hat was quite two months old.

"She is a little dowdy," the princess remarked, with a slight yawn. "But then those sort of people go in for that kind of thing, don't they? It is so hard to hit the mean, though, between untidiness and artistic effects. That girl wants a maid to show her how to do her hair."

"Would you care to take one more turn," he asked, "or shall I drive you home?"

"Home, by all means," she decided. "The roads are so horribly dusty, and I want my tea."

Sir Francis touched his leaders with the whip, the horn was blown, and they drove off smartly. Adela and Mr. Treganon watched them side by side in the shade of the lime trees.

"He has soon settled down into London life," Treganon remarked. "Do you remember that it is scarcely six weeks since I pointed him out to you at Lady Widnerton's, and he had not been in England a month then! His star has not commenced to wane yet. Six weeks; it seems longer than that, doesn't it?"

The coach was passing out the gate. Adela watched it disappear.

"Yes—it seems longer," she answered.

Chapter 11

The Prince of Hohenmahn for the first time during the season dined *tête-à-tête* with his wife. An unexpected death had broken up a great dinner party. Left with the choice of his club or his wife's company, he might possibly have chosen the former, but he was forestalled.

"I have ordered dinner at home for both of us," she remarked, looking in at his rooms on her way downstairs. "You have no other engagement until later, at any rate, and there is a matter which I wish to discuss with you."

She was gone before he could frame any objection. On thinking it over, he decided not to attempt any. A few minutes later he joined her in the drawing-room.

"This is quite an unexpected pleasure," he remarked, as he gave her his arm. "I hope we shall not bore one another to death."

"I do not think that you will suffer much in that way," she answered, smiling. And somehow he did not like that smile.

Dinner in the presence of the servants passed with a little languid conversation. The prince, to whom it was the one serious event of a generally misspent day, bestowed upon it his undivided attention. His wife, eating very little, leaned back in her chair and watched her lord through half-closed, scornful eyes. He was old and small and ugly. With every glass of wine he took—and he took a good many—his face grew redder. He had none of the physical qualities which endear a man to her sex. Yet he was a prince, the head of a noble house, and a millionaire. He represented to her at once her salvation and her bondage, but even for that salvation she could not summon up one spark of gratitude. She knew very well what it was in her that had attracted him. She watched him with disgust. Truly she had paid a great price.

With the last course he had lit a cigarette. They were dining in one of the smaller rooms at a little round table. With the arrival of the dessert he turned his chair round to the fire.

"My brougham at ten o'clock, Jean," he ordered, sipping his curaçoa.

The man bowed and withdrew. They were alone. He looked through the faint mist of tobacco smoke at his wife, and wondered whether anything unpleasant was coming. She, too, had turned her chair round, and was gazing into the fire. The white swansdown and lace at her bosom was gently rising and falling, and the fire of half hidden diamonds flashed from her hair and throat. Decidedly she was a very handsome woman, only so cold, so disappointingly, impenetrably cold. Not his style at all. He preferred something more chic. He thought of Mademoiselle Suzette, and glanced at his watch. It was barely half-past nine.

"Maurice!"

He shut his watch with a snap. It had come, then.

"I have a few words to say to you."

"I am entirely at your service, for half an hour," he said, politely.

"Half an hour will, I think, be quite sufficient. Listen, then. We have been married now for eight years; a little longer, I believe. This is the first time I have spoken to you upon a subject which few women would have left so long untouched. During that time I think that you will admit that I have kept the promises I made to you faithfully. I never pretended to love you. I never have done. But I think you will admit that you have had no cause to find fault with me."

"None whatever," he admitted. "We have got on well together, have we not? I have never complained."

She shot a single glance at him, before which his eyes fell. Such ineffable contempt stung even him.

"You complained! What I wish to remark is that I have borne in silence from you what very few women would be content to bear without reprisals. I refer, of course, to your continual and notorious infidelities."

He moved a little uncomfortably in his chair, and lit a fresh cigarette.

"Do I understand that you are bringing this forward as a charge against me?"

"I bring no charge," she interrupted, calmly. "I will do you the justice to admit that you have never attempted to conceal your—what do you call them?—amours. They have been the talk of the clubs, and the scandal of the society papers. I, your wife, have had them brought to my notice with wearisome persistence. To tell you the truth, I am a little tired of them."

"My impression is," he remarked, looking across at her, "that they scarcely form a profitable topic of conversation between you and me. If you will kindly be a little more explicit."

"I am on the point of being remarkably explicit. What I was about to say is, that for eight years I have been passive, notwithstanding unfaithfulness on your part, which has been both gross and flagrant. This is the end. From to-night I am adopting a new policy."

"A new policy!" he gasped.

"Exactly! A policy of reprisals."

He half rose from his chair, but sat down again. For several moments he was silent, watching her, and taking short, thick breaths. The unhealthy flush had partly left his face, under his eyes there was a livid streak of white. He was scarcely master of himself.

"You must explain what you mean a little more clearly," he said, closing his sentence with a quick gasp.

She shrugged her shoulders. "How is that possible, I wonder. I intend to follow your example. What can be clearer?"

"You dare not," he muttered. "Your position—"

"There are plenty of women in my position," she said, calmly, "who have done and are doing, every day what I propose to do. My wit is as good as theirs. What they do I can do. If I valued my position that much—I could retain it."

Her white, jewelled hand had flashed out between them in a gesture of contempt. The vein on his forehead grew larger.

"You would not dare!" he cried, thickly. "I would have you exposed. I would drag you into the Divorce Court. You would be an outcast. The doors of society would be closed upon you."

She smiled pityingly at him. "You are hopelessly behind the times," she remarked. "Divorces are rather the fashion just now. I am afraid there is no chance for me, though. I do not know much about the law, but, as regards the Divorce Court, you yourself have, unfortunately, a somewhat tarnished record. They do not grant divorces to men who have lived such lives as you. But, after all, that does not interest me."

He tossed off a glass of curaçoa, and come and stood over her.

"Look here, Marcia, you're talking nonsense. You've been reading some damned rubbish about new women and new laws and all the rest of it. Take my advice. I'm a man of the world. I know what I'm talking about. There may be no justice about it; I'm not defending it, but there are things a man may do and a woman may not do. I admit my unfaithfulness. But ask yourself this. Have I had no excuse? You yourself have presented me with one. Only a moment ago you said that you did not love me, and that you never had loved me."

She raised her eyes to his. "And those creatures—have they loved you?" she asked, with infinite contempt.

"They have pretended, and that is all a man wants!" he answered, bluntly. "But never mind that. That isn't for you to hear about. What I want you to understand is this. There is a license given to a man, rightly or wrongly, mind, but there is none to a woman. I may deceive you every day of my life, and no one thinks the worse of me for it. But you, you have only to compromise yourself once, and the women will hound you down. Trust them to do it. The higher your position, the more they will go for you. It's in the blood; sort of sporting instinct, I suppose. But they'll do it! Damn it, they'll do it! I'm speaking the truth. If it's a woman, it's ruin. If it's a man, well, it's his license."

"It is the license of brutes, not of men!" she answered scornfully. "You and such as you have no right to call yourselves men. I am sick and ashamed to have lived so long with so unclean a thing. When I leave you I shall feel an honester and purer woman. Oh, I'm not going to rail. I'm not an apostle. Don't be afraid. But I know this, that my purity is more sullied by the touch of the tips of your fingers, even though you are my husband, than by the arms of the man I love!"

He fell back from her. Was this the interpretation? Then he laughed hoarsely, but without mirth.

"The man you love," he repeated. "Bah! you do not know what love is. You are not a woman of flesh and blood at all. You are as cold as ice. Heart! you haven't one. Passion! you don't know what it is!"

She suddenly rose up before him. A rush of colour had flooded her cheeks and throat. Her eyes were soft and brilliant. He looked at her stupefied. It was a new woman standing there in the rose-shaded light. Her bosom was swelling, her eyes were afire. No; he could not say that the woman had no passion.

"Maurice, you remember when you pressed me to marry you, I made a confession?"

So it was the memory of that which had changed her. He nodded.

She leaned over and whispered in his ear. Again that vein stood out like whipcord. His face was purple.

"It is false!" he cried. "He was dead! You swore it!"

"He was not dead!" she answered, fiercely. "Never mind whether I lied or not. He has come back. I love him! I have always loved him! I belong to him; never—never to you. I belong to him, and if he will have me I shall go to him."

He held out his hands despairingly. "Consider—the disgrace."

She laughed in scorn. "Disgrace and the world's censure are tiny weeds beside the great tree of love!" she answered. "I have tried them and they have given me nothing. For eight years I have wearied myself by playing at being alive, and all the while I have known that the cup of life had never once touched my lips, that I was an ignoble creature of type and habit. There is no word which you can say that can stop me. I am your wife no longer. I am free of you. Be off to your dancing girl. It is ten o'-clock!"

"Tell me the man's name!" he cried fiercely. "I will know it!"

She laughed. "Why? You cannot fight him. Duelling is out of fashion. Don't be foolish. You are quite powerless. Hush!"

A servant stood upon the threshold.

"His Highness' brougham is at the door," he announced. "Sir Francis Kernham is in the hall. He inquires for Madam the Princess."

"You can show Sir Francis in here," she answered. "Maurice, it is ten minutes past ten."

He stood in the centre of the room with clenched hands. The man, with his cloak on his arm, stood respectfully by his side. After all, how lovely she was! He was blind with passion, mingled with a curious resurrection of his old admiration of her. He waved the man away.

"Marcia," he cried, in a broken voice. "I will give Suzette up! Send that fellow away. We will go abroad. I will be a better husband. I will reform. I swear it!"

"My dear Prince," she said, with a brilliant smile, "your little speech is exactly eight years too late. That is all I have to say to you!"

She touched the bell. The servant reappeared, followed by Sir Francis Kernham. The prince turned on his heel.

Chapter 12

Sir Francis looked from the closed door to the princess's face. "Something is wrong with your husband," he remarked, gravely. "He did not speak to me; he did not look in a fit state to speak to any one. Had you not better see what is the matter before he goes out?"

She shook her head. There was a flaring spot of colour in her cheek. She was standing in the centre of a little, rose-shaded halo from the lamplight, and his first thought was curiously enough the counterpart of the prince's last one. A new beauty seemed to have blossomed out in her. Even the lines and curves of her superb figure seemed to have become softer and more voluptuous. He looked into her face and wondered. A flash of the old Marcia seemed to be lighting up those dark eyes. A curious little thrill of recollection warmed his blood.

"He will take care of himself," she said. "He is very angry, and he has not very much self-control. It is possible that he may come back again. If he does, do not quarrel with him. He is not a man. He is not worth it. Leave me to deal with him."

"But why should he want to quarrel with me?"

"Come into my room, and I will tell you," she answered. "I cannot stay here. Even the odour of his cigarette sickens me. It is suffocating. Come!"

She looked at him over her shoulder as she passed—one of those looks by which a woman knows so well how to express a good deal. His heart leaped up and sank like lead. He followed her across the great hall, and when she lingered for a moment by a tall palm a sudden vision rose up before his eyes, forbidden memories burst the seal which he had placed upon them. Lower down, near the front entrance, three servants, footmen in powdered hair and in the livery of the house of Hohenmahn, stood at attention. So he followed her in silence across the marble tiles, upstairs and down a long corridor. She led him to a room where he had never been before—a room of heterogeneous appointments, half French, half Oriental, with pale green hangings.

"This is my own sanctum," she said, "and you are the first man who has ever set his foot in it. Come here by the fire and talk, or rather listen. I have a good deal to say to you."

He sank into an easy-chair, apprehensive, yet curiously tongue-tied. Between this woman and the woman of a few hours ago there was a change—a subtle marvellous change. The cadence of her voice, the soft, dreamy light in her eyes, even the rhythmic movements of her body bespoke a new and frank abandonment. Despite his will, those old memories were not altogether to be controlled. For him that one dream of love, the one passionate effort of his life, remained amongst those things of his earlier days from which time had irrevocably severed him. His sense of responsibility concerning it had never left him. It was as poignant and real to-day as on the morning when she had drifted from him into what seemed like certain destruction. The passion itself was a dead thing, yet he was a man, stronger a little, and purer a little than most men, yet a man, and she was very beautiful, and there was between them that common consciousness of a past, shrouded indeed, but never without its thrilling suggestions. That she should desire its resurrection or the resurrection of any part of it, he had never seriously believed since he had heard her name and looked into her face amongst the pictures of the New Gallery. Even now he was only bewildered with a terrible suspicion. To-night he was called upon to meet it face to face. It was true that her husband was an evil liver, that her married life in some respects must be an unholy one. Yet he could not seriously bring himself to believe that she would ever be likely to accept that offer wrung from him on his first visit to her. Since that day she had never alluded to it. He had prayed that it might be forgotten. What he had said to her then had seemed to him the right thing to say. Yet, after all, she was the wife of another man, and that man, however great a sinner, had been the means of her salvation. He was a simple-minded man, and he had no vanity. He could not believe that the passion which was dead in his own heart still burned in hers. She was the wife of the Prince of Hohenmahn, a fact which, rendering her all the more desirable to most men, to him made her sacred. In the wide world of honeycombed morals he was almost a purist. And yet behind all his reasoning there lurked sometimes an awful apprehension. He had spent sleepless nights grappling with it; it had poisoned moments when he might have felt on the verge of happiness. It had hung about him like a nameless fear. To-night, at her altered manner it had leaped up.

She sank into an easy chair close to his. The light of the fire played upon her profile, and flashed upon the jewelled hand so close to his.

"You thought," she commenced, "that my husband looked at you strangely. I want to remind you of something. Before I consented to marry him, I told him—you know what!"

With a curious shyness he dropped his eyes before hers. She laughed a low sweet laugh, sweet with the spice of the daintiest mockery.

"It made no difference. He would marry me. He thought himself very much in love. But, as you know, I told him a lie. To-night I have confessed. To-night he knows that you are alive!"

He looked up quickly.

"You have told him that I was the man?"

"He knows it—and more than that—he knows that I am going to leave him. I have borne the shackles of my serfdom long enough. You are a man. You have heard of the manner of his life."

"I have heard it spoken of," he admitted, gravely. "I had hoped that it might not have been true—that at least there might be exaggerations."

"Believe me, there are none. Do you think it right for a self-respecting woman to live with a man like that?"

He was troubled. These were matters hard to solve, and he knew that his ideas, the ideas of his youth, had long ago been laughed to scorn—that they had become the world's derision.

"I do not know," he said hesitatingly. "You are his wife!"

"My God! Do you think, then, that because the law has joined us together, the bonds which he has cast off like ropes of sand are to remain sacred to me? Do you think that I am bound to live still with a man who gives himself up to debauchery after debauchery? What hideous rubbish! Can I give my lips to his fresh from the lips of his courtezans, and retain a single grain of self-respect? No! I have borne it too long! To-night it is over—and he knows it!"

"And the future?" he murmured.

She came and knelt down by his side. Her head was bowed before his.

"Francis, when I think of your life through all these years and of mine, I am ashamed, miserably ashamed. Your words are always haunting me. Through all your long exile, when you were carving your way to fame and to fortune, no other woman's face came before you to drive out the memory of—of mine. You were faithful. And when your task was ended, and you had won your triumph—when you came back it was before my picture that I found you, and you were there to buy it at any price!"

She took his hand and smoothed it in hers. He looked into the fire with blank, unseeing eyes. His lips were sealed.

"What did you think of me when you knew that I had married another man?"

"I was glad," he answered, simply. "Remember the threat which you uttered, the terrible misery of those days, the future which you deliberately proposed for yourself. Yes, I was glad!"

She shuddered a little. "What I threatened then—I meant!" she said in a low tone. "Do you know what it was that saved me? It was you. That morning when I stole away and left you, I felt that the thing had become impossible. Sooner the river, any sort of death. I felt that I belonged to you. The old life had passed away. I started again, and I endured many things before I married that man—but your kisses were last upon my lips. There was no one else. There could not have been. I married him, and all that I promised he has had from me. Then you came back, and when I looked into your face, the old feeling returned with a rush. I was glad! I would not crush it. It was like a live sweet thing. The horror of living with him became suddenly unbearable. I know why it was. It was because you were here, and, Francis, I had not forgotten that I loved you."

Her voice sank to a whisper. She had moved as though insensibly a little nearer to him. He had only to stretch out his arms to enclose her. But he did not move. He sat still looking into the fire. The pressure of her hand was like a weight of lead to him.

"To-night," she whispered—"to-night I have broken my bonds. I am a free woman. It is like the dawn of a fresh life to me, dear. And you have been so patient, so noble. You are glad. Tell me that you are glad."

He thrust her away from him, roughly, feverishly. His bronze cheeks had paled. This then was retribution.

"Hush!" he cried. "You are forgetting—you have not thought. You are a princess. Your name, your rank—your honour!"

She smiled upon him brilliantly. She was so sure of him. It was his great love for her, this hesitation. He was so strong.

"Some day you will understand how small all these things seem to a woman compared with love," she whispered, softly. "Women are not frightened by bugbears now. The greatest shame is the shame of living with such a man as the Prince of Hohenmahn. It is to you I belong. To you I have always belonged. There is not any shame in love. Oh, Francis!" she cried, with a sudden wonderful light sweeping into her face, "I want to be loved. I am famished for love. I have been so heartsick and so weary all these years, that if you had not come, if I had lost you, I think that I should have died. Have you ever imagined, I wonder, that I dared not think of you—of our little page of love? Oh, you are wrong! I gloried in it! I gloried in thoughts of it! It made you mine! It made me yours! It gave us to one another for all eternity! If it was sin—thank God for it! Kiss me, dear!"

Still for a moment he paused. He looked away out of that dainty chamber with its silken hangings and indescribable odour of voluptuousness. He looked into the sweet, clear face of that other woman, and there was a sound of wailing in the air, and in his heart. He closed his eyes. It must go. The yoke of those soft, white arms was around his neck, her silky hair with its faint perfume brushed his cheeks. Her kiss burned upon his lips like a brand of an everlasting slavery.

Chapter 13

Adela was sitting alone gazing at her picture. She had had an hour or two of hard work, and there was an idea in her brain. She was thinking it out, her hands clasped round her knee, her faced turned towards the easel where the picture, unframed, was undergoing a transformation. The dark eyes which looked out at hers through the semi-twilight spoke of some subtle and mysterious change. A touch of genius had blended with that despairing gaze, some flashes of the fire of hope. And the solitude of the man had passed away. By his side was the sketch of another figure coming out from the dark background with outstretched arms—and it was of this figure she was thinking.

The lights of the room had burnt low, her companion had gone to bed an hour ago. Midnight a mile westward was accepted as the pivot of the day—in Coombes' Flats every one respectable seemed to have gone to bed. A silence almost depressing reigned throughout the building, and in the street below. Adela sat and thought.

The silence of the street was suddenly broken by the trampling of horses' feet. They stopped below. The front door of the place was opened and shut. Adela was only partly aroused from her little dream. She was not curious. That some one had come home late did not concern her. But in another moment she sprang to her feet startled. There was a knock at the door. Before she could answer it was opened and closed again. A man was standing upon the threshold with a long travelling coat over his evening clothes—a man into whose face she looked for a moment without any recognition. Only when he had taken a quick step forward, a little cry burst from her lips.

"Sir Francis!" she exclaimed. "You here—at this time! Is anything the matter?"

He caught hold of both her hands and held them in his.

"Look at me, and ask yourself that," he answered, with a dash of fierceness in his tone. "I was right! It has come!"

She looked into his face, and her heart grew faint and anxious. For it was the face of the man in the picture. Line for line the sorrows which she had conceived seemed branded in his haggard features. Before the black fire of his hollow eyes her own felt dim and wet with tears. Had it come to him so soon then, this despair whose shadows had haunted him, and from whose cold clasp he had shrunk with such horror? Since the afternoon there was a change. He had been pale and languid then, but at the sight of her his face had lit up, the languor seemed to have fallen away. He looked at her now with a fierce despair of one beyond the pale of hope. Something had happened.

"What is it?" she murmured. "You are in trouble. Can I help?"

"You can save me," he answered, wildly; "you only! You can save me—if you will—at a great cost."

"I do not understand," she answered, gently. "You are ill. Sit down and tell me all about it. Tell me everything!"

"I can tell you nothing," he answered, doggedly.

"But I do not understand. If you do not tell me, how can I help you?"

He threw his hat upon the table, and thrust back the masses of black hair from his square high forehead. The night was chilly, but the perspiration stood upon his forehead like beads.

"Listen," he cried. "My carriage is outside. The train leaves for Dover in an hour. Put on your hat and cloak and come with me. Make up your mind never to set foot in this country again. Come with me where I shall take you. You shall choose your own home—anywhere so long as it is far enough away. I will build you a palace—I will buy you a kingdom; but you must come with me to-night, now, without farewells, and you must trust me. We can be married in an hour at Paris. If you care for me, you will come. If you do not I am lost body and soul. No! I am not raving! You look at me as if you thought I were mad. I am not. Feel my pulse. It is steady enough. I tell you that I stand upon the border line between salvation and hell. It is you who must save me, you only can do it."

The colour had flooded her cheeks, and her heart was beating. She faced him with dim eyes and trembling lips.

"I do care for you," she said, softly. "I think that you must know it, or you would not come to me like this. I care for you so much that I will even do what you ask."

A light leaped into his face. He held out his arms with a low cry of joy. She kept him from her with gentle force.

"I will do what you ask," she continued, "on one condition. You must satisfy me that there is no other way. You must trust me as you ask me to trust you. Don't think that I am trifling with you. Satisfy me, and I will leave this house with you for ever in ten minutes."

His hands dropped to his side. "If I tell you, you will not come," he said, despairingly. "I have sinned, and I would fly from the harvest. If I tell you, you will not come."

"If you do not tell me, I shall not come," she reminded him, firmly. "You need not fear. I shall not be a harsh judge!"

"I will take my chance!" he cried. "Listen. Ten years ago, when I was young and poor and desperate, there was a girl who cared for me. She was an actress, and she was as poor and lonely as I. We were in this great city. I had tried my hand at writing and I had failed. She had tried to act, and she had failed. And one night we looked black despair in the face hand in hand, and a fire rose up in my heart. I burned my manuscripts, I turned everything I had into gold, and I swore that I would find success and wealth, the desire of the world, in a virgin country, even if I had to wrest it from the hands of fate. And she too was desperate. She, too, took a desperate resolve, and in the face of our misery and our hopelessness I had no other words with which to dissuade her. Then, somehow, in that hour of our joint despair and our joint resolution, at the parting of our ways, each on the threshold of our new lives, something in our loneliness, our isolation and our parting—what was it?—God knows—something must have fired my imagination and she—she must have cared for me even before, in those days when she was nothing to me but another waif whom chance had brought near. Women when they are lonely give their hearts so easily. On the night of our parting she gave herself to me body and soul, and on the morrow I sailed away, and for ten years she was dead and buried to me."

White and breathless he paused for a moment. A cinder dropped upon the hearth. There was no other sound. Adela was silent, but her face was pale as death. Some part of his despair seemed to have fallen upon her.

"I can't make you understand. How should I? I can't understand it myself. When the glamour of it had faded away, I cursed that meeting with her night and day. But we were on the brink of despair. There seemed no foreground for our lives. I was going away out of her life, and it seemed for ever—and she cared for me. To you it must seem like sin. But it was not sin of hers, at any rate; and as for me—I have paid the penalty. In those lonely hours when I lay under the stars outside my tent, my sense of responsibility was born. I sent money. It never reached her. What had become of her— oh, the torture I have suffered from that thought. I felt like a murderer, only it was a soul that I had murdered. And when I came back, my triumph was clouded and my success hung like a millstone about my neck. I haunted all the places where the lost souls of women congregate. I never passed one without looking into her face with fear and horror. When at last I found her my heart leaped up for joy. She had saved herself. I laughed aloud with the joy of it. It was freedom. The burden of years was rolled away. But I was a fool. My freedom was an illusion. The bonds are there still, they are there for ever unless you cut them—unless you set me free—."

And again he paused, and again she did not speak. To the bitter end she had moaned to herself. And she waited.

"I had counted myself free because she was married. It was the bitterest of all illusions. The shadow of it had been growing blacker before me. To-night I have had my final awakening. To-night I have heard read the sentence of my doom. She had saved herself after my departure because she loved me. The precipice at her feet she had recoiled from because of the memory of our farewell. Our sin had been her salvation. She faced the world again. She became a governess. She married—married a blackguard but—a prince!"

She would not help him on. She would not let him see her face. She waited.

"To-night she has told me of her misery. She turns to me to save her from degradation. 'I am yours,' she cries. 'Our union was above the marriage laws of men. I gave myself to you first, and I have loved you and only you. Take me away! I am unhappy!'"

"Adela, I have never loved her. I never knew what love was until you taught me. Am I bound to go to her? She is waiting now—to-night. Come away with me this moment. Leave England with me and cut this cursed knot. She is still with her husband. It will be the same to her as though I were dead, as though I had never come back. She is married to him. To come to me is sin. Save her! Save me! You will come! Quick! The time is flying!"

She leaned upon the mantelpiece, her face buried in her hand. The sound of her low sobbing drove him mad.

"For the love of God turn round and give me your hands!" he cried, wildly. "I will make you happy. On my soul I swear that you shall never repent."

She turned and looked at him. There was white dumb misery in her face. She was like a woman suddenly aged. Yet before her clear eyes the passion of his heart sank down.

"You must make her happy, not me. It is your duty. I cannot come. I cannot be anything to you. I cannot take her place. She has first claim!"

"You to say that!" he cried. "You, to send me to a woman who sins against the laws of God from the moment she leaves her husband. You can justify that to yourself!"

"Alas, yes. A woman who lives like that sins when she lives with any other man, even though he be her husband. She gave herself to you and you belong to her. I am outside your life forever. God help us both! Good-bye!"

He caught her roughly in his arms. His eyes blazed with a sudden triumph. He did not say anything for a moment, but he held her like a vice, and rained hot kisses upon her pale cheeks and hair and lips. The she raised her eyes to him.

"Stoop down, love," she whispered, "and I will kiss you."

The fire on his lips grew cold. There was something of reverence in that short embrace.

"You must let me go, dear."

He stood apart from her, breathless. She leaned against the table with her face turned towards him.

"Good-bye."

A sob rose up in his throat as he turned away. He walked to the door like a blind man. She moved to the window, and, clutching at the curtains with both hands, watched his carriage drive away into the night.

Chapter 14

Spring passed, summer came and lingered. The rhododendrons in the park were over, the greenness had gone from the trees, everything was white with dust. The fashionable parts of London were peopled with a new and unfamiliar throng. But in Kensington things were much the same. Adela was there, pale and heavy-eyed, fighting her battle with despair. For her the summer days were dark, the light of the sun had gone out. From early morning till dark she sat in her studio and painted. There was nothing else left.

She was alone. Her little friend, after many sad protests, had packed her easel and gone to the sea. Who but a broken-hearted woman would stay in London during a fiery September?

It was afternoon, and Adela, fearless lest her solitude might bring a return of those maddening thoughts which had made many a night a little cycle of horror, was working with a feverish, unnatural concentration. And in the midst of it the door opened and a woman walked in. Adela's brush slipped from her nerveless fingers. The pallor of her face was like the pallor of death.

She rose to her feet at once. She confronted her visitor with burning eyes and unshaken dignity.

"What do you want?" she asked, quickly. "Why are you here?"

The princess laughed softly. It was a slow, maddening laugh. She looked around her with a faint show of curiosity, at the plain walls, the plaster casts, the somewhat bare appointments of the by no means luxurious studio. Last of all, she looked at the pale, slight figure of the girl who stood before her. The eyes of the two women met. Adela's were like still fires of passionate aversion. The princess's were curious and a little wistful.

"Why have I come?" she repeated, slowly. "Really I am not quite sure even now. I wished to see you. I wanted—"

Adela moved towards the bell.

"You will forgive me," she said, quietly. "I have been ill. I am not well enough to see visitors. Will you go away?"

The princess sank into a low chair near the window. Then, as the flood of clear northern daylight fell upon her face, Adela stayed her hand. The face was scarcely the face of a triumphing woman. She gazed at it fascinated. As usual the toilette of the princess was perfect. Her gown was of the newest shade, and its fit was exquisite. Her hat, with its fresh roses, was a miracle of dainty simplicity. In the shabby little room she was like a suggestion of another world. But Adela was a woman, and she saw beyond these things.

"Tell me why you have come?" she begged. "Tell me, and go away?"

"I have come," the princess said, smoothing out her gown, "to tell you a little story. After I have told it, I shall be as anxious to go as you are to get rid of me. It has cost me a good deal to come, and it will cost me a great deal more to tell my story. You have suffered, and I have suffered. All women are born to suffer. Remember that—and don't interrupt me."

Adela held her peace and listened with bowed head. The voice of the princess was sunk lower, but every syllable was thrillingly distinct. Every word seemed charged with woe.

"It is a little history. There was a woman, lonely, friendless, and desperate, who loved a man. They were young, but they were miserably poor, and they were forced to part. The woman, who saw in the future the shadows of darker things crossing her life, gave herself to the man before they parted, that she might have at least one thing, one memory to cherish, one moment in the past common and dear to both of them. They parted. He went into exile to measure his strength with the world's forces, and won his battle. She, galvanised into life by the memory of him, and the sudden vigour of her passionate love, abandoned her more unworthy resolves, shook herself free from the fatalism which had brought her to the brink of destruction, and worked out her own emancipation. After a time she married.

"This man came back, and commenced to search for the woman. His return was the greatest joy she had ever known. She was a proud woman and she made a terrible mistake. She did not doubt but that his love had lived as hers had done. That was wrong, as you will see. Her husband was everything that is depraved and loathsome. The bonds of her marriage were as ropes of sand to her. She had given herself first to this man. It seemed to her that she was his, body and soul. She never hesitated as to what she should do. She offered herself to the man. She bade him find a home for her. She was coming to him."

She paused. Adela's face was hidden. The princess commenced nervously pulling to pieces the lace border of the handkerchief which had been rolled up in her hand.

"The woman's mistake was hideous. She had believed in the man's love. But the man never loved the woman. It was his sense of responsibility which had made him undertake that feverish search for her. It was purely a matter of conscience. That sounds strange, does it not, in connection with a man? But this is a true story. He heard her proposition and was silent. The stain upon her soul was his. It remained for him to save her from worse things. But when all their plans were made, on the very night of their leaving the country together, the man fell ill. It was in her house that he fell ill, and the woman nursed him. And one horrible night he raved and he told her the truth. She leaned over his couch, sick with horror and despair, and she gathered his story from the hot passionate words which leaped out into the dark room. There was another woman!"

"Ah!"

The cry came from Adela, and rang through the bare chamber. The princess rose. The floor around her was strewn with the fragments of that lace handkerchief.

"I have come, like the heroine of a silly story, to take you to him," she said. "Get ready quickly. I might change my mind."

Adela held out her hand with a passionate gesture. The princess shook her head.

"No," she said, calmly. "Don't make a hypocrite of me. I hate you! I shall always hate you. You have spoilt my life! You, too—what fools men are! I am handsomer than you, and God knows that you cannot love him as I do. Yet he loves you. Don't make any mistake. What I do, I do for his sake, not yours. I shall hate the very sight of your face as long as I live. Get ready, child!"

Adela crossed to her side.

"But you," she said, softly. "What will you do?"

The princess pointed out of the window. The prince was smoking a cigar in her victoria below. He wore a large button-hole, and he looked very well. On the whole he did not regret Suzette.

"My husband will be getting impatient," she said, calmly, "do get your things on."

THE END

The Reluctant Gambler

Gambler's Choice

At a corner table of the architecturally superb, but grotesquely decorated restaurant of the Hôtel de Paris, at Monte Carlo, four very distinguished local notabilities were enjoying a carefully chosen, almost Lucullian midday banquet. They were indeed men of consequence.

Monsieur Robert, the director of the hotel, was host, white-haired, but vigorous, with keen dark eyes and a presence immortalized by the leading cartoonists of Europe.

On his right sat Monsieur le Général de St. Hilaire, from the barracks at Nice, a rather short, rotund, but soldierly-looking person, with fierce gray mustaches, who wore his imposing row of ribbons with the air of one who has earned them. He was in command of the troops in the district, and with the continual frontier scares and graver outbursts of political discontent, suppressed in the local papers, but known well enough to the world at large, his post was surely no sinecure.

On the left of his host was Monsieur Desrolles, the Chef de Sûreté of Monaco, a man of mysteries, if ever there was one, tall, dark and hatchet-faced, severe of deportment, as befitted the custodian of many secrets. The fourth man at the table was Gustave Sordel, the leading spirit in the Societé des Bains de Mer, that vast organization responsible primarily for the gambling rooms, and in a minor degree for such less important institutions as the Baths, the Tir aux Pigeons, the Café de Paris, and the golf-course.

He was the youngest of the party, and he had the air of a man who welcomes responsibility with both hands, deals with it summarily, and if he makes mistakes stands by them. He was clean-shaven, with hard features, a rapid tongue, and he spoke with the tone of authority. A gathering this, indeed, of people of note—the rulers of the place, men with whom it would have been ill-advised, even dangerous, to quarrel.

The conversation was of food and its glorious corollary, wine. Monsieur Robert was engaged in the pleasing task of making the mouths of his guests water. He spoke of news that morning, over the telephone from Prunier's, of caviar, gray and small-grained, a limited shipment, alas, and at a price unmentionable—but already southward bound.

Fortunately, in Monte Carlo, the visitor's sense of money values is curiously disturbed and extravagance becomes a cult. He spoke of prawns brought in that day from the River Vesbie, large and luscious, the shells of which were soon to lie upon their plates; a consignment of woodcock from Corsica, fat with their feast of insects under the cork trees of Corte; a crate of quails from the rice-fields of Mena; some Norfolk pheasants, landed that morning at Nice from a fast aeroplane. The General, who more than any of them loved good food, and better still good wine, listened with glistening eyes.

"With the woodcock, my friends," he exclaimed, "some priceless Burgundy! Not warmed, mind, but with the chill off. A Chambertin of 1911 perhaps."

"I could accommodate you," Monsieur Robert boasted. "I have seventeen bottles in the cellar. Ah, it is our friend the General indeed who knows what is good! The Chambertin or a Clos Vougeot, eh? A perfume like violets, wine to stir the blood!"

"The General is a great connoisseur," Monsieur Desrolles declared, "but I claim to be the one who made the discovery that we were drinking the veritable vodka with our caviar."

"Ah, spirits! I have no palate for them," the General acknowledged. "The Fin? Yes, the Fin perhaps, but no others, and of that there is little now that enchants. I looked at your wine list a few days ago, Robert. Your 1812, your 1815, your 1830, they have disappeared, alas!"

Monsieur Robert smiled the smile of a wise man who knows a thing or two.

"From the wine list? Why, yes, from the wine list, perhaps, my friend. But wait!... Now with the prawns I shall give you a dry Pouilly, a fine and delicate wine. This to prepare your palate for what comes. I have not forgotten your Clicquot either, Gustave. When the champagne arrives, there is a little surprise for you.... What is this?"

He broke off with a frown. His duties with regard to the hotel were things now almost of the past. He had an excellent manager, an excellent staff of clerks, and his own advice was seldom sought save in cases of extreme necessity. Yet here at his elbow stood Henri of the reception bureau, with a paper in his hand.

"What is this, Henri?" he demanded. "Monsieur Grammont is in his office. You see that I lunch with friends? An occasion, this! Why am I disturbed?"

Henri, very correctly dressed, becoming pale, worthy, to all appearance, of his post of senior reception clerk of the Hôtel de Paris, was overweighted with apologies.

"It is Monsieur Grammont who thought that you should see this, without delay," he confided. "It is a thing incomprehensible. One does not know whether to allot the room."

Monsieur Robert produced a horn-rimmed eye-glass, and adjusted it. "The allotment of the rooms is no concern of mine," he grumbled.

"You will permit a word of explanation, Monsieur," the young man begged eagerly. "From the Blue Train there arrived, a quarter of an hour ago, this gentleman, Monsieur Andrew Tresholm, an Englishman. He had engaged by correspondence a room looking over the gardens, with bath and small salon. Monsieur Grammont suggested Suite 39. I took him to it upon his arrival.

"He was satisfied with the apartments and the price, which was none too small. All goes well, you perceive. I hand him the papers from the Bureau of Police, and invite him to sign them. He fills in his name—you see it there—Tresholm, *prénom* Andrew. His age, thirty-six. His place of birth, a county in England. He arrives at 'profession.' He leaves that blank. Monsieur Desrolles," the young man added, "will remember his recent injunction."

"Certainly," the Chef de Sûreté assented. "We wish in all cases to have this profession stated. There has been a certain slackness in this respect."

Henri bowed his grateful acknowledgments across the table.

"I desire to carry out the official request," he continued, "and I press Monsieur Tresholm to fill in the space. He protests mildly. Gently but firmly I insist. He takes up the pen and hesitates. Then he smiles. He is of that type—he smiles to himself. Then he writes. Behold, Monsieur Robert, what he writes."

The great man took the paper into his hand and stared at it for a moment as though bewildered. "'Occupation,'" he read out, "'professional gambler.'"

"*Qu'est-ce que c'est que ça?*" the Chef de Sûreté gasped.

"'Professional gambler,'" Monsieur Robert repeated, reading from the paper.

They all exchanged bewildered glances.

"A joke perhaps?" the general suggested.

The young man shook his head.

"This Monsieur Tresholm seemed perfectly serious," he declared. "I asked him if he were in earnest, and he replied, 'Certainly.... It is, the only profession I have,' he assured me, 'and it keeps me fully occupied.' Those were his words. 'Am I to send this in to the police?' I asked him. 'Certainly,' he assented. 'If they must know my profession, there it is.'"

Humor is without doubt a subtle quality. Here were four men of entirely different outlook upon life, who simultaneously recovered from a fit of astonishment and simultaneously realized that the reception clerk's announcement was very funny indeed. In his own way each laughed to the limit of his capacity. Monsieur Sordel, when he had finished, found it necessary to remove the tears from his eyes.

"You find it funny, Gustave?" his host chaffed him, as soon as he had recovered his own breath. "Yet here, perhaps, is the end of the world for us. A professional gambler, mark you. He may know something. A defeating system may have arrived. Soon you may have to close your doors, Gustave, and I my hotel."

There was a second outburst not quite so prolonged.

Henri waited patiently by. "What am I to do about the gentleman's room, Monsieur Robert?" he inquired.

"Give it to him, by all means," was the prompt reply. "See that Madame Grund adorns it with flowers, that the servants, too, show this eccentric every attention. Stop, though! His luggage!"

"He has a great deal of very superior quality," Henri confided. "There is also a motor-car of expensive make which arrived this morning by road."

"*Ma foi*! He makes it pay!" Monsieur Robert grunted. "But that is very good. Excellent!"

Henri took his leave, and they all began to talk at once.

"An imbecile without a doubt."

"Perhaps a humorist."

"Stop, stop, my friends!" Gustave Sordel begged. "There have been others who have arrived here with equal confidence. We have heard before—we of the Casino—of the invincible system. Our visitor may be very much in earnest. All I can say is, he is welcome."

The young man from the reception bureau once more approached their table.

"I thought it would interest you, sir," he announced, addressing his chief, "to see this gentleman. He has asked for a corner table for luncheon. He arrives now, in the doorway."

They looked at him with very genuine curiosity. A slim but well-built young man, of a little over medium height, carefully but not foppishly dressed in gray tweeds, with admirably chosen tie, collar and shirt. He was fair, and his hair had a slight tendency toward curliness. His complexion was sunburnt, his eyes blue, his features good, and there was a quizzical curve at the corners of his lips and faint lines by his eyes which might have denoted a humorous outlook.

"*Un jeune home très chic*," was Monsieur Robert's criticism.

Gustave Sordel looked at his victim with the eyes of the shearer who has opened his gates to the sheep. "He is of the type," he decided. "They believe in themselves, these young Englishmen with systems. We shall see."

Monsieur Robert grunted once more. "All very well, Gustave, *mon vieux*," he declared, "that man is no fool. Discoveries are being made now which have startled the world—things that were declared impossible. Why should it not have arrived at last—the perfect system?"

Gustave Sordel watched the champagne poured into his glass with a placid smile. "The gambler with inspiration," he observed, "sometimes gives temporary inconvenience, but it is upon the world with systems that we thrive. I will drink to the health of this brave man."

They raised their glasses. All unconscious of their speculations, the subject of their conversation was ordering his luncheon.

Andrew Tresholm, an hour or so later, quite unaware of the interest which his passing through the lounge had excited, stood upon the steps of the hotel, looking out upon the gay little scene. A small boy, posted there for that purpose, rushed to the telephone to announce to the *chefs de partie* and officials of the Casino the impending arrival of this menace to their prosperity. There was a little stir in the hall, and everyone neglected his coffee to lean forward and stare. The Senegalese porter approached with a low bow and a smile.

"The Casino, sir," he announced, pointing to the stucco building across the way.

"I see it" was the somewhat surprised reply. "Darned ugly place, too!"

The man, who spoke only French, let it go at that. Tresholm pointed to a quaint little building perched on the side of the mountain overhead.

"What place is that?" he asked in French.

"The Vistaero Restaurant, sir," the man replied. "The *Salles Priveés* have been open since two o'clock. The Sporting Club will be open at four."

Tresholm showed no particular sign of interest in either announcement. A moment later he descended the steps, and the four very prosperous-looking Frenchmen seated in the lounge enjoying their coffee and cigars, rose to watch him.

"The battle commences," Gustave Sordel exclaimed, with a chuckle.

But apparently the battle was not going to commence, for to the surprise of the four, of the Senegalese hall porter, of the attendants who had all gathered to see this bold stranger depart upon his mission, Tresholm stepped into a very handsome two-seated car which a chauffeur had just brought round, took his place at the wheel, and, skirting the gardens, mounted the hill.

"Ha, ha!" Monsieur Robert joked. "Your victim escapes, Gustave."

"On the contrary," was the complacent reply, "he mounts to the bank."

In less than half an hour, instead of dealing out his packets of mille notes to the ghouls of the Casino according to plan, Andrew Tresholm was leaning over the crazy balcony of the most picturesquely situated restaurant in Europe looking down at what seemed to be a collection of toy buildings out of a child's play-box. Even the Casino, its crudity effaced by distance, might have been the somewhat fanciful palace of a kingdom of dwarfs and the peaceful little port beyond, with its twin lighthouses, fitting harborage for a Lilliputian squadron. His eyes wandered appreciatively but without enthusiasm over the somewhat artificial and too much advertised beauties of the principality, to rest upon the sparking blue of the sea with its flushes of mauve and purple, its thousand scintillations where the sunlight caught the breaking waves....

A waiter at his elbow coughed suggestively, and Tresholm ordered coffee and Grand Marnier. He stretched himself out in a wicker chair, and for the professional gambler removed from the scene of his activities he seemed singularly content. The afternoon was warm, and Tresholm, who had ill endured the lack of ventilation in his so-called train de luxe the night before, dosed peacefully in his chair. He awoke to the sound of familiar voices—a woman's musical and pleading, a man's dogged and irritable.

"Can't you understand the common sense of the thing, Norah?" the latter was arguing. "The luck must turn. It's got to turn. Take my case. I've lost for four nights. Tonight, therefore, I am all the more likely to win. What's the good of going home with the paltry sum we have left? Much better to try to get the whole lot back."

"Five thousand pounds isn't a paltry sum by any means," the girl protested. "It would make things much more comfortable for us even though you still had to go on at the bank."

"Darn the bank," was the vicious rejoinder.

Tresholm, who was now quite awake, rose deliberately to his feet and moved across to them.

"Darn the bank by all means," he acquiesced, "so long as it isn't the one in which my poor savings are invested. Do I, by any chance, come across my young friends of Angoulême once more in some slight trouble? Can I be of any assistance?"

The youth, good-looking but morose, glanced across at him and scowled. The girl swung round in her chair, and a little cry of pleasure broke from her lips.

"Mr. Tresholm!" she exclaimed. "Fancy your being here! Aren't we terrible people, squabbling at the top of our voices in such a beautiful place?"

Tresholm sank into the chair which the young man, with an ungracious greeting, had pushed towards him.

"I seem fated to come up against you two in moments of tribulation," he remarked, speaking languidly, almost with a drawl, as though to give them time to recover. "At Angoulême, I think I really was of some assistance. You would never have reached the place but for my chauffeur, who fortunately knows more about cars than I do. A little pathetic you looked, Miss Norah—forgive me, but I never heard your other name—leaning against the wall by the side of that exquisite mountain road, wondering whether any good-natured person would stop and ask if you were in trouble."

She smiled at the recollection. "And you did stop," she reminded him gratefully. "You helped us wonderfully."

"It was my good fortune," he said lightly, but with a faint note of sincerity in his tone. "And this time? What about it? May I be told the trouble again? A discussion about gambling apparently. Well, I know more about gambling than I do about motor-cars. Let me be your adviser."

"Much obliged. It's no one else's trouble except our own," the young man intervened.

"Or business, I suppose you would like to add," Tresholm observed equably. "Perhaps your sister will be more communicative.

"I told you that night at the hotel at Angoulême of my reputation. I am a meddler in other people's affairs. I like giving advice, and the advice I give is pretty sound stuff too. You young people have been disputing about something. I can see it in your faces. I felt it in the atmosphere round me when I awoke. Let me settle the matter for you."

"Why not?" the girl agreed with enthusiasm. "Let me tell him, Jack."

"You can do as you jolly well please," was the surly rejoinder.

The girl leaned across the little round table towards Tresholm.

She would have been very good-looking indeed if she had not been so pale, and if there had not been dark lines under her violet eyes. Nevertheless, even as she was, Tresholm decided that this further glimpse of her was quite worth the abandonment of his motor tour and the uncomfortable train journey.

"We told you a little about ourselves at Angoulême during the evening of the day when you had been so kind to us," she reminded him. "We are orphans and we have been living together at Norwich, just on the salary Jack gets from the bank where he is junior cashier. Our name, by the by, is Bartlett. Our father was a poor clergyman and we hadn't a penny in the world, except what Jack earned.

"Then two months ago, quite unexpectedly, a distant relative, whom we had scarcely ever heard of, died and left us five thousand pounds each. We decided to pool the money, have a holiday—Jack's vacation was almost due—and, for once in our lives, have a thoroughly good time."

"A very sound idea," Tresholm murmured.

"The place we both wanted to come to," she went on, "was Monte Carlo. We bought a little motor-car—you know something about that—and we reached here a few days ago. It was lots of fun, but, alas, ever since we arrived Jack and I have disagreed. His point of view—"

"I'll tell him that myself." her brother interrupted. "Ten thousand pounds our legacy was—nine thousand we reckoned, when our holiday's paid for, and the car. Well, supposing I invested it, what would it mean? Four hundred and fifty a year. Neither one thing nor the other. It's just about what I'm getting from the bank. It wouldn't have helped me to escape, I should have had to go on just the same, and I hate the work like poison."

"Four hundred and fifty a year would have made life very much easier for us, even though you had to go on working," she remarked wistfully.

"Thinking of yourself as usual," he growled. "Well, anyhow, you agreed at first."

"Agreed to what?" Tresholm inquired.

"To taking our chance of making a bit whilst we were here," he explained. "We decided to risk a couple of thousand pounds and see if we could make enough to chuck the bank and live quietly somewhere in the country, where there was golf and a bit of shooting."

"It wasn't my idea," she ventured.

"Of course, it wasn't," he scoffed. "You're like all women. You're too frightened of losing to make a good sportsman."

"Well, we have lost," she rejoined dryly—"not two thousand but four."

"That seems unfortunate," was Tresholm's grave comment. "What is the present subject of your dispute?"

"Simply this," the young man confided. "We have spent, or shall have spent, by the time we get home, a thousand pounds of the legacy. We have lost at the tables four thousand, and sold the little car we bought for half what we gave for it. We have five thousand left. Norah wants me to promise not to go into the Casino again, and to leave for home at once with five thousand pounds in the bank. I want to go, neck or nothing— win back at least our five thousand—perhaps a good bit more. The luck must turn."

"Quite so," Tresholm agreed. "There's a certain amount of reason in what your brother says, Miss Norah."

She looked at him almost in horror. "You don't mean to say that you're going to advise him to risk the rest of our legacy!" she exclaimed.

Tresholm made no direct reply. He passed around his case and lighted a cigaret himself.

"Well," he pronounced, "I have a certain amount of sympathy for your brother's point of view. If I were in his position and had lost as much as you say, I think I should want a shot at getting some of it back, but," he added, checking the young man's exclamation of delight and the girls little cry of disappointment with the same gesture, "I should want to know that the odds were level."

"Roulette's a fair enough game," the young man protested. "One chance in thirty-five against you—and zero, of course."

"You may call that fair," Tresholm said calmly; "I don't. I am assuming that with your small capital you're backing the numbers. Very well. The bank has the pull on you the whole of the time to the extent of five or six percent. If you play *chemin de fer* the *cagnotte* amounts to about the same thing.

"I am with you in spirit, my young friend, but gambling at Monte Carlo isn't what I call gambling at all. You're fighting a man of equal ability a stone heavier than yourself. It can't be done. It's automatic. You must lose."

"That's what I say," the girl declared triumphantly. "We're simply foolish to dream of throwing away the last of our money."

"But people do win," her brother insisted. "There's that Hungarian who won half a million francs the night before last."

"The Casino takes pretty good care to advertise it when anything of that sort happens," Tresholm pointed out. "He'll probably be in again tonight and lose the lot, and more besides. Now listen to me, Bartlett," he went on. "I'm not against you in spirit. I'm against you in this particular proposal because you want to take on an impossibility.

"The people who win here are just the people who play to amuse themselves, and who go away when they've had their fun. People in your position, with a few thousand pounds left over from a legacy and nothing else to fall back upon in the world, are the people who inevitably lose."

The young man thrust his hands into his trousers pockets. His natural good looks were completely spoilt by his sullen expression.

"It's no good trying to be scientific in gambling," he said. "If you want to have a plunge, you always must have a bit up against you, of course. What's it matter so long as you win? I never mind backing a horse at odds on so long as it's a certainty."

"There is such a thing as fair gambling," Tresholm pointed out. "I'll toss you for your five thousand pounds, if you like. That's a level affair—no *cagnotte*, no zero. You can choose the coin."

The girl gave a little cry. Her brother gasped.

"You're not serious?" he exclaimed.

"Mr. Tresholm!" she remonstrated.

"I'm perfectly serious," he assured them both. "You seem to think that I know nothing about gambling. On the contrary, I am described in the police records of this principality as a professional gambler. I must live up to my reputation. I will toss you for five thousand pounds. I shall probably win as I am usually lucky, and you, I should think, are not. This moment, if you like. Shall I send for a coin?"

"No!" the girl almost shrieked.

Tresholm shrugged his shoulders. "Very well," he acquiesced. "You would like to prolong the agony. Dine with me, both of you, tonight at the Hôtel de Paris at half past eight. We will either toss, or play any game you like where the odds are level, for whatever sum you like up to five thousand pounds."

The girl looked at him reproachfully through a mist of tears. Her brother was exuberant.

"You're a sportsman," he declared. "I wanted to dine at the Paris once more before we left. We'll be there at half past eight."

Gustave Sordel paid a special visit to the hotel just before dinner-time that evening. He encountered Monsieur Robert in the hall.

"But what has arrived!" he exclaimed. "All the afternoon my chefs have been on the *qui vive*. I have reinforced every table to the extent of a hundred thousand francs. I arranged for a high table at *chemin de fer*, and, if Monsieur Tresholm had wished to take a bank at baccarat tonight it could have been managed. Yet behold the strange thing which has arrived. He has not as yet taken out his ticket."

"In the Sporting Club, perhaps?" Monsieur Robert suggested.

"Three times I have sent there. No one of his name has applied for a card."

"This affair gives one to think," Monsieur Robert admitted. "At present he dines with a young Englishman and his sister—a couple *bien distingué*, but poor. They left here last week for a cheaper hotel. Of what interest can they be to him?"

Sordel shrugged his shoulders. "After all," he pointed out, "even a professional gambler must have his moments. He waits for the night without a doubt."

Meanwhile, in the restaurant, Tresholm, to all appearance, was very much enjoying his dinner. Bartlett was excited, and drank perhaps a little more wine than was good for him. Norah, on the other hand, was very silent. She ate and drank little, and her manner, especially towards her host, was reserved, not to say cold.

"Your sister, Bartlett," the latter confided, when the second bottle of champagne was opened, "is displeased with me. I wonder whether I might ask why."

"Because you have taken his side against me," she said, looking at him with a smoldering anger in her eyes. "You are encouraging him to gamble with that last five thousand pounds. I hoped so much that you would have been on my side, that you would have told him to keep that money, for both our sakes, and not to enter the Casino again."

"And if I had told him that," Tresholm asked calmly, "would it have made any difference?"

She reflected for a moment. "Perhaps it would not," she admitted. "He is very self-willed. He would probably have had his own way, and yet somehow or other I am sorry that it should have been you who encouraged this."

"I don't think that you are quite just to blame me," he complained. "You must realize that nothing I could have said would have made the slightest difference. You know that you yourself have used all your persuasions.

Your brother would have lost every penny in the Casino if I had not offered him a saner chance of gambling with me."

"I can't explain," she sighed. "I am just disappointed."

Dinner drew towards a close, but Tresholm waved aside the waiter's suggestion of coffee.

"I have ordered it in my sitting-room," he explained to his guests. "It shall be the prelude to the duel."

They left the table, crossed the lounge and entered the elevator. In the corridor Bartlett stopped to speak to an acquaintance. The girl suddenly turned to her companion.

"Mr. Tresholm," she begged, "don't do this. Let him lose his money in the Casino if he must. I don't like the idea of you two sitting down to play against one another. I don't like it. There's something horrible about it."

"Don't you think," he asked, "that if your brother must throw his money away, I might as well have it as anybody else?"

"Do you mean—do you really mean that you are what you said?"

"I am afraid there is a certain amount of truth in what I told you," he acknowledged. "If you go to the Chef de Sûreté here in Monaco, he will show you my papers."

"Then I think it is all very terrible," she pronounced sadly. "I am very sorry that we ever came to Monte Carlo."

"Now for the terms," Tresholm said, as he and Bartlett seated themselves at a small table. "First of all, here are two tickets for the Blue Train tomorrow. It is understood that, whether you win my money or I win yours, you make use of them."

"Right-o!" the young man agreed, pocketing the yellow slips.

"I require more than a casual acceptance of that proposal," Tresholm persisted. "I require your word of honor."

"That's all right," the other acquiesced. "I promise upon my honor."

"And I am your witness," Norah intervened gravely.

"Furthermore, whether you win or lose," Tresholm continued, "you must promise not to return within twelve months."

"Agreed. Come along. Let's start."

"The game I leave entirely to you," Tresholm announced. "There are, as you see, four new packs of cards. I will cut you highest or lowest to win, whichever you like, or I will play you two-handed poker, or piquet, or any other game you prefer."

There was a sudden gleam in the young man's eyes. "Piquet?" he repeated. "You play piquet?"

"Rather well," Tresholm warned him. "I should advise you to choose something else."

Bartlett laughed confidently. "Piquet's good enough for me," he declared. "I used to play it with my old governor every night. Let's get on with it," he added, moistening his dry lips. "A hundred pounds a time, eh?"

"Whatever you like," was the reply.

It was midnight before the matter was concluded. Bartlett, white and distraught, with a dangerous, almost lunatic, gleam in his eyes, was pacing the room excitedly. Norah, unexpectedly calm, was still seated in the chair from which she had watched the gambling with changeless expression. Tresholm remained at the table. Before him lay a check for five thousand pounds which the young man had just signed.

"Ready, Jack?" she asked at last.

"I suppose so," he growled. "Come along."

Tresholm rose to his feet. "You've had a fair deal with level odds for your money, haven't you?" he asked his late opponent.

"I'm not complaining," was the broken reply. "I suppose it's no use asking you to lend me a hundred just to have one shot at the Sporting Club?"

"Not the least use in the world," Tresholm refused. "The hundred pounds would go just where the rest of your money has gone. There are some of us who are made to win at games of chance; others to lose. You are one of the predestined losers. If you take my advice, you will never again, so long as you live, indulge in any game of chance for money." He opened the door. The girl passed out, slim and dignified, without a glance in his direction.

"Good night, Miss Bartlett," he ventured.

"Good night, Mr. Tresholm," she replied. "I congratulate you upon your profitable evening."

With that they both disappeared. Tresholm mixed himself a drink and returned to his place at the table, playing idly with the cards.

The Blue Train, disturbingly early upon its return journey, just as it is usually outrageously late upon its arrival, came groaning round the bend from Mentone, snorting and puffing into the Monte Carlo station. Norah settled down sadly in her compartment while her brother made his way to the restaurant car to secure seats for dinner.

Then, glancing idly out of the window, she suddenly gave a little gasp. Very deliberately along the platform came Tresholm, calm and undisturbed. Behind him was a small boy carrying an enormous bouquet of roses.

She shrank beck in her place. Anything rather than see him! Before she could decide upon any means of escape, however, the roses were on the seat by her side, and Tresholm, neat and debonair as usual, was standing bare-headed before her.

"A little farewell offering for you, Miss Bartlett, which you must accept, and a farewell note here for you to read as soon as the train has started," he added, handing her a letter. "Will you shake hands?"

In her moment of indecision she forgot, and she looked up at him. Directly her eyes met his, clear, gray and somehow compelling, she gave in. Her fingers rested for a moment in his. Then he raised them and brushed them with his lips.

"I am glad," he said gratefully, "that you did not carry your resentment too far. You will accept the roses, I hope, as an inadequate peace-offering, and think of me as kindly as you can."

Then he was gone, and it was not until after the train had passed through the first of the two tunnels that she remembered the note. She tore open the envelope and read:

Dear Lady of Angoulême,

I very much fear that your perceptions were keener than your brother's last night, and that you realized the fact that I was playing with marked cards—part of the equipment of the professional gambler. The unexpected luxury of a qualm of conscience has, however, seized me, and I return your brother's check for his imaginary loss.

I still hold him, however, to the conditions of our bargain, and, if you will accept the advice of such an unprincipled person, keep him away from gambling in any shape or form even though the odds should seem level. There are some men who are born winners. I am one of them. There are others who are born losers. Your brother is one of those.

Fate, alas, deals out other favors to the latter class, which she denies to the former.

Which is why I must sign myself,

Unhappily yours,
Andrew Tresholm.

Fragments of a torn check fluttered across the compartment. Even in her dazed state, even under the spell of that great throbbing joy with which she waited for her brother's return, there crept into her mind a faint, wonderful doubt—a doubt which sometimes, when she looked backwards, seemed to color those hours of agony with a little halo of romance. Was it altogether by chance, she wondered, in those moments of reflection, that the only possible means by which her brother could have been induced to return to England with that five thousand pounds were precisely those which Tresholm had employed?

In his sitting-room, Tresholm found the four packs of cards neatly stacked upon the mantelpiece. He rang the bell for the waiter.

"You might return those," he begged, "to whomever you borrowed them from."

The waiter collected them with a smile, also the fifty-franc note which Tresholm passed him.

"I borrowed them from one of the clerks in the office, Monsieur," he confided. "I trust that Monsieur had fortune."

Tresholm nodded slightly, but without his usual smile.

"Yes, I am generally lucky," he confessed.

A Fool and His Money

Tresholm brought his car to a standstill in the deep pool of shade under a close-leaved magnolia tree, jammed on the brakes and lighted a cigaret. For six miles, ascending gradually all the time from the sea-level, he had climbed the tortuous mountainous road until he had reached the fruitful plateau which embosoms the slopes of the Lesser Alps. Blue and gold, the landscape lay below him, gray here and there with the shimmer of turning olive leaves, the vineyards and meadows like little squares of patchwork, the flower fields daubs of brilliant color, the river winding its way amongst them, a glittering thread of silver. In front, barely a mile distant, was one of the old hill towns, the houses of which might well have been carved out of the living rock. The air around him was pleasantly brisk. In the majestic distance, the snow still lay upon the mountains.

His resting-place was peaceful and well-chosen. On his right was a humble French domain, a trim white dwelling-house, with red roof and green shutters, separated from the road by a carefully tended vineyard, an orchard of orange trees wandering up to a plantation of pines behind. A very pleasant, sunny spot it seemed, cut off from the world by the ravine, on the farther summit of which was the old town and the precipitous way by which one climbed from the great thoroughfares below. Scarcely a human being in sight, scarcely a toiler in the fields.

An imaginary solitude. Tresholm, although his nerves were the best, started as he realized the fixed stare of a gaunt figure in blue jeans, standing only a few feet away from him in the vineyard, partially concealed by a scrubby hawthorn hedge. It was more than the ordinary scrutiny of the curious peasant; in fact, it became clear to Tresholm during those first few seconds that the man was not a peasant at all.

He was tall and thin, and there was something fine-cut about his features, sunburnt and worn though they were. The brown fingers which grasped the pruning-knife were well-formed and shapely, and as he returned that intense gaze, a queer wave of remembrance swept into Tresholm's brain. Like pieces of a jig-saw puzzle those scraps of memory mocked him: the bleak wind-swept plain; the wilderness, dotted all over with a maze of tin huts and framework buildings; the roar of a great city with its myriads of blinding lights; a room high up in a huge official building, the thunder of traffic below, the ceaseless movement of multitudes crawling like ants along the pavements.

Perhaps the two men reached the end of that unwinding coil of memory at the same moment, for the watcher in the vineyard turned abruptly away and strode off towards the house. With a muttered exclamation, Tresholm pressed the starting-button of his car, turned in at the rude gateway, drove up the rock-strewn approach to the house, and pulled up in its shadow. He descended, and waited for the man who was still climbing from below.

"You're Dows, aren't you?" he greeted him. "Jasper Dows, Naval Intelligence Department at Washington? Let me see, how many years ago?... Who cares?"

"I am Jasper Dows, all right," he admitted, "but Washington, Naval Intelligence Department—I don't know what you're talking about. All gone! I'm a small landed proprietor of Les Tourettes. Eighty acres—you can see the lot. I remember you, though. You're Tresholm. Blast you!"

"Why blast me?" his visitor remonstrated.

Jasper Dows laughed bitterly and stood for a moment in silence. When he spoke again, there was a change in his manner.

Some of the resentment had gone.

"Not your fault, of course, Tresholm," he acknowledged. "Come in and drink a bottle of wine. It's long enough since I talked my own language."

They passed into a small sitting-room, in which were some quaint pieces of old Provençal furniture, a mass of flowers in a rude china basin, but with carpetless floor and empty walls, poverty lurking even in its cleanliness. A woman rose hastily from a chair in a corner with its back to the window—a woman far too attractive for her surroundings, evidently English or American, a little startled at the sight of an unexpected visitor.

"A gentleman whom I used to know, Sara," the master of the house announced. "My wife, Tresholm. We want a bottle of last year's vintage, dear, and a couple of glasses."

She greeted Tresholm pleasantly, left them for a few minutes, and returned with a bottle of wine and two glasses upon a tray.

"The most brutal thing I ever did, to bring her over here," Jasper Dows acknowledged, as, with a word of excuse, she hurried away again. "She would come, though. She's that sort of woman."

"But what was the trouble?" Tresholm asked gravely. "When I left Washington—"

"You knew nothing about it, of course," the other interrupted. "The trouble was disgrace and ruin."

"That's rather hard to believe."

"There were a few men in my department who thought so at the time. They changed their minds though, and out I went. I got the sack, Tresholm. Cashiered—chucked out of the service. Do you know who brought it about? Of course you don't. I'll tell you. Here's one of them."

He picked up a copy of the Nice Éclaireur, which had been lying upon the table, and read a paragraph from the English and American news:

"'Considerable excitement has been caused in the Sporting Club during this week by the very spirited gambling of an American millionaire, Mr. Josh Chandler, of New York. We understand that he was successful in breaking the bank twice in one evening.' That's one of them," Jasper Dows continued, throwing the paper down. "Josh Chandler was one, and you were the other."

"Are you serious?" Tresholm expostulated, wondering for the moment whether the man had lost his wits.

"Sit down, drink your wine, and listen. You are the one man in the world to whom I can tell the story."

Tresholm listened, and it was late in the afternoon, with the sun sinking over the Estérels, when he glided down again from the farm among the mountains to take his place in the stream of vehicles panting along the lighted way.

Gustave Sordel, being at a loose end the following morning, crossed the road from the Casino about a quarter of an hour before luncheon, and took an *aperitif* with his friend Monsieur Robert, the director of the hotel. They found seats in a retired corner of the lounge.

"The doors of the Casino are still open?" the latter demanded, in gentle badinage.

"And likely to remain open, so far as regards this eccentric of yours," was the good-humored reply. "Figure to yourself, my dear friend, this Monsieur Tresholm. He rests here within a stone's throw of the Casino, he inscribes himself a professional gambler, and he has not yet taken out his card of admission. What does he do with himself?"

"I will tell you what he did yesterday," Monsieur Robert volunteered. "He left his chauffeur, and he drove out into the country. When he returned, he dined alone—the dinner of an epicure, mind you, and drank with it half a bottle of my choicest Burgundy."

"And afterwards?"

"He went to bed."

"*Imbécile*—for what does he wait?"

"For money, perhaps. One cannot storm your stronghold, my dear Gustave, without the sinews of war."

The director of the Casino moved a little nearer to his friend.

"As to that," he confided, lowering his voice, "I can tell you something. Have no fear for your hotel bill. Yesterday morning—it must have been before our friend started for his motor trip—I was at the bank, and I—I myself, mind you, was compelled to wait. An important client was with the manager.

"When he came out from the office it was this Monsieur Tresholm. They were around him as though he were a Rothschild. The manager even escorted him to the door whilst I waited."

Monsieur Robert was interested. "You ventured upon an inquiry, perhaps?"

"Up there they are discreet," was the cautious reply. "Monsieur Blunt, as you know, has little to say. In his position, he is wise. He brushed aside all my interrogations. 'Monsieur Tresholm,' he whispered in my ear, 'comes to us with excellent recommendations from the highest quarters.' What more than that can be said of any stranger? Yet that is the man who announces himself as a professional gambler, and in four days he has not crossed the threshold of the Casino or of the Sporting Club."

They spoke of other things, and as they talked Tresholm himself entered. He was in tennis togs, carrying a racket under his arm, and instead of passing directly across the lounge, he made a detour towards the restaurant which led him past the divan where the two men were seated. The hotel director greeted him cordially.

"Monsieur was successful in finding a game this morning?" he inquired.

"I found just the game I hoped for," Tresholm confided.

"Excellent! And your apartments, they are comfortable—there is nothing one can do?"

"Nothing whatever," was the courteous assurance. "Everything is as one expects to find it at the Hôtel de Paris—perfect."

He would have moved on, but his interlocutor detained him.

"Let me present my friend, Monsieur Sordel," he begged. "It is Monsieur Tresholm, you understand," he added, turning to his companion, "who has perpetrated this jest upon the Chef de Sûreté. I present, you understand, one professional to another. It is a matter of attack and defense. Monsieur Sordel directs the Casino."

Tresholm smiled as he shook hands. "Your friend then," he remarked, "is a man of many affairs."

"As yet," Sordel rejoined, "I have not had to number you amongst my responsibilities."

"That will come without a doubt," Tresholm predicted. "When I first arrived, I had some young friends to entertain. Yesterday the weather was so perfect that I had a fancy for the country. Today, who knows?"

He passed on with a nod of farewell, and the two men exchanged significant glances.

"It may be today then," Gustave Sordel observed.

Tresholm paused to interview a *maître d'hôtel* and order luncheon for two in half an hour, after which he ascended to his room, took a shower-bath and changed his clothes. He descended in time to welcome his guest—an American, Chandler by name, his recent opponent at tennis, and a man apparently of about his own age. There was a marked difference between the two, however, as they strolled together into the restaurant—Tresholm lean, bright-eyed and sunburnt, to all appearances as hard as nails, and in perfect condition; his companion, built on stockier lines, more than a little fleshy, carefully dressed and groomed, but with the air of one to whom the night pleasures of the principality had made their successful appeal. He demanded a second and a third cocktail before he commenced luncheon, throughout which he drank high-balls with the thirst of a man only recently escaped from the shadows of prohibition.

"Lucky to have come across you this morning," he remarked, as they took their places. "Don't know that I should have got a game at all. Fellows here seem sort of cliquish. Don't fancy taking a stranger in if they can help it."

"I dare say they make up their sets beforehand," Tresholm suggested tactfully.

"Maybe. Guess I'd better let a few of them know who I am. My old dad left twenty million of the best. You bet I don't have to wait long for a game at any club over on the other side."

"Twenty million dollars is a great deal of money."

"Piled it up during the war, the old man did," his son confided.

"You were over on this side?"

"Didn't get the chance. I was in the navy, but they wanted me in Washington. Seaplane stuff, most of the time. Gosh, they kept me at it, too!"

His first high-ball was beginning to loosen the young man's tongue. He was filled with placid satisfaction with himself and his surroundings.

"Say, I ought not to have let you whip me like that this morning," he observed. "Six-two, six-one. Not often I get it in the neck like that."

"A little lazy round the back line, weren't you? A late night?"

"Say, if anyone can tell me how to get to bed early in this little burg, he's a winner with me," Chandler declared gloomily. "I was playing chemie until five this morning."

"I rather thought roulette was your game," Tresholm remarked. "Didn't I see that you had a big win yesterday or the day before?"

"A hundred and thirty-eight thousand of the best, I skun 'em," the young man boasted. "I had them all scared. They don't understand having anyone up against them who can afford to lose just as much as he wants to. It don't matter a snap of the fingers to me whether I win or not. That's where I've got them cold."

"A hundred and thirty-eight thousand," Tresholm repeated softly, thinking for a moment of that poverty-stricken farm up in the mountains. "That's a great deal of money, Mr. Chandler."

"I guess it seems so over here," was the complacent reply. "See that bulge in my pocket? There it is, and they can have the lot back this evening, if they can get it."

Conversation languished for a time, and then continued upon somewhat formal lines. Towards the close of their meal, the American, who had been scrutinizing his host closely, asked him an abrupt question.

"Say, haven't we met somewhere before, Mr. Tresholm? Something about you seems kind of familiar to me ever since you came up and asked me for a game."

"I shouldn't be surprised," was the somewhat vague acknowledgment. "It's a small world, you know."

"Ever been in the States?"

"Not lately. I dare say we come across each other in Paris or somewhere," Tresholm observed. "I wander about a good deal."

"Same here. I don't have to do any work, and over this side's good enough for me. You Europeans know how to live the life. Say, that's a bully two-seater of yours, Mr. Tresholm."

"Glad you like it. How about a little run into the country this afternoon?"

"It will keep me awake at any rate," the young man agreed.

At Nice, Chandler, who had dropped off to sleep before they had reached Beaulieu, woke up and demanded a high-ball. They stopped at the Negresco bar where he relapsed into an easy chair with a sigh of content.

"Some car of yours," he admitted; "but I guess we've come about far enough, eh? This seems a pretty good spot to me."

"Only a little farther on," Tresholm begged. "I want to call on a man I used to know, if you don't mind. We can look in here again coming back, if you want to."

Chandler's acquiescence was a little ungracious, but he suffered himself presently to be escorted out to the car where he sank back among the cushions and promptly went to sleep. Tresholm drove smoothly on until they were just short of Cagnes, when he turned off the main road and crept upwards towards the ridge which encircled the lesser mountains.

Outside the little farmhouse, he pulled up and shook his companion.

"Come along in and see my pal," he invited.

Chandler sat up, blinking, and looked around him. "Where are we?" he demanded.

"Somewhere between Cagnes and Vence. We have a visit to pay."

Chandler descended grumpily, and Tresholm, opening the unfastened front door, ushered him into the bare sitting-room. The unwilling guest looked about him distastefully.

"Don't seem to me as though we'd get a drink here," he decided. "I guess I'll leave you to your friend and wait outside."

Then Tresholm did an unexpected thing. He locked the door, placed the key in his pocket and pointed to a hard wooden chair.

"You'll sit there, and wait until we've finished a little matter of business," he directed.

Josh Chandler was dumfounded. He stared first at the man who had suddenly abandoned his role of courteous if somewhat silent host and addressed these threatening words to him, and then at the no-less-alarming figure in blue overalls who had pushed aside the curtains and appeared upon the threshold of an inner room. As he stared, his memory also reasserted itself. His sleepy, drink-sodden brain cleared beneath the shock.

"Good Heavens!" he exclaimed. "It's Jasper Dows—and"—his eyes traveled fearfully towards Tresholm—"and the Englishman!"

There was a brief silence. His gaze wandered from the worn face of his former associate back to Tresholm, cold, supercilious, tight-lipped, hard yet flexible as a piece of steel.

"What's this—a hold-up?" he demanded. "I'm getting out of here."

"You'll stay just where you are," Tresholm enjoined calmly.

"Who's going to stop me?"

"I am. You can have a rough-house if you want it, Chandler. Oh, yes, I know you're a strong fellow, but I am a boxer. You wouldn't live with me for thirty seconds. No good patting your hip pocket either. I felt you over in the car. You'd better listen quietly."

"What the—"

"Oh, do be quiet," Tresholm begged a little wearily. "It isn't any use. You're up against it. You've recognized me. I know the truth as between you and Jasper Dows. You'd better look upon me as your protector. I think if I left you two alone, he'd kill you."

"Do you think I'm afraid?"

"You ought to be if you're not," was the quiet rejoinder. "If you think a thrashing will help you to listen more patiently, come outside and have it. If not, get back to your chair."

"I'm right enough here. Get on with it."

"We won't specify the actual date," Tresholm began, "but some ten or eleven years ago, not being in the financial position to which your father's millions have since boosted you, you sold copies of various plans of proposed new American seaplanes to the secret service agent of another country who happened to be in Washington."

Chandler looked around the room as though to be sure that there were no other auditors but that stern, haggard figure standing between the parted curtains.

"I sold them to you," he said hoarsely. "I've been wondering—I was wondering all luncheon-time where I'd seen you before."

"Quite right," Tresholm acknowledged. "You sold them to me, and I paid you a very handsome sum of money for them. Unfortunately, the fact that the plans had been copied leaked out, and the affair was traced either to Jasper Dows, or to you. As is usually the case, the innocent man got it in the neck, and you, the guilty one, escaped.

"Jasper Dows was considered lucky to be cashiered. His father cut off his allowance and died without leaving him a penny. His friends gave him the cold shoulder, and here he is, working himself to death, earning just enough to live on. By rights, you ought to be in his place, Chandler. I know the person from whom I bought the plans, don't I?"

The accused man leaned forward. His eyes were full of a very malicious light.

"You know all right, you confounded spy," he agreed, "but you can't tell. Supposing I did sell them to you, what about it? You can't open your mouth, and I'm not going to. There isn't another soul in the world knows the truth—and you can't tell."

Tresholm eyed him for a moment meditatively. "What a foul swine you are," he remarked, in bitter disgust. "However, either you forget one trifling circumstance, or things may be different in your country. We have a statute of limitations—ten years it is fixed at in my department. The ten years are up. Added to this, my papers went in some time ago. I am a free man, Chandler. How do you like that?"

Apparently, Chandler didn't like it at all.

"What do you mean?" he exclaimed. "Is this blackmail?"

Tresholm inclined his head very slightly. "I always said that you were not quite a fool, Chandler," he confided. "It is blackmail, and you are the victim."

The young man was dazed. Tresholm pointed authoritatively to his chair. He sat down.

"Let us consider the matter now from a business point of view," he continued. "Jasper Dows, you had better join us."

"I'll stay where I am," was the low, passionate reply. "If I'm in the same room I might kill him."

Tresholm nodded sympathetically.

"Quite so," he assented. "Well, I'll proceed on your behalf. Our friend Jasper Dows, Chandler, would have inherited at least half a million from his father, if it hadn't been for your machinations. Very well, we'll start with that. I think you told me on the tennis-courts this morning, and at luncheon today—several times, if I remember rightly—that the old man, as you called him, had left you twenty millions. We'll take half a million away from you. Half a million dollars, Chandler—not a great sum for the ruin of a man's life."

"What else?" was the gruff demand.

"Several little things. First of all, you won, as all Monte Carlo knows, a hundred and thirty-eight thousand francs last night. I can see the mille notes bulging in your pockets. You have even confided to me the fact of their presence there. You will hand them over to Jasper Dows for immediate expenses."

"What else?"

"Ah, now we come to the point. Your confession of having sold the plans, and of Jasper Dows' innocence, is drawn up here. Your signature will be witnessed by the American consul, who is now walking with Mrs. Dows in the garden, but—listen to me calmly—this is where my friend Jasper Dows is inclined to be generous. He has, as it happens, no desire to return permanently to America. Your confession, therefore, will only be used to insure the clearing of his name.

"That is to say, it will simply be placed before the authorities in Washington. His rank in the service will be restored, and that is all he desires. You have nothing to lose in this direction, for you held no commission. You were simply a skulker, placed in the department by influence to escape active service."

"I'll have nothing to do with this business!" Chandler shouted.

"Wait!" Tresholm begged, holding out his hand. "Consider for a moment what will happen if you agree. You will have made such atonement as is possible to Jasper Dows, even though it may have been under compulsion. For the rest of his life he will enjoy the comfort of which you have deprived him for the last ten years, and his honor will be re-established. Consider what a relief this will be to that sensitive conscience of yours, Chandler."

"Blast you!" the other snarled.

"On the other hand," Tresholm went on, unmoved, "if you refuse, being a free-lance in life and having a fancy for my friend Jasper Dows here, and his wife, I shall take the trouble to pay a visit to Washington myself, where I still have many friends. I shall place the facts before the authorities, and I shall place them equally before every one of those enterprising and brilliant young journalists who are apt to gather around when any social scandal or the rumor of it arises. In other words, Chandler, I'll emblazon your name on the roll of disgrace from New York to San Francisco, and never again, so long as you live, will you be able to put your foot upon the deck of a westward-bound steamer."

Chandler unbuttoned his coat threw the great pile of mille notes upon the table, produced his check-book and drew his chair up to the table.

"I'm beat," he decided.

"I always said that you were not quite a fool," Tresholm acknowledged pleasantly. "Dows, you might call in Mr. Wiseley."

At Nice, on their homeward journey, Tresholm stopped outside a garage.

"I have brought you so far, much against my inclination," he said to his companion. "You can hire a car here. Get out and look after yourself."

Chandler slouched surlily off, and Tresholm drove on to Monte Carlo.

They sat together in the sunshine outside the Café de Paris the next morning—Jasper Dows and Tresholm. The former had just descended the hill from the bank.

"So it was all right, eh?" his companion asked.

Jasper Dows had the air of a man who had been living in the darkness for years. Even his tone, when he spoke, was the tone of one half dazed.

"They didn't even hesitate," he announced wonderingly. "The money was there already to my credit—five hundred thousand dollars in French francs. I could have drawn the lot if I'd liked."

"Good! Where's the wife?"

Dows' face suddenly softened. An almost beatific smile parted his lips. One might have fancied that his eyes were a little dim.

"She's shopping," he confided. "I just pushed a handful of mille notes into her bag, and she's gone off with them like a child into toy-land. After ten years' poverty, Tresholm! Never a hundred francs to spend. Making and remaking old clothes.... And now she's shopping!"

Tresholm summoned a waiter and busied himself with the lighting of a cigaret. Jasper Dows was feeling his way back to life again.

"There was one thing yesterday, Tresholm," he said, "that puzzled me. Our Secret Service isn't quite the same as yours, of course, but—that statute of limitations now. I don't quite get that."

Tresholm leaned back in his chair and looked up at the blue sky. "Chandler's just the sort of idiot who would swallow such a story," he murmured. "You and I know well enough, Dows, that never so long as I lived could I have opened my lips."

"It was just a bluff then?"

Tresholm nodded. "It seemed the only way of dealing with him—just a gamble as to whether he swallowed it or not. I like a gamble sometimes. Rather in my line, as it happens," he added, pausing to wave his hand to Gustave Sordel, who was passing.

The Master Cheat of Monte Carlo

Tresholm stood upon the topmost step of the Hôtel de Paris at Monte Carlo, looking doubtfully out at a not very exhilarating prospect. A low-lying bank of clouds obscured the panoramic hills, the pavements were rain-splashed, there were little puddles in the road.

The chairs and tables at the Café de Paris opposite were piled up together. The *commissionnaire* outside the Casino awaited arrivals with a huge umbrella already unfurled. The Senegalese head porter, standing by Tresholm's side, showed all his white teeth in a smile of expectancy.

"A day for the Casino, Monsieur," he hazarded.

Tresholm gazed meditatively across the Place at the great stucco-fronted building, and the very fact of his hesitation seemed to create a little wave of excitement in his immediate neighborhood. The man who worked the lift to the underground passage held open the gates hopefully. A boy in buttons prepared for a dash across the Place to announce the coming event.

By intuition, or some invisible means, the rumor of this long-expected descent upon the stronghold of gambling began to spread. The chief *maître d'hôtel* of the restaurant, followed by two of his subordinates, strolled up as though casually to pay respects to an excellent client.

"A day to remain indoors, I fear, Monsieur," he ventured. "One might amuse oneself at the tables for a time."

Tresholm nodded absently. As yet he made no move. Several people in the lounge prepared to follow him if he should cross the square.

A self-declared professional gambler who had been in Monte Carlo for at least a week, and had not once entered the gambling rooms! The thing was amazing.

This morning, however, what else could happen? There was the Casino, with its doors hospitably open, through which was passing all the time a little stream of the world in mackintoshes. The thing seemed predestined.

And then there happened what can happen only upon the Riviera, and most often in Monte Carlo. A thin shaft of silver appeared from some partially hidden place and crept down from skywards. The gray puddles flashed like molten silver. A few loiterers glanced upwards and furled their umbrellas. The waiters from the Café de Paris came tentatively out and, after a look around, began to rearrange the chairs and tables.

The shaft of sunlight grew broader with the moments. Up in the sky a patch of deep, distinct blue was unexpectedly visible. The slanting drops of rain for one moment became diamonds, and then ceased. The dull, metallic sea sparkled once more. Over head, the clouds were parting like the drawing of a curtain in a theater, and were disclosing more blue sky at every moment.

And then, unmistakably, sunshine—sunshine smiling down upon the Place as though to explain that those leaden hours had been just a joke, a little effort of contrast, now exhausted. The sun shone clearly, its tender warmth chasing all the damp out of the moist atmosphere. Monte Carlo was itself again. Tresholm threw away his cigaret and lighted another one.

"Good!" he exclaimed to his Senegalese friend in the blue uniform. "I shall go out to Cagnes and play golf."

The man tried to conceal his disappointment as he summoned the car. The lift attendant turned away in disgust. The *maître d'hôtel* followed his example. The expectant little crowd in the lounge resumed their places, and Tresholm stepped into his coupé and disappeared. Later in the day, it was to mean something to him that the sunshine should have appeared at that particular moment.

Tresholm put on his brakes, stopping the car at once, while his headlights disclosed more clearly the man standing in the middle of the road with uplifted and supplicating arms. After a round of golf, he was in an excellent humor and prepared to play the good Samaritan to anyone. A broken-down car, perhaps? Someone desiring a lift? He leaned forward to scrutinize the man who had hailed him, and a very unpleasant and disturbing sight he was.

"Monsieur will descend," a hoarse voice insisted.

Tresholm, for once in his life, was utterly taken by surprise and uncertain for the moment how to act. With his hand upon the door of the car stood a person of most ruffianly appearance, wearing a narrow black mask and holding with very firm fingers an ugly-looking automatic. Not only that, but a second man had appeared out of the shadows and was hanging on the other door.

It is probable that if Tresholm had not been dreaming and required several seconds to realize the position, his impulse to make a dash for it would have been successful. As it was, however, the opportunity had passed. His first assailant had him at his mercy, and the man who had clambered up behind was in a position to deal him a nasty blow on the top of his head.

Tresholm reflected quickly. He had only a few mille with him, and he was unarmed. Discretion was certainly indicated. He held up his hands.

"I will descend," he agreed, "if you will wait while I draw to the side of the road."

"*Vite!*" was the harsh command.

Tresholm had every intention of keeping his word, but there was a sudden and most unexpected change in the situation. A flashlight illuminated the road. There was the report of a gun from behind, followed by another. The man who had accosted him, without a second's hesitation, dashed for the wood from which he had issued, followed by his companion, and the third, who had clambered into the coupé, leaped out and went down the ravine on the other side like a scared rabbit.

Tresholm descended to find them all disappeared, and the *deus ex machina* a small two-seated car with dazzling headlights, which had evidently just turned the corner. In the middle of the road stood the slim figure of a woman, with a smoking pistol still in her hand.

She remained steadily on guard and beckoned him to her. He obeyed the summons, hat in hand. The twilight was merging into night, but the moon had scarcely yet risen. He saw her only indistinctly, but he gathered she was young, and to all appearance French.

"Mademoiselle," he said, "I am infinitely grateful for your opportune arrival."

She inclined her head very slightly. "One is foolish to travel along this road at night without being prepared for trouble," she remarked. "Monsieur is probably a tourist, or he would have known that."

"It is unfortunately true," he admitted.

"You are hurt?"

"Not a scratch."

"Or robbed?"

"Neither, thanks to you, Mademoiselle."

She glanced at him for a moment intently, almost, he thought, inquisitively. He saw now that her eyes were dark and her features regular. She was sufficiently good-looking, but her appearance was spoiled by a lowering, almost sulky expression. She seemed to resent his presence, to resent having been under the necessity of offering aid. Her voice only was pleasant.

"Monsieur speaks French so well," she said coldly, "that I am in doubt as to his nationality."

"I am English. My name is Tresholm, and I am staying at the Hôtel de Paris."

For the first time, she showed signs of definite interest. She studied him earnestly, and there was curiosity in her eyes which for a moment he failed to understand.

"You are the eccentric," she asked, "who registered here as a professional gambler?"

"My little joke," he apologized.

"Nevertheless," she went on, "you must have had some reason for what you did. You play cards? You gamble at times, yes?"

"Now and then," he admitted.

"Piquet, perhaps?"

For a moment, Tresholm was oppressed with a sense of unreality. The situation seemed to him too absurdly fantastic. An attack by footpads in the center of civilisation, a deliverer so unexpected and apparently so unwilling, a question so apparently pointless!

What on earth could it matter to her or to anyone whether or not he played a somewhat neglected game? His companion appeared to realize his bewilderment; she stamped her foot at him gently in the dust and frowned at him impatiently.

"Please do not think that I am a crazy woman," she begged. "I have a reason for asking you such a question. Now will you please listen to me. You are Mr. Tresholm. Very well. You will admit that I have been of some service to you."

"A service for which I am greatly obliged," he assured her. "I should certainly have lost my temper and my money, if nothing else, but for your opportune arrival."

"Well, you shall do something for me in return," she said, still without the vestige of a smile, or any note of graciousness in her tone. "You will do me the favor of accompanying me to the villa where I live, which is near here, and taking either a whisky and soda or a cocktail before you proceed."

"I shall be delighted," he acquiesced.

She stepped back into her car and took her place at the wheel. "Will you follow me, please?" she asked. "I would ask you to drive with me, but I see that you have no chauffeur. Your car is not damaged?"

"Not in the least. The engine is still running."

The two-seated car moved slowly on, with Tresholm behind. Just before reaching the outskirts of Monaco, the girl extended her hand, and they turned down one of the narrow roads which connect the Lower and Upper Corniche. After a few hundred yards' descent her hand went out again, and she turned between two broken-down gates, along an ill-kempt cypress-bordered drive, until they reached a deserted-looking villa.

The façade, which had once been a Provençal brown, was weather-stained and shabby. Its rows of windows were like great staring eyes, uncurtained; the gardens were desolate; the whole place had an unkempt and forsaken appearance.

The girl descended from her car, turned the handle of the door, and, in obedience to her gesture, Tresholm followed her into an ill-furnished room upon the ground floor. Her first action was to throw her hat upon the table. Then she looked at the clock.

"A quarter to seven," she murmured, as though to herself. "Monsieur Tresholm, it is very kind of you to pay me this little visit."

"If I can be of any service," he ventured, more than ever puzzled.

"You may be," she answered. "I cannot tell. It depends upon what manner of man you are. You seem to have courage, although you let yourself be rescued from footpads by a girl."

He shrugged his shoulders. "I submitted to the inevitable, Mademoiselle," he replied.

She opened a deal cupboard and placed a bottle of whisky, a siphon and a glass upon the table. There were other bottles, at which she looked meditatively.

"Perhaps," she said, "you will consider that I have brought you here under false pretenses. A cocktail, I warn you, would be difficult. I do not suppose we have any ice in the house."

"I prefer a whisky and soda," he assured her hastily.

"Then you will help yourself," she invited. "Have you ever heard of this villa before, Mr. Tresholm? Do you know who I am?"

He shook his head. "I must confess my ignorance."

"Well, they talk about us sometimes," she remarked,—"not very favorably. This is supposed to be a place to avoid. I live here with my father. He is supposed to be a man with whom you should have nothing to do. You are sure that you have not heard of us?"

"Quite sure, Mademoiselle."

"My name is Brignolles—Lucie Brignolles."

He shook his head in response to the question in her eyes. "I am sorry," he confessed, "but the name is unfamiliar to me."

"You never heard of either of us?"

"The other one being—?"

"My father—Monsieur Brignolles."

"Unfortunately, no. You must remember that you yourself correctly described me as a tourist."

"So much the better," she declared. "I will tell you about my father before we begin. You call yourself a professional gambler. An effort at humor, I should imagine," she sneered, "for you seem prosperous. My father is also a professional gambler. Unfortunately, the occasion is rare nowadays when he can find anyone to play with him. His reputation is none too good. He is barred from the Casino. We have no friends. Are you listening?"

"I have heard every word," he assured her.

She looked across at him gloomily. He thought that he never had seen a more sullen expression in his life. Even the beauty of her eyes was marred.

"My father has ill health," she went on. "He cannot live very long. He has only one passion, and that is to play cards and to rob anyone who plays with him. I have to tell you this, but I am his daughter, and my sympathies are entirely with him as against any fool whose money he can take. I have been to Nice to try to find someone to come and play piquet. He is quite invincible at piquet. He can win just as much money as his opponent chooses to play for. Will you play with him?"

"Certainly I will," Tresholm accepted, with a queer little smile. "I must warn you that I am rather good at the game myself."

"You could not succeed against my father, because he cheats," she rejoined curtly. "Nevertheless, it will probably make his last few days happier, if he can win some money from you. Can you afford to lose?"

"I certainly can," Tresholm assured her.

"You are wealthy?" she insisted.

"Sufficiently."

"Remember," she told him, "you are fully warned. You will not complain afterwards?"

"I give you my promise," he replied, "that I will submit to whatever may happen to me."

She produced another siphon of soda-water and set out a card-table. "You need not be afraid of the whisky and soda," she said dryly. "This is a gambler's den, but that is the end of it. You are here to be cheated, and I am the vamp, but the drinks are all right. How do you think I play the part?"

"In an entirely original manner, if you will allow me to say so."

Her eyes flashed. For a moment he thought that she was going to strike him. She restrained herself, however.

"You are quite right," she said. "I do not suppose I should be much of a success in the places you are used to. Sit there, please, and wait while I fetch my father. Your solitude will give you an excuse to escape if you are afraid."

He mixed himself a drink and opened the door for her. She passed him as though utterly unconscious of his presence.

Tresholm resumed his seat with a little grin. He loved adventure. Although he had a sort of instinctive confidence in the ungracious young woman who had just left him, he fully realized that he might very well find himself involved in a singularly unpleasant adventure. He waited for her return, however, without any feeling of apprehension. Very soon, he heard footsteps. She opened the door and entered.

Leaning upon her arm was a tall, emaciated-looking man whose suit of ancient gray tweeds hung loosely upon his shrunken figure. It needed only a glance into the big face to convince Tresholm that the girl had been right about his health.

"This is my father," the girl announced shortly. "Mr. Tresholm. A gentleman staying down at Monte Carlo. He will play piquet with you for an hour."

"Very good of him, I am sure—very good," the old man declared, as he extended a skinny hand. "Pleased to welcome you, Mr.—what did you say his name was, girl?" he asked harshly.

She spelled it out with care.

"Tresholm," he murmured. "Quite a good name. Very kind of you to give me a game, sir. Will you sit there? I have brought the cards."

He laid two packs of cards and some markers upon the table, and lowered himself, assisted by his daughter, into the chair. He commenced shuffling, and Tresholm watched his long fingers, fascinated. One part of the man, at least, retained its old nimbleness.

"What points do you care to play, sir?" the old man asked.

"I am in your hands," Tresholm replied.

"Would twenty-franc points seem too much?"

"I think I could manage that," Tresholm agreed. "I should warn you, sir, that although I have not played lately, I am supposed to be rather good."

The old man looked across at him without expression in his face. It was as though he wore a mask.

"There is no one in the world," he said, "who can beat me at piquet. Many have tried. They lose their money. You will lose yours. You can afford it, I hope."

"I can very well afford it," his adversary assured him.

They cut for deal. Monsieur Brignolles won.

"It is permitted to smoke?" Tresholm asked, as he laid his cigaret-case upon the table.

"By all means," the girl acquiesced, "so long as you have your own cigarets. We have nothing. We have just that bottle of whisky and some soda-water, in case we can find anyone foolish enough to come and play."

"And your father?"

She shook her head. "He neither drinks nor smokes," she confided. "His state of health does not permit it."

Whatever Monsieur Brignolles' state of health may have been, his mentality, Tresholm decided, after the first few games, remained unimpaired. He discarded with brilliant intuition, and he played his cards unerringly.

Tresholm for the first time found himself outclassed. He lost with better hands; he lost heavily with hands of equal value. Each time his opponent drew as though inspired.

The last card was scarcely played before he was preparing for the next hand. It was as though he played for a great stake, and against the clock. The girl did the scoring, and every time she passed the sheet to Tresholm for his inspection, she did so with a half-malicious, half-triumphant smile.

"You must say when you would like to leave off, Mr. Tresholm," she remarked once.

"Mr. Tresholm must have his revenge," her father squeaked hastily. "It is not for you to interfere."

"I can tell you one thing, Mademoiselle Brignolles," Tresholm confided. "Your father is not only the finest piquet player whom I have ever encountered, but I can assure you that he is also the finest player in the world. I have never seen such intuition. One could imagine that he might be one of those rare people in the world who can see through the back of the cards."

The girl shot one malign glance at him and did not speak again until the next game was finished. Tresholm glanced at his watch.

"You are afraid of being late for your dinner?" she asked, with a note of sarcasm.

"Not in the least," he assured her. "I only looked at the watch to be certain that I should not be. If I leave here in another half-hour, that will suit me admirably."

"If you are sure you can afford it," she mocked. "Prosperity has come to the house. I see that you already owe nineteen milles."

"I must economize in other directions," Tresholm replied. "At any rate, I am having a wonderful lesson at the game."

They played on in silence. The old man shivered every now and then as though affected by an ague, but the cards left his hand with uncanny precision. They played by the illumination of half a dozen candles in ordinary bedroom candlesticks.

In the intervals between the deals, Tresholm ventured to glance around, and it seemed to him that he never before had sat in such a terrible room. The color wash was peeling off the walls. There was dust upon the frames of the few hideous pictures. There was not a whole article of furniture in the room.

To make matters more uncomfortable, there was a fire of huge logs burning upon the hearth, and not a single window open, but, although Tresholm felt his cheeks burn and his forehead become damp, his host's face never changed in its waxen pallor.

A sudden vigorous distaste of his surroundings, the ugliness it all, the terrible old man, the sullen girl got on Tresholm's nerves. He mixed himself a second whisky and soda, and, potent though he knew it to be, it tasted like water to him. He began to make mistakes in playing his cards and suffered for them severely. The girl smiled maliciously.

"Only ten minutes longer," she consoled him. "How glad you will be to go. Never mind, worse might have happened, if I had left you to the robbers on the hill."

"The game is very interesting," Tresholm assured her, speaking with an attempt at lightness. "I am outclassed, but so would anyone else be."

She shivered palpably. Her father's long, nervous fingers were toying with the cards which remained in the little pack. He drew them out one by one, glanced back at his own hand and hesitated. Finally he discarded, throwing three cards only, instead of five, to which he was entitled. Tresholm was rubiconed, and when the last card fell upon the table he had lost more than in any previous game.

The girl began to add up the scores. Her father looked over her shoulder, checking the totals. When she had finished, she looked at them in dismay.

"Do you know how much you have lost, Mr. Tresholm?" she asked.

"Quite a good deal, I am afraid," he replied. "Your father is a very experienced player."

"You have lost thirty-one thousand francs," she announced.

"As much as that?" he rejoined coolly.

"Have you the money in your pocket?" the old man asked, with a note of nervous harshness quavering in his voice. "If not, my daughter had better return to the hotel with you."

"I never carry more than a few milles," Tresholm replied. "I have my check-book."

"Where do you bank?" Brignolles asked.

"Here in Monte Carlo."

The old man's face cleared. "If you have not the money, I must take a check then," he grumbled. "Lucie, fetch pen and ink."

She placed writing materials upon the table—a cheap bottle of ink, and a stubby wooden penholder with a scratchy nib. Tresholm produced his check-book, and with some difficulty wrote out a check. While he was filling in the counterfoil, he was conscious of someone looking over his shoulder. He turned around and met the old man's greedy eyes.

"But what a balance!" the latter declared breathlessly. "You are a rich man, Mr. Tresholm?"

"I have enough for my needs," was the quiet reply.

The girl rose to her feet once more and threw open the door. "What does it matter to us whether Mr. Tresholm is rich or not?" she demanded. "He has enough to pay his debt."

"His debt?" Tresholm murmured.

She looked at him with challenge in her eyes. The old man shuffled across to the cupboard and took out a glass and a bottle. The girl swung around.

"Come this way," she enjoined. "I will see you out."

They passed down the wretched little hall, and she opened the front door.

"Well," Tresholm said, "many thanks for saving me from the bandits."

"Nothing to thank me for," she rejoined curtly. "You paid, all right."

She closed the door, and Tresholm drove away from the place with an infinite sense of relief. The girl returned wearily to the shabby little room. Before she reached the door, she heard her father calling her. He was standing at the table with a pack of cards in his hand.

"Lucie," he cried, "where is the other pack?"

She shrugged her shoulders. "I do not know," she answered.

"It is gone!" the old man shrieked. "Do you suppose—?"

She searched the table, turned the box upside down, looked everywhere feverishly. Then they faced one another—father and daughter.

"He has taken it away!" the former groaned. "Stop him, Lucie!"

She listened to the sound of Tresholm's horn as he turned from the avenue into the road.

"Too late!" she muttered. "You may as well tear up the check, Father."

At eleven o'clock on the following morning, the girl stood in the road below the bank and watched the great doors roll slowly back.

She looked in her bag. The check was safely there. She closed it, turned her back upon the Boulevard des Moulins and slowly entered the gardens. She chose a secluded seat and sat there in what seemed to be a sort of apathetic stupor. After some time she rose, left the gardens by the lower exit and looked up at the Casino clock. It was exactly eleven.

She crossed the road, sat down at one of the tables outside the Café de Paris and ordered a cup of coffee.

At half past eleven she paid for her coffee, adding a modest *pourboire*, and mounted the hill. At five-and-twenty minutes to twelve she crossed the portals of the bank. She made her way to the nearest cashier's window, unfastened her bag, and produced the check.

As she handed it across, she felt her heart give a great throb. For a single moment the man's face before her was blurred; everything in the bank was hazy. Then she came to. She was herself again. Even the sullen expression had returned. She was like any ordinary customer waiting for her money.

"Would you like any small change, Madame?" the cashier asked.

"A little, please," she answered, not too steadily.

He glanced at the check once more. Then he counted rapidly through three packets of ten-mille notes pinned together, pushed them across the counter, and added a mille in hundreds and fifties. The girl stuffed them into her bag.

She walked a little uncertainly towards the door. Then she came face to face with Tresholm, who was talking to the bank manager. She gave one little gasp, but recovered swiftly. She was passing on when he stopped her.

"How do you do, Mademoiselle," he said. "I hope you found that I had enough money to meet your father's check."

The bank manager laughed. An excellent joke! The girl looked at Tresholm, and for a moment he was startled. There was a curious new quality in her eyes.

"Could I speak to you for a moment?" she asked.

"Certainly," he acquiesced. "I am just leaving, and so, I see, are you."

He opened the door for her and nodded his farewell to the bank manager. She led the way across the road to the gardens.

"How is your father this morning?" Tresholm asked politely.

"He is as well as he is likely to be," was the toneless answer. "Do you mind sitting down here? I wish to ask you a question."

He seated himself by her side, immaculate in his white flannels, his pongee coat and the carnation in his buttonhole. In the rather pitiless sunlight, the shabbiness of her own clothes, well-cut though they were, was a little pathetic.

"I want to know why you did not stop payment of that check," she demanded.

"Stop payment of the check?" he repeated. "But why should I? I lost the money."

"Yes, you lost the money," she agreed, but—" She paused significantly.

"If you thought I was going to stop payment of it," he asked, "why weren't you here on the steps at ten o'clock this morning?"

"I was," she confessed. "That was what I was supposed to do—to cash it as soon as the doors were opened. I thought I would give you a chance though. I went away and waited."

"Very sporting of you!" he murmured. "Anyhow, I never meant to stop it."

"Why not?" she persisted. "You know that you were cheated; you know that my father was playing with marked cards. You even brought them away with you—as evidence!"

He turned around, so that he faced her upon the seat. There was a good-humored twinkle in his eyes.

"My dear young lady!" he expostulated. "You haven't your facts correctly, and you seem to have an entirely wrong view of the situation. It is true that I brought away a pack of your father's cards last night, but that was simply because I thought he was better without them. Besides, didn't I own up to being a professional gambler? I am always interested in the appurtenances of my profession."

"I do not believe that you are a professional gambler at all," she declared, with a sudden flame of anger in her face and tone.

"But I can assure you that I am," he pleaded earnestly. "Everyone who comes to Monte Carlo and signs his papers at a hotel has to have a profession. That is mine. Now, I don't want to seem unsociable," he went on, after a moment's pause, "but don't you think you ought to be getting home? Your father will be uneasy."

She opened her bag and dashed the little pile of notes upon the ground between them.

"You knew you were being cheated!" she cried passionately. "You knew that you had no chance. You lost that on purpose. It was charity."

He contemplated the notes lying on the ground, but he made no effort to pick them up.

"Young lady, it was nothing of the sort," he insisted. "I thoroughly enjoyed the experience. Your father's skill at the game, to begin with, is phenomenal; his technique in those other small matters was also amazing."

"Be quiet, will you!" she sobbed, stamping her foot. "One has to suffer enough without such gibes."

"Now please be reasonable," he begged. "I assure you—"

Then, for a moment he broke off and affected to be busy lighting a cigaret. His briquet gave him some trouble. When at last he was prepared to resume the conversation, the young woman's breathing was a little more normal, and she had disposed of her handkerchief.

Within a few feet of them, the uniformed garden attendant was standing, leaning upon his rubber-shod stick. His eyes were glued on the packet of notes.

"*Quelque chose est tombée, monsieur,*" he pointed out.

Tresholm peered at the notes through his eye-glass. "*Ça n'est pas à moi,*" he declared, with a little gesture of abnegation.

The man turned to the girl. "*À mademoiselle, peut-être?*" he suggested, pointing to the money.

"*Ça ne m'appartient pas,*" she echoed.

The man drew a little nearer to the notes. There was a gleam of cupidity in his eyes. Tresholm's foot fell gently upon them.

"Monsieur," he said, "believe me, the young lady is mistaken. The notes are hers. I saw them fall from her bag. Owing to a slight difference of opinion between us, she refuses to pick them up. I, too, am obstinate. What would you have! These young ladies—sometimes, no doubt, you yourself find them difficult."

He passed across a hundred-franc note, and the keeper at once decided that a hundred francs in the hand were worth more than a bundle of mille notes upon the ground.

"*Monsieur est bien gentil,*" he murmured and departed, with a little flourish of his hat.

"You see, Mademoiselle," Tresholm continued, "to leave those notes on the ground there may eventually result in trouble. If our friend had been a *gendarme*, for instance, we might have been marched off to the *commissaire* to account for the singular fact that we are sitting with a bundle of mille notes between us which neither of us will touch.

"Now, I will set you a good example," he added, coolly possessing himself of her bag, picking up the notes, unfastening the clasp and dropping them in. "That, I trust, will be the first step," he concluded, "towards our complete reconciliation. You will not deny that the *sac* is yours."

The bag lay upon the girl's knees. She said nothing. She was suddenly very white.

In her eyes was vacancy, and yet when he ventured to look towards her, was it his fancy, or were there unfathomable depths of wistfulness lurking there? He suddenly remembered the few sous, the carefully folded handkerchief of coarse linen, the single French cigaret, the little bundle of something suspiciously like bills.

"Mademoiselle," he said gently, "why make the world a gloomier place than it is? It should be a place, you know, where human beings take pleasure in helping one another and in receiving help. The fates have made me, through no merit of my own, a very rich man. I have few pleasures. One you can give me by picking up that bag and shaking hands with me and mentioning no more that ugly word 'charity,' because, after all, remember that is a phrase ill-used by all of us. You permit?"

Almost before she knew what was happening, he had risen to his feet. He raised her fingers to his lips—very well-shaped and carefully tended, he saw they were—and, with a little smile of farewell, he passed on. The girl remained in her place, her eyes following his departing figure, the bag clasped tightly in her hands.

One Night in Nice

Earlier in the day, Tresholm had brought his car to a standstill and had joined a curious little crowd of people gazing down into the harbor of Villefranche where a sinister gray monster of a battle-ship lay anchored. The reason for their mild excitement was easily apparent.

Instead of being surrounded by the usual stream of boats coming and going, the sea around the battle-ship was deserted, the gangway was drawn up, and a flag was flying which perhaps Tresholm alone among that little company rightly understood—the navy flag, warning off all visitors or tradespeople of any description. The only craft visible was the battle-ship's own pinnace, which had just left the landing-stage.

Tresholm leaned round to the back of his car, discovered his field-glasses, adjusted them and studied the scene below. The two passengers who were being escorted on board were Monsieur Desrolles, the Chef de Sûreté at Monaco, and a companion whom Tresholm chanced to recognize as the Chef de Sûreté at Nice.

Something had happened to disturb the serenity of life upon the sullen-looking battle-ship. His understanding of the flag, and his recognition of the two men in the pinnace helped him to realize perhaps a little more than his neighbors the probable nature of the event.

He watched the pinnace cutting through the water, leaving behind its trail of foam, watched the gangway let grudgingly down and the two visitors received on board, watched afterwards the immediate drawing up of the gangway and the sheering off of the pinnace. Then he sat back in his car once more, and drove on to Nice.

It was a gay night at Maxim's, Nice's most fashionable bohemian restaurant. The tables on both sides of the room were filled; the popping of corks was incessant; the cloud of blue smoke grew denser and denser. The exhibition dancers never had been received with more favor. Tresholm, inclined to wonder why he had lingered on after a late dinner to the small hours of the morning, still felt no impulse to depart.

There were two people and one circumstance in the room which interested him—the girl with the misty eyes at the table opposite and the small man who was his left-hand neighbor, a man with rather high color, a wizened face, hair as stiffly upright as porcupine quills. He was correctly dressed for the evening—which Tresholm was not—and he ate his supper with an Éclaireur du Soir propped up in front of him. These were the two people whom Tresholm, always observant of the world around him, had singled out as being of interest.

The circumstance was another matter—a long table laid for fourteen, at the end of the room, which had been unoccupied all the evening and which was now being slowly and unwillingly dismantled under the supervision of the chief *maître d'hôtel.* Tresholm leaned forward as the latter passed, and addressed him.

"You are disappointed of some guests tonight, Louis?" he remarked.

The man assented disconsolately.

"A party of officers from the battle-ship in Villefranche Harbor, sir," the man confided. "Some of them visit here most nights, but this was to be a very special affair. The wine and the supper were ordered a week ago. It was the fête-day of the one who has been our best patron here."

"The celebration has been postponed then?" Tresholm asked.

The *maître d'hôtel* approached a step nearer. "Monsieur has not heard then of what has arrived?"

"I have heard nothing at all," Tresholm replied. "I have been over to Mougins for the day, playing golf. Met some friends at the Casino at Cannes afterwards, and stayed here to dine on my way back to Monte Carlo. What is this happening?"

The man leaned forward. The music was banging out a jazz tune. A creole *chanteuse* was careening up and down the room, emitting wild shrieks of corresponding melody. The moment was propitious for confidences. The *maître d'hôtel,* however, apparently thought otherwise. The words seemed to stick in his throat. He took the bottle of wine from the pail by Tresholm's side and filled his glass.

"One knows nothing, though one hears sometimes wild stories," he said. "Leave from the battle-ship has been stopped. It is a pity, for the supper has been cooked. They will come another day."

The man bowed himself away, and Tresholm, aware of the cause of his sudden reticence, continued his meal without remark. Presently he looked across at the opposite table. The girl with the smoothly brushed dark hair and the misty eyes smiled at him slightly. With nothing in his mind save the gratification of his almost impersonal interest, he rose to his feet and crossed the floor.

"Mademoiselle will dance?" he invited.

Mademoiselle distinctly hesitated, and it seemed to Tresholm that she looked over his shoulder at his neighbor. Then she rose slowly from her place.

"If Monsieur wishes," she assented.

Mademoiselle was slim and light, and although a little languid in her movements, graceful and correct in her steps. The dance was a success, and as Tresholm led her back to her seat he was somehow confident that his curiosity concerning her was justified.

"Mademoiselle would care to share my table for a time?" he suggested. "We both seem to be alone."

She demurred. "Sit with me for a few minutes," she begged. "I like this side of the room better."

Tresholm accepted her invitation and ordered wine.

"Why do you prefer your table to mine?" he asked.

"It is your neighbor," she confided. "I do not like him. He looks at me all the time. I know very well that if we talked together he would listen."

"Why shouldn't he, if it amuses him?" Tresholm rejoined, smiling. "We are not going to discuss secrets of state, are we?"

The girl took out her vanity-case and dabbed at her lips.

"I suppose you have something to say to me," she ventured. "I do not know what it is, but I can guess. I would prefer that Monsieur did not hear; so, I should think, would you."

Tresholm showed no signs of surprise at her unexpected speech. There had certainly been no thought of adventure in his mind when he had decided to stay here for dinner. Yet old habits were strong. At the first breath of it, he felt himself back in the old life. He was playing a part, even before he knew it.

"What do you expect to hear from me?" he asked.

She finished with her vanity-case and put it deliberately away. "You will probably ask me first where Arthur is," she said, with a faint smile. "After that, you will talk business."

"Then where is Arthur?" Tresholm demanded.

"In the Casino." She paused, expectant, for his next question. Then she caught the air of bewilderment in his face, and her own expression changed. *"Eh bien?"*

"It seems to me," Tresholm confessed, "that this is where I break down. Shall we dance again?"

The girl shrugged. She was evidently ill at ease.

"Tonight I am tired," she pleaded. "I prefer not to dance any more. Perhaps Monsieur had better return to his table. I am expecting—a—a friend."

He rose to his feet. "I trust that I have not offended in any way."

She looked at him keenly. "Only by seeming to be what you are not."

She suddenly rose, and Tresholm became aware of one of the professional dancers standing at the table. She accepted his invitation to dance, and Tresholm returned to his place. His neighbor glanced up from the newspaper as he sat down, and addressed him in English, which showed only the slightest trace of a foreign accent.

"Scarcely a success, eh?"

"I am afraid," Tresholm admitted, concealing his surprise, "that I was not exactly popular with the young lady."

The little man dropped his eye-glasses, folded up his newspaper and leaned towards his companion.

"Am I right in believing that your name is Tresholm," he asked, "and that when you registered at your hotel in Monte Carlo, you described yourself as a professional gambler?"

"Quite right," Tresholm admitted. "An effort at humor which has led to several misunderstandings. The hotel clerk was persistent that I should fill in the space, and I could think of nothing else for the moment."

"Not being anxious to disclose your real profession," the other suggested.

"Having retired from it, whatever it may have been," was the swift rejoinder.

"Retired?"

"Formally and actually."

"Then what are you doing here tonight?"

"I am here entirely by accident. I had been playing golf at Mougins, met some friends at the Casino—"

"Yes, I heard you telling the *maître d'hôtel* all that," was the somewhat impatient interruption. "With me it is unnecessary."

"May I ask who you are?"

"I will tell you," the other replied, "although I expect you know already. My name is Vigaud—Charles Vigaud—not unknown to the headquarters of the police here. Now, Mr. Tresholm, we know one another. Presently I may have a suggestion to make to you. But wait. Things are about to happen."

There was a disturbance at the door, a hurrying forward of the *vestiaire*, a vision of bowing waiters, a *maître d'hôtel* hastening towards the place where the long table had been dismantled. Ten or twelve new arrivals were divesting themselves of hats and coats.

Vigaud turned to Tresholm with a queer smile.

"Our friends, the naval officers," he remarked. "The commander must be in a gracious mood."

"Do they belong to the ship that was flying the warning-off flag?" Tresholm inquired.

Vigaud nodded. "This has been their usual meeting-place for many nights," he confided. "This morning all leave was stopped, and they were not expected."

"Why?"

The other shrugged. "A robbery on board, one hears."

They came presently down the room—ten very presentable young men, the majority of them sunburnt and of excellent physique. They were popular, evidently, for shouts of welcome greeted them. The girl with the misty eyes alone looked down at her plate and never once glanced up as the long file trooped past her.

Tresholm, happening by chance to notice the fact, watched the young men curiously. The first half-dozen, either by design or accident, ignored her completely. Towards the end of the procession, however, one of the youngest-looking of the officers—scarcely more than a boy, in fact—glanced anxiously across at her table. He made no attempt to stop, but he scarcely removed his eyes from her bent head.

Tresholm's gaze followed the lad curiously. He fancied there was a certain tenseness in his expression, shared by none of his companions. They took their places noisily. The youth was the first to shout for cocktails. Vigaud chuckled.

"An idea," he commented—"without a doubt an idea!"

"What's it all about?" Tresholm inquired good-humoredly.

His companion appeared to have become less communicative. His little shrug of the shoulders was more expressive than his words were illuminating.

"One asks oneself," he murmured.

The arrival of the unexpected guests seemed to have given a new lease of gaiety to the room. The creole lady, in brilliant scarlet, alternately sang sentimental ditties and danced with the abandon of the savage. Waiters hurried up the room with trayfuls of cocktails, and the *sommelier* followed with magnums of champagne.

The young men from the battle-ship in particular settled down to enjoy themselves, and no one was more swiftly uproarious than the youth whose entrance had attracted Tresholm's attention. Ladies with inclinations towards dancing seemed to arrive as though by magic from all directions.

Every one of the party danced, including the boy. His partner, however, was a little, fair-haired Frenchwoman, from whose eyes he scarcely once looked away.

Tresholm, who was beginning to be intrigued by a situation which he utterly failed to understand, ordered another bottle of wine and postponed his intention of leaving. The girl with the misty eyes suddenly smiled across at him, with a little gesture of invitation. Tresholm hastened to her side, and she slipped eagerly into his arms.

"But your hands are cold!" he exclaimed, as they swung down the room.

"As cold as my heart, Monsieur—cold with fear," she answered.

He looked at her, puzzled. There was little doubt but that she was speaking the truth. Such natural color as she may have possessed had left her cheeks so completely that the rouge remained like an ugly daub upon her livid skin. Her body was quivering.

"Come to the bar," she begged. "I am not fit to dance. I thought at first that you brought me a message from George. We had a little code arranged—that is of no consequence—you must help me. Indeed, you must help me."

They sat on stools, and she swallowed eagerly the brandy which he had ordered. Then, with a whispered word of mingled excuse and injunction, she left him for a few moments. The barman, with whom he had some slight acquaintance, leaned across the counter.

"Monsieur knows the young lady well?" he asked.

"I never saw her before this evening," Tresholm replied.

"If Monsieur is ignorant of certain things," the man advised, "if he is not concerned, he would do well to be careful. It is a night, this, when disaster might come."

"I wish I knew what the devil you are talking about!" Tresholm exclaimed.

The man leaned a little farther over the counter. He looked furtively to the right and to the left. Then suddenly he stiffened. He examined the label on a bottle which he had been holding and replaced it upon the shelf.

"The Cognac Hennessy is always good," he remarked.

Mademoiselle stood once more by Tresholm's side. She had washed the rouge from her face, and although she was terribly pale, she looked once more herself.

"I have engaged a *salon privé*," she whispered. "Monsieur will come. I have something to say to him."

Tresholm frowned. He was sufficiently interested in the mystery with which he seemed to be surrounded, but the idea of the private room was unsavory to him. Then he realized that the mistiness in her eyes was not altogether an unreal thing. There were tears gathering there. This was no ordinary invitation.

He followed her down the passage, and the young barman looked after them anxiously. With a little sigh, the latter drew his account book from his pocket, scribbled a few lines upon one of the pages torn from it, and handed it to a gray-haired *maître d'hôtel*.

The man nodded and made his way up the crowded room to where Tresholm's neighbor was still seated. He handed the note to him without a word, and slipped away. Vigaud adjusted his eye-glass and read the few lines carefully. Then he glanced across at the empty place opposite and shrugged.

His bill was already paid as though in expectation of some such emergency.

He made his way through the throng, received his cloak and hat from the *vestiaire* and strolled out into the night.

Tresholm was a man rarely ill at ease, but a certain fineness of sensibility inspired in him a swift revulsion to his tawdry and meretricious environment—the too-ample couch which took up half the room, the bottle of champagne already opened upon the table, the locked door, the room itself, with its brazen adornments, were all alike hideous to him.

"Mademoiselle," he said, "you must forgive me, but I find these surroundings distasteful. Unless you can offer me an immediate explanation of the service which you require from me, I must leave you."

"I shall explain," she assured him quickly. "Have patience for a few moments, I beg."

"At least, let me unlock the door," he begged.

"Not yet," she insisted. "There must always be that delay. Now I explain."

He stood icily upon the other side of the table. She poured out two glasses of champagne, drank one and threw the other upon the floor.

"You know my nationality," she began. "For the last few years there has been unrest in this part of the world. I speak both languages. I have many acquaintances. In the war I was in a government bureau. Since then, the men who were my chiefs have continued to make use of me."

She paused to listen for a moment.

"Go on," he invited, a little less coldly.

"My instructions came to me a month ago, but first I had to wait for three weeks. Since then I have been working. There is a battle-ship in the harbor. My task was to make friends with one of the officers. The battle-ship is fitted with some secret device for resisting torpedoes. Half-way across the Atlantic she was submitted to tests—you understand, Monsieur?"

"Quite well," Tresholm assented. "Go on."

"The results of these tests," she continued, "were entered in the Admiral's private diary. My task was to obtain the page upon which the results were written, whilst he was away in Toulon. I succeeded."

"Are you sure you haven't been hoaxed?" he asked her.

She shook her head. "A great deal was done for me," she confided. "On the first visitors' day someone whom I have never seen in my life took a wax impression of the key of the small cupboard where the diary is kept. The key was given to me four days ago. I gave it to my friend. Yesterday, he brought me the page, cut out."

"Have you parted with it yet?"

"They won't let me," she cried, almost hysterically. "I have been driven crazy. The French police are suspicious. They have not ventured to search my rooms, but there is an agent of the police outside my door who pretends to be a fireman, and they follow me in the street so that I dare not post a letter or approach any of my intimates here. My telephone, I know, is guarded.

"I have been nearly crazy with anxiety. The man into whose hands I was to pass the page of the diary has been in the restaurant tonight, but I had to signal him to go away. Opposite me sits Vigaud, an agent of the French police. I am terrified."

"Where is this page of the diary at the present moment?" Tresholm asked.

"I have it with me," she confided. "I throw myself upon your generosity, Monsieur. My heart has ached ever since I did this thing. I repent. I sob at night with terror. That poor boy! I saw his face this evening."

"You mean the tall youth at the end of the procession?"

"Yes. They tell me if it is discovered, he will be shot. I want the page restored to him."

"What would be the good of that?" Tresholm pointed out. "You can't cut a page out of a diary and replace it."

"This is different," she told him eagerly. "The book is of a different fabrication. Each day of the week is on a separate page, with holes at the top through which two clips pass. The poor boy still has the key. He could at least take his chance of replacing it."

"How are you going to communicate with him?"

"I can't," she cried, "but you could."

"Even if I did," Tresholm deliberated, "it seems to me long odds about his being able to replace it. Has anyone discovered it is missing?"

"I will tell you, Monsieur, what has happened," she declared eagerly. "The Admiral's secretary, with whom he left his keys, had occasion to go to the safe. He found things disturbed. The alarm was given. The ship was isolated. Afterwards a search was made."

"This one page from the diary?"

"It was not noticed. The secretary—he decided that he had been mistaken in the disturbance of the papers. People were allowed once more to come and go from the ship as they willed, but tomorrow, Monsieur—tomorrow the Admiral returns. He will be told of the scare, and he will search for himself. It must be returned before midday tomorrow."

She listened for a moment with the old terror in her eyes, poured out more champagne, and moving over to the couch, disarranged the cushions.

"*Ecoutes,*" she said, returning. "I had a letter from him this morning—a pathetic letter. If only he knew how I longed to give him back the page! No harm has been done. Not a soul has seen it. Nevertheless, when the

Admiral returns, a report of the scare will be made to him and the theft will be discovered. George—he is my little friend—he will be suspected first of all because he is the Admiral's nephew and is allowed access to the cabin. Poor boy, he is not of the nature of those who conspire. He will break down. He will confess. He will be shot."

Tresholm stood considering the problem.

"You are my hope!" she cried. "Directly you came in, my heart gave a leap. You were pointed out to me at Monte Carlo. They told me that you were a great gambler. Take the risk, Monsieur. You will save this boy's life. You are English. So little can happen to you. Ah!"

She sprang away. Down the passage came footsteps which in their very tread seemed grim and official. To Tresholm she behaved like a madwoman. She flung herself upon the couch, pulled off her stockings and concealed them beneath the cushions, tore down part of her dress, rumpled her hair and burst into a senseless fit of gay but hysterical laughter.

Then there came the knocking at the door—a brief, imperative knocking. She answered. Her voice was stifled—angry, but not terrified.

"*Qui est là?*"

"Open the door, in the name of the police," was the stern reply

"*Ridicule!*" she exclaimed. "*Il y a quelqu'un. Alles-vous-en.*"

She beckoned Tresholm towards the couch, and he found himself at once obeying meekly. She leaned over and poured out more champagne. The she began to talk to herself.

"*Chérie!*" she cried. "*Ne vous deranges pas. C'est une blague. Voyez!*"

She unlocked the door and stepped back with a little cry, spilling wine from her glass in the movement. A very official-looking inspector of police had entered, followed by two *gendarmes*. They closed the door behind them. The inspector addressed himself to Tresholm.

"Monsieur," he said, politely, "I demand pardon for this unusual intrusion, but a grave theft has been committed in the neighborhood, and this lady is under suspicion."

"You arrest me?" she shrieked.

"*Pas forcément!*" the inspector replied. "If this gentleman and you will submit yourselves to a search, and the missing property is not discovered upon either of you, our disagreeable duty will be completed."

"But how impossible!" she exclaimed. "Search me—a woman? It is incredible!"

"We have a female attendant outside," was the civil response, "and an empty room."

She scowled at him, and then turned to Tresholm.

"I ask a thousand pardons, *chéri*," she said. "Shall we humor this man and then perhaps we shall be left alone?"

"I am at your disposition," he conceded.

The *gendarme* unlocked the door, and Mademoiselle passed out into the care of a woman who was waiting in the passage. Tresholm divested himself of his outer garment, handed over his belongings and saw every pocket of his clothes being turned inside out. After an even closer search of his person, the official saluted.

"A thousand pardons, Monsieur." he apologized courteously. "Permit me to play the part of valet. I trust we are more fortunate with the lady."

"What is this missing property?" Tresholm inquired.

"A packet of a hundred mille," the man answered glibly.

Tresholm smiled. "A great deal of money," he remarked, helping himself to some of the wine and passing the bottle towards the inspector.

In due course the door opened, and the woman searcher returned with her charge. A glance between the former and the inspector was sufficient.

"Perhaps," Mademoiselle demanded angrily, "we may now be allowed to finish our wine."

"There is nothing to prevent it, Mademoiselle," was the inspector's regretful reply, as he saluted and took his leave.

The door was closed and locked. Mademoiselle listened to the retreating footsteps, her hand still upon the key. Her face was drawn, and dark rims were forming under her eyes.

"But this is terrible," she murmured.

"Hadn't you better put your stockings on?" Tresholm suggested.

She continued to listen for a moment. Then she stole back to the couch and drew out the stockings from beneath the pillows and pulled them on. Tresholm watched her with surprise.

"But you already have stockings!"

She laughed at him. "It is the safest of all hiding-places," she murmured. "Monsieur may feel."

She held up her leg. He leaned forward and felt the sole of her foot. There was something stiff there.

"They are beautifully made by a friend at Lyons," she confided. "No one would ever believe that there is a double sole. And you—you consent now to help me?"

"I'll do my best," Tresholm promised.

The two cars full of noisy sailor boys were bought to an unexpected halt at the commencement of the dark descent to the Villefranche Harbor. A long-bonneted two-seater was slewed across the road, completely barring progress. They began with one accord to shout alcoholically inspired remarks.

Tresholm advanced out of the shadows. With his hat pulled over his forehead and his coat-collar turned up, he was quite unrecognizable.

"Sorry," he apologized. "I didn't see the bend, put on my brakes too soon, skidded round and stalled my engine. If you fellows wouldn't mind giving me a push onto the other road, I'll get her going somehow or other."

They all tumbled out good-naturedly enough. In the darkness Tresholm managed to slip a pocketbook into the young man's hand.

"No more of this confounded foolery, mind," he whispered.

The boy looked around. They were well behind the others.

"I swear there won't be, sir," he groaned.

"Think you'll get it back all right?"

"Certain," was the confident reply. "Tell you what, sir. You really want to know?"

"Well, you've given me a lot of trouble tonight," Tresholm acknowledged. "I'd like to feel that it wasn't for nothing."

"Stop on the hill, sir, just before the bend. My pal's on signaling duty tonight. I'll send you three white flashes as soon as the job's done. He'll think it's for a little girl we know at Cap Ferrat."

With a final push, the car was on the right road once more, its bonnet turned. Tresholm jammed on the brakes.

They trooped back to their cars, and Tresholm, starting his engine, curiously enough without trouble, mounted the hill. At the top he swung into the side of the road, lighted a cigaret and gazed downward.

The shapes of the great battle-ship and the three attendant gunboats were defined with curious accuracy by their brilliant line of lights. Everywhere was deep silence.

Suddenly, the signal came, somehow eloquently dramatic, significant of a catastrophe averted. Three times the brilliant white rays pierced the darkness. Tresholm slipped in the clutch and started off to complete his journey. Behind Mount Agel, the dawn, colorless as yet, was lightening the sky.

The Big Winner

Installed in an easy chair in a dark corner of that somberly lighted bar—a quaint contrast to the brilliantly illuminated, somewhat garish restaurant adjoining—Tresholm became suddenly tense, assailed by a wave of tantalizing, almost torturing memories. He bent forward, his lean face strained, his eyes fixed upon the approaching figure.

A strange flood of memories this, to haunt the brain so suddenly—the pungent perfume of the Campagna herbs, the April sunlight flooding the plain, even to the outskirts of the city, the dark and splendid outline of St. Peter's itself, the music of those hasty words, the longing of her dark eyes, then the thundering hoofs, the crack of the huntsman's whip—off again into the mild distraction of the hunt! But oh, that perfume; how it clung!

It was Lena who recognized him—a child when he had left Rome. She caught at the arm of her companion.

"Margherita, see, it is Signor Tresholm!"

He came forward then. The world of sweet fancies and memories had slipped back where it belonged. He smiled into her surprised, beautiful eyes, and raised her fingers to his lips in approved fashion.

"Princess," he murmured.

"You, Andrew!" she replied.

The seconds possessed their full measure of bitter sweetness. Lena claimed her few words, and the princess turned towards their companion—a somewhat weary-looking elderly man.

"Duke," she said, "let me present one of my dear English friends—Mr. Andrew Tresholm—the Duca di Michani. Signor Tresholm was at his Embassy in Rome when my husband interested himself in politics—five, six, alas, seven years ago."

The two men shook hands.

"I knew your chief very well, of course, Signore," the duke acknowledged.

A waiter and the manager himself were hovering in the background, anxious to welcome such distinguished clients. The princess turned to Tresholm.

"You are not by any fortunate chance alone?" she asked…. "Yes? Then do join us. Indeed, if you will, you will relieve me of some anxiety. Here, it is difficult to explain. This little enterprise of ours is undertaken much against my will. You would be of great assistance if you would join us."

"I will do so with pleasure," Tresholm accepted. "I must warn you though, that I seldom dance."

"Yet I seem to remember," the woman murmured, "when the music was to your fancy, there were few who danced like you."

"It may be for that reason," he rejoined, "that today I dance but seldom."

She flashed a little glance at him, and people who saw it turned their heads to look at her, for she was indeed beautiful. Arrived at their table, to which they were escorted by the manager and the head waiter, Lena floated away almost at once with her escort. The princess smiled.

"Lena is the sister of my heart," she acknowledged. "Always she understands. Now, before we speak of anything else, dear friend, before I bring myself to realize how happy it has made me—even this brief meeting—let me tell you of this embarrassment in which we find ourselves. I came here tonight because of it, in fear and trembling. With you, however, I feel safe."

"Tell me, by all means," he begged and glanced at her.

Indeed, she was as beautiful as ever in her silver gown, her famous pearls, her shining dark hair, her flawless complexion and her exquisitely shaped mouth. In the old days, when she had been kind to the young English attaché, she had been acknowledged one of the most beautiful women in Europe. It seemed to Tresholm that the years which had passed had not even disturbed the bloom of youth. Her brown eyes were as eloquent as ever. Her fingers rested upon his coat sleeve in the old appealing gesture.

"Dear friend," she confided, "last month we announced Lena's engagement to Bartoldi."

"I read of it," Tresholm murmured. "In spite of our vow not to write, I nearly sent you a line."

"The affair seemed well enough. Bartoldi is poor, but Lena is overrich already. I knew little of the young man. Like most others, he was supposed to be gay. What would you have? He is only twenty-four. It was thought that marriage would be good for him. I begin to doubt it. Indeed, I am frightened."

"Tell me exactly why," Tresholm suggested.

"We discovered one thing—he is a gambler."

Tresholm smiled slightly. The thought of his own reputation flickered into his mind.

"He must be too young for that to have become a settled vice. He is playing here?"

"Night and day—and disastrously. Disastrously, not only for his purse, but, I am afraid, for his character. Lena is in great distress. I dare not tell my husband, and the duke here has hated the Bartoldis all his life and can find no good word to say about them. We have no one in whom to confide, and we are in great distress."

"Just how do things stand at present?" Tresholm asked.

"Gastone, as I told you, is not rich," the princess explained. "He comes here as our guest. He brought with him a hundred thousand lire for gambling. He has lost that. He has drawn another hundred thousand lire from home, he has borrowed some from me, and tonight he has borrowed from Lena.

"It is not only his money losses which are so distressing, but he himself is changing. Lena and I refuse to play at all, hoping that may have some effect. We came here last night with Michani and two other friends. Gastone arrived just as we were leaving. He behaved disgracefully. He quarreled with the man with whom Lena was dancing, and declared that until she was married she must dance with no one but him. He made a scene. I am afraid he was not quite sober. I was much ashamed, and a little frightened.

"Today he has obtained money somehow, and he is playing. As soon as he has lost it all, I fear that he will follow us here. He will perhaps make himself disagreeable. He is very violent, and I feel sure that he is drinking too much brandy. Lena is in despair. I know that she is fond of him, but what can one do? Last night he behaved like a madman. He wanted to fight a perfectly harmless youth with whom she was dancing."

She broke off, to hand the menu to Tresholm, who ordered supper and wine. Almost immediately Lena and her escort returned to the table. Conversation—a pleasant farrago of reminiscences—became gay. The duke, approving alike of the caviar and the champagne, unbent. He danced again with Lena. The princess looked at her companion, and a little smile parted her wonderful lips.

"The dances are not the same, but the music—it remains. Andrew, you will dance with me?"

They danced, and he was back again in the flood of memories. There were a few whispered words, but the silence had its tumultuous charm. More than once he felt her cling to him—her slim, exquisite body yielding itself to his arms. When at last they sat down, Tresholm was a little breathless. It seemed to him that she was avoiding his eyes. Then suddenly she touched his sleeve.

"Bartoldi!" she exclaimed. "Look! In the doorway."

Tresholm turned and met the gaze of the young man who had just entered. Bartoldi was very decorative, but he was not altogether sober. He stood there, gloomy, almost ferocious-looking. The princess waved her hand. He approached with deliberate footsteps. He bowed to the women, nodded to the duke and ignored Tresholm.

"I looked for you in the club," he said. "It was arranged, I thought, that we should come here."

The princess toyed with her fan. "At twelve o'clock, dear Gastone," she reminded him. "At one o'clock you were still playing. We persuaded the duke to be our escort, and I was fortunate enough to find here one of my dearest friends... Mr. Andrew Tresholm—Prince Bartoldi."

Bartoldi looked across at Tresholm with heavy eyes. The greeting between the two men was of the slightest. There was a smile, however, upon Tresholm's lips.

"The prince occupies himself a great deal with the game," he remarked.

"I do. And you?"

"As yet, I have not played."

"But surely you have been here for some time?" the princess asked.

"Three weeks," Tresholm confessed.

The young man was staring at him solemnly. "You have been here three weeks," he repeated, "and you have not yet entered the Casino or the Sporting Club?"

"Not yet. I shall play a little before I go. I find many other amusements here."

The princess laughed softly. "You were always an original."

"Original indeed," Bartoldi muttered. "What other amusements has Monte Carlo?"

"Well, for example, I play tennis for two or three hours in the morning," Tresholm confided. "After that I motor out to some of the smaller hill villages, perhaps dine in some bohemian place in Nice or Cannes on my way home, and often I am so sleepy that I read my papers or a book and go to bed."

"Why come to Monte Carlo?" the young man queried, almost insolently. "You could lead that sort of life anywhere."

"Quite so," Tresholm assented. "On the other hand, Monte Carlo is a very amusing place, unless one is by evil chance a gambler. The climate is excellent, the scenery attractive, and one meets friends."

"I agree with Signor Tresholm," Michani declared. "I have not his energy, perhaps, but when I have lost five hundred francs in the afternoon, and five hundred in the evening, I seek to amuse myself elsewhere than in the gaming-rooms."

The music was once more alluring. Lena smiled at Bartoldi.

"We dance, Gastone, yes?"

The young man surveyed the room disparagingly. He muttered something in Italian and poured himself out some wine.

Tresholm rose. "Perhaps you will honor me," he begged.

She rose without hesitation. Bartoldi set down his glass.

"Lena!"

She affected not to hear him and would have hurried her partner off, but Tresholm lingered for a moment.

"Signor Tresholm," Bartoldi said, "I do not know who you are. The Signorina is my fiancée, and in Italy it is not the custom—"

"Pity we're in Monaco," Tresholm interrupted pleasantly, as he moved away.

The princess leaned forward. "Gastone," she said, "it seems to me that we, who may be your new relatives, will have a little more to put up with than we expected. There is one thing, however, which I warn you should never forgive, and that is your making yourself ridiculous before any dear friend of mine.

"You may make yourself at ease concerning Signor Tresholm," the princess continued. "He is an Englishman of distinguished family who was in the Diplomatic Service of his country when I knew him. Continue your supper, please. You have lost again, I fear."

"I have lost," the young man acknowledged sullenly. "I have lost all the money I could scrape together, and all the money they would lend me at the bar. Never was anyone plagued with such accursed luck."

"It is a little message from fate," the princess told him. "You are not meant to win. The man who plays against fate, plays hopelessly."

"Women know nothing about gambling," Bartoldi declared savagely.

"That may be why we win," was the suave rejoinder....

Tresholm and his partner returned in due course, and the supper-party, never a brilliant success, nevertheless drifted on without disaster. Towards its close, Tresholm found himself once more alone with his hostess. Lena and Michani were dancing, and Bartoldi had gone to the bar in search of an acquaintance.

"What am I to do?" the princess asked Tresholm suddenly. "I believe that Gastone is not so bad. It is just this gambling. And Lena, alas, adores him. Already he has borrowed all our spare money, and my hands are now tied. I have promised my husband I will lend him no more. What can one do with him? Advise me, dear friend. I want so much their happiness."

Tresholm smoked thoughtfully for a moment. "My first impression of the young man," he confessed, "led me to believe that your sister would probably be better for his loss. One must not judge hastily, though. You have known him longer than I. You find in him qualities?"

"Indeed yes, Andrew," she assured him. "Gastone has good in him. I can promise you that."

"In that case," Tresholm decided, "I will do what I can to help him. You have your car here, of course? Very well. When you leave, the duke can escort you and your sister. I will propose to Prince Bartoldi that he and I walk to the hotel. If I fail with the young man, I can at least let you know at the end of four days what I think of him."

Her fingers deliberately sought his. "You are just as sweet to me as ever, dear Andrew," she whispered. "If only I had had the courage in those days!"

He shook his head. "Your place, dear Margherita," he sighed, "was always in the great world."

They left soon afterwards. On the pavement outside, Tresholm offered his cigaret-case to the young man.

"Shall we walk?" he suggested. "It is only a few yards to the Paris, and Michani is sufficient escort for our hostess and the Signorina."

The young man assented without graciousness.

"Had bad luck at the tables, haven't you?" Tresholm asked.

"Infernal," was the disgusted assent. "It is all a matter of capital. I could have got it back, but I can't raise any more money. The old prince is a miser, my lawyer is in England, and not one of my friends is out here."

"Upon certain conditions," Tresholm proposed gently, "I will be your banker to the extent of, say, a million francs."

"You will what?" Bartoldi exclaimed.

"I will lend you a million francs," Tresholm repeated, "but on my own terms, mind."

"I will pay any interest!" the young men declared eagerly.

"I am not concerned about interest," Tresholm assured him. "If I lend you this money, you will give me an I.O.U. for it, and pay me back the exact sum, but—you won't like my terms."

Bartoldi glanced at the clock, still visible in front of the Casino.

"Could we step round to the Sporting Club?" he suggested. "We could have a drink anyway, and there might be a chemie table going."

"Certainly not," Tresholm refused. "These are my terms. You may rely upon me to keep my word—the princess will tell you, I think, that I am not likely to break it."

"The terms then, if you please."

"It is now," Tresholm reflected, "Tuesday morning. The sum I mentioned will be at your disposal on Friday at midnight. The terms are these: that between now and then you do not attempt to gamble; you do whatever I choose."

"Any restrictions after that?" the young man asked.

"None at all," Tresholm assured him. "At midnight on Friday, the money will be at your disposal. You can gamble with it, pay your debts with it, or do whatever you like, and you can return it to me when it is convenient."

"You are not going to ask that I do anything impossible during the four days?" the young man ventured.

"Nothing whatever. Most of the time I shall spend with you."

They turned into the Hotel de Paris.

"I thank you very much, sir," Bartoldi said. "It is so arranged then. To-morrow morning, I am at your service."

"Turn up at half past ten in tennis kit," Tresholm enjoined.

Bartoldi was a slow starter at tennis on the following morning, but improved considerably towards the close of the séance. Tresholm, who had won the first three sets, was obliged to fight hard for the fourth, and lost the fifth. They wandered off to the Royalty for cocktails with the princess and Lena, who had been interested spectators. The princess took Tresholm's arm.

"Dear friend," she remonstrated, "I hear that you have offered to lend Gastone money, without any restrictions as to gambling."

Tresholm nodded. "He doesn't get it till midnight on Friday though," he reminded her, "and until then he's on his honor not to play at all."

"It is not very long until Friday midnight," she sighed.

"Miracles have been wrought in less time," Tresholm replied. "Mine is just a little gamble. If I lose—well, I can afford it."

They drank their cocktails in the sunshine, and on a sudden inspiration motored out to Beaulieu for luncheon. Afterwards, the princess suggested a visit to Cannes, but Tresholm shook his head.

"If you don't mind," he begged, "Bartoldi and I want to go to the Sporting Club."

The young man's eyes glittered. The Princess and Lena were astonished.

"To the Sporting Club!" the latter exclaimed. "I thought Gastone was not to play till Friday."

"We aren't going to play; we're going to look on," Tresholm confided.

"Surely," Lena pleaded, "you would be better away from the place altogether—or rather Gastone would."

"I'm not so sure," Tresholm replied. "Anyhow we'll look in there for a short time."

At a few minutes past four, the event for which Monte Carlo had been waiting took place. Tresholm mounted the steps of the Sporting Club, accompanied by Bartoldi, and turned into the Bureau.

"Got to get my ticket," he explained.

The young Italian stared at him incredulously.

"Do you mean to say that you haven't even taken a ticket out?" he demanded.

"Haven't been in the place since I arrived," Tresholm confessed. "Come and sign for me."

Tresholm's appearance caused a sensation. His ticket was made out in breathless speed by the senior clerk, while the junior one rushed to the telephone. The news spread in all directions. When they entered the rooms, the croupiers stood up and craned their necks with curiosity. The chef of the plaque roulette table covertly counted over his capital. The chef at the trente-et-quarante board sent at once for a supply of five-mille plaques. The man whose appearance had created such a sensation, however, entered the gambling-rooms modestly. He made no attempt to change any money.

His companion stood with his hands in his pockets, his eyes on the board.

"*Quatorze*," he groaned as the spin was concluded. "Signor Tresholm, for heaven's sake, let me have a mille. I must back seven and twenty-nine after fourteen."

"What on earth for?" Tresholm demanded. "In any case, you know that under our conditions you are not playing."

"And you? You will not play either?" Bartoldi asked, a little bewildered.

"No, not at present."

The next number was thirty four, the next thirty-five, the following one six.

"You'd have lost your money, wouldn't you?" Tresholm remarked casually.

"Look at that Dutchman," Bartoldi whispered. "He must have eighty mille there."

Tresholm nodded. "Clever fellow!" he murmured. "Let's watch some of the other tables."

They wandered down to the far end of the room. When they came back the Dutchman at the plaque table was changing a bundle of mille notes.

"Soon lost his eighty mille," Tresholm observed. "Jolly interesting, isn't it. Let's look at the chemie."

The chemie game was dragging wearily along. At each table, the croupier glanced round almost wistfully at their approach. Tresholm remained blandly indifferent.

"Time for our first cocktail," he suggested to his companion.

"Thank heaven!" the other replied.

They sat down and smoked cigarets in a corner of the bar.

"Queer thing at that table that's just broken up," Tresholm remarked as he sipped his cocktail. "Eight people went to cash their chips, and there wasn't a winner among them. Cagnotte had the lot. Jolly interesting to watch, all the same! Drink up quickly, and we'll get back to the roulette."

When the time came, the young man rose unwillingly. Things at the table had changed. The Dutchman was nervously fingering the last of his mille notes. A newcomer had collected a pile of plaques. They watched for a time and then walked down to the other tables. When they came back the Dutchman had increased his stock by a few plaques. The newcomer was cashing mille notes.

"Must play badly, these fellows, I think," Tresholm observed. "They never seem to keep it. Let's go over to the Cercle Privé for an hour."

Bartoldi frankly yawned. "Why do you not play?" he reiterated. "Anything is better than doing nothing."

"I never possessed the bump of philanthropy," Tresholm answered dryly.

They wandered down the passage, crossed the lounge of the hotel, passed through the swing doors and strolled towards the Casino. A small crowd of people collected to watch them. They were met in the vestibule of the "Kitchen" by Gustave Sordel himself.

"So you have found your way here at last, Mr. Tresholm," he greeted him, with a welcoming smile.

"A very brief visit, I am afraid," Tresholm confided.

"If you will tell me which table you're going to play at, I will see that they have plenty of money," Sordel suggested.

"I'm not sure that I'll do more than look on today," Tresholm replied.

Sordel hurried off with an incredulous shrug of the shoulders. They passed through the "Kitchen," stopped to watch the play at some of the tables.

"Always gives me the hump, this place," Tresholm remarked. "To think that some of these broken-down, miserable-looking men and women were once decent folk. Came here, lots of them, with plenty of money, good homes and all the rest of it, and then set themselves to play against a certainty. Imbeciles, of course, but one can't help feeling sorry for them!"

They wandered down to the Salles Privées.

"Let's have another cocktail before we watch any more," Bartoldi proposed. "These people are getting on my nerves."

Tresholm assented readily enough, but as soon as the cocktails were consumed, he led the way out of the bar again.

"There are a couple of plaque tables in the Schmit Room," Tresholm said. "Quite high play, I believe."

Bartoldi followed his companion without enthusiasm. At first sight of one of his numbers appearing produced in him a fit of restlessness. After about an hour, however, he scarcely made an observation. Every now and then he glanced at the clock.

"We are all dining with you, are we not?" he asked Tresholm. "Is it not time we thought about dressing?"

"Ten minutes more."

They stayed for a quarter of an hour. It was Bartoldi who led the way out of the rooms. As they mounted the steps of the Hôtel de Paris, the Senegalese porter came forward with his broad grin.

"*Monsieur a fait sauter la banque?*" he demanded eagerly.

"I haven't played," Tresholm answered.

The man stared at him without comprehension. In the lounge, Monsieur Robert, the manager of the hotel, came hurrying forward.

"At last, Monsieur Tresholm, they tell me that you have entered the lists!" he exclaimed. "What fortune? The Casino is perhaps mortgaged to you?"

Tresholm smiled. "I have just been looking on," he confided. "I haven't played."

"You could watch and not play?" the other gasped.

"Why not? I find it amusing enough."

"All these people seem very interested in you," Bartoldi remarked curiously as they mounted in the lift.

Tresholm smiled. "I have a reputation," he explained, "which as yet I have not attempted to justify."

Dinner was distinctly a cheerful meal. Bartoldi was a little tired and nervous, but he improved in humor and appearance as the evening went on. The princess was puzzled.

"I do not understand," she told Tresholm frankly. "Gastone tells me that instead of keeping him away from the gaming-rooms, you have pressed him to accompany you there, and on Friday you are lending him all that money."

Tresholm nodded. "I am gambling," he confessed.

She made a little grimace. "You have the right to, without a doubt, but Gastone—he will only lose your money."

"The luck may change."

It was eleven o'clock before they left the dining-room, and everyone was in excellent humor. Lena turned towards Tresholm.

"Why shouldn't we all go straight to that little Russian place and dance?" she suggested. "Gastone doesn't mind."

"Just one hour at the Sporting Club first, please," Tresholm begged.

"And I thought you didn't play," the princess intervened reproachfully,

"It's a wonderful game to watch," Tresholm rejoined

They made their way through the passage silently. The princess drifted into the chemie room. Tresholm, with his hand resting lightly upon Bartoldi's shoulder, took up his old position at the roulette table. There were more people playing and the gambling was heavier.

"Twenty-nine!" the young man exclaimed irritably. "Oh, if only I could back the seven and the fourteen."

Tresholm remained deaf. Twenty-five turned up, then nineteen, followed by twenty-seven. An English nobleman collected a great pile of ten-mille plaques.

"Over two hundred thousand francs he's won while we've been standing here," Bartoldi murmured feverishly.

Tresholm nodded. "Let's watch the other table for a time," he suggested.

They strolled around. In half an hour they returned. The Englishman was cashing a check. He looked up and nodded as Tresholm passed.

"What's become of all those plaques," the latter asked.

"All gone," was the frowning response. "They spin too quickly."

"Yes, I suppose that's it," Tresholm agreed, half to himself. "They spin too quickly. They don't give you a chance to keep your winnings."

Lena leaned forward and passed her arm through his. "Margherita wants to go," she pleaded. "Everyone feels like dancing tonight."

"What about Bartoldi?" Tresholm asked.

"I'd like to go if you're ready," the young man assented, almost eagerly.

"Just half an hour more," Tresholm stipulated.

The princess's eyebrows were slightly upraised; Lena looked puzzled.

"So long as Gastone doesn't mind leaving," she whispered, "why do we not get away?"

Tresholm smiled. "The next twelve numbers," he begged her. "Just twelve spins."

"But you don't play," she expostulated. "Why do you like watching the numbers that turn up?"

"Because I don't play," he answered cryptically.

Even Bartoldi sighed with relief when they left the Sporting Club a short time later. There were still signs of strain about him, but he danced with spirit, and of his own accord inquired about the morrow's plans.

"Tennis at ten-thirty," Tresholm told him. "Two decent fellows want to make a foursome. And Thursday morning—what about a foursome at Mont Agel?"

"I should love it," Lena declared.

"Alas, it is so long since I played," the princess sighed.

"Nevertheless, we will give them a game," Tresholm promised....

"I wish I knew just what your idea is, Andrew," she said to him a little later, when they were alone at the table. "Of course, I know that you have promised to lend Gastone some money, and that is what makes him agree to everything you suggest, but why don't you keep him away from the tables altogether? Surely that would be best. This afternoon, and part of this evening, the poor boy was standing there in agony."

Tresholm nodded with satisfaction. "You noticed that too, did you?" he observed. "Good! The young man is to have this money I promised him at midnight on Friday. After that I shall try to explain."

She laid her fingers upon his hand. No one else in the world knew so well how to caress with a touch.

"Dear Andrew," she begged, "Lena is so worried. She is afraid you don't realize what this gambling may mean to him."

"You know that they call me here?" he asked abruptly.

"I know," she admitted—"'the professional gambler.' It was a *blague* of yours when you arrived."

"Nevertheless," he went on, "there is perhaps a little truth in it. As a professional gambler I must know something of the psychology of this—shall we call it habit or vice? I am the physician. Bartoldi is my patient. You are the amateur who intervenes. Dear lady, shall we dance?"

She came willingly enough into the clasp of his arms, and again he thought of those great bunches of Roman violets, their purple glint and their April fragrance.

Tresholm glanced at his thin gold watch and passed his hand through the young man's arm. "Come along into the bar, Bartoldi," he invited. "It is midnight on Friday, and your period of probation is up. Time for us to arrange our little business."

The young man, who had been standing patiently looking down at the roulette table, turned around with alacrity.

Tresholm led the way into the inner portion of the bar, ordered two whisky-and-sodas, and drew out a formidable-looking packet from his pocket.

"Here you are," he announced. "There's a hundred mille in each of these—ten of them. Get as much fun as you can out of it. It ought to last you a few nights, at any rate."

The young man smiled. "You don't seem to believe in anyone's winning, Mr. Tresholm."

"Oh, I dare say they do sometimes," was the casual reply,—"if they have to leave in a hurry just after a run of luck. We've been watching for four afternoons and four evenings, haven't we?"

"Watching till I'm blamed sick at the sight of the ball," the young man declared vigorously.

"Well, we haven't seen anyone win who kept his winnings, have we?" Tresholm observed.

Bartoldi stopped a young man who was passing.

"Here's the sixty mille I owe you, François," he said.

"That is excellent," the other exclaimed, in some surprise, as he pocketed the money. "You have been winning, yes?"

"I haven't played for the last few days."

Bartoldi excused himself and made his way to the bar, summoning Joseph to a conference. Joseph approached, glum, and with regrets already framing themselves upon his lips.

"I will take my I.O.U.'s, Joseph," his patron said. "Sixty mille, I think."

The sun broke through the clouds. Joseph's famous smile illumined his face.

"The I.O.U.'s are here, Monsieur le Prince," he said, producing them.

Bartoldi tore them up. Tresholm was talking to the princess and Lena, who were just leaving the room with the Duca di Michani.

"Margherita," Bartoldi announced, "I owe you fifty thousand. *Voilà*. And you, Lena, thirty thousand. You have room in your bag, I hope. Now I have only one creditor."

"My dear Gastone!" the princess exclaimed. "Now I shall be able to play again."

"You are sure that you wouldn't like to keep this a little longer?" Lena asked wistfully.

"Not for a second," he assured her.

"I was suggesting to the princess an hour or two at the Carlton," Michani proposed.

"Well, we've gone there for several nights," Tresholm observed. "Tonight I think we ought to stay for a little time to see Prince Bartoldi play."

Michani indulged in a significant grimace. There was distress in the princess' face. Nevertheless they trooped out to the roulette table. As though instinctively, Tresholm and his young companion stood where they had watched the game hour after hour for the last four days. Tresholm's eyes followed the whirling of the ball.

"Nineteen," he announced. "I should never have thought of nineteen. What are you for, Bartoldi? Maximums on seven, fourteen, twenty-nine, I suppose?"

Lena's hand stole through the young man's arm.

"I may stand by you?" she whispered. "I do not disturb?"

Tresholm was watching his companion closely. Bartoldi's attitude was that of a genuine spectator—if anything a trifle bored. He held a packet of notes in his hand, but he was whispering to Lena and they both laughed. Then he leaned forward and watched the croupiers for a few seconds.

"What a silly game!" he exclaimed suddenly. "I say," he added, turning to Tresholm, "do you mind if we go on up to the Carlton? You and I have to play against those fellows at tennis tomorrow at half past ten, so we ought not to be too late."

The little procession passed down the stairs, Lena's arm through her ancé's, the princess' head close to Tresholm's.

"But you are a magician, dear friend," she murmured.

Later in the evening they found themselves alone for a few minutes.

"Ever since I knew you, dear Andrew," she said, "you've been helping people out of trouble. There was that second secretary who had an affair with Signor Catoni's wife. And then—"

"Don't make me out too much of a busybody," he begged. "Dear Margherita—you permit?"

"Margherita, and nothing else, for always," she whispered.

"Then, Margherita," he went on, "believe me, this little episode has given me real pleasure. It is a hobby of mine to speculate upon human nature and its byways, of which gambling is one. I figured to myself that, after the first agony of watching a game of chance when one was hopelessly without the means of joining in, the flatness of it would begin to depress. That was my theory.

"Afternoon after afternoon, night after night, we watched that stupid mechanical toy, and every time the young man has become more bored. At first he suffered, but only for a short time. Since then, I think he has felt all the surfeit of the cigaret-smoking youth set to watch over a tobacconist's shop and given *carte blanche*. By comparison, the tennis we arranged for him, the golf, the companionship of your delightful Lena gained every hour in value. Tonight I am certain he was honest. The game did not attract him. I am proud of my patient."

"And you, the wonderful physician!" she murmured. "Is there no one who can pay your fee?"

Then the lights went down; shadows crept through the place. The music which began like the rustling of leaves, the sighing of a south wind, stole into form. Without a word, they rose.

"The last thing the true physician thinks of is his fee," Tresholm confided.

Her lips almost brushed his in that subdued light. "So the patient has to offer," she whispered.

The Gambler's Road

Pierre Gourdain, son of the Niçois millionaire jeweler, and one of the young elegants of the Sporting Club at Monte Carlo, presented himself at the main Bureau de Change with only a weak effort at that immobility of expression which, in the life of the Casino, is counted part of the equipment of the chic gambler.

Both his hands were filled with enormous red plaques, and he had no sooner deposited them upon the desk than, from his bulging pockets, he produced two more handfuls. The cashier, with a little skilful manipulation, spread them before him in rows of ten.

"*Un—deux—trios—quatre—et soixante, monsieur. Quatre cent soixante mille francs.*"

"*C'est ça!*" the young man murmured, struggling to keep the elation from his tone. "*J'ai touché le zéro trios fois avec les maximum. Il faut gagner de temps en temps.*"

The cashier produced an incredible pile of mille notes, done up in series of tens. He turned them over with agile forefinger, pausing to examine more closely a small portion of them.

"There is some sealing-wax which has fallen upon the backs of these," he pointed out. "Monsieur objects?"

"Not in the least," the young man assured him.

The forty-six packets were in due course transferred to the pocket of the fortunate young man. There happened to be no other client for the moment; the two were alone. The cashier leaned forward.

"Monsieur returns to Nice tonight?" he inquired.

The young man nodded. "Naturally."

The cashier looked up and down the room. "Monsieur will play tomorrow night?"

"Without a doubt. While the Sporting Club is open, I play nowhere else."

The Gourdains were a well-known local family, and the cashier was a born Monégasque. He leaned forward once more.

"Why not leave a portion at least of the money, Monsieur Gourdain?" he suggested. "I will give you a note for it and you can collect it when you arrive tomorrow."

The young man shook his head. "Why should I do that?" he protested. "My banker thinks that I gamble too heavily. Tomorrow I shall show him: I shall deposit half, and bring the remainder away with me. He will believe then that it is possible to win. It will amuse me, this!"

"Four hundred and sixty thousand francs is a great deal of money take with you from here to Nice at three o'clock in the morning," the cashier warned him.

"Why, my friend," the young man expostulated, "this is one of the safest roads of Europe. I have traversed it a hundred times without molestation. Besides, in a car at a hundred kilometers an hour, what can be done? I stop for no one. That I can promise."

There was a rush of business, and the fortunate gambler passed on. He lingered at the bar for a word with Joseph and a final whisky-and-soda. The popular barman leaned across the counter.

"Monsieur has had good fortune tonight?"

Pierre Gourdain smiled. "Good enough to ask you to take one of those boxes of cigars home with you, Joseph."

"That is very kind of Monsieur," was the grateful acknowledgment. "But Monsieur Gourdain, why not leave some of your winnings with me? It goes into the safe, or I can get you a Casino check."

"What on earth for? I am going straight back to Nice and, as you see, I am, as always, sober."

"Naturally," was the reply; "but the road between here and Nice—"

"Why, it is the safest in the world!" the young man interrupted. "I pass along it at all hours of the night and morning, four times a week. I ought to know. I have never heard anything more than a rumor of any attempt at robbery."

"*Écoutez, Monsieur Gourdain,*" Joseph begged eagerly. "Up till last week, yes; since last week, even the night before last, there has been trouble on the road."

"What do you mean? Robbery?"

Joseph nodded. "There is an American who was staying at Nice, in hospital at the present moment. He was robbed of fifty thousand francs— as yet he is not able to explain how."

"I have heard nothing of this," Pierre Gourdain declared. "There has been nothing in the newspapers."

"The newspapers, no," Joseph remarked meaningly. "Do we read much in the newspapers, Monsieur Gourdain, of what happens in Monte Carlo, save of the galas, and the brilliant crowd at the Sporting Club, and the great winnings? Nevertheless, this is the truth. Besides the American, there was a man found dead two mornings ago, in the road near Cap d'Ail, and not a sign or a word as to how he got there—a man in evening clothes, with empty pockets. What does one think? I ask you, Monsieur Gourdain."

Joseph stepped back to yield smilingly to a call upon his till. The young jeweler sipped his whisky-and-soda thoughtfully. How did these people hear such things? he wondered. And, stranger still, how was it that the other people did not hear them? Joseph presently returned.

"Who is to know, Joseph," Gourdain asked him, "that I leave here tonight with my pockets full of money?"

It was evident that the conversation was distressing to the barman. He hesitated for a moment, and his manner became reluctant. Nevertheless, he answered his young client's question.

"Monsieur Gourdain," he confided, "it has been said, and it would appear that there might be truth in it, that there are spies about here; that when a large win comes to anyone out of Monte Carlo, like you, the news is passed on by telephone. I speak more than I should, perhaps, but I have my ideas."

One of the perambulating deities of the place crossed the threshold of the bar and looked around the room. Joseph faded away like a ghost.

Monsieur Gourdain paid one of his linen-coated assistants for his drink and made his thoughtful departure. As he struggled into his heavy overcoat, a person whom he had passed on the stairs entered the telephone-booth.

Four o'clock glowed upon his illuminated timepiece as Tresholm, home-ward-bound from Toulon, swung round one of the last of the terrible curves of the Lower Corniche close to Cap d'Ail.

Against the high bank on his left, all the elements of tragedy were dis-closed to him by his cautiously operated headlight. He turned it off and descended. His chauffeur, jumping from the seat beside him, was already in the road.

"An accident, I'm afraid," Tresholm muttered.

"It's that Lancia car from Nice, sir," the man volunteered.

They both hurried forward. An overturned car was leaning against the bank, with an ambulance wagon drawn up just short of it; upon the ground a prostrate form, over which were bending a woman in a nurse's costume and a man who had the appearance of a doctor. A gendarme in the Moné-gasque uniform turned towards the two new arrivals.

"What is it that has arrived?" Tresholm asked quickly.

"A motor accident," the man replied. "Monsieur would do well to proceed. There is by chance here a doctor and a nurse. Further aid is not necessary."

Without a doubt, but for that last sentence, Tresholm would have climbed back into his car, would have passed the sad little scene and proceeded on his journey to Monte Carlo. He had years of experience behind him, how-ever, and in the days when life and death were always in the balance he had learned to suspect a superfluous sentence.

"You are of the gendarmerie of Beaulieu or Nice?" he inquired, looking at the man's uniform.

"It is of no consequence, that. Monsieur will please proceed. My orders are to allow no one to loiter."

"Your orders? From whom?"

"Monsieur le Docteur Earnshaw," was the prompt response. "It is a question whether the injured man will live. A crowd around him would be fatal. Pass on, if you please."

"I myself have some knowledge of medicine," Tresholm persisted. "I may be of assistance."

He deliberately avoided the man's outstretched arm and approached the prostrate form. The doctor, a clean-shaven, gray-haired man, swung round at the sound of his footsteps. The nurse, who was leaning down on the other side, pushed her veil back and looked at him with startled eyes.

"There has been an accident, I fear. Can I be of any assistance?" Tresholm asked.

The doctor hesitated for a moment. There was a look of distress in his face, and his black coat and dark trousers were covered with dust.

"You and your chauffeur can help us to carry this unfortunate fellow to our ambulance, if you will be so kind," he suggested.

"What happened?" Tresholm ventured.

"We scarcely saw," the doctor replied. "He passed us, traveling at a tremendous speed at the beginning of the turn here. Perhaps he did not allow himself quite enough room. Perhaps he had drunk too much. He gave a tremendous skid, hit the side of the bank, and the car turned over. We found him lying by the roadside here."

"Is he seriously hurt?"

"I can find no signs of life."

The four men picked up the injured man with ease, and carried him to the ambulance. The nurse arranged the pillows for his head. Still he gave no sign of life; the blood coming through the bandage on his head trickled down on his clothes.

"How far do you go?" Tresholm asked.

"To Nice," the doctor answered. "I have a small clinic in the Boulevard Dubouchage. My name is Doctor Earnshaw."

"I seem to know the young man by sight," Tresholm reflected.

"He is quite well known in Nice," the doctor confided gravely. "He is the son of a rich jeweler—a great gambler I fear. Thank you so much for your help sir."

Tresholm returned thoughtfully to his car. He paused to light a cigaret and watched the departing ambulance thread its careful way round the curve.

"We'll get along, Johnson," he called out to his chauffeur, who was examining the wreck of the Lancia.

"Queer things, them skids sir," the man remarked. "The road's as dry as a bone at the turn here, and there ain't too much dust. Besides that, the front of the car's all smashed in, as though it had hit something solid. The bank's soft enough. No more than an odd bit of rock or two that wouldn't hurt anything."

Tresholm crossed the road at once and examined the car with his chauffeur. The terrible condition of the bonnet and the smashed front-springs were difficult to understand.

"It does seem queer," Tresholm ruminated.

"I've never seen the front of a car buckled up like that before, sir, just with running up a bank," the man commented. "Looks to me as though there might have been a bit of dirty work before the doctor and the ambulance came along. He wouldn't think anything about that, naturally, seeing the car overturned here, and the man dead or unconscious."

Tresholm walked a few pace, along the road. They were some distance from any habitation, except the ghostly Château d'Ail, whose empty windows had looked down upon the road for forty years. Tresholm studied them meditatively. Then he returned to his car.

"The young man's face was familiar to me," he repeated, as he climbed into the driving-seat. "I fancy he's been pointed out as a gambler from Nice."

"I know the car, sir," Johnson confided. "I've seen it doing a cool hundred along this road more than once. Never ought to be allowed, the way they drive on these curves. That was one who got what was coming to him, anyway."

Tresholm, the rare and unwilling victim of a gala dinner a few nights later, unfolded his napkin and glanced sideways at the card of the woman on his left. She caught his eye, smiled, and adjusted the strip of pasteboard so that he could read it more easily.

"Earnshaw," she murmured. "Isobel Earnshaw. That is my name. Yours I know, but I wonder whether you can remember where we met last."

Tresholm was genuinely intrigued. Something about the woman's eyes was vaguely reminiscent. She was a handsome woman, beautifully dressed in one of those elusive black frocks which to the uninitiated seem simple, yet which cost famous dress designers many hours of anxious thought. Her pearls were beautiful, her plainly coiffured hair attractive. The sense of familiarity was there, but for once Tresholm was at a loss.

"I have seen you somewhere recently," he admitted. "The amazing thing is that I cannot recall where."

"I will not spoil your dinner by leaving you guessing. Those were tragical moments in which we met. Three or four o'clock in the morning, it must have been, a mist over the moon, the commencement of a mistral—and that terrible accident"

"You were the nurse!" he exclaimed.

She nodded. "And my husband was the doctor. You can see him on the other side of the table. It was a great grief to both of us that we were unable to do anything for that poor young man. He must have been dead several minutes before we arrived."

"It was a horrible tragedy," Tresholm said gravely.

"It was indeed," she assented. "I cannot think, Mr. Tresholm, why we English people do not try to bring our influence to bear upon the authorities to stop this reckless driving. They estimated that he must have gone round that corner at eighty kilometers an hour."

"What I find even more difficult to understand," Tresholm confided, "is the extraordinary reticence of the newspapers when an accident of this sort takes place. One single paragraph in the paper is all that I have seen—just a brief account of a motor accident, and the death of the driver. Yet it seems to me the affair has been too easily dismissed."

"In what way?"

Tresholm, glancing idly down the table, suddenly caught the eye of a man whom he recognized as the doctor. They exchanged friendly nods.

"Well," he explained, "in England there would have been a terrible fuss. We should have had diagrams of the road and photographs of the smashed car. We should have had pages of your evidence, and your husband's, and a dozen theories as to the cause of the skid."

"The French are not like that," she observed. "An accident such as this in the center of a great pleasure-spot is, from their point of view, a thing to be glossed over, to be dismissed in as few words as possible. I am not sure that they are not right. It is simply pandering to the sensation-mongers to dilate upon a tragedy. Besides, in a police affair—which this, fortunately, is not—what a help the newspapers in England are to the criminal."

"In the case of a crime, I agree with you entirely," he assented. "In this case, however, when there is no suggestion of anything of the sort, one might have expected a few further details."

She shrugged her shoulders and turned to answer a remark from her left-hand neighbor. Tresholm leaned towards his hostess, Lady Westerton.

"We were speaking of that poor young man's motor accident on his way back to Nice," he explained. "One has seen so little of it in the papers."

"I was remarking the same thing to my husband this morning," Lady

Westerton agreed. "Have they found any trace of all that money he was supposed to have with him?"

Tresholm turned once more to Mrs. Earnshaw. "Lady Westerton was saying something about the young man's having had a large sum of money."

"An exaggeration, I should imagine," she commented thoughtfully. "He was undressed at the clinic, naturally. The night-sister took my place, but I am sure I should have heard of it if he had had any unusual sum."

She leaned across the table, and spoke to her husband. "Lady Westerton has been telling us that that poor young man Monsieur Gourdain was supposed to have a considerable sum of money in his possession."

"Seven mille and some odd change," her husband replied. "I know, because I locked it up."

"There are always rumors of that sort," Isobel Earnshaw reminded them. "In this case, however, it must have been a mistake, for there was certainly no time for anyone to have robbed him and to have gotten away, before we arrived on the scene."

A guest from the other side of the table intervened. "There is no doubt that the young man won a large sum that night," he said, "but he probably left it somewhere in Monte Carlo."

"He had plenty of time," the doctor remarked. "They say that he left the Sporting Club at three o'clock. It couldn't have taken him more than ten minutes to get to Cap d'Ail, and it was nearly four when we came upon him."

Tresholm opened his lips, but closed them again. Someone spoke of the new supper place everyone was going to. Finis with poor young Monsieur Gourdain!

The party broke up as usual with a general exodus to the Sporting Club. Tresholm found himself afflicted with a curious fit of uneasiness. He watched the play for a time, and then, acting upon a sudden impulse, descended the stairs and strolled out into the soft night. He walked the length of the terrace, and returning found himself in front of the Casino. He joined the thin stream of entrants and made his leisurely progress through the "Kitchen."

Suddenly he came to a standstill. Mrs. Earnshaw was seated at one of the tables, playing—and playing for high stakes.

He watched her closely. She had a book in her hand which she studied before each bet, but she was losing constantly. He changed his place and strolled round behind her. She must have had four mille in stakes on the table, mostly around twenty-one and red. Twenty-two and black turned up. Her reluctant fingers stole into her bag. She drew out a packet of notes and passed five of them to the croupier.

Tresholm for a moment almost betrayed himself. On the backs of the notes were little spatterings of red sealing-wax.

Tresholm watched the note disappear into the tronc of the table. Then he walked silently away.

The sordid, crowded room existed no longer. He looked into the darkness; he saw the flickering beams of moonlight upon the white road, the little groups of figures, the young man sobbing out his last breath—watched those white, cool fingers stealing in and out of his pockets.

Tresholm made friends with the Chef de Sûreté of the principality. It was rather a one-sided affair, for that functionary was reserved though polite, and Tresholm was on the borderline of being inquisitive. He persisted in discussing the tragedy of the Lower Corniche Road.

"You see, Monsieur," he ventured, "it is not as though it were the first affair of the sort. There have been two others presenting similar characteristics."

"From whom have you that information?" Monsieur Desrolles demanded.

"I gathered it with difficulty," Tresholm replied evasively. "Nevertheless, there was Monsieur Pierre Lavalle, the contractor from Saint Raphael, who was found dead, with a burst tire on his car, not a mile from the scene of the present tragedy. He, too, is reported to have been winning at the Casino, yet when he was discovered he had barely a mille note upon him.

"Then there was the wine-grower from Juan-les-Pins—I have forgotten his name—and his was a small affair, but when he left the Casino he certainly had seventy or eighty thousand francs in his pocket, of which there were no traces when his body was found at the roadside.

"It may be as you say, a dangerous road, Monsieur Desrolles, but it is odd that these three accidents should have happened to men who left Monte Carlo with large sums of money which were never seen again."

"The affairs in question are occupying my department," the Chef de Sûreté declared. "At the same time, let me remind you of this—there is no direct evidence that any one of these three men whom you have mentioned actually had a large sum of money in his possession when the accident occurred.

"Young Monsieur Gourdain, for instance, is known to have called somewhere in Monte Carlo on his homeward way, and also at a dancing place in Cap d'Ail. Lavalle sat in a café two hours on his return journey and the person from Juan was, according to the medical testimony, sodden with drink. All these might well have been robbed elsewhere than upon the scene of the accident."

"That is true perfectly," Tresholm admitted, "but as against that, no traces of the money have been discovered."

"How do you know?"

"Well, there has been no word of it in the papers."

"In England," the Chef de Sûreté pointed out, "you are foolish people with your newspapers. You often make escape from justice an easy thing for the criminal. You show him in what direction the police are working, and against whom their suspicions are directed. That is not our method."

"Admitting all this," Tresholm insisted patiently, "do you honestly believe, Monsieur Desrolles, that these three tragedies which have taken place within the last few weeks are ordinary accidents?"

"My answer to you, Monsieur Tresholm, is that we have no reason to suppose otherwise," was the dry rejoinder. "In your case, as you are a friend of Monsieur Robert's, I will treat you with some confidence, and I will venture to remind you of one fact. The amateur detective does not exist in France. We find that official business proceeds more satisfactorily without interference from outsiders."

"Monsieur Desrolles," said Tresholm, "I am not an amateur detective, and I have no wish to force your hand in any way. For anything I know, you may be on the point of making an arrest in connection with the *affaire* Gourdain. If that is so, your caution is justified, but unnecessary. I will walk away from here with a seal upon my lips. If it is not so, please listen to what I have to say."

"I will listen to what you have to say, Monsieur Tresholm," the other decided.

"The clerk at the *caisse* who handed Gourdain notes for some of his winnings is reported to have apologized for the fact that a number of them had been spattered with small drops of red sealing-wax. I have seen notes spattered in the same fashion within the last twenty-four hours."

The expression of Desrolles had undergone no appreciable change but there was a keener light in his eyes. "Where?"

"In the Casino."

"You would recognize the person who passed them?"

"Certainly I should. I could tell you her name, if you would like to hear it."

"I am listening."

"Her name is Isobel Earnshaw. She is the wife of the doctor whom I saw upon the road bandaging the young man's head that night."

Tresholm was confused at the result of his words. Whether from shock or for some other reason, Desrolles was incapable of speech. Tresholm had the queer feeling that the man was personally affected.

"The lady in question," Tresholm went on, "was gambling in the 'Kitchen' for sums which, for a doctor's wife, were enormous. I suggest, sir, that you look up the dossiers of Doctor Earnshaw and his wife."

The functionary was himself again. There was a new and rasping note in his voice, however.

"There is no one in the neighborhood," he announced scornfully, "who needs to look at a police dossier of Doctor Earnshaw, or his wife. The doctor has practiced in Nice for at least seventeen years, served in the war, and has amassed, without doubt, a comfortable fortune. He has been married for twelve years and his wife enjoys the respect of the whole community. She won every distinction that was possible for a woman during the war. She was decorated by the President."

"A wonderful record," Tresholm admitted.

"So wonderful," Desrolles continued, "that your suggestion, I must say, took my breath away. There are many bundles of mille notes, Monsieur Tresholm, which bear traces of sealing-wax."

Tresholm rose unwillingly. "After what you have told me, Monsieur—"

"No, sit down," the other interrupted. "We must consider this matter apart from the sentimental view. Any theory you may have formed concerning Earnshaw and his wife is of course absurd, yet tell me what was in your mind. What had you to propose?"

"Simply this. I am fond of an adventure—a gambler outside of gaming-rooms, you understand. I had an idea of leaving the Sporting Club a heavy winner one night, and testing the affair by going to Nice myself. If you approved of my plan and were willing to help me, I thought we might perhaps solve this mystery."

Desrolles was scribbling with his pen upon a scrap of paper, his head leaning on his hand, his face half hidden.

"Your plan is worth trying," he conceded. "See me later, and we will work out the details. In the meanwhile, Monsieur Tresholm, let me impress upon you one thing—the necessity for entire and inviolable discretion. Upon that condition alone we work together."

"I agree," Tresholm assented.

On the following night, Tresholm justified himself, at least in the eyes of all Monte Carlo.

The news went flashing from the Sporting Club back to the hotel and through the Casino. The attack upon its resources was opened. Tresholm had bought a million francs' worth of plaques, and was playing a steady, systematic game of roulette in maximums.

An hour later a further bulletin was issued. Affairs were going ill with the intrepid gambler. He was half a million down, and losing steadily.

Gustave Sordel, hurrying through the passage, chuckled to himself. It was a tardy triumph, but worth while.

Tresholm backed the same numbers and every possible combination of them without flinching his losses. His luck began to turn when a vacated place next to the croupier on the opposite side of the table was taken by a woman.

Their eyes met as she sat down. Whatever surprise Tresholm may have felt, he succeeded in concealing it. His greeting was friendly.

Following her first smile, however, was a look in her beautiful eyes which puzzled him. He had suddenly become of some account to her. So might she have looked at him if, by some incredible chance, she had overheard his conversation with Desrolles. She had betrayed only a trace of it but, she was afraid.

Luck at the tables is a singular thing, or the world's interest in that mechanical toy, the roulette-wheel would long since have evaporated. The woman opposite him was playing on black numbers of low denominations. Tresholm, with every stake, was directly opposed to her.

From the moment of her sitting down, his numbers dominated the board. In five spins he won *en plein* three times. His luck was prodigious. The heap of disks in front of him grew and grew.

As be won, his vis-à-vis lost; as his pile of plaques increased, hers diminished. Once or twice she looked across at him. Their contest seemed to have affected her nerves. Her lips were trembling; her fingers shook.

"You are invincible, Mr. Tresholm," she murmured.

"You are playing against the table," he rejoined. "The run of it is for my numbers."

At one o'clock she left off playing, and at a quarter past Tresholm rose. The cashier handed him back his check for a million, which he had cashed at the beginning of the evening, and over a million in mille notes. For once he broke through his habit of silence.

"It is perhaps as well for the Casino, Monsieur Tresholm," he said diffidently, "that you are only an occasional player. Would you like me to send one of the clerks up with you to your room?"

"Thanks very much," Tresholm replied, "but I am staying at the Negresco at Nice—moved in there yesterday."

"You are not going to make that journey, Monsieur Tresholm, with all this money?" the man expostulated.

"As a matter of fact, I must. I am a careful driver, though. I do not think that anything is likely to happen to me."

"Leave the money with us," the man urged. "We'll telephone it to you at Nice tomorrow morning."

"You know what they call me here, Monsieur," Tresholm confided—"'the professional gambler.' That is because I like to take an occasional risk."

He stuffed the most magnificent offering which the desk had ever received into the depository provided for it and strolled away. In the bar he called for a whisky-and-soda. Joseph welcomed him.

"Walk quickly through the passages, Monsieur," he advised. "A million francs burn in the pocket."

"I'm not going through any passages," Tresholm said. "I am going to Nice. I'm staying at the Negresco for a few days."

"Leave your money with me, sir," Joseph begged. "It will be safe."

"I think it will be pretty safe with me," Tresholm rejoined sipping his drink.

Joseph was worried. "Mr. Tresholm," he pleaded, "you are a brave man, like most great gamblers. Do not be foolhardy. Monsieur Gourdain—"

"But Gourdain was driving a motor-car round a corner at eighty kilometers an hour," Tresholm argued, "and I'm not going to do anything of that sort."

There was a rush of custom, and Joseph moved reluctantly away. Tresholm finished his drink and turned to leave the room. In the entrance he came face to face with Isobel Earnshaw.

"Better luck now I've left?" he asked.

She ignored his question, laid her long nervous fingers on his arm and drew him into the little recess.

"Mr. Tresholm," she said, "you will think that my nerves have all gone because I have been losing tonight, but it is not that. I have a superstition—a real one. Don't go to Nice tonight."

"But my dear lady!" he protested. "Why not? I am not like these young men—a reckless driver—and I shall call nowhere on the way."

"Nevertheless, I implore you—do not go."

Their eyes met for a single moment. Hers fell.

"Madam," he said, "this, I believe, is kindness, which I shall always remember and for which I thank you. Good night!"

He strode out, and down the stairs. As he stood waiting for his hat and overcoat, someone hurried into the telephone-booth.

The Sporting Club was still crowded, an hour and a half later, when Tresholm made his unexpected reappearance. He strolled into the bar and made his way towards a vacant stool. Joseph stared at the newcomer as if he were a ghost and asked breathlessly:

"You changed your mind, sir?"

"Not exactly that," Tresholm admitted. "I found the road just beyond Cap d'Ail practically in the hands of the police, and such a hullabaloo going on that I thought I'd come back."

Gustave Sordel, who had been at the bar, leaned forward. "What, then, has arrived?" he demanded.

Tresholm paused for a moment, and in that moment he heard soft movements; a waft of perfume crept his way. The woman's dress was almost touching his knees. He had no need to turn his head; he knew who had stolen up onto the vacant stool by his side.

"Well," he replied, "do you happen to know a sort of deserted château on the road near Cap d'Ail?"

"Naturally. All the world knows it," Sordel assented. "Proceed."

There was a little indrawn breath on his other side—almost a sob. Tresholm was merciful. He avoided the temptation of a dramatic recital.

"I found a barrier across the road there," he recounted. "The Nice police had got possession of the place. From the little I could gather, it seems to have been temporarily in the possession of a doctor. Someone had gotten hold of the place before him, I suppose, though, and just round the bend there was a most diabolical affair, worked by an engine from a secret opening in the wood, which dragged an iron structure up to the right-hand side of the road. That's the thing young Gourdain ran into, of course, and probably others. As a matter of fact, it was out tonight—for me."

There was a babel of questions.

"Can't you see that Mrs. Earnshaw isn't well?" Tresholm protested. "Give me some brandy, Joseph."

"Was anyone arrested?" someone asked eagerly.

The fingers of the woman gripped his own. She had recovered. She was deathly pale, but her eyes commanded.

"Go on," she insisted. "Tell your story."

"There is not so much to tell," he obeyed reluctantly. "Half a dozen arrests were made, among whom—it was ridiculous, of course," he added, "but your husband was nominal owner of the property—so, as a matter of form—"

"What else?" she interrupted.

"Let me take you home," he begged.

"If you don't tell me everything," she gasped, "I shall die. Can't you see? I must know!"

"There was another tragedy," he confided. "Monsieur Desrolles—no doubt it was a point of honor with him—he thought that the Nice police had been too officious; he drove up, passed me on the way, in fact, found out what had happened, and blew his brains out."

There was a little shiver of emotion. Isobel Earnshaw stretched out her hand for the brandy.

"You have yourself received a slight wound, Monsieur," Sordel remarked.

Tresholm dabbed his cheek with a handkerchief and nodded. "A bloodthirsty night," he observed. "Someone took a pot-shot at me from a car. I had just turned my head, fortunately."

The woman dropped a white pellet into her glass. There was a furor of conversation. She drew closer to Tresholm.

"It was Armand Desrolles who tried to shoot you," she confided. "He was my lover. I am glad he didn't. You're a brave man anyhow, although you deceived Armand and went for the Nice police."

She drained the contents of her glass. Tresholm suddenly saw the cloudiness of the liquid and snatched at it, but he was too late. She leaned over and kissed him.

"An affair of sixty seconds," she assured him. "You took a gambler's chance, anyhow, and I like you for it."

"Tresholm!" someone called out.

He turned his head. Another voice was raised above the general hubbub.

"Look out! What's happened to Mrs. Earnshaw?"

She slipped from her stool, clinging to his shoulder to break her fall. Her arm dragged him down, her pale lips whispered.

"I was a gambler from birth, through life—to death," she faltered. "You, too. Good-by!"

12 Stories

Darton's Great Picture

All that we knew of her was that her name was Bertha, and that she was Darton's model. As for me, I had never spoken to her in my life. When she knocked at my door at considerably after midnight, and brushed past me into my room without a word of explanation, I naturally concluded that something was up.

"Anything wrong with Darton?" I asked quickly. "Is he worse?"

"No."

I was out of candles, and, owing to a difference with a myrmidon of the gas company, my supply had been cut off. Therefore I was sitting in the darkness. But I had a great north window, curtainless and blindless, and a flooding shaft of yellow moonlight lay diagonally across my floor. She had stopped in the very centre of it, and I smoked my pipe and looked at her. For the first time I understood Darton's enthusiasm. I looked at her with a new respect. Her black gown was shabby and untidy, and the hall-mark of what usually passes for profligacy was upon her cheeks. She was swaying, too, a little unsteadily—perhaps she was drunk. But all the same, I looked at her with new eyes.

"Take a chair," I suggested, placing one by her side. "It's all right if you sit down carefully, and keep your skirts off the broken canes."

She shook her head, but drew the chair towards her, and leaned over its back. I looked at her and sighed. There was immortality in that pose. If Darton failed, it would be his own fault. By-the-bye, perhaps he had heard. Perhaps that was why she was here.

"Any news of the picture?" I asked.

She took not the slightest notice of my question. I don't think she even heard it. I smoked on and wondered. Not that I was in any hurry. The longer she remained like that the better I was pleased. As a whole, she was beyond my powers of reproduction, but the lines of her half-crouching figure, the pose of her drooped head, one faint suggestion of the writing upon her face, was capital to me. My personal curiosity was already gone. There was something greater in the room, and I was being drawn into it. I cared not why she had come. I was only anxious that she should not go. When she spoke, I was sorry.

"Do me a service!"

I nodded. What did she want? Not money! People knew better than to come to me for that. Nevertheless, there was a half-sovereign in my pocket— my last—and it was hers for the asking. My fingers closed upon it that I might be prompt in offering, but it was not money.

"They say that you are clever at making rapid sketches. Come and make one for me."

I took up a block of paper and a couple of pencils.

"Whereabouts?"

"In Darton's studio."

I nodded. "Half a minute!"

I filled my pipe, and handed her a cigarette. She took no notice of the proffered box. She was looking through me, through the walls of my room, away into some dark corner of the world. She did not see me, or hear my voice. I would have given that half-sovereign, and gone dinnerless for a week, to know what thoughts were rushing through her brain—what she saw behind that lifted curtain. For a moment I envied her. She was living! The limits of her little life had fallen away. She was in that shadowy second world where the great winds of fate go roaring over the sterile plains, and the flames of passion leap up to the dark sky. How I envied her! To have felt like that with my brush in my hand would have meant immortality. To her, the model, it came; and me, the artist, it passed by. I sighed, and struck a light.

She left the room, and I followed her down on to the second landing, where Darton's studio was. She held up a warning finger, and opened the door softly. I passed by her side across the threshold. A tallow candle was burning upon a box. She took it up and held it over her head. I stood by her side.

I knew then why, for the last month, we had all been excluded from Darton's studio. I knew what had been thrown under the mighty wheels of the Juggernaut of success, what had gone to the making of Darton's great picture. Poverty had swept me bare enough—we were all poor together in our little colony. Most of us had kept starvation off with pot-boilers, and renovations, and hack-dealer's work of some sort or other; but Darton, since his great picture had come to him, had put away all these things as unholy. How he had lived had been a mystery to us. Now that I looked around his room, and at the girl by my side, things seemed clearer to me. Every article of furniture was gone, except the easel. The walls and the carpets were perfectly bare. There was no fire in the grate, nor any signs of food. On the box, close to where the candle had been, was a pile of pawn-tickets. There was the brand of starvation in the room, in the spiritualised thinness of the figure by my side. The first glimmerings of the truth commenced to dawn upon me.

In the far corner the foot of an iron bedstead protruded from behind a torn and faded curtain of red baize. Shading the candle in her hand, she glided from my side, and drew it back along the bending string. Darton was sleeping there upon the bare frame of the bedstead, his body covered by a woman's brown ulster, his head resting upon a rolled-up skirt. His face was so white and thin that, for a moment, a new terror seized me. Then I saw that he was breathing heavily. His hand, drooping down to the floor, clutched a letter, retained even through his sleep by the spasmodic clasp of those long, delicate fingers. She let the curtain fall, and came back to my side.

"Draw it for me," she whispered. "Everything! Him"—she pointed to the bedstead—"the letter, those"—she pointed downwards at the pawn-tickets. "Everything! Softly! Let him sleep; he is worn out."

I did her bidding. It was a trick of mine, this rapid sketching. Sometimes it brought me money when my art failed me. So I did her bidding.

She moved to the curtain. "Put me in."

She turned to face me, and my heart was sick for a north light, for my palette and brushes. But, as the thing seemed to me by the miserable light of that single candle, I put it down on the paper. When I had finished, I looked at it almost with awe—for the first time my knack had come into touch with what there was of the artist in me. There was a tragedy there, in those few hasty strokes. I looked at my work, and I coveted it.

"Is it finished?" she asked, looking half-fearfully towards the bed.

"It is finished."

She came to my side, and held out her hand; but I hesitated.

"Let me make you a copy. This is so rough, and it would be useful to me."

"There must be no copy. Let me have it!"

She raised her eyes, and I hesitated no longer. I gave it to her.

She offered no thanks, for which I was grateful. How the night was passing with them below I could not tell. But I sat over my fire till its white ashes were cold, and the chill dawn-light filled the room.

Next morning we all knew the news. The Royal Academy had been graciously pleased to accept Darton's great picture, and by almost the same post he had received news of a legacy of three thousand pounds. I am free to admit that the last piece of news had an immensely exhilarating effect upon me. He came up to my room with a fat bundle of notes in his hand. He had been to see the lawyer.

"How much is it, old chap? You haven't kept my I.O.U.'s, have you?"

I laughed at him, and we sat down together and pondered over the matter. He made it at least fifty. I put it down at thirty. We struck a balance at forty, and I stuffed the notes into my trouser pockets with a feeling of great wealth. It was more money than I had possessed all at once for many years.

Darton was excited. He walked backwards and forwards across my bare floor, with a scarlet spot burning in his pale cheeks, talking incessantly. Every now and then he stood where she had stood last night. I looked at him, and I longed to ask a question. But my tongue was tied. So he talked, and I listened. He was to become famous; his pictures were to fetch great prices; he was to build that wonderful studio of which he had dreamed, and in it there was always to be a corner for me, or any of his old pals who chose to come to him. The world of which we had talked and wondered over together was to be opened for him, and, through him, for Fred, and for Dick, and for me. And still I listened, and listened in vain. He did not speak of her.

But it came in a day or two. Darton was giving us a dinner at Mariette's—he had spoken of the Savoy, but we had laughed in derision. Where were our dress-coats, our patent boots—even our tall hats? We were not of the world of the Savoy diners. Besides, had not Mariette trusted us, one and all, in our direst straits? There was not one of us who had not owed him for many dinners—as a matter of fact, there was not one of us who was not at that moment in his debt. Mariette had treated us, and Mariette should have our cash. Besides, was there not Burgundy in his cellars—old Burgundy, with a yellow seal and a cunning flavour; and as for the dinner, Mariette himself would put on his white apron and cook for us! What could be better? So Mariette's it was.

We were all there, Darton at the head of the table, in the wildest spirits, Fred at his left hand, and I at his right. Dick had come late, and sat by my side. A dandy was Dick, with a great bunch of violets in his coat, and a flavour of the West End in his clothes and bearing. Anyhow, we were all there, and dinner was half-way through, when I could stand it no longer. I tossed off a glass of Burgundy, and looked at him.

"And Bertha?"

His face clouded over. He set down his glass with a gesture of annoyance.

"She has left me."

I looked at him hard. We all looked at him. He helped himself to an *entrée* with nervous, shaking fingers. No one went on eating; no one spoke. He threw down his knife and fork like an angry child, and looked at us defiantly.

"How can I help it?" he exclaimed. "I did not drive her away. She left me of her own free will. I offered her half my legacy, yet she went."

"Tell us," Dick said quietly, and I echoed his word. We were all grave. Eating had become a farce.

Darton poured himself out wine and drank.

"Well, I will tell you then. You should hear the whole story. You shall be my judges and hers. You know that I took her for a model. Where she came from, and who she was, God only knows! But her face is the soul of my picture. You see, I admit it. Not only that; I was poor; I could not pay her. She came still. Presently, she gave up her rooms and came to me. Her little odds and ends of furniture she sold, and the money came to our joint housekeeping account. You know what that meant. It went into my picture. She was in the chorus of the Frivolity, and every penny she earned went the same way. I earned no money for months, as you fellows know. My picture absorbed me; I was drunk with it. Bertha found me food, and drink, and tobacco, and she paid the rent. She was my model, and I simply lived upon her. But that isn't the worst."

He threw himself back in his chair, and wiped his forehead. The perspiration was standing out upon it in beads. Fred leaned forward encouragingly.

"Never mind, old chap; you can make it all square with her now. What luck!"

Darton took no notice. I do not think that he heard him.

"Towards the end," he went on, leaning forward, and speaking in a thick whisper, "things went worse. Her play was taken off at the Frivolity. Bit by bit, we sold every stick of furniture. When my picture was finished we were half starved—and there was the frame. I went to David's; the fellow had lost faith in me—he would not advance a penny. All one night we sat and looked at one another. The picture was finished, but we were faint from want of food, and there was no frame. I had borrowed from all you fellows. There was no one else in the wide world. We looked into one another's faces, and Bertha—she had been so plucky all along—burst out sobbing, and then I'm afraid I wasn't what you'd call manly myself. Then she sprang up, and threw her arms around my neck and kissed me. When I looked up, she had gone.

"Well, in less than an hour a commissionaire brought me an envelope, with a sovereign in it. I knew that it came from Bertha, for the address was in her handwriting, and I thought she must have found out some old acquaintance and borrowed it. I bought food and drink, and it was life to me! Presently she returned. She came in, followed by one of David's men, and, without looking at me, she pointed to the picture. The man took it away, and I went with him. The frame was paid for; she had paid for it— and the money—was stolen!"

He poured out a glass of wine and drank it. The look of gaiety had fallen from his face. He was ghastly pale. And we were all silent. We waited.

"It was not until I came back from David's that I knew the truth. She was lying sobbing upon the bed, and when I would have gone to her she pushed me away. I must not touch her! she moaned. I must never touch her again. And then at last I saw her face—"

He held out his hand across the table.

"D—m! Let me finish! She did not go away! I fainted and for many days I was scarcely conscious. All the time she watched me, brought me food and wine, and kept me alive. And when I got well—she was in prison!"

I tried to raise my glass to my lips, but it fell shattered upon the table. We scarcely noticed it or the little stream of red wine. Dick retained presence of mind enough to wave away the advancing waiter. We were all breathless.

He looked from one to the other of us, and swore a deep oath.

"Haven't you fellows a single grain of sympathy to offer me?" he cried. "Why do you all look at me like that? Am I a culprit? Are you my judges? They were very lenient with her. She was not in a fortnight. I showed her my letters. Half of my legacy was hers, I told her. What in the name of all that is horrible could I do more? Could I keep her with me? Would you have had her here with us?"

"In the seat of honour!" cried Dick, his eyes all ablaze. "At your right hand, now and for ever!"

"That's d—d nonsense! She had behaved nobly. I know it, and I told her so. But how could I go on living with a woman who had been—who had been—in prison? A thief!"

I got up and struck him across the lips, so that the blood came through my fingers. Then my hands were held. The others hesitated; but I went away, for I knew more than they knew.

Perhaps, after all, the blow was a mistake. At any rate, the breach between Darton and myself was not final. We met afterwards, and spoke for the sake of those days of wonderful good-fellowship, when we four had fought our great battle with poverty so cheerfully. So it was that Darton sent me a card to see his pictures, when his new studio was built.

Darton had become fashionable, and he was engaged to a rich girl. I stood in a corner of his long reception-room, watching the throngs of people passing through, until I hated the man. I could not go and speak to him. That night still stood out from all others in my memory. Across the daintily tinted walls I seemed to see, in letters of fire, the price of his great picture, his great success—a woman's soul!

A rustling of skirts, the floating into the air of a familiar cheap scent, the uplifting of a closely drawn veil! I looked around in horror, but there was no one to see us.

"You have not forgotten me yet, I see," she said, with something of the old softness in her tone. "Well, you see, I am here! Don't you think it is time?"

She held up a little roll she was carrying. I recognized it, and my heart stood still. It was my sketch. Now I understood. I looked away from her, over the heads of the people, to where Darton was standing, with one hand resting upon his easel, talking to a tall, handsome girl. "He's going to be married, they say," she whispered.

"I have heard so."

She opened the sketch, and looked at it. Then she glanced up at me with an old smile.

"Will you show me the young lady?"

I waved my hand around the room.

"It's all your doing," I said softly; "the picture was yours; it was your flesh and blood."

"And my soul," she murmured.

"Is it worth while to undo it all? You have made your sacrifice; why render it useless? Let him alone."

"You are right," she said quietly; "it is not worth while. Here!"

She tore the sketch in pieces, and placed them in my hands. There was a dampness in my eyes as I took them. When I could see clearly, she was gone.

I hurried after her. Darton's butler stopped me in the doorway.

"I trust that that person did not annoy you, sir," he began, anxiously. "She had a card, and I could not catch Mr. Darton's eye, so I was forced to admit her."

I pushed him on one side and hurried down the steps on to the pavement. She was out of sight. There was a grey mist hanging upon the pavements, and somewhere she vanished into it. I have never seen her since. I do not expect to see her again. Darton and I are strangers.

The Reformation of Circe

"For the last time, then—"

"For the last time, no!"

Ransom looked sorrowfully into his friend's face. The note of finality in that brief negative was unmistakable. And the pity of it! Immense! Inexpressible!

"I shall not come again, Derrator. But now that you are sending me away—we shall likely enough never meet again—you are going to hear the truth!"

Derrator bowed.

"Be patient, my dear friend," he murmured, with a faint note of irony in his tone. "I am going to hear your view of the truth."

"I do not accept the correction," Ransom answered, quickly. "There are times when a man can make no mistake, and this is one of them. You shall hear the truth, and when you have spun out your days here to their limit, your days of sybaritic idleness, you shall hear it again—only it will be too late. Mind that—it will be too late! You are fighting against Nature. You were born to rule, to be master over men. You have power—the gift of swaying the minds and hearts of your fellow-creatures. Once you accepted your destiny, your feet were planted firmly upon the great ladder, you could have climbed—where you would!"

"My friend," Derrator murmured, "it was not worth while."

Ransom turned upon him fiercely.

"Not worth while! Is it worth while, then, to loiter in your flower-gardens, to be a dilettante student, to write fugitive verses, to dream away your days in the idleness of purely enervating culture? Life apart from one's fellows must always lack robustness. You have the instincts of the creator, Derrator. You cannot stifle them. Some day the cry of the world will fall upon your ears, and it may be too late. For the place of all men some time or other is filled."

Derrator lit a cigarette, and took his friend by the arm.

"Come," he said. "You have plenty of time for the train. I will tell the carriage to go on to the top of the hill. I want to show you my possessions."

Ransom recognised the purpose in his friend's invitation. Together they climbed the mountainous path. At the summit Derrator paused.

"Look around," he said.

"It is a beautiful view," Ransom admitted, coldly.

Derrator laughed softly.

"Look again," he said. "There is the sea, the moor! Turn your face to the wind: can you smell the heather? We have left the rose-gardens below, Ransom. This is Nature—the mother, the mistress beneficent, wonderful! You are a man of cities. Stay here with me for a day or two, and the joy of all these things will steal into your blood—and you will know what peace is."

"Peace is for the dead," Ransom answered, fiercely; "the last reward, perhaps, of a breaking life. The life effective, militant, is the only life for men. Break away from it, Derrator, for God's sake! Yours is the *fainéant* spirit of the decadent. Were you born into the world, do you think, to loiter through life an idle worshipper at the altar of beauty? Who are you to dare to skulk in quiet places while the battle of life is fought by others?"

Derrator smiled quietly—the smile that Ransom hated.

"Dear friend," he said, "the world can get on very well without me, and I have no need of the world. The battle that you speak of—well, I too have been in the fray, as you know. The memory of it is still a nightmare to me."

"You were ill-treated, Derrator," Ransom interrupted; "but your return would be all the more a triumph. You will go straight into office. The Premier himself is your suppliant."

Derrator shook his head.

"Let us confine our conversation to generalities," he said, dryly. "Do not think that I nourish any resentment against the Party for whom I laboured. I owe them nothing but thanks for driving me out. Only, I have learned my lesson. The strenuous life which you would glorify I have tried and found wanting. All the great causes of life are honeycombed with the disease of man's ambition and vanity and greed. For me the bottom has been knocked out of the whole thing. I have found here the life that satisfies me. Come and see me when you will, Ransom, but never again as an ambassador."

And Ransom was silent, because he had no more to say. The two men stood side by side, watching the carriage from below crawl up the hill. Before it reached them, however, the horn of a motor-car, approaching in the opposite direction, drove them to the side of the road. They both turned. A slow, enigmatic smile transformed Ransom's face. After all, there was hope, then.

The car passed them—without undue speed, but enveloped in a cloud of dust. Derrator watched the woman, and Ransom watched the man who had once been his bosom-friend. He saw the woman's languid curiosity flash from her deep-blue eyes, Derrator's arrestment of all expression, his sudden, faint start as the woman's lips curved into what, with longer waiting, might have developed into a smile. The episode, if it was to be ranked as such, was over.

Ransom, from his seat in the carriage, leaned over to say a final word.

"My mission, Derrator," he said, "must be written down a failure. Yet I am one of those who cling to thin chances, so I want you to remember this: All that I have said remains in force for six months from to-day. The solitude which has brought you a certain measure of madness may carry in its bosom its own antidote. Therefore, I shall not despair. *Au revoir*, Derrator!"

"Farewell!" Derrator answered, with a wave of the hand.

She came to the boundary-hedge, a gleam of white, tall, a little ghost-like with the smooth grace of her silent movements. She was bareheaded; she came to him out of the late twilight as one walking through a mist. As she walked she sang softly, at first to herself, then to him. He heard her, frowning. He was pale and nervous.

"Is it true," he asked abruptly, "that you are going?"

"But why not?" she answered, with gently upraised eyebrows. "One does not come to such places as these for always. One sleeps through the night, but the daytime—ah, that is different!"

"You have been contented here?"

"More than contented! I have been almost happy," she answered.

"Then why go back?" he asked, with a sudden fierceness in his tone. "What is there in the world so beautiful, after all? Here are the sun, and the sea, and the wind—it is the flower-garden of life. Stay and pick the roses with me!"

She shook her head.

"I am not like that," she answered, slowly. "Life may have its vulgarities, its weariness and its disappointments, but it is the only place for men and women. The fight may be sordid and the prizes tinsel—yet it is only the cowards who linger without."

"Still, you have been content here," he repeated, hoarsely.

"Content to rest," she answered; "but one does not sleep for ever. We were, neither of us, born to linger in a maze of abstractions. The contemplative life is for the halt and maimed of the world. We others must carry our burden into the thick of the battle."

"You speak to-night in allegories," he said. "You mean that you will return to London?"

"Of course!"

"And leave me here, after these days together—after everything."

Her eyes sought his, and the man's heart beat to passionate music.

"That," she murmured, "is as you will, Sir Hermit. Only it is certain that I must go. As for you—well, you are a man. It is for you to choose."

He sprang over the low paling. She swayed towards him with outstretched arms. Together they passed away into the world of shadows.

"You wonderful woman!" Ransom murmured. "What can we give you? A peerage in your own right, a diamond tiara—?"

"Don't talk nonsense!" she interrupted, a little sharply. "The Governorship for Herbert was all that I asked, and that he has. For the rest, I wonder sometimes—I wonder whether I do not regret."

Ransom stared at her in amazement.

"Regret?"

"Yes. I do not believe that he is happy."

Ransom sighed meditatively. After all, the ways of women were indeed mysterious.

"Pardon me," he remarked, "but that sounds a little sentimental, does it not?"

"If it is—what then? Am I too old or too world-weary for sentiment?"

Ransom was not at his ease.

"You amaze me, Adelaide," he said. "I regard you—we all regard you—as Derrator's saviour. He had committed moral suicide; it was you who disinterred him. The world owes you much for that; we owe you more; Derrator, perhaps, owes you most."

"Perhaps," she murmured; "perhaps not."

"But I do not understand your hesitation," Ransom persisted. "Derrator's career was ended. It was you who brought him once more into touch with great things, and you can see for yourself the outcome. Did you ever know a man grip the helm more firmly? He will be Prime Minister in five years."

"Prime Minister, perhaps; but will he be happy?" she asked.

Once more Ransom looked at her in surprise.

"Happy, Adelaide! I do not understand you. The man's career was ended. It was you who brought him back before the footlights. Of all your achievements I think that was the greatest."

"And of all my achievements," she answered, "it is the one of which I am least proud. You and I are both worldly persons, Ransom, but I yield the palm to you. To tell the truth, I am not happy about Derrator."

"You lingered too long with him in his lotos-land," Ransom said, with a subtle note of mockery in his tone. "His rose-gardens were very beautiful, but there was poison in every blossom—the 'poison of honey-flowers,' you know. I trust that none of it has found its way into your veins."

"I am not so sure," she answered, a little defiantly. "After all, a man is great by what he is, not what he does."

"Hush! He is coming," Ransom said, quickly. "I am going to look for Milligan. Find out what he has decided about Duncan's offer."

Derrator sank into the seat which Ransom had vacated. He was a little tired and there were dark lines under his eyes. The woman watched him closely.

"You are weary," she whispered.

"It is nothing," he answered. "Already I have forgotten it. I have been looking for you."

For once she was tongue tied. She knew well that the psychological moment had arrived. Every muscle of his face seemed set into nervous lines.

"I have been looking for you," he repeated, in a low, deep tone, his eyes fixed steadfastly upon her. "I have something to say."

"Well?" she murmured.

"I think," he continued, "that to-night I may speak. I have obeyed your call. For your sake I have broken a vow which had become to me almost a holy thing. The time has come, Adelaide, when I claim my reward."

For the moment she was evasive. Her eyes were fastened upon his face, as though she would read his unspoken thoughts.

"My friend," she said, "that sounds a little like an accusation. I persuaded you to break your vow because I honestly believed that you were wasting your life. I thought that you only needed to feel yourself once more in touch with the great world, and your only regret would be for the years which you had wasted. To-night I have been watching you, and I am not sure that I was right."

He looked straight ahead. Could he, too, she wondered, be wandering once more in the world of shadows where the cedar-trees drooped low and the perfume of the roses hung heavy upon the air? Underneath the lace of her gown her bosom was quickly rising and falling. She leaned forward and touched him on the arm.

"You shall have your answer," she whispered, "and it shall be 'yes.' But there is a condition."

The momentary flash of joy in his face died away. "Another!"

She leaned a little forward.

"Do not be afraid, dear," she whispered. "The condition is only this—that you take me back to where I found you. Only a little while ago I was a missionary; to-day I am myself a convert. Let us go back together—and hear whether the nightingales are singing still!"

So Derrator was never Prime Minister, after all.

The Little Grey Lady

Stourton forgot at once the gloomy, half-lit appearance of the house, the cold, uninhabited air of the hall and passages, the somber bearing of the solitary manservant who had ushered him in. This grey-headed old lady, with the delightful face and quaint air of having stepped out of some medieval picture, but whose unfortunate deformity was only too apparent, charmed him at first sight. She sat in a great chair before a fire heaped with logs of wood, whose pleasant heat seemed to strike a reassuring note after the draughts and general chilliness through which he had passed. Her smile of welcome lent her features a sweetness which was more than sufficient compensation for those misshapen shoulders. A cloud of vague misgivings vanished as he bent over her outstretched hands.

"It is Mr. Ronald Stourton, I am sure!" she murmured. "You've done me so great a kindness that I scarcely know how to welcome you."

He laughed good-humouredly and began to unfasten his travelling coat. "You expected me, then?"

"Max, my nephew, telegraphed that you would bring me the letter. I cannot tell you how important it is to me, how thankful I am to you."

He produced a long, leather case, and taking a letter from it, carefully replaced the portfolio in his pocket.

"It is a very small matter, this, for gratitude," he said. "Only I am afraid that I must ask you to excuse my remaining here, even for a moment. Technically I believe that I am guilty of a misdemeanour in paying even this hurried call. I have to be in Downing Street as quickly as possible."

She poured out a cup of coffee from an arrangement of wonderful appearance which stood by her side.

"Do not stay for a moment longer than you wish," she murmured: "but you must positively have something to warm you before you go. I am sure that you are cold. I know what crossing is like in such weather. Ah! I see that you are smiling at my machine. Well, coffee is one of my hobbies. I always make it myself, and my friends are so good-natured as to pretend that they like it. You must give me your honest opinion. Will you pardon me if I just glance through this letter? There is a question, then, which I want to ask you about Max."

He accepted the cup of coffee, as he would have accepted almost anything from such a delightful old lady. He sipped it first. It was strong and of a delicious flavour. He drank it off and set down the cup. Suddenly, as he stood upright again, a queer giddiness assailed him. His hand went up to his head and he staggered back. The floor rose beneath his feet. Strange sounds throbbed in his ears. He clutched at the air with outstretched hands. He tried in vain to drag his limbs toward the door.

"Good Heavens!" he cried. "Let me out! I am ill! Let me out! Send—for a cab! Eighteen—Downing Street!"

He collapsed and lay stretched upon the floor. The little old lady sat and watched him over the top of her letter. The smile which parted her lips now was of altogether another order.

"For your muscles," the girl said, looking up at his averted face with a quiet smile, "I must always entertain a most profound respect. But as for your manners, I think they are abominable!"

The man was a little startled. He looked at her quickly, and meeting the laughter in her eyes, drew himself up stiffly.

"I am sorry if I have given offence," he said. "May I ask in what way I have laid myself open to such a rebuke?"

She leaned a little forward, as though to look into his face, but his broad-brimmed hat was pulled well over his forehead, and his profile was expressionless as though carved out of stone. She raised her eyebrows in humorous self-expostulation. The man was impossible, but so tantalising.

"Well," she said, "your first appearance upon the scene was opportune enough. I came round the corner running for my life, and after me the tramp. I was so overjoyed to see you that I forgot to look where I was going, caught my foot in the root of a tree, or something horrid, and over I went."

"I trust," he said, "that you are not going to attribute your sprained ankle to my appearance."

"Don't be foolish!" she answered. "It is your manners I am attacking now. There I lay stretched upon the ground—a pretty object I must have looked—waiting for someone to help me up, and you, well, you ignored me in favour of the tramp. It was detestable!"

He bit his lip—it might have been to check a smile.

"I had an idea," he said, "that you were in no hurry. The tramp was!"

"In no hurry!" she repeated. "Heavens! have you ever tried lying on your face, with half of you in a furze bush, your skirts all disarranged, and no positive assurance that your leg wasn't broken?"

"I have never tried it," he answered simply; "but I was very anxious to make the acquaintance of your tramp."

"So anxious that you ignored me!" she remarked.

"I felt," he said, "that you would wait."

The girl leaned right forward this time. She meant to look into her companion's face. What she saw to some extent satisfied her.

"You took a great deal for granted," she remarked. "And I think you were very brutal to the tramp."

The man's lip curled slightly.

"Shall I go back and apologise?" he asked. "As for being brutal to him, that is nonsense. He deserved a thrashing, and he got it."

"And I had to pick myself up!"

"My dear young lady," he exclaimed testily, "the other affair was more important."

The girl frowned slightly. After all, there was something of the boor about this man.

"My name," she said, "is Esther Stanmore. My father will wish to add his thanks to mine. Will you let me know your name, and where he will find you when he returns?"

Then the man really smiled. He seemed for the first time to find a grim humour in the situation.

"My name is John Paulton," he said. "I am a friend of your father's game-keeper, Heggs, and he has lent me his cottage for the summer. I believe your father has taken him up to Scotland for a few months."

If he had expected to surprise her, he was disappointed. She accepted his information as the most natural thing in the world.

"I remember hearing about your coming, Mr. Paulton," she said, "and I have seen you in the woods. I am ever so grateful to you, of course, but I wish you would notice that I am limping."

He slackened his pace at once.

"I am very sorry," he said. "Is there anything I can do to relieve you? Will you rest here while I go up to the house for a pony?"

"How can you think of such a thing," she exclaimed, "after the fright I have had?"

"Then I really don't see—" he began.

"You might offer me your arm," she suggested. "I don't think that I can walk any further alone."

He did as she asked in silence. She leaned heavily upon him, and they moved slowly along the path. He seemed determined not to encourage any conversation. She, however, was of another mind.

"Are you quite alone in Hegg's cottage?" she asked.

"I have a friend with me," he answered.

"A dark, clean-shaven man, rather pale?" she inquired.

"Yes."

"He was standing at the gate when I came by," she remarked.

He frowned.

"And I recognised him," she continued.

"Indeed!"

"He used to be my cousin's servant," she remarked. "The best man he ever had, I have heard him say."

He bit his lip.

"It is quite probable," he answered shortly. "I believe that he used to be in service, before—before he saved some money."

They emerged from the wood. The footpath which crossed the field in front of them led past a cottage built of grey stone, and with an ancient, red-tiled roof. A man was leaning over the gate, smoking a pipe. Directly he saw them, he thrust his pipe in his pocket and disappeared. The girl smiled.

"Your friend," she remarked, "is shy."

The man muttered something underneath his breath. The girl's smile deepened. She pointed to the cottage.

"I shall not try to walk any further," she said. "I am going to beg the hospitality of your porch. Do you think that if we asked your friend very nicely, he would go up to the Hall for me, and tell them to send a groom down with a pony and a side-saddle?"

He opened the gate and motioned her to enter, with a gesture of grave politeness.

"I will find you a chair," he said, "and then, if you will permit me, I will go myself to the Hall."

His anxiety to escape was a little too obvious. She answered him coldly.

"That must be altogether as you wish," she declared. "I am only sorry to give you so much trouble. If my foot were not very painful, I would struggle on somehow or other; but I am sure that I could not manage the stiles."

"If you will excuse me for a moment," he answered, "I will fetch you a chair. There is not the slightest necessity for you to walk any further."

She heard his voice inside—quick, imperative, alert, the other man's smooth and respectfully acquiescent. The girl smiled to herself. This was so like the conversation of two friends! Did he really think that she was to be so easily hoodwinked?

Presently he came out, carrying a chair, which he placed carefully in a corner of the tiny lawn overgrown with wild flowers.

"You will excuse my not asking you in," he said shortly. "The rooms are small and stuffy. It is much pleasanter out here."

"I have no wish at all," she answered stiffly, "to intrude upon your hospitality. Thanks very much for the chair, though."

"Is there anything I can do for your—ankle?" he said uncomfortably. "Would you like some—er—some hot water?"

She looked down at her foot gravely.

"You might feel whether it seems to you very much swollen," she answered, lifting it a few inches from the ground.

He stooped down and took it carefully into his hand. It was a long, slender foot, very soundly but daintily shod, and there was a faint silken rustle as she moved it carefully backwards and forwards. He held it for a moment very lightly—perhaps for a little more than a moment. Then he rose abruptly to his feet.

"I cannot feel any swelling at all," he announced.

She was much relieved.

"I dare say, then, that it is nothing serious," she declared cheerfully. "I am so glad. If there is anything I detest, it is having to stay indoors."

"It is certainly tedious," he admitted. "I do not think that you need fear anything of the sort in this case, though."

"I am so fond of walking—in the woods," she murmured.

Left rather abruptly alone, the girl found herself confronted with a moral problem. Mr. John Paulton, as he had called himself, had excited her curiosity. The means of gratifying it were close at hand. Was she justified in using them? The man inside the cottage was, of course, his servant. He had stayed once at the Hall with her cousin, and would doubtless answer any of her questions. It was not, she admitted to herself reluctantly, a nice thing to do; but, on the other hand, Heggs had no right to lend his cottage to mysterious strangers who might be hiding from their creditors, or from even worse things. It was inconsiderate of Heggs, especially as she was alone at the Hall. She decided that she had the right to investigate the matter thoroughly. And of course she did nothing of the sort. Even when the man came out a few minutes later to once more offer her some tea, she let him go without a single question. It was not possible.

He was back again in less than half an hour, followed by the groom with a pony. He helped her into the saddle and stood bareheaded to see her go.

"I feel," she said, looking down at him with a very expressive light in her soft, grey eyes, "that I haven't thanked you half enough."

"Please do not think any more of such a trifle," he protested. "Your gamekeeper would have done all that I did just as effectually."

"But my gamekeeper was not there," she objected.

"It was my good fortune," he answered gravely. "Nothing more."

She gathered up the reins and smiled down at him. The men whom Esther Stanmore smiled upon seldom forgot it.

"I shall have to confine my afternoon walks to the home woods," she remarked. "They are just as pretty, really. Good afternoon, Mr. Paulton. We are such close neighbors that we are certain to come across one another again soon, I hope."

But Paulton, though he bowed, did not echo her wish.

And yet in less than three weeks they had reached the end, the last barrier through which one looks into Paradise. They were seated on the trunk of a fallen tree, in the sunshine distorted into queer, zigzag stripes and gleams playing away from their feet into the heart of the silent wood. A squirrel had just scampered across the path. From the hidden places beyond, a pigeon was calling softly to his mate, a woodpecker was busy amongst the branches of a beech-tree, and all the while the west wind sang in the rustling canopy above their heads. They alone of all the living things were silent.

"I think," he said, at last, "that up to now I have dreamed, not lived. The commencement of life is here."

She looked at him a little wonderingly.

"You are losing your sense of proportion," she remarked, smiling. "It is here, if you will, that one may dream of life and be happy. Yet it can be nothing save an interlude. Life is not in these woods—no, not the commencement or the end of life. It is the Paradise of dumb beasts, this. We, alas! have to seek for our Paradise in different places."

"A month ago," he said slowly, keeping his eye fixed upon the ground, "I should have needed no one to have told me where Paradise lay. If I were the Ronald Stourton of a month ago, I should not hesitate for a single second to grasp it—now."

"Ronald Stourton!" she repeated softly. "So you are Ronald Stourton!"

"Yes," he answered. "I have heard you speak of my people."

"I thought you were in Paris."

"I was. I came to England on an important mission from the chief to the Prime Minister a month ago. I bungled it hopelessly. I was taken in by a trick which should not have deceived a child. There isn't any particular secret about it now. I brought across a draft of the proposed understanding between France and England as to their neutrality in the Russo-Japanese war. The draft was stolen from me by an agent of the Russian Government or by someone who means to dispose of it to the Russian Government. I am suspended for the present. Immediately the draft is transferred to the Russian Ambassador, and the thing comes out, I shall be dismissed from the service."

She looked at him—as a woman knows how to look at such times. Her hand rested lightly upon his shoulder.

"Oh, I am so sorry," she said softly. "I felt all the time that you were in trouble. But can nothing be done? Can't the person be found who stole the paper?"

"The cleverest detective in England has the matter in hand," he answered, "and it was at his particular request that I disappeared. The person whom he strongly suspects is being watched day and night, and it is supposed that he has not yet had an opportunity of disposing of the papers. That is why I am still merely on leave. It is a sickening story, but I am glad that you know the truth. You will understand now why I must go away."

"I understand nothing of the sort," she answered decisively. "Of course, it is shocking bad luck; but even if you have to give up your profession, there is plenty of other work in the world for a man, isn't there? How old are you?"

He smiled. He thought her manner charming, but it was certainly original.

"I am thirty-four next birthday. Too old, you see, for any of the services. I might go abroad, of course; but it is a far cry from diplomacy to ranching."

She looked at him thoughtfully.

"You are well off, aren't you?" she remarked. "Most of your family are."

"Yes," he answered dryly, "I am well off. I am spared the luxury of having to work for a living, at any rate. But I am a sorry idler."

"Quite right!" she assented. "I detest men who do nothing. It always ends in their dabbling in things which they don't understand at all."

He groaned.

"Don't!" he begged, digging his stick savagely into the ground. "I can see myself—a J.P., perhaps a county councillor, a director of City companies— Heavens knows what!"

"Aren't you a little premature?" she said, smiling. "You are not sure yet that you have finished with diplomacy."

"I am perfectly certain that diplomacy has finished with me," he answered ruefully. "Pardon me!"

He picked up the letter which had slipped from her waistband and handed it to her. His eyes by chance fell upon the address, and he started.

"Miss de Poulgasky!" he repeated. "Forgive me, but I could not have helped seeing. It seems strange to see that name here."

She nodded sympathetically.

"It is her father, of course, to whom those papers will be sent," she remarked. "I was at school with Corona, and we write to one another now and then. My uncle, who came down last night, seems very friendly with them. This letter is really from him. And that reminds me. I am no longer without a chaperon. I want you to come and dine with us to-night."

He shook his head.

"Don't ask me! I am not in a fit humour to meet people."

"There is only my uncle, and I think that perhaps he may amuse you. He is such a thorough cosmopolitan. I believe that he is equally at home in every capital of Europe, and he has the most marvellous collection of anecdotes. Come and dine, and afterwards I will show you my rose-garden."

"If you will—" Their heads came very close together. He seemed to have a good deal to say, and she was very well content to listen. In the end he forgot for a brief space of time all his troubles. And she forgot to post her letter.

He was watching the sunset from the terrace. Behind him was the empty drawing-room. He had arrived, after all, a little early; eight o'clock was only just striking by the stable clock. She could scarcely be down yet. He had left her barely an hour ago, and he was in no humour for a *tête-à-tête* with this wonderful uncle. So he leaned over the worn, grey balustrade and wondered which way the rose-garden might lie. Were other men so much the sport of Fate as this, he asked himself bitterly, that the greatest joy of life should shine down upon him whose feet were fast set in the quagmires—a tantalising dream—an impossible—yes, an impossible—?

Then the chain of his thoughts was snapped. Each pulse of his body seemed to cease beating. He was listening. Behind, in the drawing-room, someone was talking to Esther, and the voice—what folly! He turned slowly round as one who expects to confront a ghost. Esther was standing in the window, and by her side a smooth, clean-shaven old gentleman in glasses, who smiled benevolently upon him and went on talking. What folly! He dragged himself to meet them. He was ill at ease, scarcely conscious of where he was. But he watched Esther's uncle. His manner was certainly queer, but he watched. He saw things which sent the blood rushing through his veins at fever heat.

Dinner was served at a small, round table drawn close up to the open window. The Stanmore cook was famous, and Esther's uncle had had a word or two with the butler about the wines. Nevertheless, it was an ill-balanced trio, and Stourton especially was talking all the time at random. Mr. Heslop Stanmore was quietly entertaining, but Esther was too worried at her guest's strange demeanour to find much pleasure in her uncle's conversation. She made several attempts to establish more natural relations between the two men, but without the least success. She felt all the time that there was nothing they both of them desired so much as her absence. At last she got up and left them.

"I shall give you a quarter of an hour, no more," she said, glancing at Stourton. "You can smoke where you choose here."

The butler with great care set the Château Yguem and port upon the table and withdrew. Then Mr. Heslop Stanmore leaned back in his chair and laughed softly.

"My dear fellow," he exclaimed, "you have my sympathy. You have indeed. All the time you have been getting surer and surer, longing to get up and take me by the throat; and instead you have had to swallow your dinner and make polite speeches. Come, you can relieve yourself now. All your suspicions are correct. I am the little hunchbacked lady of Hyde Park

Terrace. I stole those papers—it is my profession, you see. I am very sorry indeed to have inconvenienced you; but one must live, and I am a younger son."

"Where are they?" Stourton asked between his teeth.

Mr. Heslop Stanmore shrugged his shoulders.

"My young friend," he said, "I am thankful that you did not ask me that question a few hours ago, or I might have been compelled to have resorted to subterfuge. I have had the utmost difficulty—by the by, you really ought to try this Château Yguem. No?—the utmost difficulty in disposing of them. I have been watched day and night, and so has Poulgasky's house. However, I have managed it at last. My niece Esther, with whom, by the by, you seem to be on remarkably good terms, is an old school-friend of Corona Poulgasky's, and I got her to enclose my papers this morning in a letter to her. The post went out, I believe," he continued, raising his wine glass and looking critically at its contents, "at four o'clock. A delivery is made in London to-night. It is just a question—rather a near thing, I should imagine—whether those papers are not already in Poulgasky's hands."

"Did Es—Miss Stanmore know what she was doing?" Stourton groaned.

"My dear fellow," her uncle remonstrated, "do you think that I should dare to give away my secrets to a child? She has not the slightest idea!"

Esther stepped suddenly in through the window. Her forehead was slightly wrinkled. She held something in her hand.

"My dear uncle, will you ever forgive me?" she exclaimed. "I started for the post, but I forgot all about my letter."

What followed was probably the most amazing thing Esther had ever witnessed. Her uncle made a spring for the letter which she held in her hand, only to find himself caught by the throat and flung back into his chair. Stourton stood over him, grim and threatening. Just in time he saw the glint of steel. The revolver fell harmlessly upon the floor; a strong hand held him like a vice. Then Ronald turned to the girl.

"Esther," he said, "will you give me that letter?"

She was very pale, but she did not hesitate for a moment.

"I do not understand why," she answered; "but if you ask for it, of course I will."

Mr. Heslop Stanmore, with Stourton's knuckles very near his throat, did not find speech easy. But he said one word!

They opened his wedding present a little dubiously. It was a copy of Harrison's "First Steps in Diplomacy." They looked at one another and laughed.

"I am afraid," she said, wiping the tears from her eyes, "that my uncle is a very black sheep, but he certainly has a sense of humour."

Stourton put the book carefully on one side.

"We will treasure this volume," he remarked. "Some day, when your uncle has a birthday, I will send him a little textbook I have on the art of 'Making Up.'"

The Two Ambassadors

Stourton, for the first time since he had left Downing Street, released his hold of the despatch-box. Both doors of the railway carriage in which he was seated were locked, on both windows was pasted a modest oblong label announcing that the compartment was reserved. There was no lavatory, and he had already looked carefully under the seats. Outside on the platform a liberally tipped servant of the company stood before the carriage door to prevent any attempt at intrusion. Stourton, with a little sigh of relief, set down the box on the middle seat opposite him, lit a cigar, and opened the evening paper.

The great black headlines, which for the last four hours had been placarded all over London, took up one half of the paper.

CHINA AND JAPAN.
DECLARATION OF WAR.
JAPAN APPEALS TO HER ALLY.
BARON NAGASKI AT THE FOREIGN OFFICE.
CABINET COUNCIL NOW SITTING.

The headlines themselves told all that was known. The news had come without warning, and following hard upon a slight Japanese reverse on the Yalu. But the news itself was incomplete. Already the mighty engines of Fleet Street were at work. To-morrow morning's papers would provide even more sensational reading. Barely two hours ago startling intelligence had been flashed across the Channel. Orders for the mobilisation of the French Fleet had already been posted. The two great Powers, who had, only a few weeks ago, amidst a shower of congratulations, concluded an agreement which seemed likely to ensure a permanent peace, were, with a suddenness which had no parallel in the modern history of nations, on the very brink of war.

The whistle sounded for the departure of the train. Suddenly Stourton was aware of some disturbance upon the platform. A tall, fair-haired woman, whose long opera-cloak imperfectly concealed her evening clothes, was trying to make her way past the official who stood before the carriage door. Stourton, with an exclamation of alarm, sprang to his feet and let down the window. Even in that moment of astonishment he did not forget his caution. He caught up the despatch-box and held it in his left hand.

"Esther!" he exclaimed. "What is it?"

The official stood aside. The train was already moving. She had almost to run to keep up with it.

"Heslop Stanmore is in Paris!" she cried breathlessly. "I found my maid sending him a telegram. He wanted to know—exactly—when you left. Take care!"

She could keep up no longer. She was already flushed and panting. He waved his hand reassuringly and shouted a farewell. Then he fastened the window and resumed his seat. "The little grey lady," he muttered to himself. "Esther's maid bribed—made friends with her down at ——, of course. He can't think that I'm such a blithering fool as to walk into another trap. If he tries it—" Stourton's fingers clasped something in the pocket of his overcoat, and his face was suddenly hard. He was thinking of the weeks of misery which this man had caused him less than a year ago. Another conflict might end differently.

Stourton's nerves were almost perfect, but he would scarcely have been human if he had not been conscious of some anxiety. Any successful tampering with his mission might mean the kindling of the war torch throughout the world. It might mean the pouring out to waste of the accumulated millions of centuries of industry, it might retard the whole progress of civilisation for many decades. The bare possibility of the thing was appalling. And yet when he stopped for a moment to reflect, the absolute security of his position was borne in upon him. He carried a fateful message with him, but it was a verbal one. There were no means of wresting from him words which his memory and tongue could alone make real. He had important papers, too, but they were in cipher—not the ordinary cipher of the Foreign Office, but a simple variation of it, to which, again, the only key had been committed to his memory and destroyed. The worst that could happen to him would be delay, and it was hard to see how even that could be engineered. These reflections brought him a certain amount of consolation, but he did not for a moment relax his watchfulness, though the train was speeding now on its way to Dover without any intervening stop. He sat quite still. The despatch-box was within easy reach, a loaded revolver upon his knee.

At the pier station he descended, making his way along the platform and across the gangway to the steamer. Two men of unobtrusive appearance, quietly but unfashionably dressed, were his nearest neighbours, one walking a little behind, and one in front. No sign of recognition passed between Stourton and them, yet he knew very well who they were and what their presence meant. On board the steamer he made his way at once to the cabin which had been reserved for him. The two men ordered deck-chairs outside. With the cabin door locked, and two of the shrewdest detectives from Scotland Yard within a few feet of him, Stourton felt fairly secure against even such a man as Heslop Stanmore, yet he never relaxed his watchfulness. He neither ate nor drank. He simply sat and watched the despatch-box.

At Calais the same programme was repeated, only this time, without speech but as though by previous arrangement, the two men shared his *coupé* in the train. Stourton, ignoring their presence, behaved exactly as though he had only himself to rely upon. With the despatch-box upon his knees, covered over by a thick travelling-rug, he sat alert and sleepless throughout the whole of the journey. Still nothing happened. Paris was reached without incident.

Here on the platform the two men closed in upon him, one on either side. Although they had no luggage, they chartered a small station omnibus, and a few minutes after the arrival of the train they were on their way to the British Embassy. The grey twilight of dawn was already breaking over the city, but there were traces still on the *boulevards* of the excitement which throughout the night had kept the streets and *cafés* thronged with people. The news from the East had stirred Paris in the same degree as London. Everywhere it was agreed that a favourable reply from England to the appeal of her ally must mean war, and already momentous steps had been taken. Stourton smiled slightly as he looked in upon one of the still brilliantly lit *cafés*. He carried the news which was to decide the question of peace and war. A word from him, and these people might have gone quietly home to their beds. And that word was to be spoken during the next few minutes.

The omnibus drew up at last before the great white stone front of the Embassy. The three men alighted, and his two companions watched Stourton admitted. Then, raising their hats slightly, they turned away. Their errand was finished.

Stourton breathed a sigh of relief as he stepped inside the hall.

"Is Sir Charles better, Morton?" he asked the man who admitted him.

"His Excellency is complaining of his head a good deal, Mr. Stourton," the man answered. "Monsieur Camillon sent for him about midnight, and has only just returned. You will find him in the study, sir. He gave orders that you were to go straight in immediately you arrived."

Stourton did not hesitate for a moment. Already he was beginning to think of his bath and a whisky-and-soda. A few more such errands as this, and even his nerves would suffer. He crossed the hall at once and entered the study.

The room was dimly lit, but a familiar figure rose at once from the couch.

"At last, Stourton. Come here to my desk, and we'll have some more light. You have the despatches?"

"You are better, Sir Charles?" Stourton asked, as he drew out his keys and laid the box before him.

"Better, but abominably ill," the Ambassador answered wearily. "Everything here is in a ferment. Camillon has lost his head. There isn't a man in the Cabinet who can discuss the position of affairs calmly. What is it to be, Stourton?"

"Peace, Sir Charles," Stourton answered. "The whole thing will fizzle out in a few days. As a matter of fact, I think even you will be surprised at the message you will have to carry to Camillon."

"You have it there? Good! Ring the bell and order a carriage. I am nearly beside myself with pain, but Camillon is waiting."

Stourton glanced at the clock. It was barely six. Sir Charles was certainly in a very queer way. His voice sounded hoarse and unnatural. His movements were the movements of a man racked with pain.

"It will take me an hour, sir, to reset the cipher," Stourton said. "In case of urgency I have the gist of the whole matter in a verbal message. Would it not be well if you delivered that unofficially to Monsieur Camillon, and I would undertake to have the despatch copied for you by eight o'clock?"

"It is a good idea," Sir Charles said wearily. "Give me your message."

"It is short enough," Stourton answered. "You are to assure Monsieur Camillon that England refuses absolutely to recognise China as a Power, and the fact of her alliance with Russia, although a source of regret to us, does not come within the scope of our obligations. We pledge ourselves not to move a single warship Eastwards or to act in any way so as to disturb the present balance of power."

"The news," Sir Charles said quietly, "is good. Be so kind, Stourton, as to ring the bell. I will be off at once."

Stourton moved to the bell, and Sir Charles, drawing up the blind, for a moment looked down upon the street below. But though his fingers rested for a moment upon the knob, Stourton never pressed it. When Sir Charles turned round, he looked into the muzzle of a revolver.

"Are you mad, Stourton?" the Ambassador asked, taking a quick step back.

"I am not sure," was the calm answer. "At any rate, I am taking no risks. If you move a step backwards or forwards, I shall fire!"

Sir Charles became at once as motionless as a lay figure. Stourton leaned forward and switched on the electric light all round the room. Then he moved towards Sir Charles. He was beset by a horrible perplexity. He had either made a most ghastly blunder, or he was the victim of an extraordinary piece of necromancy.

"Tell me the cipher exchange for March!" he asked with dry lips.

Sir Charles shrugged his shoulders.

"Your journey seems to have upset you, Mr. Stourton," he said calmly. "Be so good as to address me, if at all, with more respect."

"The cipher exchange—for March," Stourton repeated doggedly.

Sir Charles laughed shortly.

"Do you imagine," he said, "that I am going to submit to a cross-examination from you? Have done with this folly, Mr. Stourton. Stand aside and let me pass!"

"You do not go alive from this room," Stourton answered hoarsely, "until—until—"

He leaned forward, and a sudden cry broke from his lips.

"If you attempt to escape, I shall shoot you like a dog!" he cried. "You are not Sir Charles. You are a wonderful masquerader, I admit, but that is what you are—an impostor. Come, off with your mask! Who are you, and what do you expect to get by this? Remember, you are covered, and I shoot straight. What have you to say?"

Sir Charles laughed—and at the sound the sweat broke out on Stourton's forehead.

"You there!" he gasped. "Where is Sir Charles? If you try to escape, I'll kill you!"

"Escape, my dear nephew-in-law?" was the smiling reply. "How is it possible? I am not armed, and I am not fond of firearms. Escape! Why should I think of such a thing? I am interested here—interested and even amused."

Stourton was past taunts. To think that he had been outwitted after all was maddening, but his anxiety kept him cool.

"Where is Sir Charles?"

"Doubtless at Monsieur Camillon's," was the suave answer. "I believe that the first arrangement was that he should wait there for your coming. Unfortunately a violent attack of headache compelled Sir Charles—in my person—to return unexpectedly."

"And what do you propose to do now?" Stourton asked grimly.

Heslop Stanmore shrugged his shoulders.

"My young friend," he said, "I have no plans. I am in your hands. Lock me up, if you will. Put me anywhere, so that it is not necessary for you to stand with that diabolical little weapon pointed at my head."

Stourton walked to the door, locked it, and put the key in his pocket. Then he sat down in an easy-chair and tried to think. All the time his eyes were fixed upon the pseudo-Ambassador.

"By means of a trick more or less ingenious, certainly lucky," he said thoughtfully, "you have obtained from me some very valuable information. The question which puzzles me is, how are you going to profit by it? That information will be placarded all over Paris by midday, and until midday you will certainly remain—my guest."

Stanmore smiled.

"I see your difficulty, my young friend," he remarked. "Let me help you, if

I may. I had a use for your information, provided its tenor had been different. Five minutes earlier knowledge of war might have meant a good deal to me. The pacific intentions of your Government are simply of no interest to me. Take my parole, dispose of me as you will. I simply am not interested. If it had been more fateful news—that which you have so kindly vouchsafed to me—it might have been worth my while to have risked something to have got away. As it is, you may treat me as a harmless lunatic."

Stourton suddenly sprang up. He heard a familiar voice in the hall and a sound of footsteps. He unlocked the door, and almost immediately it was thrown open. Sir Charles entered. He addressed Stourton sharply.

"What infernal muddle is this?" he exclaimed. "Surely my instructions were clear enough? I have been waiting for you at Monsieur Camillon's."

"The explanation, sir, is there," Stourton answered, pointing to the further end of the room.

The Ambassador and the pseudo-Ambassador were face to face. Sir Charles gazed at his double in horrified silence. The latter, with a gently deprecating smile, appeared to be making a deliberate examination of the details of Sir Charles's dress and person.

"Heavens, sir! who are you?" Sir Charles exclaimed at last.

Stanmore waved his hand toward Stourton.

"This young gentleman will explain," he said suavely. "Forgive my close observation; I am always interested in these little studies of mine. I perceive that I have libeled you in one or two small details. The height and presence I could not hope to gain—I was obliged to remain seated; but it vexes me extremely that I should have parted my hair at least an inch too much to the left. Nevertheless, Sir Charles, I trust that you will not consider me altogether a caricature."

Sir Charles had regained his composure. He eyed him up and down grimly.

"On the contrary, sir," he said, "I congratulate you. The resemblance is at any rate close enough to warrant your acquaintance with a French prison. Now, Stourton."

Stourton explained rapidly. An immense relief came into the Ambassador's face as he delivered his message.

"Thank Heaven!" he exclaimed fervently. "I will go at once to Monsieur Camillon's, and take this effigy with me. No, I can't do that. We mustn't give ourselves away. Keep him under lock and key, Stourton, till the news is on the *boulevards,* and then kick him out. Work out your draft despatch and send Blount round with it. He will be here in half an hour."

Sir Charles hurried away. Stourton took his troublesome connection up to his own quarters, made him relinquish his wig and moustache, and brought him back to the study. He established himself in an easy-chair with a little sigh of relief.

"If one might venture to suggest a cup of coffee—" he remarked: "and—Sir Charles does not smoke. I do. I have been suffering for the last two hours."

Stourton ordered the coffee and threw him his cigarette-case. He made himself quite at home. When he had finished his work, Stourton rose and faced him sternly. Already the din on the *boulevards* had commenced.

"Stanmore," he said, "this is the second time you have tried to ruin me. Now it is my turn. What is to prevent my handing you over to the police? You are here under false pretences. In the eyes of the law you are a burglar."

Stanmore shook his head.

"My young friend," he said quietly, "you know very well that you cannot do it. You dare not admit that you were—pardon me—so easily deceived. Your Embassy would be the laughing-stock of your fellow diplomats. Besides, the French police know me. They would examine the charge with perfect gravity—and release me!"

"If I let you go," Stourton said, "will you give me your word of honour to leave me alone in future? Try your tricks on someone else, if you will. I've had my share. I am fond of the Service, and I have had two narrow escapes—through you. Give me your word of honour that this shall be your last escapade where I am concerned, and you can go."

Stanmore shook his head gravely.

"My dear Stourton," he said, "believe me, in your own interests, I cannot do this. You are, I am pleased to say, a connection of mine, and I am very much interested in your career. The two—er—incidents to which you have referred have brightened you up amazingly. You have no idea how much you have improved already. If I were to give you that promise, you would relax your vigilance at once. No, no! It is much better as it is. Always be on your guard against me. I may turn up at any moment."

Stourton opened the door in silence. His uncle-in-law walked out.

Sir Charles asked Stourton to lunch with him next day. The Ambassador was in the nervous state of a man just recovering from an immense strain, and in the midst of a shower of congratulations there was one point on which he was particularly irritable. He alluded to it as soon as they were alone.

"I don't like these stories of enormous buying of English Consols and French *Rentes* just an hour before Camillon issued the news," he said. "They say that it was one man on both markets. They watch that sort of thing at Downing Street. I only hope they don't suspect a leakage."

Stourton answered Sir Charles's unspoken thought.

"I did not let him go," he said, "till the news was on the *boulevards*."

Sir Charles grunted and dismissed the subject. But it came into Stourton's mind again when at breakfast-time one morning, about a fortnight later, Esther, with a cry of delight, opened a large morocco case.

"Ronald! Did you ever see anything so beautiful?" she exclaimed breathlessly.

Stourton was reading the note.

"My dear Niece—and Nephew-in-Law—

"I have always felt that my wedding present was the most inadequate offering, and I hope that you will allow me, now that Fortune has been more kind, to make atonement. I do not often speculate, but I am thankful to say that my last venture was crowned with complete success.

"My best regards to your husband. I envy his luxurious quarters at the Place Diplomatique. The view from Sir Charles's library down the Boulevard St. Antoine especially commends itself to me.

"Believe me, my dear Esther,

"Ever your affectionate Uncle."

Esther looked over her husband's shoulder.

"What does he mean, Ronald?" she asked, perplexed.

Stourton threw the note into the flames.

"I have not the least idea," he answered.

The Lord of Crersa

A whirlwind of small snow flakes and a wind which roared through the mighty forests of pines, snapping the strongest of them as though they had been saplings. A wild night in the plains and cities, here among the mountains a pandemonium of terrors. Clouds as black as ink brought impenetrable darkness, the clamor of crushing boughs and howling wind sank every now and then into insignificance before the roaring of deep-throated guns, whose red fire flashed out across what seemed to be a bottomless abyss. Below, the army of the Turks decimated in numbers, yet still a host, within the walls of Crersa, the defenders of an oppressed and brave country making their last stand in their ancient stronghold.

Three men stood on the walls, holding to the ramparts for dear life, talking eagerly together. Every now and then they paused, and strove to see what lay beneath in the red, lurid light of the cannon flames. Hohenloff, who spoke, was general of the forces, and in command of the defense.

"Prince," he said, "there is no longer any doubt. Crersa, unconquered for a thousand years, will fall now through treachery. Perhaps to-night, perhaps to-morrow. Who can say?"

Prince Maurice of Herania, who saw a kingdom, the kingdom of his forefathers, passing away, groaned aloud.

"Hohenloff," he said, "may God grant that you are mistaken. They are bold, and they have ventured very near the walls, as you know. It may be chance."

"It is no chance," Hohenloff answered, roughly. "On Monday the southern buttress was hit. Outside we covered the weakness, inside alone it was apparent. Yet all day they poured in a merciless fire upon that one weak spot. On Tuesday, we moved the powder magazine. Their guns follow, and Crersa was very nearly blown to atoms. On Wednesday we planned a sortie to drive in a herd of goats. We left the gates in darkness as black as pitch, and never a sound was made, yet without warning they were waiting, fell upon us, and only half a dozen escaped. I could give you a hundred proofs were they needed, yet there are enough. My Prince, there is a traitor here, and unless we find him Crersa is doomed."

Once more the thunder of cannon—this time from a new spot in the darkness. From below came the crashing of masonry, and the crying of wounded men. Hohenloff stamped his foot in bitter anger.

"This, then, accounts for their long silence," he cried. "They have heard of our attempt to rebuild the north wall, and they have moved their guns to command it. Oh, to think that brave men should be the jest and the victim of a cursed spy."

Then Romakoff spoke, chief minister of Herania, a small man with sallow features, but with the forehead of a lion.

"Hohenloff," he said, "our secrets are not the secrets of the whole garrison. How many have known of these things?"

"Not more than a dozen," Hohenloff answered. "It is a cursed thing to say, but the traitor is one of our inner counsel."

"Their names?"

"Helkoff."

"A clumsy man but faithful."

"Mentz."

"A true man."

"Rottenick."

"I would answer for him with my life."

"Petroff."

"As true as steel."

"Melakoff."

"An honest man."

"Ulmul."

"Wounded to death yesterday fighting like a lion. Traitors are made of other stuff."

"Sirka."

"Also wounded. Has been unconscious for three days."

"Myself."

"Well."

"Yourself."

"Well."

"The Prince."

There was silence. Then Hohenloff spoke:

"The traitor is not amongst these."

"Then in the name of God," cried Romakoff, "where shall we find him?"

Only the Prince was pale and thoughtful.

"Tonight," he said. "I watch without the gates."

"And I with you," Hohenloff cried. "You may need my sword. The dogs are close at hand."

But Prince Maurice shook his head.

"I watch alone," he answered. "It is my wish."

"It is not safe," Hohenloff cried. "I, at least, will bear you company."

"I watch alone," the Prince answered. "It is my command."

As the night drew on the storm increased. The gunners worked at their task with numbed fingers, the watchmen on the walls were like moving pillars of snow. Every now and then the roaring of cannons drowned the fierce wind, the red belching fires lit up the snow-clad country. Round the northern gate were gathered a company of soldiers, and into the midst of them a muffled figure in military cape pushed his way. At a word from him they fell back with respectful salute. He passed through to the very archway of the gate. For a while he stood talking to the officer in command. Then came the clanking of bolts and the creaking of bars. Prince Maurice passed out alone.

There was a good deal of whispering amongst those who saw him go—many surmises—for outside the gate were dangers of many sorts such as it seemed rash indeed for their Sovereign to face alone. But he left no hint behind as to his destination, and although gracious to the lowliest of his subjects, he was never one who suffered others to question him as to his doings. So they whispered together, and wondered. As yet no rumors of treachery had stolen abroad, for Hohenloff had kept his own counsel even from the House of Advisers. The spirits of the people must be maintained, and there is nothing in this world so chilling, so apt to discourage the beleaguered as the very suggestion of a traitor within the gates. So neither the soldiers nor the citizens knew anything of this new cause for anxiety, and their Prince's quest was a mystery to them. Only they peered out into the darkness, and waited for his return, ready to throw open the gates, or to sally out to rescue at any sound of fighting.

Outside the city the storm was raging more fiercely than ever. The wind swept down the ravine with a roar like thunder, and for all his great strength Prince Maurice was more than once hurled breathless against the wall. He was making his way, step by step, to the northern boundary, where a few watchers were stationed, and no system of defense attempted, for here, at least, the town was impregnable. The walls overhung a great ravine—there was not a single spot from which an attack could be even attempted. But Prince Maurice took up his station in a sheltered nook facing a high tower, and, crouching back amongst the shadows, waited.

As the hours passed on his brow became less clouded. He even ventured to draw a sigh of relief. His had been a hateful task, and nothing but a stern sense of duty to his suffering people had induced him to undertake it. He was playing the spy upon a woman, watching her house, and a woman dependent upon his hospitality—a prisoner also in his unhappy city. Not only this, but the woman was the Countess of Merguillon, the wife of the French resident, who was even now seeking in Paris to win aid for him. Not only this, but she was the woman whom Prince Maurice, although no word of it had ever passed his lips, very dearly loved.

His veins were almost frozen with the cold, and his fingers were numb. The snow was thick upon his military cloak and peaked hat, he had become a figure invisible—a human icicle. Yet as the night passed on his heart grew lighter. Death and disaster he could face as a brave man should, fighting for his people and his kingdom with his sword red in Moslem blood. The dishonor of the woman whom he worshiped would have been harder to bear. So he listened to the guns and watched the red fires leap out into the darkness with lightening heart, and something which was almost a smile upon his blue lips. In an hour his vigil would be over. In an hour he would banish forever those vague but horrible suspicions.

But before the hour was passed strange things happened. Up in the topmost window of that tower which he had been watching there flashed for a moment a faint light. It flickered, went out, and reappeared. Prince Maurice felt his heart stop beating, and a cold more deadly than anything he had yet felt went shivering through his veins. Someone was there waving a lamp, and from the side of the ravine came the answering signal.

He looked no more at the window, but watched the dancing light come nearer and nearer. A man carrying a torch—nothing more—but a tragedy in itself. The light in the window was extinguished, but its purpose had been accomplished. Prince Maurice moved slowly along by the side of the wall until he stood immediately in the shadow of the tower.

Soon there came a sound—a man's footsteps muffled in the snow. A torch was thrown hissing forward upon the ground, a man's head and then his body appeared, as, with a final effort, he pulled himself up the side of the ravine. A tall man, breathless with his climb, and disheveled. Prince Maurice could have thrust his sword into his body from where he was, but remained motionless. He was waiting.

The newcomer set his heel upon the torch, first lighting a cigarette from its embers. Then he stood upright, and looked impatiently toward the tower. He hummed a tune, shook the snow from his clothes, and walked restlessly backward and forward. At last he came to a sudden standstill, and a little exclamation of relief broke from his lips. A small nail-studded door at the base of the tower had been opened, and a woman was standing there.

She held the lamp above her head, and from where he stood Prince Maurice could see her plainly. She wore a fur cloak which left revealed her pink satin slippers and her face. There were diamonds flashing in her black hair, the hand which held the lamp was ablaze with rings. The man stepped forward confidently, as though he would have entered, but she pushed him back.

"Not tonight, my friend," Prince Maurice heard her say, and he saw, too, that wonderfully alluring smile upon her lips which had befooled many men before him.

"It is not safe. Do you know that there are men watching my house from the street, and I am almost afraid to come to you for even this moment? See, I have written down here what you wanted to know. I have kept my word, but I am ashamed of it. Now go."

He bent over her, and the lamp-light fell upon his dark, sallow face, with the black moustache and coal black eyes. Then Prince Maurice recognized him, and ground his teeth with bitter rage.

"Not without a word at least, Sophie," he cried, lightly. "A curse upon this obstinate Prince and his mulish people!"

They whispered together for a moment. Prince Maurice's hand stole beneath his cloak and grasped the hilt of his sword. Then there came the sound of the door being softly closed.

"To-morrow," the Turk whispered.

Then Prince Maurice stepped out, and threw aside his cloak.

"To-morrow, Menid Bey," he cried, "you will spend in hell. Draw and defend yourself, man. Quick."

The Turk recognized him with a little cry. He sprang back, but the Prince's sword was upon his throat.

"On guard, General," he cried, "or I shall forget my manners, and spit you like a dog."

The Turk shrugged his shoulders, and drew his sword slowly.

"Prince Maurice!" he exclaimed. "My friend of the *boulevards*. Come, be reasonable. We are old friends. Why try to kill one another?"

"I have no friends amongst my country's enemies," Prince Maurice cried. "The old days in Paris are gone. I was a citizen then. I am a sovereign now. Draw, Menid Bey, or by Heaven I will remember only that I have found a spy sneaking his way into my city, and have you hanged from yonder turret."

"We cannot see to fight," the Turk cried.

"Then have at you in the darkness," Prince Maurice cried, fiercely, with a lunge forward. But the Turk was prepared, and the sparks flashed from their swords.

"'Tis a madman's contest," he cried. "Come, Maurice, mine was but an idle errand. The Countess and I were friends in Paris. I wished but to show her the way to safety."

But Prince Maurice only scoffed as he thrust his naked sword into the darkness.

"Be silent," he cried, "unless you wish to die with a lie upon your lips."

Then the little door in the wall swung suddenly open, and the Countess, who had heard their voices, stood there, holding the lamp over her head.

A cry broke from her white lips as she recognized the two men—a cry which changed swiftly into a scream of terror. For the light of her lamp, dim though it was, and flickering with the wind, was sufficient to show them each other's whereabouts. The Turk sprang upon his opponent like a wildcat. Prince Maurice parried his blows with the skill of a practiced swordsman. The result was never for a moment doubtful, even to the woman who stood there still with the lamp in her shaking hand. Menid Bey, with the sick fear of death at his heart, called out to her.

"Throw away the light, Sophie. Throw it down."

But the Countess only laughed—a hard, unnatural laugh, and held it out a little more into the black night.

"Kill the dog, my Prince," she cried. "Kill him, for he is a spy."

Prince Maurice took no notice, but he held his opponent, now unnerved with terror, wholly at his mercy.

"Menid Bey," he cried, "if we had met thus in fair fight I would have spared you for the sake of old days when we were friends. But you have come here secretly, a traitor and a spy, and you must meet the death you merit."

Once more the swords clashed, a whirling flame of steel, and then the death yell of Menid Bey rang out above the storm of wind, above the booming of the never-silent guns. Prince Maurice's sword dripped red upon the trampled snow. He turned toward the door, where the woman was still standing transfixed with fear.

"With your permission," he said, "I will return to the city through your house."

She motioned him to pass her, and locked and barred the gate. They passed up a narrow passage into a great square hall. Several servants were cowering before the great door. When Prince Maurice appeared his sword still in his hand, they fled screaming to different parts of the house. The Countess threw open the door of her own apartment. He caught a glimpse of a room where a great open stove was burning—a room full of cushions and lounges, a mandolin here, books there, flowers everywhere. But Prince Maurice did not enter.

"I have no wish to linger in this house," he said sternly. "Tell your servants to unbolt that door and let me out."

She laid her white hands upon his shoulders, and turned her beautiful, distraut face upward to his.

"Maurice," she said, "listen to me."

He threw her arms roughly away.

"What have I or has Crersa done to you?" he asked bitterly, "that you should plot for our ruin? Come, answer me that, woman. Have you been ill-treated—have you found us inhospitable?"

"No, a thousand times no," she moaned. "I have been to blame, and I know it. Yet, is it much wrong I have done? I have suffered Menid Bey to come to me as a friend, for I knew him years ago, and he found his way here by stealth a few nights ago. I have been weary to death of my life here, Prince Maurice. Do you wonder at it? Day after day I have spent here alone, seeing nothing but grim, famine-stricken faces, and hearing nothing but the roaring of guns and the shrieks of the wounded. Was it for this, do you think, that I left our beautiful Paris, that I strove to get Henri the appointment here, to be left alone with never a soul to speak to—not even— Prince Maurice."

Her eyes forced his to look into them. She knew then that she was safe. Yet he held her coldly at arm's length.

"Sophie," he said, "if I have kept away—you know the reason. Your husband is absent on a mission in our interests—to save us—and I have sat at his table and he has treated me as his friend. Need I say anything more?"

"And why," she asked, "should my husband receive all your consideration, and I—none?"

"There was no middle course," he answered.

Her eyes leaped to his.

"Then you—cared?"

"For the woman I thought you were—yes," he cried. "For the woman you are—no. If Hohenloff and the others had seen what I have seen tonight, not even I, the Prince of Crersa, could save you."

She shuddered, and even at that moment there came a great knocking at the front door and a tramping of feet outside. She called aloud, and stopped those who would have answered the summons. Prince Maurice watched her with a heavy heart, for her terror was the terror of a guilty woman.

"Ask what they want, Francis," she cried to a servant outside. "Tell them that it is too late for me, an unprotected woman in a beleaguered city, to open my doors."

Even whilst she spoke the shouts from the street told her what she dreaded most to hear. Others besides Prince Maurice had found her out.

"Bring her out—the traitress."

"Come and show yourself, you who are selling Crersa to the Turks."

"We will hang her from the walls."

"Set fire to the place and let her roast."

She fell upon her knees and clutched him frantically.

"You will save me, Maurice, from these people? You will not let them kill me? You will not desert me?"

"I will do what I can for you," he said coldly. "Listen. Is there any place from which I can speak to these people without opening the doors?"

"There is a balcony on the next floor," she gasped. "They will obey you,

Maurice. Tell them to go away."

"Show me how to reach the balcony," he answered.

She caught hold of his arm and hurried him upstairs. It was her bedroom from which the balcony projected. Prince Maurice set his teeth and swore hard to himself. For the first time in his life he faced his people with a doubtful heart.

Below, the street and courtyard were full of a yelling mob—beyond, pandemonium reigned. The palace had caught fire, and red tongues of flame were leaping into the night. The roaring of the guns was nearer than ever, and more fierce, mingled every now and then with the crashing of masonry and the shrieks of dying men. Prince Maurice lifted his voice, but not a soul below heeded him. They swarmed around the door like madmen. They were drunk, with their lust for vengeance. He stepped back again into the room at last, breathless and heart-broken.

"They will take no heed of me," he said. "For the moment they are mad. We must try and keep them out."

She crouched closer to him. Though her face was as white as marble, her hair dishevelled, and her eyes large with terror, she seemed more beautiful even than ever. Only Prince Maurice looked upon her for the first time in his life coldly. She had been dear to him, but Crersa and his people were dearer, and it seemed to him that the stain of treachery apart from all else must keep her an unclean thing forever.

"Save me," she murmured. "You won't leave me? Promise."

And he remembered that she was a woman, and promised. A storm of bullets beat against the shuttered windows. Splinters of wood flew into the room. He saw that they must gain an entrance before long, and he drew his sword, still wet with the blood of Menid Bey.

"Can we get out on the roof?" he asked. "We might escape from there."

She showed him the way, but the house stood by itself, and all around was an island of blank space.

"It's no use," he said. "We must face them boldly when they enter."

"You will not desert me?"

"No."

"Will you kiss me—once?"

She raised her pallid lips. He touched them with his, coldly. They made their way into the hall. He stood waiting with a revolver in his left hand and a sword in his right. He had thrown off his cloak, that the people might recognize at once his uniform. So they waited whilst the very walls about them seemed to reel, and the great door groaned upon its hinges. The servants had fled away terrified. They were alone in the place.

"Will they listen to you?" she whispered, hoarsely.

"They may," he answered, "or they may not. If you know a prayer you had better say it."

Then there came the crash of falling timber, a yell of triumph, and the huge door fell inwards with half a dozen of the foremost sprawling upon it. Others trooped over them, a rush of cold air, and a storm of snowflakes swept through the halls. But when they saw their Prince standing there with drawn sword and flashing eyes they hesitated and looked behind. Through their parted ranks came Hohenloff and Romakoff, with a small guard of Palace soldiers. When they saw Prince Maurice they too came to an amazed stop. But Hohenloff stepped forward.

"You, too, sire," he cried. "You have discovered the traitress. Let us away with her to the rampart. Arrest her, sergeant."

But the Prince held out his hand.

"You are too hasty, Hohenloff," he said. "The Countess is a subject of the country whose friendship we seek. She has demanded my protection, and I have granted it. She shall be tried if you will, but by proper tribunal."

But Hohenloff's face grew black as night.

"My Prince," he said, "we have proofs of her guilt sufficient to justify us in hanging her a hundred times over. There is no tribunal for such a case. Our courts are broken up, and at any moment we may expect the Turks upon us. We have sworn to have her life first, and have it we will."

The sword of Prince Maurice touched the throat of the man who had sprung forward.

"The blood on my sword," he said, "is the blood of Menid Bey, the Turkish General, whom I have slain. Without him they will make no movement. We are safe for to-night, aye, and tomorrow. I make myself responsible for the keeping of this woman."

But a roar of discontent and angry mutterings arose from the throng, and Hohenloff grew pale with rage.

"We have promised the people," he cried raising his voice, "that justice shall be done, and our word must be kept."

"And what of my word," Prince Maurice answered. "I have pledged it to her husband for her safety during his absence, and I have pledged it to the lady herself. Officers of the Guards, I call upon you to protect your Prince against this rabble."

The soldiers hesitated. From the throng of half-starved men came running two, who sprang upon the Countess. But the woman's shriek of terror was mingled with their death-cry, and once more Prince Maurice's sword dripped with blood. With a cry of rage the rabble closed in. Then, indeed, it seemed as though the end was come. There were hundreds of them armed and athirst for blood. Prince Maurice lowered his sword and held up his hand.

"You want a victim," he cried. "Very well, take the one who deserves death. This woman is innocent, I am the traitor."

There were cries of amazement, of disbelief. Prince Maurice waved them aside.

"It is I who would have bought your safety and my own," he cried. "I mean to give the city over to the Turks on favorable terms, for no hope remains of saving it. I would have done it so that the honor of our citizens might be preserved. The Countess was my tool, nothing else. Now you have foiled me. I have broken my word, and there will be no quarter."

Hohenloff rushed at him with his sword shortened.

"Traitor!" he cried.

But Prince Maurice struck him with his fist and he fell heavily upon the ground.

"Do what you will with me, my people," he cried, "but remember that the Countess is innocent."

Romakoff turned towards them.

"Men of Crersa," he cried, "we have been betrayed, and by him in whom we trusted most. Let us not soil our hands with his blood. Send them forth to the Turks. Let them live and suffer the eternal torment of a dishonored life. Close the gates of the city upon them and then to the ramparts. For every Turk that enters Crersa another shall see hell."

"To the gates with them," cried the mob. "Romakoff is right."

So in the twilight of a windy dawn the people of Crersa drove out their Prince, and with him the woman whose life he had saved at such a bitter cost.

A Turkish sentry found them and dragged them into the camp. It was the old father of Menid Bey to whom Prince Maurice, without faltering, told his story, and when he had finished there was silence. The old man rose up, dry-eyed but terrible in his anger.

"The Countess of Merguillon," he said, "is our honored guest, and we will find means to send her before long to her country. To you, Prince of Herania," he continued, "shall be dealt out such punishment as befits the murderer of my son, an obstinate enemy and a traitor to his natural suzerain, the Sultan."

"The Sultan is no suzerain of mine, nor ever has been," cried Prince Maurice. "Neither am I a traitor."

The old man ignored him.

"Today," he said, "is a feast day with you, Christian dogs—the feast of Christmas. You shall spend it fittingly, I promise you. Away with him, guards."

The Countess fell on her knees.

"My lord," she cried, "have mercy upon him. Your son fell in fair fight, as

I myself saw. If anyone is guilty of his death it was I, for he came to see me. You are a brave man and a soldier. You will not disgrace your country and your profession."

Menid Pasha thrust out a yellow, skinny forefinger toward her. There was no yield in his face.

"Remove this woman," he said, "and see that she is securely lodged. As for the Prince of Herania, he shall help his people keep their Christmas."

When morning broke they who stood on the wall of the city beheld a strange sight. Not a mile away, between the camp of the enemy and the city, on a slight hillock, a rude cross of pine wood had been built, and upon the cross was stretched the figure of a man bound with cords. They gazed at it for long in wonder, and then a fearful whisper went round, and they gathered together with pale faces and doubtful hearts. The man who was bound there, the victim of a slow and horrible death, was their Prince Maurice of Herania, their Prince whom they had driven forth as a traitor. Would the Turks treat thus a friend? They fetched Romakoff and Hohenloff to gaze upon the hideous sight. Some of them even fancied that they heard faint cries of agony borne upon the icy wind. The people of the city grew restless; and many dark faces were turned upon Romakoff. The muttering grew into a storm. They gathered together at the southern gate, before his house, and there someone found a fainting woman, her delicate hands clasping the iron bars, her clothes sodden, her feet bloodstained. And until she opened her eyes and spoke no one recognized the beautiful Countess of Merguillon.

She staggered to her feet. Whence came her sudden strength she could not tell, but she found voice and courage enough to stand up and speak so that her voice traveled to the farthest of them.

"Men of Crersa," she cried, "it is your Prince whom they have bound there. He is no traitor. It is I alone who am guilty. I made him swear upon his honor to save me, so he took the blame of what he knew nothing of. It is the father of Menid Bey who has planned this horrible thing. Listen! Are you men to let your Prince suffer a frightful death and never strike a blow?"

Then came hoarse cries from amongst them.

"What can we do?"

"Their guns sweep the plain."

A spot of color flared in her cheeks.

"Listen," she cried, "and I will tell you a secret. I will tell you why the Turks are so desperate, that they have done this thing to make you sue for peace. Their ammunition is spent. Their guns are as useless as old iron."

A murmur of excitement thrilled through them.

"Men of Crersa," she said, "you have fought a valiant fight, and you are in desperate straits. Strike one great blow for your freedom and for your

Prince. I know a side of the Turkish camp where never a scout is posted, and where you can fall upon them without the slightest warning. Their guns are useless. You will cut them to pieces like sheep. Be men, and live to remember this night as the greatest in your history."

There was a roar of acclamation. They gave her food and wine, and under cover of the darkness the men of Crersa—aye, and many of their women, too—stole out by a roundabout way to the Turkish camp. The story of that night is history—only before daylight a few scattered handfuls of Turks were flying across the mountains, leaving behind them a slaughtered host. Of the Turkish army nothing remained. When they looked for the woman who had led them out, they found her with a cold, motionless figure wrapped in her arms, lying underneath the cross, striving to keep him alive by the warmth of her body.

Two years later all Paris was crowding to the reception of the Mme. Le Comtesse, the first since her husband's death. Many guests had passed through her rooms and left. The evening grew late, and the last guest had taken his leave. The Countess was alone, when her major-domo, recalled to his duties, threw open once more the door of her apartment.

"His Royal Highness, Prince Maurice of Herania."

A little cry broke from her lips—or was it a sob? He took her outstretched hands and looked down into her startled face.

"Are you surprised?" he asked.

"Very," she answered. "I had no idea that you were in Paris."

"I arrived only last night."

"And Crersa?"

"Crersa is herself again. My Ministers tell me that we need only one thing now—a Princess. That is why I have come to Paris."

The color flooded her cheeks and left them again almost immediately. She remained silent.

"There is only one woman, Sophie, whom my people would welcome, and there is only one woman whom their Prince could marry. So I have come to you. You will not send me away?"

She looked up at him, radiant with happiness. Yet for a moment she hesitated.

"You are sure, Maurice, that your people—"

"They have canonized you," he answered, laughing. "They remember only that you are the woman who saved Crersa."

"And you—is that how you also remember me?"

He took her hands into his.

"I remember also," he said, "that you are the woman who saved my life, and the woman whom I have always loved."

One Shall Be Taken

Across the broad flower-strewn land and fields of waving corn, never altering his course or swerving from the high hedges, through which he plunged, a man was steadily running for his life.

The sweat from his forehead and the blood from his thorn-scratched cheeks had trickled onto his collar and shirt. His clothes were white with dust and torn in many places. A slight froth was upon his indrawn lips, his breath was coming in sobs and the gray pallor of utter fatigue had whitened his face even to the likeness of death.

He was clearly upon the point of exhaustion. Once or twice he reeled, but recovered himself without falling. Once he threw up his arms and earth and sky and the tall hedges swam together before his fainting sight, and the film of unconsciousness had well nigh set its darkening seal upon his eyes.

He was running steadily toward the sea, as he had run for 20 miles or more, meeting never a soul all the way, save a few village folk, who had looked up at him in blank amazement, who never thought of making any attempt to stop him.

An hour ago the sun had set. The soft twilight began to cool the freshening air. The man was hatless, but he raised one hand and thrust the heavy hair back from his forehead with a little choking cry. It was only a momentary weakness. The breath of fresh air seemed to revive him wonderfully.

Was it his fancy or was there really a salt odor about the fluttering wind? The very thought nerved him.

It could be no more than a mile or two now. Yonder, marked with a little cairn of unhewn stones, was the beacon hill, against whose base the gray Atlantic dashed its long, thundering rollers.

The he girded himself up for one supreme effort. The way was longer and harder than he had dreamed of—he was running a close race with death. But first he turned finding himself upon a level stretch of grass, and looked with scared white face and haunted eyes over his left shoulder.

There was not a soul in sight, no sign of any human being stirring, nor any habitation. If it was pursuit he feared, he might at least take heart, for before him stretched the highway of the unknown, and behind him was no living person.

He stumbled against a piece of loose rock and nearly fell. Recovering himself, he ran steadily on and looked no more behind.

Soon his lips parted, and he gave a little gurgling cry. Through a gap in the hills yonder was a little vista of blue-grey sea, bordered far away on the horizon by a long trail of black smoke from a passing steamer. He was nearing his goal in earnest now. If only he could hold out a little longer he was safe.

Once more he glanced over his shoulder. This time his heart sank like lead, and the blood in his veins ran cold. Striding along in the shadow of the tall hedge which bordered the great cornfield across which he had come, was a man on horseback.

Well, it was, after all, only one more danger to be faced, one more difficulty to be met and conquered. He measured with his eye the distance which lay between the man and the sea, and, with a shrug of his shoulders, he accepted the inevitable.

He sank down on the mossy turf and, taking a handkerchief from his pocket, wiped his face and forehead, and moistened his lips with the contents of a small silver flask. Then he drew a cigar from his pocket and striking a match with firm fingers, began to smoke.

Meanwhile his pursuer, finding himself observed, struck out into the open and galloped his pony up the hill. In a few minutes the two men were at close quarters.

The newcomer was a young man, tall, fair and sunburnt. He was carefully dressed in a tweed riding suit, and he wore a red rose in his buttonhole. He rode fearlessly up the hillsides, with stern set face and an angry gleam in his dark eyes.

"You will consider yourself my prisoner," he cried. "I am a magistrate for the county, and my men are following. You can either return with me to meet them, or remain here until they come."

The man, who had not risen or moved from his seat, knocked the ash from his cigar.

"I am exceedingly obliged to you, Mr. Maxwell," he said. "I think that as I have arrived so far as this at considerable personal inconvenience, I will remain where I am—at any rate, for the present."

The newcomer looked up in surprise at hearing himself addressed by name. He gazed with some curiosity at the man who lay stretched out at his feet, the personification of repose, his head resting upon his hand, the cigar between his shapely fingers giving out a faint, fragrant odor.

This was not at all the sort of person he had been imagining to himself. There was nothing whatever of the criminal in his face or manner.

"You know my name," he remarked, "but you are a stranger to the neighborhood and to me, I am sure."

The other smiled thoughtfully.

"Yes, I know your name," he replied. "You are called Philip Ruscombe Maxwell of Maxwell Court, in the county of Devon."

"You are quite correct," Mr. Maxwell admitted shortly, "but, after all, that has nothing to do with the present affair. I must warn you again that you are my prisoner, and in your own interest I should advise you to be silent."

The man knocked the ash quietly from his cigar, and raised himself into a sitting posture. Notwithstanding his sang-froid, however, he kept a careful watch upon the open country, across which Mr. Maxwell had come. As yet there were no signs of any further pursuit.

"Mr. Maxwell," he said, "I have a word or two to say to you! You are a man of modern ideas. You are a man of senses. I believe that you are capable of taking a broad view of the difficult question.

"If you saw an adder in your path, you would set your foot upon its neck and crush it, not only for your own sake, but for the sake of your fellows. It is true that I killed Vincent Lee. It was a fair fight, but I lay no stress on that. I made him stand up to me, but his poor fingers shook so that he could scarcely grasp the pistol that I had forced into his hand.

"I killed him. I admit it. I had come some distance for that sole purpose. I don't repent it. I should do exactly the same again. His death was a charge upon me."

"He was your enemy, then?"

"Not mine," the man continued, "more the enemy of every decent human being upon the earth. He was one of a cursed class! He was what his kind would call a man of the world—a man of pleasure. He was what I should prefer to call a vampire, sucking his pleasure from the lifeblood of honest and pure men and women.

"I make no secret of this—it was for a woman's sake I killed him, a woman whose life he had wrecked. I killed him as you would an adder, for the harm which he had done, and the harm which he yet might do, had he lived.

"Of course, it was a risk. I placed my own life in peril, it is in peril now! Yet, so far as you are concerned, I have no fear! You will let me go!"

The twilight stillness was suddenly broken; from below the cliffs, breaking away again seaward with many rolling echoes came the booming of a gun. The man rose to his feet.

But Maxwell stood still in the path. He was in some degree moved, but he saw still that white, dead face upturned to the skies, and the horror of it had taken deep root in his heart.

"He may have been a worse fellow than he seemed," Maxwell said, "but none of us are without fault. Bad though he may have been, you cannot compare the life of a human being with the life of a reptile. I am sorry for you, sir, whoever you may be, but I must do my duty. I cannot help you or suffer you to escape!"

The man shrugged his shoulders.

"The hopelessly bad in humanity," he said, "do more harm upon the earth than any reptile. Their removal is not only justifiable, it is a solemn duty.

"But I have no time to argue with you. Vincent Lee was a blackguard. The catalog of his crimes is a long and dreary record. He has been false to all his friends—false to every single person who trusted him. His presence under your roof last night was in itself a crowning piece of blackguardism!"

"You are mistaken," Maxwell answered. "I scarcely knew him. He was an artist, staying in the village, and I was decently civil to him."

"I am not mistaken," the man continued. "He was a blackguard to have thrown himself in your way, to have accepted your hospitality; he called himself Vincent Lee. His real name was Maurice Dubois."

Mr. Maxwell of Maxwell Court was a strong man, and a man of nerve. His face was tanned with the hot suns of India and the winds of Cornwall, but at the mention of that name he grew suddenly pale to the lips, and the hand which grasped his riding whip trembled.

"And I let him go," he muttered. "He was in my power, and I let him go."

"I admit," the other continued, "that to a certain extent I usurped your place. The hand which forced a pistol into his trembling fingers and sent a bullet through his cowardly, fluttering heart should have been yours. Yet I had an account of my own to settle with him. You can do your share now. You can lend me your horse and let me go free. Come! It is justice which I have dealt out. I am no murderer. Let me go!"

"What was your quarrel with him?"

"My quarrel was your quarrel—or rather hers!"

A dull spot of color burned in Maxwell's cheeks. His eyes were very bright.

"Her quarrel," he repeated. "Her quarrel! Speak out man! We have no time for riddles. Whose?"

"Your wife's."

"I have no wife."

His companion shrugged his shoulders.

"On the contrary," he said, "one of the best and sweetest women God ever made bears your name, and is—your wife."

"It is a lie," Maxwell answered fiercely. "The woman whom I married is my wife no longer! She is dead."

But the other man shook his head.

"The woman," he said, "who was unfortunate enough to marry such a thick-headed, obstinate mule as you is alive! Further, she is foolish enough to care for you still, notwithstanding your hateful and abominable mistrust of her, and your idiotic pride.

"Maxwell, a few minutes are all that I can spare in this country. There is somebody moving down there in the cornfield yonder—I shall want your horse, to get away as it is. Listen!

"Your wife is living in Allsbad! Save for myself, she is alone and friendless. She permits me to call myself her friend, and I am proud of it. Now I have brought you a message from her! She has sent for you! She bids you go to her!"

Maxwell's heel was ground into the turf and his eyes were flashing.

"Never!" he cried, passionately.

There was a moment's silence. The man whose life was in danger was gazing steadily at a moving speck in the open country. Was it his fancy, or were those men yonder, by that distant flush of yellow gorse? One, two, three, four of them he counted.

Yes, they were men, either soldiers or policemen, for the light was flashing upon their metal headgear. He must delay no longer. There was no more time to lose. He turned sharply to Maxwell.

"You are a fool," he cried. "As regards the past—as regards Maurice Dubois. I have sworn to her that I will speak no word to you. I am not her defender—God knows she needs none. Such women as she need no champions. I will not break my promise to her, but I say this to you as from man to man.

"If she were my wife, though the proofs against her were as black as night, and the whole silly world were cackling with stories about her guilt, I would believe nothing except from her own lips."

"There was never any possible doubt," Maxwell began.

"Doubt!" the word quivering with scorn, seemed almost to bite the air. "Never mind. I have finished, thank God. I have said to you more than she would have had me say. You have your chance. Will you come to her?"

"No!"

The man's face was suddenly bright.

"You are the greatest fool that ever set foot on God's earth," he said. "But it is yourself who must pay the price for your own folly. Now listen to me! I have spoken fairly to you—I have almost stooped to plead her cause, who is as far above you as one of God's angels.

"I love your wife! She does not know it, and I dare not tell her. It was for love of her that I killed Maurice Dubois, for love of her that I have said these things to you.

"Now, here's a warning for you. I'm going back to her a new man! She's the woman I love, and I want her!

"I have given you her message. Pray for her forgiveness now, and you may gain it. She carries your likeness next to her heart. I have seen her look out toward the hills at dusk, and I have heard her murmur your name! She loves you!

"Today she is yours, you have your chance. Take it, or never dare to complain if the time comes when you find you have lost her forever."

And then there was another brief, tense silence between the two men. Maxwell was without doubt shaken. He thought of those gloomy years of bitter loneliness, of his aching heart, his wounded pride.

But suddenly there was a change. Maxwell drew himself up—his face became dark and stern.

"I have nothing to say to you or to her," he declared coldly. "You had better go! You can take my horse. My people are close upon you."

The man sprang into the saddle. The red sun flashed in his face, all alight with joy.

"You poor fool," he cried. "Farewell!"

Then he rode down the hill at a thundering gallop and Maxwell stood watching him, half inclined even now to call him back.

A little puff of white smoke shot up from the inlet below; there was the sound of splashing oars and muffled orders. The man would get away safely enough. Already he must have reached the beach. To Maxwell, as he stood there, lost in thought, the air seemed full of the echoes of those last scornful words—"Fool, fool, fool!"

Maxwell rode slowly home across the moor, his bridle loose, his head bent.

He had held a murderer in his grasp, and he had let him go free. Not only that, but the murder had been one committed almost under his own roof, the victim his own guest.

It was true that the man was an imposter and a scoundrel, that his presence there had itself amounted to an insult—yet these things, by the side of death, seemed to lose so much of their significance.

The man, in a sense, had deserved his fate. There had been ugly stories about him, he had coldly pursued the path of his own pleasure with undeviating and unscrupulous selfishness. But, after all, was there any crime in the whole world which deserved death, the sudden extinction of all sensation, death so swift that repentance could be but dreamed of?

He could picture to himself that little scene in the corner of the park. Dubois dragged almost from his bed to meet, with ashen face, the cold sneers of the avenger, to face his agony in a grey twilight, peopled with the ghosts of his abandoned victims.

Despite his own knowledge of the man's baseness, his sympathy for him, touched with horror though it was, was deep and sincere. For death after all was an awful and unrealizable thing.

A few hours ago he had been playing billiards with the man; they had spoken of the morning's fishing—he realized with a certain sense of responsibility that Dubois had been his guest, had gone out from his own roof to his death. After all he had done a wrong thing to let the murderer escape.

He turned in his saddle and looked seaward. The yacht was standing now well out to sea, already its long trail of black smoke blackened the horizon.

After all it was only a chance that he might escape. Every port would be closed against him. He would find it very hard indeed to land in any civilized country. Nowadays the arm of the detective reached from hemisphere to hemisphere—the man would scarcely find a hiding place where the telegraph wires had failed to flash out the news of the crime.

Life henceforth must be a thing of jeopardy for him, and with that thought came the memory of those parting words of his. He had run the risk for the love of—her.

Maxwell's eyes were suddenly blinded with tears. She had fooled him, too, then—for the man was honest; there was no doubt about that. He believed in her. "Would to God!" Maxwell sobbed, as he bent lower still over his horse's head, "would to God he could!"

For he loved her still. He would always love her. There was no escape, no hope! Through life he must carry this burden—the burden of his love for a woman who had deceived him.

At the door his servants pressed him for the news. Maxwell shook his head.

"The man has escaped me," he said shortly. "He reached the coast, and got away on a steamer."

There was a little murmur of disappointment, which, curiously enough, irritated Maxwell. He went straight to his room.

"Have any telegrams come—anything been heard from any of Mr. Lee's friends?" he asked the servant.

A telegram was brought him—it was from the bankers, whose address had been found in the dead man's pocket book. Maxwell tore open the envelope, and read it slowly.

"Deeply shocked to hear of Mr. Lee's death. We know nothing of his family or friends. Wire when funeral."

Maxwell changed his clothes, and ate a lonely dinner. It seemed that the dead man's half-jocose, half-cynical account of himself had been a true one. He was alone in the world. He had neither wife nor child to be horrified at the sudden and awful catastrophe.

And she—well, she was far away, enough now, at any rate. He thought of her for a moment almost tenderly. The thing had unnerved him.

Later on in the evening he entered the gunroom, where the body of Vincent Lee had been carried. He was about to perform the task from which he shrank with a distaste for which he despised himself.

The papers found in the pocket book and on the person of the dead man were there together on the table by his side. He turned up the lamp and drew them over toward him.

After all, it was a lighter task than he had feared. There were a good many invitations, mostly hailing from Bohemia, a few bills, and several letters from women. These he felt justified in destroying, with a brief note of their addresses.

But there was one over which he lingered. It was signed Maud, and at the sight of the name his heart gave a sudden throb. He read it through eagerly. The handwriting might be hers   at any rate, there was a similarity!

He laid it down and looked once more into the still, cold face of the dead man. Death was terrible enough—but such death as this, the sudden arresting of a life of selfish vice, too sudden for repentance—it was a very awful thing.

His own anger towards the man was gone. Death had wiped it out, and with it had come a renewal of that terrible heartache, the miserable desire to look once more into the face of the woman who was still his wife, still the only woman he had ever loved.

Was this letter hers, he wondered fearfully. Word by word, he read it through, rightly interpreting its story of sorrow—a very grim story, indeed, it was, read by the side of that dead man.

Had he answered it? Scarcely likely. It was not the sort of letter that such a man would answer.

Glancing over to where his head appeared above the coverlet, Maxwell felt a sudden impulse of savage hatred towards the man who could never more make any amends for the hearts he had broken, and the lives whose happiness he had sapped away.

For five years he had lived and suffered in miserable isolation—strange that tonight more poignant and bitter than ever should come again that flood of bitter memories which had many a time wrung his heart.

He looked once more at the letter in his hand. At least he would soon know. Some one must tell her of this awful thing—he would go himself. It would be only ordinary humanity. And if it should, indeed, be his Beatrice—well, who could tell?

Maxwell was a proud man, and the separation from his wife had been the one great blow of his life. For the first time the thought of reconciliation and forgiveness assumed a definite place in his consideration.

She must have been terribly tempted, she must have bitterly repented. Who was he, after all, so immaculate as to stand aside for ever from a woman who had sinned, if, indeed, she were repentant.

Once more he glanced through the letter which still remained between his closed fingers. Yes, there was regret there—there was surely enough unhappiness. He would find this woman out, and if it should be Maud— well, his heart warmed at the thought of ministering once more to her wants, of relieving her at any rate from all anxiety.

Almost she seemed to glide into the room, as he sat there gazing with blank eyes into the fire, he saw her again, pale, sweet and graceful, with her deep, serious eyes and delicate mouth, he heard the music of her voice and the soft swish of her gown as she crossed the room toward him with outstretched arms and a world of yearning tenderness in her mobile face.

Bah! what a fool he was! He crushed the letter up in his fingers and rose to his feet. Such memories as these were maddening, unworthy. He would have no more of them!

But one resolve he had made, and he would keep it! He would seek this woman out, and afterward—well, he would at least know where Maud was.

Maxwell, for an unemotional man, found himself curiously disturbed as he walked along Bloomsbury Street a week later, toward the address of the letter which he had found upon the dead man a week ago.

He was in a part of London of which he knew nothing. The secrets of those tall, gloomy rows of closely-built houses were hidden from him. He only knew that in one of them dwelt the woman who had written this letter, the woman who had been living in close association with Maurice Dubois, and whose handwriting had brought to him that sudden rush of old memories.

He had not written to her—he had undertaken this journey at the first possible moment. If he had written, there was the risk that he might have learnt nothing.

Afterward he wondered at the eagerness which he undoubtedly felt to visit this woman. Was it destiny, he wondered, which had provided that the events of this day should change the whole tenor of his life?

He had not arrived in London until 2 o'clock, and it was barely 3 when he reached his destination.

The door was opened after a few minutes' delay by an ill-dressed untidy-looking servant, who answered his inquiry glibly enough. Yes, the lady was in! He could come upstairs. She was sure to be disengaged.

He followed her up the stairs on to a stuffy little landing, and into a room which bore many signs of feminine occupation, such as Maxwell was not accustomed to see displayed.

After that first swift glance around, he knew that the likeness of this woman's handwriting to his wife's was an accident. She had never been, could never become the inhabitant of such a room as this. Even as he was telling himself this, an inner door opened and a woman came in. She was a complete stranger to him.

She was dressed not too tidily in a loose gown, and her copper golden hair, which to a man more versed in such matters would inevitably have suggested peroxide, was coiled up in fluffy disorder at the back of her head.

She was good looking in rather a showy way, but her face had the pastiness which comes from the habitual use of cosmetics, and her eyebrows were obviously darkened.

"You are Mrs. Montrose, I believe?" he said. "My name is Maxwell. I am sorry to say that I have been called to bring you some rather bad news."

She looked at him anxiously.

"Well, what is it?" she said. "I don't know you, do I? Are you from Mme. Melisse? Because, if so, it is no use bothering me. I haven't got—"

He stopped her.

"No; I live in Cornwall," he said, "and I found a letter from you on a man who met with an accident near my house."

"What? Vincent Lee?" she exclaimed.

"Yes! I am sorry to tell you that the accident was a very serious one—in fact, he is dead."

She flopped into an easy chair, and looked at him for a moment in a dazed sort of way. He was much relieved to find that she did not scream or show any signs of fainting.

"Dead!" she repeated. "Him dead! O my! Good gracious!"

"He was shot," Mr. Maxwell explained.

"Who shot him?" she asked quickly.

"The man escaped," he answered. "We do not know who he was."

She extracted from her pocket a small handkerchief reeking of scent, and dabbed her eyes with it.

"Poor Vincent!" she murmured. "Poor old chap."

"I gathered," Maxwell continued, "from the letter which I found in his possession, and which it became my unhappy duty to examine, that you and he were upon somewhat intimate terms. I thought it best therefore to bring you the news myself. I am sorry to be the bearer of it."

She looked at him with a grim smile upon her lips.

"You needn't be," she said.

"I—I don't quite understand," Maxwell said, puzzled.

"Didn't I speak plainly?" she asked. "Well, is this plain enough? It isn't bad news at all, and I'm glad he's dead. I'm glad some one had the pluck to shoot him. I sometimes wonder that I didn't do it myself! I have felt like it many a time."

Maxwell was shocked, and his face showed it.

"O, you perhaps don't know him," she went on. "I did. He was one of the wickedest men that ever breathed. He did evil for the love of it. I knew him years ago—when things were different. I sometimes think that he only kept on with me for the pleasure of taunting me with my misery— for the pleasure of seeing me suffer. O, he was a bad man."

She was crying now, but it was for herself—not for him. Maxwell remained silent. He was heartily sorry that he had come. He was too horrified to say anything.

"He came to see me," she went on, "now and then, because he knew that I hated him. It amused him. If I had cared for him he would never have come to me. It was his way. I am glad that he is dead. He will do no more harm. God knows how he will answer for all he has done already."

She sprang up from her easy chair and walked up and down the room with clenched fingers.

"You don't understand, perhaps. You look like a good man. There are some in the world, thank God. I am not good—and it was his fault. You don't understand the side of life to which I belong. It is the underneath side. It is splendid to think that there are some men who loathe it. You look strong and manly and good. Have you a wife?"

"I had," he said, softly. "I have lost her."

"What did you say your name was?" she asked him suddenly.

"Maxwell—Philip Maxwell," he answered.

Her face lit up with a strange excitement. She looked around at the closed door. Then she came close up to him.

"Did you kill him," she whispered.

He started a little at the abruptness of the question.

"I? No. Why do you ask that?"

"He was your enemy."

"I did not know it until after he was dead, or he would never have set foot over my threshold," he answered. "He called himself Vincent Lee."

She was obviously disappointed.

"I hoped that it was you," she said, with a sigh. "You look as though you were brave enough, and no man had a better right."

"How do you know that?" he asked.

"I am going to tell you," she said. "It was kind of you to come here, and you are going to be rewarded. Wait here for a moment."

Maxwell was puzzled. She disappeared into the inner room. In about five minutes she came back with a little packet of letters in her hand.

"You said that you had lost your wife, Mr. Maxwell. You did not mean that she was dead, did you?"

He looked away, and his voice was scarcely natural.

"No."

"I had to ask you! Don't mind! Read those letters."

One by one Maxwell read them, and piece by piece the evil plot of the dead man, against the woman who had despised him, became revealed.

Then he gave a sharp little cry. He had reached the last letter, and it bore a date which he remembered too well.

"You say that you have compromised me, that my husband is already estranged, and you dare to offer me your love as a refuge. You are a scoundrel, Maurice Dubois, and I have no other feeling for you than one of intense loathing.

"What you say may be true. You may have succeeded in ruining me, but we have met for the last time, thank God!

"My husband will be home tomorrow; I shall go to him, and I shall tell him everything. If he will not believe me—well. I can live! But he will!"

The rest was torn off, but it was sufficient! The letter fluttered from Maxwell's fingers. She had come to him, and he had declined to listen to her! She had written letters to him, and he had declined to read them. He had been a harsh, short-sighted fool—the victim of an evil plot. And she— his wife was guiltless! O, what folly! What idiocy!

He looked up and became conscious of the woman who sat watching him.

"Where did you get those letters?" he asked.

"It was five years ago," she said. "I found them in his rooms and hid them. I hated him, and I knew from his anger when he discovered their loss that they were very important.

"He had every carpet up, every drawer ransacked, every corner turned out. But I held them safely. If they were as precious to him as all that, I knew they must be part and parcel of one of his villainous schemes.

"When he was gone I read them. I understand now that they are a record of one of his failures. You believed your wife guilty, Mr. Maxwell?"

"I did," he groaned. "I was a poor, miserable fool!"

"Well, you had better set to work and try to find her. She will forgive you! Women always forgive, and she must be—a very good woman."

He looked up at her with a sudden sense of gratitude.

"How can I ever repay you?" he cried warmly. "I loved my wife, and I have never been happy for an hour since we parted. You have given me something to live for just at the time when I was most unhappy. Cannot I help you somehow? Is there nothing I can do for you?"

"Nothing," she answered. "Go away and find your wife! Do not delay a moment!"

He lingered at the door! His alacrity after all seemed a little brutal.

"You must think me," he said, "very ungrateful."

"I do not," she answered earnestly, "but indeed there is no way that you could help me, and I would rather you went away."

He wrote his address upon a card and gave it to her.

"Will you keep this?" he said. "Some day you may need a friend, and you have only to send to me."

"Some day," she answered, "I may be starving. It is very possible! If it comes to that I will write and ask you for money. Good-bye. I hope that you will find her."

And that was the prayer on Maxwell's lips when he left England a few hours later.

"Women," her friend was saying, "forgive too easily. A man is always sure of them. It is a great mistake."

"Do you think so?" Maud Maxwell answered softly.

"I am sure of it. Give me another cigarette, please. I wish the echoes from those wretched guns would not toll amongst the hills so. I can stand the noise, but I don't like it second-hand. What a crash."

The girls both stood up and looked across the valley to the hill beyond. Little puffs of white smoke had suddenly shot out from a dozen places around its base, and the roar of answering guns from beneath shook the still morning air, and sent it vibrating about them.

The two girls drew close together. This was war in earnest then. The elder one looked across at the tent a few yards away.

"There will be work for us before long," she said. "You will not be nervous, Maud?"

Her companion smiled sadly.

"There is no fear of that," she said. "This is not nearly so terrible as the accident ward in a great hospital. I have seen some dreadful sights there— and then war is different. Out here men are fighting for a great cause— they go into battle knowing their risk. It is the suddenness of an accident which is so awful. No, I shall be ready for work when it comes."

"There will be nothing to do for some time, at any rate," her friend remarked. "Let us forget that we are waiting for dying men, and talk about the living."

"I would rather talk about anything else," Maud said sadly. "Men do not interest me."

"Yet you wear," her companion remarked, with a sidelong glance at the white, slim fingers clasped now around her knee, "a wedding ring."

Maud smiled bitterly.

"Every night," she said, "for five years I have meant to take it off, but when the time comes I lack the courage. It is foolish to keep it on, for my husband and I are parted for ever. Yet—it remains there, you see. I begin to think now that it will stay there as long as I live."

"Poor little woman," her friend said smiling. "However, you are wise in your generation. Take my advice, Maud, and never part with it."

The two girls both started round at the thunder of horses' hoofs close behind them. A single rider was galloping up the steep hillside. As he reached the summit he leaped from his horse, which was covered with foam and quite exhausted, and stepped eagerly forward to the edge of the precipice.

Down below in the valley were dark masses of men steadily moving toward one another, from the hills around the plain came little puffs of white smoke and flashes of fire. It was a picturesque panorama, an admirably chosen battlefield from a sightseer's point of view.

But the newcomer was evidently no ordinary spectator. He whipped out a note-book from his jacket and began to sketch. He had not even glanced toward the two women.

"He is a newspaper correspondent," the elder woman whispered. "How interesting. Let us go and peep. He is too absorbed to notice us."

Maud did not answer. She was standing with her eyes fixed upon the man, whose tall, slim figure was silhouetted so distinctly against the background of empty air. Her lips moved, but she did not speak. Her companion, glancing carelessly around, was amazed at her expression.

"Why, Maud, are you ill?" she cried. "You look as though you had seen a ghost."

There was a dead silence for several moments. The women were looking at one another. The man, who had not glanced at either of them, was sketching as though his very life depended upon the swift completion of his work. Then Maud's white lips moved in a half whisper.

"I have seen a ghost," she said. "Come with me into the tent."

The two women moved away. As they passed the man he spoke to them without even glancing up.

"Have you such a thing as a glass of water?" he asked. "I have ridden hard for the last six hours in the sun, and I've nothing but neat brandy in my flask."

"We have plenty of water," Maud answered mechanically. "I will send you a glass out."

His pencil stopped suddenly and he looked quickly round. The two women were just disappearing into the tent, both of them clad in the quiet, gray uniform of the Red Cross sisters, and wearing long aprons. There was nothing to distinguish the one from the other.

The man drew a long breath and picked up the pencil which had slipped from his fingers.

"It must have been fancy, of course," he said to himself, "and yet—yet, there was something in that voice."

He sighed wistfully, and recommenced his work. Below, the roar of artillery had grown in volume, and was mingled now with the sharper rattling of rifle volleys and the far-off shouting of the attacking army.

"Here is your water. Shall I set it down on this piece of rock?"

Note book and pencil, too, fell from his nerveless fingers. He turned swiftly round, and caught the grey figure by the arm. She did not protest, but she looked up at him proudly. A sob shook him for a moment.

"Maud!" he cried. "Thank God! At last I have found you, then."

She echoed his words bitterly.

"At last! Has the search been so long a one, then? Have you spent so many years in looking for me?"

He shook his head slowly.

"Only six months, Maud," he said, "six weary, disappointing months. I searched for you in London and Claybrook and Paris. If you were really trying to conceal your whereabouts you succeeded very well indeed."

"May I ask," she inquired steadily, "why you have been searching for me?"

He came a step nearer—he held out his hands and took hers! She did not resist, nor did she make any movement of yield.

"To ask for forgiveness. To take back all the hard and brutal words I have spoken to you. To beg you, Maud, my dear, dear wife, to come back to me. I have been very lonely."

Her own cheeks were flushed now with emotion and her eyes were wet.

"You—you believe in me now, then?"

"Implicitly! I have had proof! I was deceived by a villain! Everything has been made clear to me."

"Before you—began to look for me?"

"Yes."

"How did you, then, discover the truth?"

"Maurice Dubois is dead," he said solemnly. "Did you know that?"

"I—had heard it."

"He came," Maxwell said, "to an awful end. As you know he was a stranger to me, and I had entertained him unawares—he was passing under a false name. After his—death it became necessary for me to go through his papers. It was then I found the clue!"

"So you did not start your search for me—until afterwards?"

"I am bitterly ashamed of myself," he said slowly. "I have ruined years of my life, years of your life! If you will forgive me, Maud, I will do my best to make you forget it."

"Forget it!" She laughed heartily. "Could life be long enough for that? No, Philip, I cannot forget."

"At least," he cried, "you will come back to me."

"No! I have lived through these years of agony—I have lived down my suffering. I have found a way in which I can do a little good in the world. I dare not trust myself to you again!"

He stood before her—a proud man all his days, humbled and ashamed.

"I have loved you always," he pleaded.

"Loved me! Loved me!" she exclaimed with bitter scorn. "Well, you may have done so after your way, but it was a very little love and a very little way. Your own pride and your own jealousy were stronger things than this love of yours!"

He looked up at her suddenly. His face was white with anxious fear.

"There is—someone else!" he faltered. "Some one else whom you care for! For God's sake, Maud, tell me that it is not that!"

She looked at him curiously, as though trying to measure the anguish so plainly written in his drawn face.

"You really care like that," she said. "Well, if there is—can you wonder at it?"

"It is the man," he cried bitterly. "The man who killed Maurice Dubois, the man whom I helped to escape from Dunkery Beacon. He spoke to me of you."

"Tell me what he said."

He had a wild impulse to ride down the hillside and plunge himself into the fight. Somewhere there might be a bullet for him—and death, just then, would have been a very welcome thing.

And the woman watched him trembling. She had come very near to the limit of her strength.

"He is a brave man," she said, "and he has been very good to me—and believed. It is good for a woman to have a man believe in her."

"Where is he?" Maxwell asked with a sudden fierceness.

She pointed below with shaking finger.

"He is down there—fighting," she said, "as a volunteer. They have given him a regiment."

"He shall have all the fighting he wants," he muttered. "Goodbye, Maud. I don't blame you. It was my own wretched folly. God bless you."

He sprang on to his horse, and a sudden roar filled the air. The little sob, which somehow stuck in his throat, and her cry, were drowned in the rattle of the artillery.

"Philip, come back. I—I want you, Philip, dear."

He was already far out of hearing, urging his horse down the perilous descent, his white set face fixed upon the distant battlefield.

High above, on the hill-top, a woman leaned toward him, with out-stretched arms, and tear-stained face, calling to him passionately, idly measuring her voice against the rolling thunder of the guns. But there was no good genius to whisper in his ear, and bid him look behind.

Her eyes still followed him—he was riding straight towards a rolling cloud of white smoke drifting across the valley. Now he had reached it—there was another great roar of artillery. He had disappeared.

By nightfall the battle was over, and the hills were covered with the remnants of the defeated army. The little ambulance tent was filled to overflowing. Maud and her fellow nurses had no rest since sundown.

Tired and faint, she staggered at last from the tent out into the open air, and away in the east, morning was breaking. She stood on the edge of the mountain and gazed downwards on to the plain. It was strewn now with the bodies of dead men, with dismantled guns and burning fragments of shells and debris of all sorts.

Yonder she could see the exact spot where he had disappeared. She watched it wistfully—but for her work she would have scrambled down the rough path and made her way there.

A shower of rolling stones below and the struggling of a horse making the ascent disturbed her. She looked over the mountain edge, and her heart stood suddenly still.

Out of the gray twilight a man was riding slowly upwards, with a heavy burden stretched across the pommel of his saddle. She knew him at once—it was Maxwell. His face was as white as death, save where a great splash of blood has stained his cheek, and his lips were moving slowly as though he were talking to himself.

He saw her and reined in his horse. Then he tenderly lifted the body of the man which he had been carrying up, and held it out to her, speaking in strange, unreal tones.

"Take him," he said. "It is—my atonement! I brought him out of the Turkish lines. There were two of us against a hundred. Take care of him!"

She laid the body tenderly upon the ground. Then she started back with a shriek of horror! She had seen dead men before, but never such a sight as this. His body was riddled with wounds, and his face almost unrecognizable. He must have been dead for many hours.

"Is—he badly hurt?" Maxwell asked thickly. Then with a sudden groan he fell forward on to his horse's neck, and before she could help him he had lost his stirrups and sank on to the ground.

"I did my best," he murmured, "but they were thick around us, and they fought like devils! I did my—best!—Maud—dear!"

On very staid occasions, Maxwell sometimes wore by the side of his Indian cross, a small crescent-shaped medal, set with a brilliant diamond; and one night in the smoking room a privileged guest asked him a question.

"Maxwell," he said, "do you mind telling me where you got that curious little decoration of yours?"

Maxwell laughed and lit another cigar.

"Ask Lady Maxwell," he said.

"Exactly what I have done an hour ago," he answered. "She referred me to you as to its history, but she rather whetted my curiosity by saying that she would not part with it for all the Maxwell diamonds."

Maxwell smiled.

"It was given to me," he said, "by a Turkish general for attempting to save the life of an Englishman in the Greek war. As I was fighting his own men I have always looked upon it as a specially generous impulse. My wife and I are both very proud of it."

"It is," the guest remarked, "a very interesting relic. Some day I should like to hear the whole history."

"Some day," Maxwell answered with a laugh, "we may tell it to you."

A Strange Conspiracy

The governor's wife rose suddenly from her chair, and waved her fan toward me. It was a summons not to be disregarded. I hastened to present myself before her.

We passed across the room, dexterously avoiding several interruptions. Directly we were by ourselves Lady Marsham's manner underwent a change.

Assured that there was no one within hearing she leaned forward in her chair and looked at me with a gleam of anxiety in her blue eyes.

"Philip," she said, "I want to ask you a question."

"There are several I should like to ask you before I leave Jamaica," I said in a low voice.

"Don't be foolish," she said. "I am in earnest."

Lady Marsham was really a very pretty woman, and I was extremely fond of her. So I looked up reproachfully.

"In earnest. I, too—am very much in earnest."

"Once and for all, Philip, I did not bring you out here to talk nonsense. Why, I'm old enough to be your mother, and—"

"Oh!"

"Don't interrupt me, please. I want most particularly to ask you a question. Have you received any anonymous letters during the last few days?"

I was honestly amazed.

"Why, yes, I have," I admitted. "Two most extraordinary ones."

"You haven't them with you by any chance?" she asked eagerly.

I felt in my breast pocket, and produced them. Here and there the terrace was lit with Japanese lanterns. I detached one, and held it so that the flame, steady enough in the breathless air, shone full upon the sheet of heavily-scented and strangely-woven note-paper.

There was neither address or orthodox commencement—only a few lines hastily scrawled in a feminine but evidently disguised handwriting.

"You are a stranger to me, Philip Atherstone, but I have a fancy to do you a good turn. Your passage is booked in the *Aurora*, which leaves Jamaica Nov 2. If it is in any way possible for you to do so, leave instead by the *Argonaut* Oct. 24. If you are not able to do this, let nothing prevent you from leaving on Nov. 2. It is possible that other plans will be proposed to you. Remember my warning, and do not accept them."

The second letter, which was shorter, had only reached me two days before. It was written on the same sort of note paper, and apparently in the same handwriting.

"The *Argonaut* has sailed, and you are still here. I hope most earnestly that you will not disregard my warning. If your life and honor are dear to you, if you ever wish to see England again, leave on the *Aurora*. Efforts will be made to prevent you. Disregard them. Those who will propose other plans to you are not trustworthy. These are true words, and the writer runs a risk which you know nothing of in sending you this warning. May it not be in vain."

"Well," I said, "what do you think of them?"

"Extraordinary," she declared.

"And how on earth," I asked, "did you know that I had received them?"

"Because I myself," she answered, in a low tone, "have received a precisely similar one."

"It is either a hoax," I declared, "or someone here is very anxious to see the back of me. You didn't write them yourself, did you Lady Marsham?"

She looked at me reproachfully.

"I feel convinced that the whole thing is a myth."

"And I am equally convinced," Lady Marsham said, firmly, "that it is nothing of the sort."

"At any rate," I said, "I am sure to avoid this threatened calamity, for I am most certainly sailing tomorrow on the *Aurora*."

"You are going direct to London?" she asked.

"As fast as steamship and express train can take me," I declared.

"Do I know her?" she asked.

"There is no her. It is just a fit of homesickness. I am longing to walk along Pall Mall, to drop into the club for lunch, to see a few old faces again, and find myself inside a London theatre."

She sighed ever so slightly.

"You are quite right, Philip. This is nothing less than banishment. If I had understood that diplomacy, as Sir William called it, was likely to turn out such a pitiful apology for a career, and—well—"

I straightened myself instinctively. Sir William was standing a few yards away from us, fumbling with his glasses. Upon his arm was a lady who was a stranger to me.

"Dear me, dear me!" he exclaimed. "I am quite convinced that her ladyship is close at hand. I regret very much that she should not have been in her place to receive you."

The lady answered him, and at the sound of her voice I rose to my feet and looked eagerly in her direction.

The voice and the speaker were alike unusual. I looked eagerly through the darkness. I could see nothing but a white face and diamonds, before whose brilliancy Lady Marsham's gems seemed but the poorest paste. But the voice, slow, deep, strangely musical, was unusual enough to provoke more than curiosity.

"Lady Marsham can scarcely be everywhere, and I for one do not blame her for desiring to escape if only for a moment from what I am afraid she must find a very thankless task."

So I saw for the first time the woman who was to become the enigma of my life. I stood on one side for a moment whilst the usual small courtesies were proceeding. Then Lady Marsham turned toward me.

"Let me present Mr. Philip Atherstone to you, Miss Hoyt," she said. "Mr. Atherstone will execute any commission in London for you. He leaves Jamaica to-morrow."

Now in an ordinary way I am not an observant person, but Miss Hoyt was one of those young women who anywhere and at any time have the powers to rivet attention upon themselves. I had been watching her closely from the moment she had appeared, not of my own will altogether, but of necessity.

At the mention of my name there had come into her face a singular change. I was quite sure that save myself no one had noticed it. But I had heard the quick breath indrawn between her teeth, I had seen the startled light which flashed for a moment in her deep, still eyes.

"I am glad to know Mr. Atherstone," she said. "I think that I have heard of some of his work."

"It is more than likely," Sir William remarked. "Mr. Atherstone is one of those who bring water from the mountains to the cities, and build bridges in impossible places. My dear," he added, turning toward his wife, "there are others of our guests who may think our presence desirable. Will you permit me?"

Lady Marsham rose wearily up and took his arm. So I was left alone with Miss Hoyt.

"Tomorrow, then, Mr. Atherstone," she said, turning towards me at last, "you are going home."

"We sail at daybreak," I answered.

She roused herself as though with an effort, spoke of my work in Jamaica and passing lightly on to larger subjects, showed herself to be a girl of unusual intelligence, cultivated, and well-read. We talked perhaps for half an hour.

"What times does the *Argonaut* sail?" she asked again.

"At daybreak."

"And what time does the American boat arrive?"

"It is due about midday tomorrow," I answered, "but it is generally 12 hours late."

What satisfaction she could derive from this intelligence I could not then imagine. But she certainly seemed pleased. A gun boomed out from the point.

"What is that?" she asked, sharply.

"It is usually the signal for the arrival of the mails," I said, "but there is no steamer due tonight. Watch for the lights on the hill over there."

Presently a blue light flashed out, and immediately afterward a red one.

"Why, it's the American boat," I exclaimed, "in 12 hours before her time. Such a thing has never occurred since I have been on the island. Let us go and tell the governor."

She detained me. Her face in the moonlight seemed white and drawn, her dark eyes were filled with fear.

"Do not go," she exclaimed. "I want to talk to you!"

"By all means," I answered. "I was coming back."

"Do you know what that means?" she asked, looking fixedly at me.

"It means a very fast passage," I answered doubtfully.

"It is you," she said, "who are the cause of it."

I looked at her in blank amazement. She met my gaze without flinching.

"Yes! There are men on her who wished to intercept you. The captain has been bribed."

"To intercept me," I repeated, vaguely. "Dear Miss Hoyt, you are mistaking me, I am sure, for someone else. I am Philip Atherstone, engineer, a person of no consequence whatever. I have few friends certainly, but no enemies."

"Listen to me," she said, "listen very carefully, for I speak for your own good. Before you leave tomorrow an offer will be made to you to undertake some work for a country which you have probably never visited before. On no account must you accept this offer. Do you hear? Promise me that you will sail in the *Argonaut* whatever happens. They will try to tempt you. You must be resolute. Promise me that you will."

I plucked the letters from my pocket.

"You wrote these?" I exclaimed.

"Yes! You should have gone by the *Aurora*."

I hesitated. I was 35 years old, and had not yet outlived the love for adventure which had sent me roving over the world as soon as I had escaped from my teens. And while I hesitated I heard Lady Marsham's voice from the other end of the terrace.

"At least," I said hastily, "I will promise this. I will accept no offer without very careful consideration, from whomever it may come. And I can assure you that nothing will prevent my first visiting London."

"You will sail on the *Argonaut*, whatever happens?"

"Whatever happens," I repeated.

Past the silent white houses, I rode into the city and made my way to the hotel. A sleepy-looking clerk came out to meet me in the hall.

"There are two gentlemen here to see you, sir," he announced. "They arrived by the *Manhattan* tonight."

I took the letters which he had handed me, and passed on to the smoking-room. There was a babel of conversation in many languages. I stood upon the threshold for a moment looking round. Then I felt a touch upon my elbow, and a voice in my ear.

"It is Mr. Philip Atherstone, I believe!"

I had pictured to myself something sinister—the result this, no doubt, of Miss Hoyt's warnings. Almost I felt inclined to laugh at myself. The young man whose hand was already outstretched was about my age, or less, irreproachably dressed in white ducks, with dark, oval face, the complexion of a girl, and a smile which, if a little foreign in its pronouncement, was at least friendly.

"My name is Anthony. I and a friend who is with me have a matter of business to discuss with you if you can spare us a few moments."

Then rose up from before a small table, on which stood two tumblers and a bottle of champagne, a short, thick-set man, with skin as yellow as old parchment, black eyes set close together, a black beard brought to a point and black hair close-shaven to his head, standing up from the scalp like the bristles of a blacking brush.

"This is Mr. Gorrino, of whom, doubtless, you have heard," my new acquaintance said.

I endeavored to look as though the name of Gorrino was a household word with me.

"I am at your service, gentlemen," I declared. "I will only remind you that the *Argonaut* sails at daybreak, and I have my clothes to change and still a little packing to do."

Mr. Anthony looked around him. The room was certainly full of all sorts and conditions of people.

"If you will do us the honor," he said, "to grant us a short interview in my friend's sitting room, we will endeavor to detain you but a few moments, whatever the upshot of our conversation may be."

Now I had stayed in the hotel more than once, but I had never yet penetrated to the part towards which I was now led. We passed along many passages and out of the back of the building. Then along a covered way through the gardens to a sort of single-storied annex which I had seen more than once, but never explored.

The annex was gloomy, and had a generally unoccupied look. I had an idea from its appearance that we were the only persons in it.

The younger man, who came last into the room, lingered for a moment with the handle in his hand. I turned sharply round in time to see him turn the lock.

He met my look of amazement with a smile which broadened into a laugh. He held the key out to me.

"Pray do not think I am endeavoring to compel a hearing from you," he exclaimed. "It is simply that I do not wish to be disturbed, and there is one who might find it to his interest to break up our little council."

He laid the key upon the table by my side, and busied himself with one of the champagne bottles.

"You will take a glass of wine with us, Mr. Atherstone—and there are cigars at your elbow."

"You are very kind," I answered. "I won't refuse, but really I should be much obliged if you would let me know the nature of this business."

"You have no idea as to its nature, then?" he asked quickly.

"None whatever! Why do you ask?"

"Come, come," Mr. Gorrino said, "we must be quite candid with our young friend. O, yes! There is a person now upon the island who might. O, yes, she might have given you one hint. Yes, indeed, we expected it."

"If you mean Miss Hoyt," I said, thoughtlessly, "all that I have heard from her is a warning to depart by the *Argonaut* tomorrow, and to listen to no propositions whatever which would involve any change in my plans."

I could have bitten my tongue out immediately afterwards, for the glance which passed between the two men was like silent lightening with none of its harmlessness. They seemed for the moment transformed.

The girl-like smoothness of Mr. Anthony's face, and the calm courtesy of his manner seemed rent aside. His face was convulsed with anger, his eyes had narrowed, and were evil things to look upon.

And the older man looked back at him with a fierce return of his anger, a glance once satyr-like and full of the promise of vengeance.

All this seemed to come and go in a space of time which only a thought could measure, and then sat there once more a harmless looking fat little foreigner, with humorous eyes and bland features, and a man whose clear, fresh boyishness and light smile would have won him a second glance from any woman in the world. But my eyes were opened.

"Not that anything which Miss Hoyt said could have affected my plans in the slightest," I continued with emphasis. "They are already irrevocable."

Anthony sipped his wine and looked at me with forehead wrinkled in protest.

"We must hope, Mr. Atherstone," he said, "to hear you change that word. For frankly our purpose is to induce you to make some alteration in your plans."

"I am sorry," I said, "but it will be useless."

"Come!" he said, "we must remember that virtually we are unintroduced to you. We can scarcely hope to possess your confidence. You came into the smoking room holding letters in your hand—and I think a telegram. Will you be so good as to refer to them? It may be that the recommendation which we have asked from some of your friends are amongst them."

I looked through the little bundle at once. I opened first the cable. It was from London.

> "Recommend serious consideration of any offer made you by government of Brazil.
>
> > "Moulton."

Now, Sir George Moulton was the head of the firm of engineers with whom I was a very junior partner, and I must admit that the reading of that cable somewhat reassured me.

"You, then," I asked, "are representing the government of Brazil?"

Anthony looked at me with wide-open eyes. Then he laughed softly.

"My friend here," he explained, "is minister of public works, and I am the private secretary to the president."

One other among my letters referred to their visit, and that was sealed and signed by a very great man. It was short enough:

> "My Dear Atherstone—The Brazilian minister has paid me a call today for the sole purpose of asking whether your quasi official position would stand in the way of their making you a very exceptional offer to undertake some work in Brazil. After some consideration I have decided that in your interest it is only fair to allow you a free hand. I have, therefore, supplied your address to Mr. Ferraro, who is cabling it to Brazil, and you have my best wishes should you decide to accept the offer. I am, yours most sincerely,
>
> > "Powerfield."

I laid the letter and the cable down.

"I am very much flattered, gentlemen," I said, "that you should have thought it worth while to take this trouble to procure my services. Perhaps you will explain exactly what you require of me."

"Our country is passing through an era of unexampled prosperity. Large sums have been voted for public work which for many years have been neglected. We want an irrigation scheme, an aqueduct, a bridge which will be the longest in the world, and several less important matters.

"We are willing to pay, but we want the best man. We have engaged Colquohuon, and we want you to work with him. We are empowered to offer you £10,000 a year for five years, and an honorarium of £40,000 on the successful termination of your work."

"Gentlemen," I said, "this is a most extraordinary offer. I have been, it is true, successful during my last few undertakings, but I cannot help feeling that my work and experience do not warrant anything of this sort. I am really only a mining engineer, and—"

Anthony turned to me seriously.

"Mr. Atherstone," he said, "we who make you this offer have satisfied ourselves as to your fitness for the work. The offer is a bona fide one."

"Then I have no option," I answered, "but to accept it most gratefully."

"I must confess," the younger man remarked, "that we did not contemplate any different decision. It has been fortunately within our power to offer you terms which we believe to be almost unique."

"The final agreement," I remarked, "I can doubtless arrange with your minister in London."

"In London!" Anthony looked up at me as though in surprise.

"But, of course. Why not!" he exclaimed. "That reminds me, though," he continued, "that we wish you to return to Brazil with us tomorrow, and discuss all details of our schemes with the president. Afterwards, if you wish, when things are on the way, you can take a few months' holiday in London."

For a moment I was back again in the residency. I saw amongst the shadows a dark, languid face. I heard her speak—every word a warning. I saw her eye, pleading, insistent.

I shook my head.

"I am afraid," I said, "that whatever happens I must visit London first. I must sail this morning on the *Argonaut*."

"Let me see," Anthony remarked thoughtfully. "It would mean a delay of—how long?"

"Three months at least," Gorrino said, shaking his head. "We must talk to our young friend, Anthony. The president is very impatient. We must try and persuade him."

"I am sorry," I said, "but I am really overworked. A few days in London are absolutely necessary for me."

"For rest," Anthony suggested, suavely, "what could be better than a sea voyage?"

"It is so hard to make you understand," I said slowly, "without seeming ungrateful. But indeed I am not a free agent in this matter. My passage is booked in the *Argonaut*, and my sailing by her has become a necessity."

Anthony shrugged his shoulders. They both seemed to regard me as a spoilt child with whom reasoning had become futile.

"At least, Mr. Atherstone," the former said, drinking up his wine, "you will always be able to say that you refused the most liberal offer ever made to a man of your youth. It will be something to be proud of. I trust you will never repent it."

I was staggered.

"I am to understand, then," I said blankly, "that your offer is withdrawn if I do not accompany you to Brazil from here?"

"It is absolutely necessary that there should be no delay at all," Anthony said. "For this reason: The government of Brazil is stable enough and soundly established, but it is not, of course, so firmly established as the government of your great European nation.

"The vote for granting the money was carried after a fierce struggle, but it is liable to be rescinded. If the works are commenced—well, the matter is ended. Nothing can be done then, of course.

"That is why the president is so anxious. Colquohoun is already there. A start must be made within the month. That is why we went to the expense of having a special steamer sent here to take you back."

There was a short silence. Both men watched me covertly. I believe that they reckoned upon my resolution giving way in the face of their quietly professed ultimatum.

This offer was amazing enough, it is true, but in the face of my cable and letter from London it was not possible to doubt its genuineness.

There remained that single moment of betrayal on the part of these two men when I mentioned Miss Hoyt's name. Yet what did that amount to? I knew nothing myself of Miss Hoyt. Beautiful women have been on the wrong side before now. So I sat reasoning the matter out, and presently Anthony drew from his pocket a roll of papers.

"I am a bungler," he declared, with a charming air of candor. "For the moment I had forgotten that this was strictly a matter of business. Even among those who know nothing of commerce these things of course have to be put on a proper basis. Here is your formal appointment, sealed and signed. The president and the subcommittee have passed the terms which I offered you."

I glanced through the agreement. It appeared to be in scrupulous order.

"You have only to put that in your pocket," Anthony said, "and the thing is done."

I placed it upon the table with a sigh of regret.

"It is just what I cannot do," I said, firmly but with reluctance. "My word is passed to sail on the *Argonaut*. If you can suggest any means whereby I can do this and accept your offer, well and good. If not—well, I can only try to express to you my most profound regret."

They were satisfied at last that I was not to be moved. Anthony rose to his feet.

He caught up the key and moved toward the door, swinging it lightly on his forefinger. I followed him, and behind came Gorrino. He fitted the key into the lock, but seemed unable to make it turn. It seemed to me that he was trying to turn it the wrong way.

"Let me do it," I said, bending forward. "I think I know how it works."

I bent forward. Almost immediately, and like lightning, an arm was thrown round my neck. I had no time to utter a cry or strike a blow. The speed with which it was done was marvellous.

I was garroted, and my wrists were bound together with a cord which cut deep into my flesh. The thrust must have been made and the knot tied with a single movement.

Gorrino came stealthily to my side, and before I could even guess at his purpose a wet silk handkerchief was pressed against my face. The sickening fume of chloroform crept up my nostrils. There followed a buzz in my ears—then darkness.

The rushing of water through my half-opened portholes was the first sound of which I was distinctly conscious. I sat up in my bunk, looked about me in amazement.

A sudden flood of memory came to me. I remembered Anthony and his friend, our interview at the hotel. I had been drugged and brought on board this steamer unconscious. It was incredible, but it was true.

Then I sprang from my bunk in a towering rage. I tore on my coat and waistcoat, and without waiting for tie or collar I pushed aside the sheet which hung in front of my door and hastened upon deck.

And face to face with me in a suit of spotless ducks and smoking a cigarette of Havana tobacco was Anthony.

"What the devil is the meaning of this?" I exclaimed. "How dare you bring me here?"

"My dear Mr. Atherstone, I do not understand. We are only carrying out our last night's arrangements."

"Don't talk such rubbish," I interrupted fiercely. "You and that other blackguard gave me chloroform and got me here somehow, but by heaven you shall suffer for it."

"But, my dear sir," he exclaimed, "you are under some extraordinary illusion. O, I am sure that you are. Last night you agreed to sail with my friend and myself for the purpose of considering a proposition to be laid before you by the minister of the country to which we belong. You were taken ill. We drank, it is true, two magnums of champagne. The night was so hot. But our starting time was fixed, delay was impossible. Consider yourself, my dear Mr. Atherstone, the nature of our dilemma."

"You mean to insinuate, then, that I was drunk," I cried fiercely.

Anthony was distressed.

"To-morrow," he said, "you will surely remember everything. It will be unnecessary for me to explain further."

"You will have a good deal of explaining to do, my young friend," I declared, "when I get you before an English consul."

"It is so unfortunate," he murmured, "but I do not think that there is an English consul where we are going."

"Now, between you," I said, softly, "you must contrive to tell me the truth. Where are we bound for?"

Mr. Anthony shrugged his shoulders.

"My dear sir," he said deprecatingly, "why assume that there need be any concealment about it? There should, indeed, be none. We are bound for the Island of Morcaqua!"

"Morcaqua!" I exclaimed. "And where the mischief is that?"

They looked at one another in well simulated astonishment. Gorrino even raised his fat hands.

"You do not know where Morcaqua is," he protested. "Impossible! O, impossible!"

"Geography," I remarked, "is not my forte. I must confess that I never heard of the place."

"It is amazing," Gorrino exclaimed, with a leer. "Anthony, do you hear? Our young friend here—he has never heard of Morcaqua, the island of untold riches."

"Come," I said, "let us have no misunderstandings. You have kidnapped me. You are taking me to Morcaqua. What you expect to gain from it I can't imagine. But I want to warn you of this. I'm only a civil engineer, but I belong to a country which doesn't permit these sorts of liberties with her people, and further, although I myself am of no account, I have an uncle who is a cabinet minister, and another in the foreign office. So you see, I am not altogether friendless. I demand that you make for the nearest port of any nation and land me. If you refuse—well, there will be trouble."

Anthony laid his hand lightly upon my shoulder.

"My dear Atherstone," he said, simply, "don't make us feel like jailers. You know what discipline is. Well, we are acting under orders."

"From whom?" I demanded.

"From one whose acquaintance you will soon make," he answered.

"Let me know his name," I insisted.

The two gentlemen exchanged glances. It was Gorrino who answered me.

"Why not?" he exclaimed. "Why not, indeed. It is indeed Morcaqua whom we serve. It is the ruler of Morcaqua to whom we are taking you."

They left me, and I walked to the side of the steamer and leaned over the rail. Jamaica was now but a blue mist, that far away trail of black smoke upon the horizon might very well be the *Argonaut*.

Who was Miss Hoyt? Who was the ruler of Morcaqua? What could possibly induce him to believe that I should be willing to work for him after an outrage so gross as this?

The philosophy of youth reasserted itself. I resigned myself to wait for events, and remembered that I was hungry. I descended the stair to my stateroom, and completed my toilet.

In the saloon Anthony and Gorrino received me with effusion. The coffee was good. The breakfast which was set before me excellently cooked. My hosts made somewhat labored efforts at sustaining a conversation which should contain no references to the peculiarities of our position.

The humor of the thing for the first time began to dawn upon me. Anthony and Gorrino joined boisterously in the laugh which I was no longer able to repress.

I lit a cigarette, and looked thoughtfully into the cloud of blue smoke.

"On deck," Gorrino declared, suavely, "it is verra hot. Have you informed our honored guest, my dear Anthony, that his luggage is in the stateroom next to the one in which he this morning found himself?"

"My luggage!" I exclaimed, incredulously. "What luggage?"

"You give us credit," Anthony said, softly, "for very little consideration. We wish your journey and your stay in Morcaqua to be as comfortable as possible. We consequently arranged for the whole of your luggage which was at the docks waiting shipment on the *Argonaut* to be transferred here."

I made my way amidships. To my surprise the whole of my belongings were there, packed in an empty stateroom.

However, I unpacked a few things, found out the bathroom, and changed into a suit of white duck. Then I went up on deck, with an armful of books, and promptly dropped them all over the place. For coming along the deck towards me was Miss Hoyt.

I found a deck chair, and spread it out for her.

"Come," I said, "you will at least be able to tell me many things which I am anxious to know. It seemed to cause you no surprise to see me here. I, on the other hand, am amazed to see you."

She looked nervously around her.

"Never mind the chair," she said. "We shall be interrupted in a moment. Have you mentioned my name to them."

"I believe that I did—to Anthony."

"I was afraid so. You see that awning and rope? I am to keep to my own deck cabin, and the little space in front of it. These may be the only words we shall have alone together during the voyage. Listen! Is there any way in which I can help you?"

"Shall I need help?" I asked. "I am going no further with these men than the first port we land at. I scarcely see what difficulty I can have in getting away."

She looked at me in faint pity.

"You underrate the cunning of these men," she said. "Morcaqua is a desolate island in a wholly unfrequented route. There will be no one to whom you can appeal. A letter to your friends I might try to dispatch."

"If you would really do me a service," I said, "for heaven's sake relieve my curiosity. I am utterly bewildered when I ask myself what possible object these men can have in making a prisoner of me like this. What use can they expect to make of me?"

"Do not ask me," she begged. "You will find out soon enough."

"At least tell me—do they expect me to work for them?"

"Assuredly. That is why you are being taken there."

"And you?" I asked. "What have you to do with such people as these?"

"Don't ask me," she begged. "Only remember what I have said. These men will take you to Morcaqua. Be on your guard when you meet their master. Do not trust him."

"The intercourse between us is not likely to be a very friendly one," I said. "But let my affairs go for the moment. Let me ask you this. Shall I see you in Morcaqua?"

"Probably as much as you desire to," she answered. "I have not been allowed to take such a journey as this for years, and if he ever knows that I tried to warn you against coming I shall never be allowed to leave the island again."

"From me," I assured her, "he never will. At least, if I am to see something of you, life in Morcaqua cannot be all misery."

"When you see the part which I have to play," she murmured, "you will forget that little speech."

"I wish I could persuade you to the contrary," I said. "Nothing could lessen my pleasure in being allowed to see you now and then."

"You should not say that," she said. "You know nothing of me. I can make no real difference to you."

"Promise me your friendship, and I shall be almost reconciled to losing my holiday, and to this extraordinary adventure."

"You had better be careful," she said, quietly. "Do you know that I am supposed to be acting as a sort of decoy? They have lost confidence in me for some reason, but that was my original position."

"I am willing," I assured her, "to be decoyed. If you say the word I will give my parole and come to Morcaqua."

"I will not say it! If you have the slightest chance of escape, seize it. If you can avoid coming to Morcaqua, even at the risk of your life—take that risk. Remember my words. Be silent now."

Barely a moment had passed before Anthony's soft voice sounded in our ears.

"So you two have met before. It is, perhaps, the renewal of an old acquaintance?"

"Miss Hoyt and I met at the government house at Jamaica," I said.

Anthony bowed.

"The carpenters are busy with your awning," he said, turning to her, "and need your instructions. Will you allow to make a suggestion—if Mr. Atherstone will excuse us?"

She followed him across the deck, and presently he returned alone.

"It is very fortunate," he said, "that you are already acquainted with Miss Hoyt."

"Why so?" I asked.

"Surely you know," he said, "it is Miss Hoyt's father who is so anxious to have the honor of making your acquaintance."

Early on the fifth morning of our voyage I awoke in my berth with a peculiar sense of stillness, the cause of which was readily apparent. The engines had stopped.

I dressed and hurried on deck. On the port side of the steamer was what looked to be a barren rock of an island, ornamented with a fringe of scanty herbage. Anthony, with a quiet smile, extended his hand toward it.

"Welcome," he said, "to Morcaqua!"

"What in the name of all that is marvellous," I said, "can I have been brought here for?"

A soft voice from behind answered me.

"You will know very soon."

I turned around. Margaret Hoyt was by my side.

"You will know very soon now," she said. "Look, the pinnace is coming out for us."

"The sooner the better," I answered.

"In which case," Anthony remarked suavely, "you will perhaps be so good as to see that your luggage is ready for transport to the island."

"Do you really mean," I asked, "that I am expected to land upon that rock?"

"Without doubt," Anthony answered coolly. "Mr. Hoyt is awaiting you there with impatience. We are almost a day behind time."

In a very short time Miss Hoyt and I were seated side by side in the stern seat of the pinnace.

"You have told me nothing about your father," I remarked, as we drew near to the landing place.

She looked at me again as she had looked on the balcony of the government house. Again I was conscious of potent things unsaid. I asked her no more questions. Only just before we landed her fingers sought mine for a moment.

I am not sure whether at that moment I would have exchanged my seat in that little boat for the empty stateroom in the *Argonaut* plowing her way homeward.

My introduction to Margaret's father was in some respects a curious one. She herself led me to him, and I saw at once from his instinctive movement in my direction, and the curious poise of his head, that he was blind.

"Father," she said, bending over him and kissing him lightly upon the forehead. "Mr. Atherstone is here. I had no share in bringing him, as the others will doubtless tell you. If he had taken my advice he would not be here. I will leave you alone."

Mr. Hoyt extended a very white hand toward me, but he did not rise from his seat. By the side of his basket chair stood a pair of crutches.

"You are welcome to Morcaqua, Mr. Atherstone," he said, in a rich bass voice. "I am delighted that my emissaries were able to prevail upon you to pay us this visit."

"Their persuasions," I remarked, "consisted chiefly of a locked door and a chloroformed handkerchief. I have been brought here a prisoner, Mr. Hoyt. I am naturally anxious to know for what reason."

"You are joking, of course, my dear sir. The very suggestion of such means of compulsion sounds prehistoric."

"What do you want of me?" I asked, bluntly.

"You shall hear," he said. "You are a junior member of a great firm of engineers, and I am informed that a branch of your business is devoted to mining. You may wonder why I have chosen to make a summer home in what seems to be a very barren island. I will tell you. It is because these few miles of soil contain the richest gold mines in the world."

I looked around me incredulously.

"Impossible," I exclaimed. "There is not the slightest trace of auriferous soil."

"Appearances," he murmured, "are so deceptive. You will change your opinion. I am sure. Do me the favor to read this."

He handed me a few sheets of manuscript paper pinned together. I glanced them through. The language was cold and studied enough, but the story they told was Arabianesque.

It was a wonderful report of the Morcaquan gold mine, but it was unsigned. I laid it down with a little laugh.

"It is," I said, "a marvellous work of imagination."

"It will sound better," he remarked, "when your name is at the foot."

I stared at him for a moment in blank amazement. Then the situation began to dawn upon me.

"You had better," he suggested, "for form's sake make a brief investigation of the island. I will send for my daughter. She shall accompany you."

He struck a bell, and a colored servant came out, whom he dispatched in search of Margaret. She came at once, in a cool white linen dress, and swinging a large sun hat.

"I want you to show Mr. Atherstone round the island," Mr. Hoyt directed.

She beckoned to me to follow her. When we were out of sight she turned, and I saw that her eyes were full of tears.

"You understand?"

"Perfectly," I answered. "I think that we will not waste our time looking for gold."

"I am so sorry," she said.

"It is not your fault," I answered, "and I think that I would rather be here than on the *Argonaut*, after all."

"Well," Mr. Hoyt remarked, lifting his head as we approached.

"There is not an ounce of gold upon the island," I said.

Mr. Hoyt motioned to Margaret, and she left us.

"I will give you £20,000," he said, "to sign that report."

"If your condition," I answered, "did not prohibit such measures, I should punch your head."

He smiled.

"Exactly the answer I expected," he remarked. "Well, we shall save the money. The Press is a great power. By now it is announced in England that you have left Jamaica for the Morcaqua gold mine. That is quite sufficient for us. The signature which will adorn this report may not be yours, but I promise you that it will be a very fair imitation. I only regret," he added with a faint smile, "that it will be necessary for you to become my guest here for some time.

"Franks," he called, "my crutches."

I saw servants on their way to the little harbor with luggage, and Mr. Hoyt was himself evidently prepared for a journey.

"You mean to leave me here?" I exclaimed.

"It is regrettable, but necessary," he answered.

I was unarmed, but in any case resistance would have been absurd. There were at least a dozen men waiting for a signal from him.

An hour later there was nothing to be seen of the steamer but a thin line of smoke upon the horizon.

"Miss Hoyt!"

I stopped short and stared at her in amazement. It had never occurred to me for one moment that there was the slightest chance of her having been left to share my imprisonment. Besides, I had seen her trunks go down to the beach, and herself in their wake.

Yet here she sat in a shady corner of the veranda, a book upon her lap, her dark eyes inscrutable as ever raised to mine.

"Well," she said, quietly.

"I don't understand," I faltered. "Has the steamer come back? Has your father changed his mind?"

"My stepfather," she said, "does not change his mind. The steamer was out of sight hours ago."

"But I saw you in the pinnace—and all your luggage."

She smiled faintly.

"I have had to sacrifice my wardrobe," she remarked, "but I had never any intention of leaving the island unless I was obliged—with them."

My imprisonment seemed no longer a terrible thing. It was amazing what a change had come over everything.

"What will they say when they know?" I asked.

"My stepfather—will be annoyed," she remarked calmly. "They will not know, however, until tomorrow. My maid is on board, and she will keep my door locked. My father knows that I am a bad sailor."

"Will they come back, do you think?" I asked with sudden fear.

"I think not," she answered. "Mr. Hoyt is too anxious to get to England."

"I believe you stayed for fear any harm should come to me," I ventured boldly.

"Perhaps I did," she admitted, flashing a sudden look at me. "Are you not gratified?"

"More than that," I declared; "I am reconciled."

She looked at me coldly.

"It is possible," said she, "that your detention here may not be as long, after all, as my stepfather thinks. You have very good friends in Jamaica, and they will know something of your disappearance."

"It seems to me," I answered, "that I have a very good friend here. If I was not a perfect idiot your first warning would have been sufficient to keep me out of this scrape."

She smiled.

"You admit that it is a scrape, then?"

"I admit nothing of the sort," I declared. "I would rather be here at this moment than on the *Argonaut*."

"I am afraid, after all, that you are a very foolish person," she said. "I shall go away and leave you. It is too hot to be out of doors."

"I am quite sure that you are a very tantalizing one," I answered. "When shall I see you again?"

"Perhaps—at dinner," she said. "In the meantime," she added, more seriously, "have nothing more to say than you can help to the servants, and keep your revolver in your pocket. I do not think that they would dare to try and harm you, but it is as well to run no risks."

I lit a cigar, and appropriated her vacant chair. It was astonishing how everything had changed with me. I could think of Mr. Hoyt and the trick which he had played me with positive amusement. This barren rock of an island had suddenly become to me the most desirable place in the world.

Later on I felt even more at peace with my absent host. Something of a sybarite himself, he had left behind him his cook with generous instructions for my comfort. Margaret came down to dinner in a white muslin gown, and if a little informal, our meal was none the less delightful. Afterwards we went out into the deep, cool darkness, and she beckoned me to follow her.

"Let us climb up the hill," she said. "We shall get a breeze there."

Once she let me help her over a difficult place, and as her hand touched mine I tried to draw her to me.

"Margaret!" I murmured.

She snatched away, and flitted along the path at such a pace that I had hard work to keep anywhere near her. When I reached the summit I found her looking intently seaward. She stretched out her hand.

"Look," she said, softly, "is that phosphorus—or is it a light?"

It was hard to say. It was hard to believe, too, that I was utterly indifferent.

"Margaret," I said, "I must—I must tell you something."

"It is a light," she exclaimed suddenly. "Look!" it was certainly a ship's light, and as though to make assurance a certainty there came to us as we stood there the sound of a gun booming over the water.

"I knew that they would send for you," she said. "After all, you see, Mr. Atherstone, your imprisonment has not been a long one."

"It has not been imprisonment at all," I answered.

"You will be able to leave at daybreak," she said, cheerfully.

"I shall not leave at all," I answered, boldly, "unless you come too."

"You are absurd," she protested.

I felt for her hand. It rested passively in mind.

"You will come, Margaret," I begged.

"I—I suppose I must," she faltered.

Then I took her into my arms and I blessed Mr. Hoyt and all his schemes.

It was exactly two months and a day before I saw Mr. Hoyt again. At 7:15 on a dull, cold morning, I stood on the dock at Liverpool, watching the passengers leave the great liner which had just arrived.

A last I saw them come down the gangway. Anthony in front and Gorrino behind helping Mr. Hoyt. I accosted them at once.

"Welcome to England, Mr. Hoyt," I said.

Gorrino shook like a jellyfish, and Anthony stared at me as one might at a ghost. Mr. Hoyt alone received the blow of my presence with perfect composure.

"You are a wonderful man—or a very lucky one, Mr. Atherstone," he said.

"There is a boat leaving for New York in two hours," I answered.

"An admirable suggestion," Mr. Hoyt declared. "By-the-bye, I am really curious to know how you got here."

"Your daughter left a note for Sir John Marsham, to be opened in case I did not leave by the *Argonaut*," I told him. "A government sloop came for me."

He nodded his head slowly.

"I ought to have thought of that," he murmured.

"Your daughter," I added, "is now my wife, so you see I am not afraid to tell you the truth. Might I suggest—"

I pointed to the dock, towards which the people were already hurrying. Mr. Hoyt nodded thoughtfully.

"My dear son-in-law," he said, "I wish you every happiness. Pray convey the same message to Margaret. Anthony! Gorrino!"

They moved down the landing stage, a strange, dejected-looking trio. I saw them off, and Mr. Hoyt repeatedly waved his hat to me. Then I returned to breakfast with Margaret.

The Girl From Manchester

The senior member of the firm had himself left the mysterious privacy of his inner office to offer a few stereotyped but honeyed remarks to the young lady from the highly-esteemed Manchester firm of Messrs. Harrison and Peters, Limited. The salesman, the assistant-salesman, and Mr. Henry Podmore, manager of the department in which the young lady's purchases had been made, stood by during the process ready to smile at the slightest provocation, eager to pounce once more upon their customer the moment their chief should think fit to retire. But the chief was in no hurry. The young lady was trim and smart and bright. She was also remarkably good-looking.

"I should like," Mr. Bedells said—Mr. Bedells was the senior partner in the firm of Messrs. Bedells, Clumber, and Company— "to glance through Miss—Miss Gray's order, just to see if anything occurs to me."

Mr. Podmore dexterously whipped an order-book from under his arm and laid it open before his chief.

"This is as far as we have gone at present, sir," he pronounced, with some emphasis upon the last phrase. "We still have hopes of interesting Miss Gray in our more expensive jet ornaments."

Miss Gray, who was lithe and supple, raised herself lightly on to the mahogany counter and swung her feet backwards and forwards. She wore grey stockings and grey suede shoes, and her ankles were irreproachable. Mr. Podmore caught her eye and glanced away hurriedly. For a partially-engaged young man he was a little ashamed of himself. Miss Gray continued to swing her feet. Her right fingers were clasped now around her right knee, and her left—well, there was more than her ankle to be seen in her new position. Mr. Podmore distinctly blushed. Miss Gray stared at him curiously. This was in London, and Miss Gray came from Manchester. She had been warned against London young men. Besides, she knew Mr. Jenkins, who was traveller to the firm and who came to Manchester. She knew him quite well, and she had never seen him blush.

"Very satisfactory, I am sure," Mr. Bedells remarked, having completed his perusal of this most interesting order. "Some of the prices are just a little fine—those bugles, Mr. Podmore."

"Quite so, sir," Mr. Podmore admitted, "but I can assure you that we found Miss Gray most difficult on the subject of bugles. I explained that the price upon which she insisted left us barely a living profit."

"Same price as I can get them at within a hundred yards from here," the young lady informed him.

"Really!" Mr. Bedells sighed. He hated the mention of rivals. "Profits, as we used to understand them in the old days," he continued, sorrowfully, "no longer exist. Disappeared entirely, I can assure you."

"You seem to do pretty well," Miss Gray remarked, consolingly. "Nice motor-car you got out of as I came in."

Mr. Bedells coughed. Was it his fancy, he wondered, or was this young lady inclined to be a trifle familiar?

Miss Gray prepared to depart.

Mr. Bedells again coughed. It was an old-fashioned firm and it had old-fashioned methods, especially with country customers.

"Mr. Jenkins's absence is indeed regrettable," he said. "He was compelled to go to Leeds quite unexpectedly, or I know he would have been delighted to offer you the hospitality which it is the custom of the employees of our firm to tender to our friends from a distance."

"Told me he'd be here all the week," the young lady remarked, with the slightest possible toss of her head.

"If you would allow one of my other young gentlemen to take his place," Mr. Bedells continued, soothingly; "Mr. Podmore—the manager of the department—would, I am sure, be delighted to offer you the usual hospitalities. London, Miss Gray, is no place for a young lady alone."

"Quite so," Miss Gray agreed. "I've found that out already. A girl can't even go to a decent restaurant without being stared at, much more the Exhibition, or anywhere like that. If Mr. Podmore is free, then?" she added, glancing questioningly toward that young gentleman.

Mr. Podmore was tall and fair and inclined to be thin. He had a pink and white complexion, and, although when in business his zeal made him oblivious of it, he was really exceedingly and painfully nervous. He met Miss Gray's confident little glance with something akin to positive apprehension. He said absolutely nothing at all. His mouth was slightly open, his ears seemed suddenly protuberant. He was glib enough in the discussion of business details, all of which he had at his fingers' ends, but the prospect of spending an evening alone with this attractive young woman reduced him to a state of speechlessness. Besides, there was Millicent!

"Of course, if you have any engagement," Miss Gray began.

"Mr. Podmore, I am sure, has no engagement that he cannot easily break," Mr. Bedells said, a little severely.

"Quite easily. No engagement at all," Mr. Podmore protested, suddenly conscious of his failure to meet the situation. "Delighted, Miss Gray! Anything I can do, I am sure! Great pleasure!"

"Very well, then," the young lady remarked, "that's settled. You can take me downstairs now, please, and get me a taxicab."

Miss Gray made her adieux. Mr. Podmore, a trifle awkwardly, escorted her to the ground floor in the lift, and more awkwardly still piloted her across the warehouse and past the offices. He sent a porter for a taxicab, and they stood together upon the step until it arrived.

"No. 8, Eden Street, Bloomsbury, my address is," the young lady declared. "Not a minute later than a quarter-past seven, mind, and I should like to see the new piece at the Gaiety. You needn't bother about stalls; dress circle will do quite well."

Mr. Podmore, who did not, as a rule, visit the theatre, and who had certainly never visited any part of it except the pit, looked a little vague.

"You'll dress, of course?" she added, as the cab arrived. "Good-bye!"

The cab drove off. Miss Gray, leaning out of the window, waved a daintily-gloved hand at him. Mr. Podmore slowly withdrew into the warehouse. He felt that he had a lot to think about.

First of all there was, as he had remembered once before, Miss Millicent Woodward. As he passed the glass-enclosed offices on the ground floor his attention was attracted by a sharp tapping. He obeyed the summons without hesitation. Miss Woodward, who was the senior typist, and sat at a small table alone, wished to ask him a question.

"Whatever were you doing with that strange-looking young woman, Henry?" she inquired, with some curiosity, not unmixed with acidity.

Mr. Podmore straightened his tie.

"Important customer of the firm," he answered in a stage whisper— "Miss Gray, a buyer from Harrison's, of Manchester. We've just booked a capital order from her."

Miss Woodward arched her eyebrows. She was rather an insignificant-looking person, undersized and with sallow complexion. Her eyebrows were, perhaps, her best feature.

"What an extraordinary idea to send out a young woman like that to buy things!" she exclaimed.

Mr. Podmore smiled.

"Come," he said, "I don't quite see why you should be the one to object. You're always on about women being able to undertake any work a man can do. How about your paper the other night on 'Careers Open to a Woman'? It's trimmings and bows she buys, and that sort of thing—just what you suggest a woman ought to be able to buy better than a man."

Miss Woodward tossed her head.

"Certain women," she declared, "are, without a doubt, suited for a great many posts at present given to men. The young lady whom you are speaking of was a different type. For one thing, I should say that she was much too stylishly dressed for the part."

"Well, I don't know about that," Mr. Podmore replied. "When we send a man on the road he wears a silk hat and black coat-dresses a jolly sight better than we stay-at-homes."

Miss Woodward reflected—and Mr. Podmore looked at her with new eyes. Certainly she was plain, according to his new standard. Her face was rather long and thin and entirely colourless. Her eyes and eyebrows were moderately good, but the former were spoilt by a pair of spectacles, which she confessed that she wore from preservative reasons rather than from any actual necessity. Her attire was unfashionable and unbecoming, though neat. Her smooth hair was brushed back from her forehead in uncompromising stiffness. Mr. Podmore was compelled to remind himself vigorously of her intellectual gifts.

"The matter," she remarked, drawing her notebook towards her, "is not worth arguing. Don't forget the Mutual to-night, if I get away first. I hear that Mr. Smith's paper will be most interesting."

The thing had to be done. Mr. Podmore plunged.

"I sha'n't be able to come to the Mutual to-night," he said. "The governor's ordered me to entertain the young lady who has just gone out—Miss Gray. She's up from Manchester on business, and has no friends in London."

There was a moment's silence.

"Do you mean the young lady who was with you just now?" Miss Woodward asked.

Mr. Podmore signified that such was the case.

"Jenkins should have looked after her," he explained, "but he's away—gone to Leeds on a special trip. You know, the governor always insists upon having customers of the firm entertained. I didn't volunteer. He simply pitched upon me because she'd been buying in my department."

"Couldn't you have told Mr. Bedells that you had an engagement for this evening?" Miss Woodward asked, severely.

"It would have been most unwise," he replied. "The governor doesn't like anyone even to hesitate when he suggests anything. There is the question of my salary pending, too."

Miss Woodward struck a key of her typewriter vigorously and recommenced her work. Mr. Podmore departed to enter up his order. To all outward appearance, the establishment of Messrs. Bedells, Clumber, and Company remained otherwise unaffected by the visit of the young lady buyer from Manchester.

Shortly after seven Podmore, who had walked from the nearest tube, and who was a little splashed about the feet, presented himself at No. 8, Eden Street, Bloomsbury. He was admitted by a neat little maid-servant, and confronted in the narrow passage by a spectacle at once alarming, miraculous, and beautiful. It was Miss Gray, in an evening dress of blue chiffon, with a broad band of blue satin around her waist, the end of which hung down almost to her feet. She was carrying a grey silk theatre coat, also lined with blue satin. Her neck and shoulders were bare, her hair was ornamented with a band of blue ribbon. She was wearing shoes and silk stockings of the same colour. Mr. Podmore had read of such costumes; he had even seen them in the lobbies of the theatres. But it had never occurred to him as a reasonable possibility that he might be brought into actual and personal association with the wearer of one.

The rain ran from his umbrella into a little pool upon the floor while he stood and gaped at this unexpected vision. Miss Gray, in the meantime, from her position underneath the swinging hall-lamp, was eyeing his costume with considerable surprise, not to say disfavour.

"I thought we agreed to dress?" she remarked, a little tartly. The significance of her speech dawned tardily upon him.

"I am sorry," he answered, humbly; "I haven't got a dress-coat. I didn't think you meant that."

Miss Gray was not only a good-natured girl, but she possessed a sense of humour. The dismay in the face of this fresh-coloured, gawky young man, so painfully conscious of his ill-cut frock-coat, grey trousers, and thick boots, appeased her irritation. Perhaps his obvious and almost worshipful admiration helped. She gave him her cloak to put on, which he did very clumsily. His eyes all the time were fixed upon her shoulders. There was an odd little perfume from her hair and clothes which disturbed him.

"I suppose you kept your cab?" she asked.

"I walked from the tube," he replied. "I have an umbrella."

"Whistle for a taxi," she ordered the maid-servant. "My dear young man," she continued, a little irritably, raising her skirt a few inches, "you don't suppose I could walk to the tube in these shoes, do you?"

Mr. Podmore might with justice have reminded her that he had not, previous to his coming, seen her shoes, or any others like them; but he imagined silence to be more discreet. A taxicab was brought, and he held his umbrella over her whilst she crossed the pavement. She manipulated her skirts in such fashion that there was not the slightest chance of their getting wet—and Mr. Podmore got a little pinker in the face.

"Where to, sir?" the chauffeur asked him.

"Trocadero," Podmore replied, with more confidence. Here, at least, he felt that he was on sure ground. He had sought advice upon the subject. Nevertheless, Miss Gray made a little grimace.

"Regular rendezvous for us poor people from the country," she remarked. "Is there anywhere else—?"

"I prefer the Savoy," she interrupted; "but perhaps the Trocadero to-night is more suitable."

Podmore was once more conscious of his attire, but from that moment her good-nature returned. She only laughed at him when he discovered, to his dismay, that he was the only one in the restaurant not in evening clothes. She helped him tactfully out of all the embarrassments of ordering the dinner. These, however, were scarcely over when a gorgeous person with a chain around his neck produced a volume bound in calf, which he tendered to Podmore.

"We've ordered," the latter apprised him.

"The wine, sir!" the man whispered, reproachfully.

Wine! Podmore took the volume and fingered it doubtfully. The man had deftly opened it at champagnes.

"Something quite dry, please," Miss Gray murmured.

But her request only left Podmore in a worse plight than ever. The man took pity upon him.

"Number seventy-eight is an excellent wine, sir," he whispered, confidentially. "Quite a lady's wine, too. You couldn't do better, I am sure."

"Bring that, then," Podmore ordered, closing the book with a sigh of relief.

"On ice, sir?"

"Just the same to me," Podmore declared, waving him away.

"On ice, certainly," the young lady directed.

Podmore looked around him with an expression almost of awe. Miss Gray, who was drawing off her gloves and who looked very superior, was more puzzled at her escort than ever.

"Do you mind my asking you a few questions?" she began, leaning a little forward.

"Not a bit," he replied.

"Sure you won't mind?"

"Go ahead and try," he begged.

"Have you ever taken a girl out to dine before?"

"Never," he answered, promptly. "I've taken Miss Woodward to tea at Lyons's once or twice."

"And who is Miss Woodward?"

"Senior typist at Bedells.'"

"A great friend?" Miss Gray asked, insinuatingly.

"I'm sort of half-engaged to her," he admitted, with a curious reluctance—"only half."

"Oh!"

Miss Gray was thoughtful for a moment.

"How do you manage when you're half-engaged?" she inquired.

He looked a little vague.

"Well, we go about together," he explained. "We go to the Mutual Benefit Society two evenings a week, and generally sit together at church."

Miss Gray bit her lip.

"Anything else?"

"Nothing, except that I suppose we should spend holiday times together," he went on, doubtfully. "You see, I haven't known her very long. We are both interested in the Mutual Benefit."

"Is she pretty?" she asked presently.

Mr. Podmore shook his head.

"Oh, no! She isn't a bit like you," he added, and his eyes and tone were very expressive indeed.

Miss Gray was pleased.

"So you think I'm nice-looking?"

"I think you're—you're wonderful!" he declared, marvelling for the first time at the poverty of the English language.

She changed the subject.

"You don't mind my going on asking questions? I'm afraid I am rather inquisitive."

"Not a bit," he assured her.

"How much do you get a week?"

"Two pounds eighteen," he replied, promptly. He was rather proud of it, and watched her a little anxiously to note the result of his admission. Miss Gray, however, turned up her nose.

"Two pounds eighteen, and manager of your department!" she exclaimed. "It isn't enough. Any commission?"

"No! I've been there since I was fourteen; started with three-and-six-pence," he wound up.

To him it seemed, as it always had done, a thrilling example of a brilliant and meteoric rise. Miss Gray, however, shook her head.

"Your firm is not given to generosity," she remarked. "Do you save any-thing?"

"Half my salary," he declared. "I haven't spent more than half for over ten years."

"Thinking of getting married soon?"

Mr. Podmore blushed. She was certainly a bold young lady. Neither Miss Woodward nor he, in their frequent conversations, had ever so much as mentioned the word.

"No!" he assured her, fervently.

The dinner which was presently served to them was like a dream of fairyland to him. A band played voluptuous music, he tasted champagne for the first time in his life, and it amused his companion to be kind. They went afterwards to a music-hall instead of the theatre, again on account of his costume, and Mr. Podmore saw things upon the stage which took his breath away. He had been brought up by a maiden aunt only recently deceased, and his surroundings since then had been such that it had never occurred to him to take advantage of his liberty. Hence his three hundred and forty-two pounds in the bank; hence, too, that tolerant interest which Miss Gray certainly took in him. After the performance she insisted upon supper—more fairy-like tables, illuminated only with rose-shaded lights, more music, more visions of other beautiful women with white necks and bare shoulders. He felt the influence of all these things, but his eyes seldom left his companion's face. After all, she found it quite an amusing evening.

"Remember," she enjoined him, as they entered the taxicab to drive homeward, "you're to charge up every penny you've spent to the firm. I'm their guest, you understand? Mr. Jenkins always did."

He suddenly hated Jenkins with a fierce and determined hatred. He was in a very bad way indeed.

"Very well," he said. "If I—if I buy a dress suit, will you come out with me next time you are in London?"

She laughed at the suppressed eagerness in his tone. "What would Miss Woodward say?" she murmured.

"I don't care," he answered. "I want you to come with me. Will you?"

"I think perhaps I may," she promised. "You really are quite nice, and it is such a relief to meet a young man who doesn't know everything."

They were side by side in the cab. Outside it was raining and the window-panes were blurred. She leaned a little towards him. His heart was beating like a sledge-hammer.

"If you like," she whispered softly, "you may give me just one kiss—here!"

She indicated the spot on her cheek with her forefinger. He sat quite still. Only his eyes glowed. She laughed mockingly.

"I shall have to show you how, I suppose. Give me your hand—no, the right hand. You put your arm gently around my waist like that, you take off your hat—that's right, throw it on the opposite seat. Now you lean over and you may kiss me once, quite gently, where I told you."

She turned her cheek towards him. Suddenly Mr. Podmore discovered himself. She felt herself held as though she were in a vice by a pair of exceedingly strong arms. Mr. Podmore kissed her not once but at least half-a-dozen times—and not at all on the spot to which he had been directed. When at last he let her go, she was breathless.

"Oh!" she gasped, and looked out of the window. She was also, for the first time during the evening, speechless.

Mr. Podmore was triumphant.

"I'd like to do it again!" he declared, daringly.

She turned slowly towards him. Her face was flushed and her eyes were twinkling.

"I wonder what Miss Woodward would say to that!" she murmured.

Mr. Podmore found out, for on the next evening he told her. She listened to his faithful narration of the whole evening's proceedings with grim disapproval. When, however, it came to the ride home—and she cross-examined him with such skill that there was very little which remained untold—her sallow cheeks were almost pink. Mr. Podmore, notwithstanding the remnants of his partiality, was forced to admit to himself that she looked spiteful.

"After that, Henry Podmore," she decided, tossing her head, "I prefer to go to the Mutual alone."

"I was afraid you'd feel like that," he confessed, with an immense sense of relief; "but I had to tell you."

"A common, over-dressed creature!" Miss Woodward continued. "Coming to London alone to buy things, indeed! A woman commercial traveller! Henry Podmore, I'm ashamed of you!"

"I won't listen to a word against her," he declared, hotly.

"Then you'd better go away or stop your ears," Miss Woodward retorted.

Mr. Podmore obeyed, and that episode of his life was closed.

Mr. Podmore bought his dress suit and made other additions to his wardrobe. He discontinued his subscription to the Mutual Benefit Society and visited several of the theatres mentioned by Miss Gray as being deserving of his notice. He sat in the gallery and strove conscientiously to cultivate a liking for what he saw. Sometimes he succeeded, at other times he failed. He really had a very correct taste, distorted a little by the cramped culture of his ill-directed self-education, undertaken for the most part hand in hand with Miss Woodward. He also read certain books recommended by Miss Gray, and in this direction he was even more successful. Novels up till now he had deliberately avoided, especially modern ones, and he was amazed at the quality and interest of what he read. He quickly went through her list and commenced on others. All the time he counted the days as they dragged by. Business was reported good in the north, and no orders by post had come in from the firm of Harrison and Peters, Limited. At any day she might appear.

One morning Jenkins came in. He had just returned from a journey, and he was a very important man indeed. He spent an hour or so with Podmore, looking at his orders and bustling about generally. The latter waited as long as he could, and then asked the question which had been trembling upon his lips for so long.

"Anything for Harrison and Peters?"

"Buyer's coming up this week," Jenkins replied, consulting his notebook—"Thursday or Friday morning, most likely. Remind me to be in the way. Likes plenty of attention that young woman does."

"We managed to do fairly well with her when she was here the time you were in Leeds," Podmore remarked, contriving somehow or other to keep his voice steady.

Mr. Jenkins nodded.

"They were wanting the stuff badly. By the by, did anyone take her out from here?"

"I did," Podmore replied.

Jenkins stared at him for a moment. Then he burst out laughing.

"Lord, what a joke!" he exclaimed. "Excuse me, Podmore, old chap, but it is funny, you know. Where did you take her? Did you try the Mutual Benefit, or was there a conversazione at the Y.M.C.A.?"

"If there had been," Podmore answered, "I should not have taken her there."

Mr. Jenkins once more gave himself up to a hearty appreciation of the joke. He was a big, dark man, with sallow cheeks, black eyes, of which he was particularly proud, a carefully-waxed moustache, and a bustling manner.

"By Jove, that`s funny, though!" he repeated. "Where did you take her to dine anyhow, Podmore, eh? To one of the select tea-rooms? I wonder she didn't tell me about it. It must have been dashed amusing!"

"Why?" Podmore asked, quietly.

Mr. Jenkins wiped his eyes.

"Don't ask silly questions," he replied, patting Podmore upon the shoulder in a patronizing fashion. "I must get her to tell me all about it when I take her out this time."

Podmore was silent because he had no words. A new terror oppressed his life. For four days Mr. Jenkins would be at home, and on any one of those four days Miss Gray might come. He was shaken with jealousy. Perhaps they had arranged it so! He found himself watching the door every time it opened. Friday was the last day. Mr. Jenkins strolled in about eleven o'clock, with a flower in his buttonhole and smoking a cigarette. It wasn't allowed, but when he was at home these odd days he gave himself the airs of a visitor. He looked about the warehouse with a slightly disappointed expression.

"Thought Miss Gray might have been here this morning," he said. "She knows I'll be away next week."

And Miss Gray walked in! She looked very neat and smart indeed in her blue serge suit and trim little toque ornamented with a single quill. She shook hands with Podmore very sweetly, but Jenkins seemed to have expanded. He seemed, indeed, to grow visibly larger and larger. He gave himself the airs of a principal, and while things were being fetched at his instigation for Miss Gray's approval he whispered to her aside. Miss Gray, however, proved herself to be at least kind-hearted. More than once she went out of her way to appeal to Mr. Podmore, asking his advice, consulting him as to the suitability of a certain article, and all the time, whenever she addressed him, laying a slight emphasis upon the "Mr." which Jenkins somewhat patronizingly and ostentatiously omitted.

"Now about this evening," the latter remarked, amiably, when at last the business was finished. "Lucky I'm free. What do you say to a little dinner at Romands and a couple of stalls at the Gaiety, eh?"

"Very kind of you," Miss Gray replied, promptly. "I think Mr. Podmore is going to take me out, though."

Podmore's heart gave a great leap. His agony was at an end. The long, stuffy room expanded to the dimensions of a palace, the fog outside was pierced by the glorious sunshine. Miss Gray was smiling towards him with gently upraised eyebrows, and Mr. Jenkins was looking from one to the other, half furious, half stupefied with amazement.

"It's very nice of you, indeed, to remember," Podmore declared, gratefully.

It wasn't much to say, but he looked the rest. Jenkins, however, like all big and conceited men, was slow of apprehension. After his first gasp he only laughed with confident scorn.

"Podmore!" he exclaimed. "Oh, I'll fix that up for you, Miss Gray! Don't you bother. I can quite understand. You gave him a sort of half-promise last time, I suppose. Look here, my dear fellow," he went on, turning to Podmore and laying his hand upon his shoulder, "Miss Gray and I are old friends, and, you'll forgive my saying it, but I'm more used to these little jaunts than you are. You won't mind standing down, I'm sure?"

"Mr. Podmore might not mind, but I certainly should," Miss Gray asserted, briskly. "I shall expect you at a quarter-past seven, same address, Mr. Podmore. Are you going to see me off the premises? Good-bye, Mr. Jenkins! See you in Manchester again soon, I suppose?"

Mr. Podmore did see her off the premises, although he scarcely knew how he walked down the stairs, and he was very punctual indeed at a quarter-past seven that evening. Miss Gray, who was a vision of loveliness in black net, with a black band of velvet in her hair, appeared to him more distinguished than any Princess Royal of England or fairyland or any other country. She welcomed him with a little exclamation of pleased surprise. Barber and general outfitter had laboured their best for him, and the dress suit most certainly did fit well.

"Well, I never!" she exclaimed, squeezing his fingers as he handed her into the taxi. "I always did say that there was nothing like evening dress for a gentleman. Such a compliment, too! You'll turn my head, Mr. Podmore."

"You've turned mine already," that young gentleman declared, with absolute sincerity.

An evening so auspiciously begun could scarcely fail to be successful. They dined remarkably well, and Podmore, inspired by the confidence given him by his new clothes, proved himself to be an attentive host and an excellent listener. After the theatre they went into a great restaurant and had a light supper whilst they listened to the music. Mr. Podmore was beatifically happy, and Miss Gray looked perfectly satisfied with her companion. They became very confidential.

"Do you know," she told him, firmly, "that you ought to be getting more salary? Two pounds eighteen isn't enough for anyone in your position."

"I've applied for a raise," Podmore told her. "It's under consideration. I think myself I ought to have more, but it's jolly slow work getting a rise indoors at our place. The governor always asks the same stereotyped question—'What results can you point to, Mr. Podmore, to justify me in this increase?' Of course, if you're on the road, you can point to a larger turnover, and then you're all right. In my position it's more difficult."

"I see," she remarked, understandingly. "You want to do something out of the way. Not sure that I couldn't help you. Would you trust me?"

He smiled at the futility of her question and squeezed her hand under the table.

"You buy all your trimmings at Offenbach, don't you?" she asked.

He was a little startled, but he answered her promptly.

"All of them."

"Bring me a list of the houses you are doing business with, and the prices you are paying, to-morrow, at one o'clock sharp, to Brown's, in Cludwell Alley. You can have lunch with me there, if you like. And listen— about that money of yours; don't you ever try to make a little more of it?"

"I never have tried," Podmore admitted.

She smiled at him just a trifle patronizingly. He really was very simple!

"Would you trust me with it for a few weeks?"

"With every halfpenny, ten times over," he assured her, emphatically.

"How much did you say there was?" she inquired.

"Three hundred and forty-two pounds," he replied.

"Draw out three hundred and forty pounds, and bring it with you to-morrow in bank-notes," she directed. "If what I'm thinking of doesn't come off, you must put it back again and wait for another opportunity. It can't do any harm, anyway."

"It's awfully good of you," he declared. "I'll bring it."

"And now," she concluded, rising regretfully to her feet, "we must really go home. I've never been out so late from my rooms before, and I've a reputation to keep up. Come along."

"You haven't missed Mr. Jenkins?" he asked, as soon as they were in the cab. "Please say you haven't."

She drew off her glove and gave him her hand—such a tiny, soft, warm little hand. Very timidly he put his other arm around her waist.

"I'm afraid of you," she declared, smiling at him. "Can't help thinking of last time! You were bold, you know! Supposing anyone were to see! Stupid! Do mind my hair!"

Mr. Podmore walked home up the staircase which leads into Paradise.

Miss Woodward looked at the list doubtfully.

"You want me to copy this?" she asked, in surprise.

"If you please," Mr. Podmore replied. "I want it for a special purpose."

Miss Woodward studied the list for a few moments, and then glanced up at her late admirer covertly. He was looking very spruce and unusually masculine. Something had certainly changed him. Besides, she was very sure that he was not wearing that bunch of violets for nothing.

"What have you done to Mr. Jenkins?" she inquired.

"Nothing particular," he answered, airily.

"Is it true that you took that young woman from Manchester out to dinner and the theatre last night?"

"Quite true," Podmore assented. "Enjoyed myself immensely."

Miss Woodward turned her left shoulder upon him. Her expression was not at all amicable.

"I suppose," she said, acidly, "that you are beginning to prefer the theatre to the Mutual?"

"I am quite sure I do," he admitted. "The Mutual's all very well in its way, but it's a terrible grind going there all the time. The theatre's much more amusing, and there's no harm in any of the plays I've seen."

"That depends!" Miss Woodward snapped, and surreptitiously slipped a carbon and sheet of paper into the machine.

Mr. Podmore was busy for the next hour or so. Miss Woodward handed him his list a few minutes before one, and immediately his back was turned sent for the under-manager of his department. After a good deal of whispering they entered, with some trepidation, the private office of Mr. Bedells.

When Podmore returned from luncheon, flushed but happy, he was at once summoned to that sanctum. On the table before Mr. Bedells was a copy of the Offenbach list. Mr. Bedells greeted him solemnly.

"I sent for you, Mr. Podmore," he began, "to ask you to clear up a little matter which, on the face of it, certainly seems—er—er—to require some explanation. This list!"

He handed it to Podmore, and Podmore knew at once that he was in deep waters.

"That is a carbon copy of a list which I asked Miss Woodward to type for me this morning, sir," he said.

"Precisely! With what object?" Mr. Bedells asked, dryly.

"It was for the good of the firm, sir," Podmore replied, feeling unexpectedly calm.

Mr. Bedells looked at him over his spectacles.

"There must be no misunderstanding about this matter," he declared. "With whom have you been lunching to-day, Podmore?"

"With Miss Gray, sir."

"Precisely! May I ask if you are aware, Podmore, that there is a persistent rumour in trade circles that Miss Gray's firm—Harrison and Peters, Limited—are going to open a branch for the purchase of trimmings and findings generally, instead of procuring those articles from us?"

Podmore felt suddenly cold. He stared at his employer in blank despair. It was too terrible, this! It was unbelievable!

"I had not heard the rumour, sir," he replied, "and I do not believe it."

Mr. Bedells sat down at his table and wrote out a cheque.

"I shall ask you to leave these premises at once, Mr. Podmore," he said, handing it to him. "You have betrayed the confidence which the firm has reposed in you. After all these years, I am sorry. You have probably been made a fool of by a designing and dishonest young woman—"

"It's a lie, sir!" Podmore interrupted.

Mr. Bedells shrugged his shoulders and pointed to the door.

"After that, Mr. Podmore," he declared, "our discussion is at an end."

Podmore took up his hat.

"I repeat, sir, that it is a lie!" he said, firmly, and left the room.

Mr. Podmore entered upon an exceedingly hard time. He had drawn out his money to the last penny, and when he had paid his bills he had only a few shillings left. He started out, however, in search of employment confidently. There seemed very little trouble about getting a berth until the question of references cropped up. There, however, Bedells, Clumber, and Company were adamant. Mr. Podmore had been dismissed for divulging trade secrets to a competitor. That was all they had to say about Mr. Podmore, but it was quite enough. In three weeks the dress suit was in the pawnshop. In six weeks its late owner had known what it was to sleep out of doors, and had felt a sensation at his stomach which was unlike anything he had ever experienced before.

Then he wrote to Miss Gray, as casually as possible, and added a postscript that if it was possible to get at twenty pounds of his money he could make very good use of it in a little scheme he had on. He said nothing about his dismissal, nor did he happen to mention that he paid for the stamp on the letter out of a threepenny bit earned by carrying a bag from Cannon Street Station to Moorgate. He had given up his lodgings, after getting three weeks into debt, but he was on friendly terms with his late landlady and he was able to have his letters sent there.

No reply came from Miss Gray, and for the first time in his moments of hunger and despair some faint doubts assailed him. One day he met Jenkins outside Cannon Street Station.

"Halloa, Podmore!" he exclaimed, looking him up and down.

"Halloa, Jenkins!" Podmore replied, thrusting his hands into his trousers pockets and pretending to whistle.

"Bad job about that young woman you were sweet upon," Jenkins remarked, with an unpleasant grin.

"About what young woman?" Podmore asked, fiercely.

Jenkins shrugged his shoulders brutally.

"Hit as hard as that, were you?" he jeered. "Well, I'm sorry for you. She's run away with someone. Gone on to the Continent and left no address."

"If Miss Gray is on the Continent," Podmore declared, "she probably had excellent reasons for going. In any case, I do not care to discuss her with you, Jenkins."

"Just as you like," the other replied. "What the dickens are you up to, hanging about here, Podmore?" he went on. "You look as though you were touting for a job."

"I am waiting for a friend."

Mr. Jenkins thrust his hand into his trousers pocket. "If a bob or two—" he began.

But Podmore had walked away.

The days passed, but no word came from Miss Gray. His letter remained unanswered. Podmore had the most aggressive ill-luck. If he could have given a clear explanation of his dismissal there were several who would have given him a job out of pity, but on this point he remained obstinate. The pawnshop now held all his effects except the one suit he stood up in, and that, for all his care, showed signs of his desperate straits. He was thinner, too, and weaker, so much so that when he set down a bag which he had carried for twopence from Ludgate Circus to St. Paul's Churchyard he leaned against the wall, gasping. There was a small restaurant opposite, if only he could reach it. He made an effort and ran into Miss Gray. She stopped short and her pretty mouth remained for a moment wide open. Her eyes grew larger and larger.

"Mr. Podmore!" she gasped.

He suddenly remembered and half turned away. His collar he had discarded when it was no longer clean, and there was an awful hole in his boot. Miss Gray looked around her and spotted the restaurant.

"Come along," she ordered sharply, though the tears were in her eyes. "Don't stand there staring at me. I'm just up from Manchester and I want my lunch."

It was only eleven o'clock, but he was too far gone to notice. The restaurant was deserted, but Miss Gray had a manner as well as a tongue, and they were eating something within a few minutes. She poured out the burgundy herself and watched him drink it in doses. She would have cut up his food for him, too, but he laughed off his momentary weakness. She waited until she saw the colour in his cheeks before she let him say a word.

"Got your letter last night," she began. "Sent you a telegram. You haven't had it, of course?"

He shook his head.

"Never mind," she went on. "Meeting you was a stroke of luck. Our little spec is over—paid out last week. I've got an account here. Three hundred and forty pounds you handed over—four hundred and fifteen pounds here."

She opened her satchel and counted out the notes upon the table.

"Might have been more if we'd had a bit of luck," she declared. "I hadn't time to explain it all to you, but we advanced the money on some machinery. Fellow paid us back the last day or we'd have cleared another hundred. Put the notes in your pocket."

She watched him stuff them away. Then she poured out another half-glass of burgundy and made him drink it.

"Now, then," she said, in a matter-of-fact tone, "out with your story. No good saying you haven't got one, because you must have. What's happened? I've got to know. I shall sit here until you've told me every word."

There was crisp and unalterable decision in her tone. Podmore hesitated only for a moment. Then he told her the truth—every word of it. When he had finished she was holding his hand. She was also suffering from a violent fit of coughing, which seemed to require the frequent use of her handkerchief.

"Very good," she said. "I understand everything. Now, then, do you feel half a man?"

"I feel a lion."

"Come along, then," she ordered. "I've paid the bill. This way."

He looked down at his clothes.

"Idiot!" she declared. "As if they mattered! You wait a bit."

She marched him straight into the private office of Mr. Bedells. Mr. Bedells was unfeignedly pleased to see Miss Gray, but he stared in astonishment at Podmore, whom at first he scarcely recognized.

"Mr. Podmore!"

"Mr. Podmore it is," Miss Gray admitted; "but he's under a promise not to open his lips till I give him permission, so don't you speak to him, if you please. I want a few words with you, Mr. Bedells."

"The more the better, my dear young lady," Mr. Bedells assured her.

"You dismissed Mr. Podmore for disclosing the firm's secrets?"

"A course in which I was perfectly justified," Mr. Bedells pointed out. "We were credibly informed that your firm thought of opening out a branch in our own line."

"Who told you that?" Miss Gray snapped.

"Mr. Jenkins, for one."

"Then Mr. Jenkins lied," the young lady answered, promptly.

Mr. Bedells began to look a little troubled.

"In any case," he insisted, "Mr. Podmore had no right to supply the information he did to anyone on earth."

Miss Gray nodded.

"Mr. Bedells," she said, "I am not an unreasonable person. There I am not at all sure that you are not right. Where you are all at sea is as regards the reason for my seeking that information. Mr. Jenkins told you a lie, and knows it. You'll kindly see that he never enters the doorways of Messrs. Harrison and Peters again. My uncle's firm has no idea whatever of interfering with your business. It's too small a thing to be worth our while. We'd sooner pay you your profit. Mr. Podmore's salary wasn't half what it ought to have been, and he explained that the difficulty was in doing something out of the way so as to force a rise upon you. Well, I thought I saw a chance of doing you people a good turn through him. I have a cousin in one of the factories at Offenbach. I sent your list out to him to have it brought right up to date. Here it is. Lots of information for you—new firms, new offers, keener prices. Make what use of it you like."

Mr. Bedells picked up the paper with some eagerness. He was quick enough to see that she had spoken the truth.

"The firm, my dear Miss Gray," he declared, "is very much your debtor. I have been for some time considering the question of sending a representative out to Offenbach."

"Mr. Podmore's debtor—not mine," the girl replied, sharply. "Now, if you're the man I think you are, shake hands with him and beg his pardon."

Mr. Bedells extended his hand without hesitation.

"Mr. Podmore," he said, "I think you will admit that from the point of view of commercial morality I was entirely justified in dismissing you. On the other hand, I am bound to confess that after your many years of faithful service I ought to have had more confidence in you."

"Entirely my fault, sir," Podmore admitted; "entirely."

Mr. Bedells coughed.

"As regards the future—" he began.

"No need to talk about that," Miss Gray interrupted, briskly. "Mr. Podmore is taking my place—buyer for Harrison and Peters, Limited. I came up to London to arrange it specially. I am thankful to say that we can give him two pounds a week more than you did."

"And what about you, then, young lady?" Mr. Bedells inquired.

She held out her hand to Podmore. She spoke firmly enough, but her voice had suddenly lost its businesslike ring. A very delicate flush of colour stole into her cheeks. Her eyes were quite soft. "I," she replied, "am going to marry Mr. Podmore!"

The Storming of Eve

Sir Austen Malcolm was sitting in the middle of the public seat, his legs crossed, his attention entirely engrossed by the small volume of poems which he held between his shapely and well-manicured fingers. He had the air, perhaps justifiable, of being perfectly satisfied with himself and his surroundings. He was dressed in all respects as a country gentleman of studious tastes should be. From the tips of his polished brown shoes to the slightly rakish angle of his Homburg hat, he was entirely satisfactory. His air of patronizing the seat upon which he had ensconced himself was also, perhaps, in order, as it was he who had presented it to the town.

At his feet—he was sitting on the summit of a considerable hill, crowned by a plantation of fir trees—was an old-world market town, a picturesque medley of grey-stone buildings, red-tiled, melodious, without a single modern discordancy. Beyond, yellow cornfields and green meadows rolled away in billowy undulations to a line of low hills fading into a blue mist. It was not a landscape to excite rapture, perhaps, but it was typical English country, serene, well-ordered, peaceful.

Up the hill, a little breathless, climbed Stephen Glask, a young man of somewhat pleasant appearance, humbly dressed as fitted his station, but carrying himself with a certain not unbecoming ease. After a moment's survey of the view he sank with a brief exclamation of content upon the other end of the seat occupied by Sir Austen Malcolm. There were other vacant seats not far away—and the baronet was obliged to uncross his knees. He turned and glanced at the newcomer. Sir Austen was, without doubt, as his appearance indicated, the great man of the neighborhood, but he was a reasonable person and his glance was not one of annoyance. It was not, however, altogether free from a certain mild surprise; he was accustomed to a great deal of respect from the townspeople. He was perhaps satisfied to observe that this intruder was a stranger to him.

"Quite a climb up here, isn't it?" the newcomer began, affably.

The voice was pleasant enough but its affability seemed to Sir Austen Malcolm a little uncalled-for. He answered without removing his eyes from the pages of his book.

"It is certainly a considerable ascent."

The young man very properly remained silent. The affair might reasonably have ended there. A slight liberty had been taken and a slight rebuke administered. Sir Austen should have gone on with his reading and the young man, after a few moments of uncomfortable reflection, should have passed on his way. As a matter of fact, however, things turned out differently. Sir Austen Malcolm, after a vain effort to return to his former train of thought, glanced a little irritably toward his interrupter. Entirely unabashed, the young man smiled blandly at him.

"Awfully good of you to give these seats," he remarked, in a conversational manner.

"You know who I am, then?" Sir Austen inquired, dryly.

The young man's eyes twinkled.

"Doesn't everyone in Faringdon know Sir Austen Malcolm by sight?" he answered.

"You have the advantage of me, sir," Sir Austen declared, with some slight emphasis on the last word.

"Naturally," the young man admitted briskly. "I have been here only a week or so and you have been up at Oxford most of that time, haven't you? My name is Stephen Glask. I bought old Johnson's iron-mongering business, you know. Bad egg, I am afraid, unless things alter."

Sir Austen dropped his eyeglass and polished it for a moment. It was quite absurd, of course, but he was conscious of a feeling of positive toleration toward this young man, for which he was entirely unable to account.

"Johnson, I am afraid, neglected his business sadly," he said. "He unfortunately developed bad habits toward the close of his career."

"Drank a bit, you mean?" Stephen Glask remarked. "Poor old chap, I don't wonder at it. You all of you bought your things from the Stores, sent to London for your cartridges, and got your petrol from Swindon. Glad I've met you, Sir Austen. I am a local man now and I want some of your trade, please."

Sir Austen stiffened a little.

"My chauffeur buys his own petrol," he said, "and my cartridges are specially filled for me by my gunmaker. As to domestic articles, my sister keeps house for me."

"I'll call in and see her," Stephen Glask declared, promptly.

Sir Austen opened his lips—and closed them again. Why should Eve be deprived of an encounter with this extraordinary young man? It would certainly amuse her. It might also be good for the young man! Sir Austen resumed his reading without remark. Mr. Stephen Glask, however, had not finished with him.

"Poor stuff, that," he pronounced, nodding his head toward the volume that his companion was perusing.

The latter stared at the young man, this time in real surprise.

"A poetaster," he remarked, with faint satire, "as well as a specialist in hardware?"

Mr. Stephen Glask was unabashed.

"I've read those verses, if that's what you mean," he answered, "and you'll think the same as I do of them when you've finished. There are a few pretty thoughts—the snowstorm in the cherry orchard, for instance—but most of the things are too florid, and the fellow hasn't a single original meter. It's the music of Swinburne and Keats to an inferior and uninspired setting—*vide* the *Athenaeum*."

"You find time to read the *Athenaeum?*" Sir Austen inquired slowly.

"And the *Ironmongers' Weekly Record*," Stephen Glask admitted, cheerfully. "I have a catholic taste in literature. Good afternoon, Sir Austen. I wish you'd speak to your chauffeur about the petrol. I'll call in and see your sister myself about the other things."

Mr. Stephen Glask strolled off, not by any means an unpleasant figure to watch although his blue serge suit was ready-made, his boots thick, and his cap shabby. He was certainly a most original young man and an exceedingly difficult one to put in his place. As he disappeared Sir Austen suddenly smiled; his eyes positively twinkled.

"I would give," he murmured to himself, "a great deal to be at home when he calls on Eve!"

Sir Austen returned to his very delightful home about an hour later. He passed up the beautifully kept avenue, lined with handsome shrubs and adorned with a wonderful border of scarlet geraniums, entered the long, white-stone house through some open French windows, looked in vain into one or two of the charmingly furnished rooms, and finally made his way out again into the garden. Attracted by the sound of voices, he crossed the tennis lawn and turned into the paddock. Here he came to a sudden and stupefied standstill. Eve, with her sleeves rolled up and a mashie in her hand, was obviously receiving a golf lesson from—Mr. Stephen Glask.

"Look out, Sir Austen," the latter exclaimed, pleasantly. "We're approaching onto the lawn there and you're just in the line."

Sir Austen stepped mechanically out of the way. He was too surprised to make any remark.

"Lucky thing I happened to call in just now," the man continued with satisfaction. "I chanced upon Miss Malcolm just as she was developing the very worst possible fault in golf. Now a little more over the ball, please," he went on, devoting his attention to his pupil. "Wrists quite stiff, and the heel of the club well on the ground. Learn this stroke and shorten your swing a little and you'll be a scratch player in a month. Now, then."

The young lady—she was exceedingly good-looking and much younger than her brother, of whom as yet she had scarcely taken any notice at all— gave herself up once more to her task. Her instructor, who greeted her efforts with only a moderate amount of approval, finally took the club from her hand and himself played a few masterly shots. Sir Austen, who was beginning to recover himself, joined them.

"Apparently," he said dryly, "you are a young man of many accomplishments."

"Oh, I like to understand something about the things I sell," Mr. Stephen Glask answered, carelessly. "We used to get through a lot of golf clubs at my last place. I am so glad to find there's some sort of a course here. I can get the agency for Minton's clubs—best irons in the world—and I shall order a mashie down purposely for Miss Malcolm, if she'll allow me."

"I should love you to!" the young lady exclaimed, eagerly. "You seem to know exactly what I want, Mr.—Mr.—"

"Glask—G-l-a-s-k," her visitor interrupted. "The name's being painted up today. And you won't forget the other things your promised to buy from me, Miss Malcolm?"

The girl smiled at him in a somewhat puzzled manner.

"Certainly not, Mr. Glask," she assured him, stiffening slightly. "I will speak to the housekeeper. I am sure—we are always most anxious to procure things locally when possible."

The butler opened the paddock gate and walked toward them. Like everything else associated with the Malcolms, he was a most correct and dignified appendage.

"Tea is served, miss," he announced.

They all turned together toward the house. The young man, who had lingered for a moment to pick up the golf balls, walked between them. His ready-made clothes and many other slight evidences of his station were there, but never in this world did any young man seem so unconscious of them. On their way out they had to pass the tea table. The young man was obviously hot with his exertions. Sir Austen glanced stealthily at his sister and found his sister stealthily watching him. Sir Austen coughed. The slight smile that had flickered for a moment at the corners of his lips vanished. He spoke with perfect gravity.

"You must let my sister give you a cup of tea after your exertions, Mr. Glask," he said.

"Yes, please do stop," she begged. "It is so hot this afternoon."

The young man accepted the suggestion without hesitation. Further, he accepted it quite naturally and as a matter of course. He sat in a wicker chair between the brother and sister and consumed bread and butter with an appetite that he took no pains to conceal.

"Rather skimped my luncheon today," he remarked. "I was busy opening some cases—a new sort of lamp, Miss Malcolm. I hope you'll let me show you when you come in. Do you mind if I have some more tea?"

Then, without any warning, the vicar's wife descended upon them. Mrs.

Randale was stout and middle-aged. Her complexion was florid, and she wore a *pince-nez* which seemed always balanced on the extreme tip of a rubicund nose. She greeted Austen Malcolm and his sister with the easy familiarity of old acquaintance. It was just about this time that a long dormant sense of humor in the latter leaped permanently into life.

"And who," the newcomer asked, smiling graciously, "is our young visitor? We see so few strangers in Faringdon."

"This is Mr. Glask—Mrs. Randale, our vicar's wife," Eve hastened to explain. "Mr. Glask cannot properly be termed a stranger. He has come to live in Faringdon."

Mrs. Randale's features exhibited the liveliest interest. She also seemed a trifle puzzled.

"To live here!" she exclaimed. "How delightful! But whose house have you taken, Mr. Glask? Curiously enough, the name seems familiar."

"Have you been in the town this morning, Mrs. Randale?" the young man asked.

"I—yes, I have been in the town," Mrs. Randale admitted.

"That's it, then," Stephen Glask declared, helping himself once more to bread and butter. "I bought old Johnson's ironmongery business, you know. You very likely saw them painting the name up."

Mrs. Randale was not used to shocks; neither had she any idea how to deal with situations. Consequently, she stared at this cheerful young man with her mouth open, and she looked neither agreeable nor a lady.

"Why, you're the new ironmonger!" she exclaimed.

The young man smiled genially.

"And I do hope," he begged, "that you are going to be kinder to me than you were to poor old Johnson. I may as well tell you at once that I shall expect your custom, Mrs. Randale. Miss Malcolm has promised me hers."

At this precise moment Sir Austen strolled away with a muttered excuse about fetching some matches. Eve always insisted, however, that she heard his chuckle as he went and loved him for it. Mrs. Randale was still unable to cope with the situation.

"I leave such matters with my husband, Mr.—er—Glask," she said. "By-the-bye," she added, as the thought struck her, "you are, of course, a member of the Church of England? I do not remember to have seen you in church."

"To tell you the truth," Stephen Glask explained, agreeably, "I haven't been anywhere yet. I've scarcely been in the place three weeks, you know. Mr. Wills, the Wesleyan minister, has just ordered a cooking range from me, so I did think of looking in there next Sunday night. I've got that order, though, so I don't know that I need bother. Call me Church of England if it makes any difference, Mrs. Randale. I am all for business."

Eve's face had temporarily disappeared behind the shelter of an illustrated paper that she had picked up from the lawn. She had met the young iron-monger's eye and there was something there that was certainly most out of place.

"I am afraid that I can make no promises, Mr. Glask," Mrs. Randale said, stiffly. "We deal with the members of our congregation so far as possible, but we prefer to believe that it is their religious impulses and not their self-interest which brings them to worship."

"Capital!" Stephen Glask declared. "Good sentence, that. You're quite right, Mrs. Randale. We'll leave my church-going alone for a time. It will pay you to patronize me, apart from that. I want you just to notice my prices, and the way I am going to cut oil—especially kitchen oil. I'll guarantee to save you two shillings a week before you know where you are. You'll excuse me now, Mrs. Malcolm, won't you? I must hurry along or there'll be no one to close the shop. Good afternoon, ladies!"

The young man took an easy and not ungraceful leave. Mrs. Randale stared after him blankly.

"Eve!" she exclaimed. "Why on earth—what on earth—your brother, too! Sir Austen—the most exclusive man I ever met! For goodness' sake, explain. Has Austen turned socialist?"

Eve was wiping her eyes. "I don't know," she murmured, weakly. "Austen found him on a seat on the hill. He tried to sell him petrol and cartridges and household things. Austen told him I kept house, so he called in here and stayed to give me a golf lesson."

Mrs. Randale became very severe indeed.

"My dear Eve," she said, firmly, "Austen ought to be ashamed of himself. No wonder the lower orders forget themselves! Austen, too, of all men; the most punctilious, the most aristocratic person. He ought to be ashamed of himself."

"He is good-looking, though, isn't he?" Eve faltered, still wiping her eyes.
"Who? Austen?"
"No, the ironmonger!"

Stephen Glask pushed his assistant out of the way. He had seen the pony cart stop outside and he was behind the counter ready to greet Eve when she entered.

"Good morning, Miss Malcolm!" he exclaimed, heartily. "I am glad to see you. I thought you'd be coming in one morning this week, somehow."

Eve looked at him steadfastly. She wore a fresh white linen dress, a charming straw hat wreathed with flowers, and white buckskin driving gloves. Her shoes and stockings were, as usual, perfection. She looked exactly what she was—a thoroughbred young Englishwoman with an un-usual knack for wearing her clothes; clean, a trifle spoilt, a trifle supercilious.

The young man behind the counter was wearing the same ready-made suit of clothes, his hair was tumbled, for he had been in the cellars, and there was a smut upon his cheek. She fully meant, when she came in, that he should be abashed, and she was a young woman of resolution. Nevertheless, although she looked at him for several seconds with uplifted eyebrows, she failed. He returned her gaze with bland and pleasant interest. She turned away, biting her lips.

"I want some kitchen lamps," she said, "a saucepan, if you have the sort we use, and a few other oddments. I should like, too, to compare your prices for oil."

For a quarter of an hour Eve was overwhelmed with the sheer flood of eloquence. At last the young man paused for lack of breath. His assistant, a son of his predecessor, was listening, rapt in admiration.

"I seem to have bought a lot of things," Eve remarked.

"You have bought just what you wanted, and you have given no more for anything than you would have done at the Stores," the young man replied, with conviction. "Don't you bother any more. I'll see that you get the things all right. And you shall have the full cash discount if I get the money within a month."

"I pay all the household bills on Monday mornings," Eve explained.

"Quite satisfactory," Stephen Glask declared. "Going to the cricket match tomorrow, Miss Malcolm?"

She looked at him in precisely the manner in which she was accustomed to look at Simpkins, the grocer—only it didn't seem to produce in the least the same effect.

"I always go to the cricket matches," she answered, coldly.

The young man nodded.

"They've asked me to play," he remarked.

"Are you any good?" she inquired, a little eagerly.

He smiled at her confidently. "I am fairly useful," he replied. "I very nearly went in for being a pro.'"

She abandoned for a moment the attitude she had thought well to assume.

"Then do play," she begged. "We want to beat Fairford. They are horribly stuck up about their cricket, and the two Sinclairs always play for them."

"What, Charlie Sinclair?" the young ironmonger asked. "The one who played for Hampshire?"

Eve stiffened again. "It is Lord Riverstone's second son," she answered, "who always gets the runs."

"We'll see about that," Stephen Glask declared. "Supposing I promise you that for every run he gets, I get a dozen—"

"Well?"

He looked steadily into her eyes. Eve felt her cheeks burn, and snatched up her gloves from the counter.

"Good afternoon, Mr. Glask," she said. "Please see that the things are delivered today."

"And thanks ever so much for the order, Miss Malcolm," the young man replied, briskly. "Hope I'll see you again soon. If I play in the cricket match, I promise you I'll do my best."

Eve and her brother exchanged stealthy glances—then they laughed. Sir Austen seldom laughed. Just now he was laughing long and heartily. The young ironmonger had bowled Sinclair with the last ball of his first over, and though he had asked to be taken off almost immediately afterward, he had gone in first for Faringdon and had carried his bat for a faultless century. He was now walking around the ground with Evelyn Randale, the vicar's daughter, and it was evidently no fault of hers that they were on their way toward the pavilion.

"I don't know what we shall do with your young ironmonger," Sir Austen declared. "I expect we shall end by asking him to dinner."

"My young ironmonger, indeed!" Eve retorted, indignantly. "I like that! Who found him first, I wonder, and sent him to the house?"

"I never told him to give you golf lessons," Sir Austen protested. "I simply sent him to acquaint you with the price of oil."

"He's sold me more than we can use for three months," Eve murmured, weakly. "Told me the price was certain to go up."

Once more their eyes met and once more they laughed. Then Stephen Glask strolled up to them.

"I kept my word, you see, Miss Malcolm," he remarked.

"I noticed it," she admitted. "Why didn't you go on bowling?"

"All rabbits except Sinclair," he explained easily. "You see, as I told you, I nearly became a cricket pro' instead of an ironmonger. By-the-bye, there's a matter about one of those safety lamps, Miss Malcolm, I should like to explain to you. It's a question of wick."

Sir Austen turned away. His sister hesitated for a moment, but finally remained.

"A question of wick," she repeated demurely.

He looked at her with a smile that she was beginning to find delightful.

"After all, need we bother about that?" he begged. "I am a privileged person for this one afternoon. Even Mrs. Randale has shaken hands with me! Couldn't we sit down for a little time over there?"

She glanced toward the seat. It was in a shady spot and had an air of seclusion about it. Really, the whole thing was too absurd! Lady Riverstone was watching, and Austen, and—

"Oh, I suppose so," she answered, "if you want to. I don't know that any-thing matters much."

Austen Malcolm and his sister dined *tête-à-tête* that night. Dinner was a meal served at Faringdon House with some formality. The round table, small though it was, glittered with fruit and flowers and glass. Eve wore always a low-necked dress, and her brother seldom descended to the in-formality of a dinner jacket. The butler was assisted by a footman and the trimmest of parlor-maids. Nothing was scamped or done hurriedly. The Malcolms, a country family of real antiquity, believed in themselves and in the things they represented. Even Austen, with his fellowship at Oxford, his long and leisurely travels across the world, believed in Faringdon House and the things that it represented. No Malcolm had ever committed a real indiscretion.

Dinner was concluded with the service of coffee. The servants left the room. Through the open windows, brother and sister looked out over a gray-terraced front, across flower-bordered lawns, to a lake and wood be-yond. The night was warm and the moon was shining from behind the trees. Austen lit a cigarette and broke the silence that had been a little un-duly prolonged.

"With reference, my dear Eve," he began, looking fixedly at the end of the cigarette he had just lit, "to this young ironmonger. You will not mind discussing him with me for a moment or two?"

Sir Austen carefully avoided looking at his sister, but for all that he was somehow conscious of the deep flush that had stolen into her cheeks. She bent over her finger-bowl. Her eyes were very bright. She was perhaps an-gry.

"The fault, of course," he continued, "was entirely mine. I have been sometimes accused by my critics of being deficient in a sense of humor. The coming of this young man has justified me to myself. He really was ir-resistible. He criticized the volume of poems that I was reading and tried to secure my custom for petrol in the same breath. He put me in such a po-sition that I was compelled to offer him hospitality here, and a few moments later he was trying to sell crockery to Mrs. Randale—Mrs. Randale, of all persons! In all my life, Eve, I have never known anything so completely and absolutely humorous."

She suddenly looked up at him.

"But is it funny, after all?" she demanded. "Why is it funny? Why should we conclude, because he is a tradesman, that—that there is humor in being forced into recognizing him—for a time—as an equal? He talks as though his education were equal to ours—"

"And he has a price list of saucepans in his pocket," Sir Austen interrupted, "which he is perfectly willing to discuss with anyone likely to become a customer, at any moment."

Eve sighed. Her own lips were beginning to quiver.

"He certainly does seem interested in his business," she admitted.

"He is one of the overdeveloped products of our modern system of education," Sir Austen remarked, didactically. "He represents just a foretaste of the difficulties with which the next generation will have to grapple. I really think, for his own sake, it would be kinder—you understand me, I am sure, Eve—if we were to abandon, both of us, that, shall I say spirit of latitudinarianism, with which we have regarded this young man. To put the matter plainly, I think it would be better if he were kept in his place."

Eve was looking out of the window. Her face was expressionless.

"I have no doubt that you are right," she said, calmly.

"By-the-bye," Sir Austen continued, "Hensham is coming down tomorrow for the week-end. You will be glad to see him?"

"Of course," she answered. She flitted away into the gardens a few minutes later, and Sir Austen went to his study. She passed through the rose gardens to the laurel walk bordering the path which led to the hill, and at the end of it Stephen Glask was waiting.

She hesitated when she saw him and glanced half fearfully toward the house. He vaulted lightly over the iron railing, however, and she had no time to retreat. She looked at him for a moment. She was half fluttered, half frightened. She was frightened because she had come, frightened because she had wanted so much to come.

"Mr. Glask," she protested, "you mustn't come in here—you mustn't, really. If Austen were to see you, he would be terribly angry."

Stephen Glask looked puzzled.

"But why?" he asked. "I have been to your house before as his guest. Why should I not be here now? I want to talk to you. I have something to say—indeed I have something to say."

Once more she looked nervously behind. The figure of the young man stood out so boldly in the soft, clear twilight. He seemed to have no idea of concealment—he did not even lower his voice. There were two alternatives before her. One was to pick up her skirts, turn toward the house, and run; the other, to take that little turning to the left and walk with this rash intruder along the laurel-bordered walk. She hesitated; so once did her great namesake.

"Please come," he begged, suddenly lowering his voice. "Won't you?"

She forgot altogether that she was a Malcolm. She felt curiously weak— and she went. They passed down the sheltered walk, between the rose bushes and the drooping lilac blossoms. She was ashamed and frightened and happy. His attitude was not in the least correct. He was leaning over so that his lips almost touched her hair.

"I think," he said, softly, "that you are the sweetest thing that ever breathed."

His fingers were in hers.

"You mustn't!" she murmured. "Oh, please don't! I—I trusted you."

He released her at once.

"But I love you," he whispered. "Don't you know that?"

For a moment she was angry—angry with Fate, herself, and him.

"You must not talk like that," she declared. "You ought to know that you must not. It is wrong of you."

"Because I am an ironmonger?" he asked, with a slight twitching at the corners of his lips.

"Yes!" she answered, fiercely. "Because—oh!—how dare you be an iron-monger!"

He laughed outright. This time she was really angry. She slipped along a dark path and before he could pursue her she was on the lawn, the center of a little halo of light streaming out from the house. For more than an hour Stephen Glask remained lingering in the shadows. But Eve did not return.

Hensham arrived on the following evening and at dinner-time they talked about books. In his way he was a very important person, editor of a well-known review, and reader to a great firm of publishers.

"Enderby's the man my people are going for, just now," he remarked, as the little party of three lingered over their fruit and wine. "Of course, theirs is the commercial point of view, but I must say that for once I am with them. I find his novels the most interesting fiction of the day."

Sir Austen nodded approvingly.

"Enderby writes excellent English," he pronounced. "His stories, too, are wonderfully lifelike."

"That's because he is so thorough," Hensham continued, cracking a walnut. "A month or so ago we had a tremendous discussion on the effect of a sense of humor upon instinctive and hereditary snobbery. Enderby had a theory of his own and he was so keen upon it that he has buried himself somewhere in a small country town, turned himself into a tradesman— an ironmonger, I believe—to make experiments. That's going into the thing thoroughly, isn't it?"

There was a brief but very intense silence. The brother and sister sat looking at each other.

"Does Mr. Enderby—play cricket?" Eve asked, calmly.

"Rather," Hensham replied. "He played for the Varsity and for Middlesex. I really wonder in what part of the world he's hidden himself. We shall not hear a line from him till he turns up with his new novel."

Eve rose slowly from the table and made her way through the French windows and across the shadowed lawn to the laurel walk. At the end of it Stephen Glask was waiting. He stepped forward to meet her, eagerly.

"So you have come, after all!" he exclaimed. "I am to be forgiven, then?"

She gave him her fingers and smiled sweetly into his face.

"I have come to the conclusion," she said, "that it is snobbish to keep you out of sight because you are an ironmonger. You can come and sit down with my brother and his guest, and drink port with them. Then if you have anything to say, later on—well, he can listen."

Stephen Glask moved forward readily enough, but he was puzzled.

"I hope Sir Austen won't be rude to me," he ventured, with obviously affected uneasiness.

Eve drew a little closer to him.

"It depends," she replied, demurely, "upon the effect that his sense of humor may have upon his inherited and instinctive snobbery."

The Road to Liberty

The house was set in a cleft of the pine-covered hills, fashioned of mouldering white stone painted pink, struggling against its inborn ugliness and succeeding only because of the beauty of its setting—the orchard, pink and white with masses of cherry-blossom, in the background, the brown earth with its neatly-trained vines. Félice's window faced east, and as usual, when the sun came from behind the hill and lay across the faded carpet of her room, she rose with a yawn, sat up in bed for a moment or two, slipped softly out, and stood before the window.

It was always the same, what followed. She stood and looked for a while at that towering wall of stony, pine-hung mountain, at the blue-smocked men and women crouching in the vineyard, at the white church upon the hill, the orchard touched with snow, and the corner of a field of violets, bending a little with the morning breeze. And then she sighed. It was always the same.

Félice bathed and dressed, daintily and carefully, herself like some exquisite pink and white flower slowly opening her petals. She left her room— as bare almost it was as a nun's cell—spotlessly neat, with the breeze sweeping in through the wide-flung window, a breeze which brought a perfume of mimosa to mingle with the fainter odour of lavender which hung about the linen and the plain white muslin curtains of the little chamber.

She took her morning coffee, served by an apple-cheeked, sour-faced domestic, in a corner of the wooden balcony which had been built out from the one habitable living-room. The petals from a climbing rose-tree fell upon the coarse but spotless cloth, bees hummed around the drooping jasmine, the soft sunshine every moment grew warmer. Félice finished her breakfast, yawned, and dreamed for a time with her eyes lifted to the hills. Then she rose, shook out her neat white skirt, fetched a pink parasol, wandered for a little time in the garden and orchard, and then, turning her face southwards, went out to meet the adventure of her life.

She walked down the straight, cypress-bordered path—a mere cart-track across the brown-soiled vineyard—down a narrow lane until she reached the one spot which she never neared without some quickening of the blood. For Félice was nineteen years old, and beautiful, though no one but the glass had ever told her so. And this was the road to liberty, the main road to Toulon and Marseilles on one side, to Cannes and Monte Carlo on the other. She had told herself repeatedly that if ever freedom came to her it would come along this road. And because her worn-out invalid father had been a little more peevish and trying than ever on the night before, and because of other things, freedom seemed to her just now so specially desirable.

Her adventure came to her in a cloud of dust—a long, grey motor-car, with luggage strapped on behind, and two men. Unrecognizable though they were, she caught the flash of their curious eyes as they passed. Then she stepped back with a little gesture of dismay. A cloud of dust enveloped her. She bent her pink sunshade to protect herself; she was disposed to be a little irritable. Then her heart suddenly commenced to beat fast. She had heard the grinding of brakes; quick footsteps were approaching along the road. Was this, perhaps, the adventure at last?

"Mademoiselle!"

She moved the parasol from before her face. She had self-control, and there was nothing in her gravely-inquiring eyes—beautiful, soft brown eyes they were—to indicate the turmoil within. Her first instinct was one of reassurance. It was a boy who addressed her, a boy of little more than her own age, bare-headed, not altogether at his ease. He spoke in halting French.

"Would mademoiselle be so good as to inform a traveller whether this is indeed the road to Cannes?"

Félice answered him with perfect gravity—in excellent English.

"There is but one road, monsieur, as you see, and it leads, without doubt, to Cannes," she told him.

The boy remained embarrassed, but he was very resolute.

"We thought it might be the right road," he admitted, "but, to tell you the truth, you looked so awfully jolly and all that sort of thing, you know, I couldn't help stopping. Don't be angry, please," he begged.

She lowered her parasol momentarily—he stooped anxiously to see if indeed it were to hide a smile. She said nothing.

"You speak English awfully well," he continued, "but you are French, aren't you?"

"I am French," she assented. "I have just returned from what you call a boarding-school in Brussels. We always spoke English there."

"And now?"

She motioned with her parasol.

"I live in the valley there," she told him. "It is—a little dull. That is why, I suppose, I permit myself to talk with you. My father is an invalid, who rises only for two hours a day, and there is no one else. But your automobile returns. You know the way to Cannes, and you must go."

The car had slipped slowly back in the reverse until it had stopped almost by their side. An older man was leaning back amongst the cushions, a man whose hair was turning grey at the temples and whose eyes were tired. He looked out upon the two with a faintly sardonic smile. The girl returned his gaze with frank curiosity, and his expression gradually changed. For all his cynicism, Maurice Londe had a soul for beauty. The girl, with her neatly-braided hair, her exquisitely undeveloped figure, her clear complexion, her large, soft eyes, her general air of sweet and spotless childhood, was immensely and irresistibly attractive.

"This is my friend—Londe," the boy said, with a wave of the hand. "My name's Arthur Maddison. I say, couldn't we persuade you to come just a little way with us? You don't seem to have much to do with yourself, and we'll bring you safely back."

Félice looked longingly along the road. She pointed to where it disappeared in the distance around a vineyard-covered hillside. To her that disappearance was allegorical.

"Farther than that," she sighed, "I have never been."

"Come with us to Cannes for lunch," the boy begged. "We'll bring you back. Do! It's only an hour's run."

She looked wistfully at the cushioned seats. The boy was already taking off his motor-coat.

"But—I have no hat," she protested.

"We'll buy you one," he laughed.

"I have no money!"

"It shall be our joint present," he persisted, holding out the coat. "Come. We'll take great care of you, and we'll have a splendid time. You shall hang the hat in your wardrobe to remind you of this little excursion."

She sat between them and the car started. To her it was like an enchanted journey. When they began to climb she held her breath with the wonder of it—the road winding its way to dizzy heights above; the vineyards like patchwork in the valley below; the mountains in the background, gigantic, snow-capped; Cannes, white and glistening with its mimosa-embosomed villas, in the far distance.

"Oh, but it is wonderful to travel like this!" she murmured. "What beautiful places you must see!... If you please!"

She withdrew her fingers quickly from beneath the rug. She seemed scarcely to notice the boy's clumsy attempts at flirtation. The light of worship was in her eyes as she looked towards the mountains. The boy felt the presence of something which he did not understand, and he began to sulk. Maurice Londe frowned slightly, and for the first time made some efforts at polite conversation. And so they reached Cannes.

They bought the hat, for which she let the boy pay, although the fact obviously discomposed her. She carefully chose the least expensive, although one of the prettiest in the shop. At the Casino the boy, whose further efforts at primitive flirtation had been gravely, almost wonderingly, repulsed, began to tire a little of his adventure. He spent much of his time paying visits to neighbouring tables, and made the acquaintance of a dazzling young person in yellow, from Paris, who kept him a good deal by her side. It was Maurice Londe, after all, who had to entertain their little guest.

Afterwards, when they had walked outside for some time upon the little quay and the boy failed to re-join them, Londe made some sort of apologies for his companion, to which she listened with a little shrug of the shoulders.

"So long as it does not weary you, monsieur," she said, softly, "I am content. I think that Mr. Arthur Maddison is rather a spoilt boy, is it not so?"

"Perhaps," his older friend admitted.

"Tell me some more, please, about the countries you have visited," she begged. "But one moment. Let us watch the people land from this little steamer."

"Trippers," Londe murmured, with a glance towards them. "An excursion from somewhere, I should think."

She clutched at his arm. A short, fat man, with bristling black hair and moustache, descended suddenly upon them. He addressed Félice with an avalanche of questions. Londe fell a few paces behind. When she re-joined him she was very pale, and there was something in her frightened eyes which touched him strangely.

"It is Monsieur Arleman," she faltered. "He is a *rentier*—a friend of my father's. It is he whom my father wishes me to marry."

Londe, a tired man of the world, thirty-eight years old, was suddenly conscious of a feeling of unexpected anger.

"Impossible!" he exclaimed. "Why, the little beast must be sixty at least."

She clung to his arm. He could feel the trembling of her fingers through his coat-sleeve.

"It is of him that I am afraid," she half whispered, half sobbed. "Oh, I am so afraid! Sometimes the thought—drives me mad. I cry to myself, I wring my hands. I felt like that this morning. That is what drove me down to the road. That is why I came when your friend asked me. That is why I would do anything in the world never to go back—never."

Londe drew a little breath. Her words seemed to ring in the sunlit air.

"But the thing is preposterous!" he exclaimed, indignantly.

"We are very, very poor," she continued, under her breath, "and Monsieur Arleman is rich. He has an hotel and much land. He has promised my father an annuity, and my father says that one must live."

Once more they drew close to the front of the Casino. In the distance they saw the boy with the young lady in yellow, on their way towards the shops. He was bending over her, and his air of devotion was unmistakable.

"He has forgotten all about me," Félice sighed. "I hope—there won't be any trouble, will there, about my getting back? Not that I mind much, after all."

She looked at Londe a little timidly. It seemed to him that he had grown younger, had passed somehow into a different world, with different stand-points, a different code. The things which had half automatically presented themselves to his brain were strangled before they were fully conceived.

"There shall be no trouble at all," he assured her. "I shall take you back myself now. Perhaps it is better."

They got into the waiting car and Londe gave the man his orders. Soon they were rushing back once more towards the hills, on the other side of which was her home.

"You are very silent," she murmured once.

He turned towards her.

"I was thinking about you," he replied; "you and your little pink and white house amongst the hills, and your father, and Monsieur Arleman. It is a queer little chapter of life, you know."

"To you," she sighed, "it must seem so very, very trivial. And yet, when I wake in the mornings and the thought comes to me of Monsieur Arleman, then life seems suddenly big and awful. I feel as though I must go all round, stretching out my hands, seeking some place in which to hide. I feel," she added, as her fingers sought his half fearfully and her voice dropped almost to a whisper, "that there isn't any way of escape in the whole world which I would not take."

Londe made no response. The appeal of her lowered voice, her wonderful eyes, seemed in vain. He was an adventurer, a hardened man of the world, whose life, when men spoke of it, they called evil; but his weak spot was discovered. He sat and thought steadily for the girl's sake, and at the end of it all he saw nothing.

"Perhaps," he suggested, "this Monsieur Arleman is not so bad when one knows him. If one is kind and generous—"

She looked at him reproachfully.

"Monsieur," she replied, "he is *bourgeois*, he drinks, he is old. His presence disgusts me."

Once more Londe was silent. The sheer futility of words oppressed him. They were climbing the hills now. The patchwork land was unwinding itself below. Only a few more turns, and they would be within sight of her home. Then, because he was a man who throughout his life had had his own way, and because there were limits to his endurance, he changed, for a moment, his tone.

"Little girl," he said, "if I were free I think that I should take you away, just as you are, in this car, on and on to some place at the end of the road. Would you rather have me for a husband than Monsieur Arleman?"

She said nothing, but she had begun to tremble. He felt the instinctive swaying of her body towards him. He laid his hand upon hers.

"It was wrong of me to ask you the question," he continued, "because, you see, I am not free. I have not seen my wife for years. I am not a reputable person. If you met with those who understood, they would pity that boy for his companion, and they would be right. They would tremble for you, and they would be right. So, Mlle. Félice, I cannot help you."

"You have helped me, and you will help me always," she whispered, her eyes filled with tears. "You will help me with what you have said—with the memory of to-day."

Then again there was silence. They were at the top of the hill now, and below them the sun-bathed landscape stretched like a carpet of many colours to the foot of those other hills. Her fingers tightened a little upon his.

"When you asked me that question—when you said that you would have married me yourself," she continued, hesitatingly, "does that mean that you could care just a little?"

Londe was only human. He leaned over, and she stole very quietly into his arms. She lay there for a moment quite passive. Then he kissed her lips once.

"I always prayed," she whispered, as he set her down at the corner of the lane, "that love might come like this."

Londe and his youthful companion went on to Monte Carlo, where for a week or so they had the usual reckless time. Then suddenly the former pulled up. He strode into the boy's sitting-room one morning, to find him red-eyed and weary, looking distastefully at his breakfast.

"Look, young fellow," he said, "I have had enough. So have you. Do you understand? I am going to take you back to England."

The boy stared at him.

"Are you mad?" he asked. "What's the use of going back to England in March, just when we are getting into the swing of things here, too?"

"The good of it for you is that you'll get back to your work," Londe answered, curtly. "How do you suppose you're going to pass your exams if you waste your time like this? What do you suppose you're going to do with your life if you commence at twenty years old to live the life of a profligate?"

Arthur Maddison set down the cup of coffee which he had been trying to drink and gazed at the speaker blankly.

"Well, I'm hanged!" he exclaimed. "What's come to you, Londe? Why, it was you who first of all suggested coming out here!"

"And I was a fool to do it," Londe retorted, coldly. "They were right, all of them, when they advised you not to come with me—right when they called me an adventurer. I don`t get much out of it. I have lived free and done you for a few hundreds. I've had enough of it. It's a disgusting life, anyway. Back we go to England to-day."

"You're mad!" the boy declared. "I am not going. I've got a dinner-party to-night."

"We go to-day," Londe repeated, firmly, "and don't you forget it."

"Do you think you're going to bully me?" the boy began.

"I don`t know what you call bullying," Londe replied, "but I shall wring your neck if you don't come. Your man has begun to pack already. I've got seats on the *Luxe* for three o'clock, and I've wired your mother."

The boy collapsed.

Londe left him at his mother's house in Grosvenor Square two days later, and drove the next day into the City. He called upon a firm of old-fashioned lawyers, and was at once received by the principal of the firm. The greeting, however, between the two men was mutually cold. The lawyer looked questioningly at his visitor's grey tweed suit and Homburg hat.

"We wrote you four days ago, Mr. Londe," he said, "to acquaint you with the news we had just received from America."

"My wife?"

"She has been dangerously ill," the lawyer replied. "The habits of her life, I regret to say, are unchanged. It is necessary that she remains under restraint."

"Is there any money left at all besides the four hundred pounds a year that goes to her?" Londe asked.

The lawyer sighed.

"It is always money," he said, grimly. "There is the Priory still."

"I won't sell it," Londe declared.

"Then there is nothing else worth mentioning."

"If you were to sell everything else that belongs to me," Londe inquired, "how should I stand?"

"You might have a thousand pounds."

"Then I'll take it," Londe declared. "I am going to emigrate."

For a moment the grim lines in the lawyer's face relaxed.

"As an old friend of your father, Mr. Londe," he said, "it would give me great pleasure if I thought you were tired of the life you are reputed to live."

"I am heartily sick of it," Londe assured him.

"Then I will do my best to straighten out your affairs," the lawyer promised. "It will take a month. Shall you remain in town?"

"I expect so," Londe answered. "You know my address. I will call here a month to-day."

Londe spent three restless weeks. The sight of the City was hateful to him. The clubs, where he was received coldly, the shadier resorts which he had been wont to patronize, were like nightmares to him. He turned his back suddenly upon them all, left London at two-twenty, and late in the afternoon of the following day arrived at Hyères. He took a room at the hotel and wandered restlessly into the Casino. There was a variety entertainment going on in the theatre, which he watched for half an hour with ever-increasing weariness. Then a juggler came on and began the tricks of his profession. Londe leaned forward. The girl who stood at the table, assisting him, had turned her face to the house. He watched her with a little start. Something in the shy grace of her movements, the queer, half-frightened smile, seemed to have let loose memories which were tugging at his heart-strings. He got up with a little exclamation and left the place. To divert himself he strolled down to the gambling saloon and threw his francs recklessly away at boule. Presently the audience streamed out for the interval. He made his way back again to the promenade and came to a sudden stand-still. Before him on a chair the girl was seated, looking a little wistfully at the people who passed. There were traces of make-up still about her face; her clothes were very simple. Then she saw Londe and gave a low cry. He came to a standstill before her, dumbfounded.

"It is you!" she murmured.

A hot flush stole over her face. As though instinctively, she glanced down at her skirt.

"You saw me just now?" she murmured.

He took a seat by her side. He was a little dazed.

"My child," he exclaimed, "what does it mean? It wasn't really you?"

She nodded. She was over her first fit of shyness now.

"The night I got home," she explained, "Monsieur Arleman came to the house. He had had too much to drink. He tried to kiss me. I—I think that I went mad. I ran out into the fields and I hid. That night I walked miles and miles and miles. I came to Hyères in the morning. There was an old servant here. I found her house. She was very poor, but she took me in. She lets lodgings to the people who come here to perform. This man was staying there, and the girl who travels with him was ill. On Monday I—I took her place. I earn a little. I have no money. I cannot be dependent upon Aline."

She looked at him with trembling lips. He patted her hand.

"My dear child," he said, "it—you did right, of course; but it is not a fit life for you."

She was suddenly graver and older.

"Will you tell me how in this world I am to live, then?" she asked.

He led her away to a table and ordered some coffee. The performance was over. She was sitting there only to listen to the music. He talked to her seriously for a time. There were no other relatives, not a friend in the world.

"Monsieur Arleman," she explained, "has been ill ever since that night, but he has sworn that he will find me. My father doesn't care. He has his coffee, his brandy, his *déjeuner*; he dines and reads—nothing else. He never cared. But, oh, I am terrified of Monsieur Arleman! Why do you look so gravely, Monsieur Londe?" she whispered, leaning across the table towards him. "Say that you are glad to see me, please!"

"I cannot quite tell you how glad," he said.

He was on the point of telling her that he had come back to Hyères only to catch a glimpse of her, but he held his peace.

"I only regret," he added, "that you should have had to take up work like this. There are other things."

"There is one thing only I can do," she cried. "Jean!"

She called to the violinist. He came across, bowing and smiling. She took the violin from his hand and commenced to play. Her eyes were half closed.

"They let me do this," she murmured. "Listen. I will play to you."

When she had finished many of the people had gathered around. Londe slipped a five-franc piece into the hand of the violinist.

"I see now, little girl," he said, "the way out. I am going back with you to your lodgings. I am going to talk to Aline. Afterwards we shall see."

She left him on the platform at the Gare du Nord three weeks later. She was placed with a highly respectable French family. She was a pupil at the Conservatoire, with her fees paid for two years and the remainder of Londe's thousand pounds in the bank. She took his hand and the tears came into her eyes.

"If only you had not to go!" she whispered, clinging to him. "You have been so good, so dear, and you won't even let me love you; you won't let me tell you that there isn't anything else in the world like even my thoughts of you."

He kissed her lightly on both cheeks.

"Little girl," he said, "it is well that you should love your guardian. Remember that I am old, and married, and a very impossible person. The little I have done for you is absolutely nothing compared with the many things I have done wrong or have left undone. Mind, I shall return some day soon to hear you play."

The train bore him back to London. He sat in his rooms that night and reviewed his position. His little income, such as it was, was gone now for good. He had twenty-four pounds left in the world. He went to see his lawyer the next morning.

"And when," the old gentleman asked, kindly, "do you start for Australia?"

Londe, when he had signed all the papers which were laid before him, held out his hand to the lawyer.

"Mr. Ronald," he said, "shake hands with me for the last time. When you have heard my news I am afraid you will have finished with me. I am not going to emigrate at all."

The lawyer's face fell.

"The fact is," Londe continued, "I have spent that thousand pounds you sent me in Paris."

"Spent it?" the lawyer gasped.

"I have either gambled with it or invested it," Londe sighed. "I can't tell which. That is on the knees of the gods. I have twenty pounds left, and I am off to the States —steerage—on Saturday. I am going to see my wife and find work out there, if I can."

"Gambled with it or invested it?" the lawyer repeated, puzzled.

Londe nodded. "Very likely," he said, "I shall never know which myself."

When, two years later, Londe found himself once more in Paris, a strange servant opened the door of the little French pension in the Rue de Castelmaine. She shook her head at Londe's inquiry. Mlle. Félice was certainly not amongst the inmates of the pension. Londe, bronzed with travel and hard though he was, felt a sudden pain at his heart. He pushed through into the little hall to meet Mme. Regnier, the proprietress. She held out her hands.

"But it is Monsieur Londe at last, then!" she cried. "Welcome back once more to Paris."

"Mlle. Félice?" he asked, eagerly.

Mme. Regnier became suddenly grave.

"Ah, that poor child!" she exclaimed. "She has gone. It is eleven months ago since she came into my little sitting-room one morning. 'Madame,' she said, 'I have finished with music. I have finished with Paris. It is of no use. Never will they make a musician of me. Herr Sveingeld has told me so himself. There are other things.' She left the next day."

"But do you know where she went?" Londe demanded.

Madame shook her head. "She left no word."

"But why on earth was that?"

Madame shrugged her shoulders.

"Mlle. Félice," she said, "was discreet always, and careful, if one can judge by appearances; but she was far, far too beautiful for Paris and to be alone. The men I have thrown almost from the doorsteps, monsieur, the men who would wait till she came out! For a week there was a motor-car always at the corner!"

Londe set his teeth firmly.

"Do you think," he asked, "that Mlle. Félice has found a lover, then?"

Mme. Regnier once more shrugged her shoulders.

"All I can say is," she pronounced, "that whilst she was here mademoiselle was, of all the young ladies I have ever known, the most discreet. Whether she has stolen away to escape, or the other thing, who can tell?"

Londe went to Herr Sveingeld. The old musician did not recognize him at first. Then he gripped him by the hand.

"I remember you perfectly, monsieur," he declared. "The little lady—she gave it up. She was clever enough, talented in a way, perhaps, but without genius. She worked hard, but there was little to be made of her. Unless they are of the best, there is no call for girls who play the violin, especially with her appearance. A public *début* would only have been a nuisance to her."

"Do you know where she has gone?" Londe demanded.

"I have no idea," Herr Sveingeld replied. Londe braced himself for the question he hated.

"Do you know anything of any admirers she may have had?"

Herr Sveingeld shook his head.

"Why should I?" he asked. "It is not my business. I think only of music. As for my pupils, they are free to come and go. They can do what they like. I am not the keeper of their morals. I am here to teach them music."

So Londe wandered back to his hotel. He spent three days in aimless inquiries leading nowhere. Then he took the train to the South. He stayed at an hotel in Hyères, and the next morning he hired a motor-car and drove over the mountains and along the straight, white road which led once more to the hills. He leaned over and touched the chauffeur's shoulder as they came nearer to the place where he had first caught a glimpse of the little pink sunshade. The car slackened speed. He looked around him. It was all very much the same. Then the car came almost to a standstill at a corner. They met a market-cart filled with huge baskets of violets, and on a seat by the side of the driver— Félice!

Londe left the car whilst it was still crawling along. He stood out in the road, and Félice looked down at him and gave a little cry. She set her feet upon the shafts and sprang lightly into the road. The only word that passed between them was a monosyllable, and yet a hope that was almost dead sprang up again in the man's heart. Félice was very plainly dressed in trim, white clothes, a large straw hat, and over her dress she wore a blue smock such as the peasants wore in the field. In her eyes was still the light of heaven.

"But tell me," he begged, "what does it mean? I went to Paris. No one could tell me what had become of you."

She laughed, the laughter of sheer happiness.

"Listen," she explained. "What was I to do? Half of the money was gone. There was no hope for me. I can play the violin like others—no better, no worse. And— don't laugh—but Paris was a terrible place for me. There were so many foolish people. They gave me so little peace, and it would always have been like that. And then one day I read an article in one of our reviews, and I had a sudden idea. There was three hundred pounds of your money left. I came back. My father had died. The little house and an acre or so of vineyard belonged to me. Well, I hired more. I am a market gardener. Behold!"

She pointed to the fields. Londe followed the sweep of her fingers. Everywhere was an air of cultivation. The vineyards were closely pruned. A wonderful field of violets stretched almost to the village. In the distance was the glitter of grass, rows of artichokes and peas, an orchard of peach trees in blossom.

"It is our business," she laughed; "yours and mine. See, I have no head for figures, but since I returned I have added four times to our capital. We keep books. I have a manager, very clever. I was going to look at a little piece of land which is for sale and leave these violets at the station. It is nothing. Walk with me here up home, and while they get *déjeuner* ready I will show you. Come this way. You must see the almond trees."

They passed across the field, where twenty or thirty blue-smocked peasants were at work. Félice stopped once or twice to speak to them. Finally they entered another gate and passed through an orchard, pink and white with blossom. The air seemed faint and sweet with a perfume almost exotic. The sunshine lay all around them. When they came out, she turned a little to her right and pointed to the road, straight and dazzlingly white—painted to where it disappeared over the hills.

"After all," she said, "it meant something to me—the road to liberty."

They were at the edge of the orchard. He took her hands firmly in his.

"Félice," he murmured, "it may mean so much to you, if you will, for I have come back—I am free—I am no longer a wanderer. I, too, have worked, and I have been fortunate. And the day when I commenced my new life—and the whole reason of it—was the day we travelled over that road together."

She came closer and closer to him, and her eyes were softer, and she seemed to him like the fairest thing on earth.

"I have prayed," she whispered, "oh, I have prayed all my days that you might return and bring back love with you—like this!"

A Lesson for Mr. Cutts

At twenty minutes past eight on a dark, pleasantly warm autumnal evening, Mr. Lionel Cutts sallied out into the streets of Norwich in search of adventures. His mind was pleasantly free from all sense of responsibility.

Mr. Cutts had glanced in at the boots' office to be sure that his sample-cases were in order, and a porter and barrow duly commanded for the following morning. He had written a full account to his employers of his doings in a neighboring town, had enclosed a very creditable sheet of orders, and the usual grumble as to the immoral competition indulged in by a rival firm—which competition, he managed to hint delicately, might have resulted in a serious loss of business but for his own personal popularity with his customers.

Mr. Cutts was fortified by the recent consumption of his favorite meal—a hearty meat tea—a repast of which he was secretly ashamed but to which he still clung; and he was conscious more than ever of that curious and most unaccountable thrill which nearly always stirred his pulses when he sallied out after his day's work into the gas-lit streets of some little known town. For Lionel Cutts, although an excellent commercial traveller, and a young man of regular habits and blameless life, was an exceedingly romantic person.

The direction which his wanderings took was in itself a proof of his eccentricity. He deliberately avoided the crowded main street. The moving-picture theatres, so far as he was concerned, displayed their flamboyant signs in vain. The huge advertisements of a world-famed circus left him unmoved. He wandered instead around the Cathedral Close, gazed up at the gloomy, ivy-covered houses, listened to the rustling of the wind in the elm trees, pursued for some distance the path which skirted the turbid river.

Mr. Cutts never could explain, even to himself, the satisfaction which he undoubtedly derived from such peregrinations. He only knew that he lost count of himself, felt imbued with a vague sense of superiority, was dimly conscious of the existence of many things in life which had nothing whatever to do with the admirable career of "Our Mr. Lionel Cutts," of the great firm of Merryweather, Jones & Co. And all the time there was the unexpressed, perhaps unrealized hope of an adventure—a hope utterly vague but sufficiently inspiring to lead him often to the silent places when the crowded streets, the hum of many voices and the popular music called loudly to his kind. A light in the window of a silent house, the strains of a violin from the door of some remote public-house, had all possessed their allurements for him. He had had many disappointments, some laughable, some humiliating, all commonplace. To-night was to be different!

It started, of course, with a girl. She passed him at the end of an empty street leading out from the Close, a slim-figured, graceful girl, with pale, impressive face and large, dark eyes, which swept him over modestly, yet not without some interest as she paused at the edge of the curbstone. It was a lonely spot—there was scarcely another soul in sight—and notwithstanding her undoubtedly refined appearance, her eyes had not been immediately withdrawn from his eager gaze. Lionel Cutts took his courage in both hands. He removed the cigarette from his mouth and lifted his tweed cap. These things were done with the best possible air.

"Can I be of any assistance, miss?" he inquired.

She looked at him, not angrily but with some surprise.

"Assistance?" she repeated, and from the first sound of her voice Lionel Cutts felt that his adventure had arrived.

"Thought you'd lost your way or something of that sort," he continued.

She actually smiled at him: a curious, apologetic little smile.

"To tell the truth," she confessed, moving a little nearer to him, "I have."

"May I try and put you right?" he begged. "I'm a stranger here myself, just strolling about for a bit, but I know a few of the streets."

"You don't live in the city, then?"

He shook his head. By this time, owing to his skillful manoeuvres they were walking side by side.

"Just passing through," he explained airily. "I am taking a little motor tour through the eastern counties—looking for a shoot for next year."

"How lovely," she murmured.

"What about yourself?" he inquired.

"Oh, I'm staying down there for a night or two with my father," she replied, motioning back with her head toward the Close. "My father is a clergyman on the other side of the country, and we are staying—with the Dean."

Lionel Cutts didn't know exactly what a dean was but he felt that it was something exceedingly superior. There was no doubt now about the adventure.

"Would you honor me by taking a little walk?" he asked.

She seemed dubious. The shadow of her ecclesiastical relative seemed to lean down over her.

"I don't think I dare," she murmured. "You see, I don't know you. Which way?"

"First turn to the left, round here," he replied promptly. "It leads right out into the country. Let's pretend we're old friends, been introduced by the bishop and all that sort of thing. My name's Montressor—Lionel Montressor."

She sighed.

"I can see that you are used to having your own way," she observed resignedly. "Mine is Hardcastle—Nancy Hardcastle. I came out for a few minutes because all the rooms were so hot. Now you must tell me about your motor tour and about your shooting. How lovely to have a shoot of your own."

He smiled in a superior sort of way.

"I'd rather hear about your father's parish," he replied.

They had a very pleasant walk and they exchanged many confidences of an interesting and personal nature. When they parted at the corner of the Close, the young lady became almost solemn.

"Mr. Montressor," she pleaded earnestly. "I want you to promise me, upon your word of honor, that you will forget this evening—that if we should ever meet again in society you will treat me as a stranger. I have never in my life done such a dreadful thing as this, but I won't regret it—if you will give me that promise."

He gave it, much impressed, and although she seemed at first terribly distressed by the condition which he imposed, she eventually paid—well way from the gas lamp. Lionel Cutts walked back to his hotel with his feet on air. He had spent a thoroughly satisfactory evening.

Their next meeting was not in society. It took place at about five minutes past nine on the following morning, when Lionel Cutts was personally assisting in the unloading of his sample-cases and their disposal inside the premises of Messrs. Hyde Brothers, drapers and haberdashers. Miss Hardcastle was standing behind the counter upon which he had just deposited, with some effort, his heaviest case. He looked at her, breathless, his mouth a little open, his healthy color deepening, perspiration not wholly born of his exertions standing out on his forehead. As usual in such a situation, the woman triumphed. She smiled at him sweetly.

"Out early, aren't you, Mr. Montressor?" she remarked. "Are you motoring far to-day?"

"How's the Dean?" he managed to stammer.

She leaned across the counter.

"Don't let's be sillies any longer," she said earnestly. "If you want to see Mr. Orton, the new buyer, he's just over there, through that door; and Mr. Creatrex, of Brown & Horris, is in the next department, waiting to get hold of him, with four truck-loads of samples. If you slip through that door you'll just get in first."

Mr. Cutts, notwithstanding his romantic disposition, was all for business. He was off like a shot and he beat the enterprising representative of Messrs. Brown & Horris by a short head. An hour later, on his way out after a most successful interview, he approached with some temerity the counter behind which Miss Hardcastle was standing.

"Will you please—" he began.

"Same time and place to-night," she interrupted, glancing over her shoulder, "and my name is Nancy Grey. Don't let them see you talking to me. It won't do you any good."

Lionel Cutts lifted his hat and left the place, somewhat cheered. He kept his appointment that night with a certain amount of trepidation, but he found Miss Grey a most delightful young woman.

"Idiotic, wasn't it!" she laughed, as they shook hands. "But I can't help it. Being in business all day, a girl does sort of get fed up with commonplace things, and I'm confessing right away that I like to make believe. I was making believe all last evening. It came just as natural as anything."

"Same here," he acknowledged heartily. "I can't keep off it. I don't care for the ordinary sort of amusements at all after my work's done. I like to wander off and make believe, too."

"Now isn't that queer!" she exclaimed, stopping short upon the pavement for a moment. "I never met any one else like it before. It's exactly what I do myself. I can't keep from it," she asserted impressively. "Last night I was pretending that I had been dining at the Palace and my car had broken down. I was looking for assistance when I met you, but I had to change things just a little because I suddenly remembered that I wasn't in evening dress."

"Seems to me we ought to hit it off together," he declared confidently. "What shall it be to-night—moving-picture or the theatre?"

"That's just what ordinary people would do," she objected.

"Anything you like to suggest," he remarked gallantly.

She reflected for a moment. Then her face lighted up.

"I know what!" she decided suddenly. "I'll take you to where I went this morning before breakfast. I saw something which has made me imagine things all day. I've made up nearly a dozen stories about it. We'll have to go by tram. Do you mind?"

"Not I!" he answered. "I don't care how far it is—the farther the better."

They traveled out of the city on the top of an electric car, and during the whole of the journey she never mentioned their destination. Arrived at the terminus, she led the way down what seemed to be a country lane in process of transition into an urban street. On either side were recently-built small villas of Garden City type, each standing in a little plot of garden. The pavement had only just been put down. The whole neighborhood, in the gloom of the evening, at any rate, was new and uninspiring. Many of the houses were empty—unfinished. Lionel Cutts stumbled against a pile of bricks. He relieved his feelings by an expression to which his companion remained politely deaf.

"You don't live down here, do you?" he asked her doubtfully.

"Not I," she replied; "only Father's a builder and this last house belongs to him. I came down on my bicycle early this morning with a note, and—well, wait just a moment."

They had reached the end of the street now—a street which terminated in the open fields—and she pushed open the gate of the house in front of which they had paused. They groped their way up a little gravel path to the stuccoed front of the little villa. There was no light shining from any of the windows. Only the outline of the building was dimly visible, rising out of a desert of immature garden. Beyond was the untouched country, a dark, uneven chaos, with a few trees close at hand standing up like black sentinels.

"Anyone living here?" the young man whispered.

She nodded.

"A retired colonel in the Army. He is Father's tenant. I came down with a note this morning about some alterations, but no one answered the bell, so I strolled round and just glanced in at the window—this side one here. Step softly on the grass border. Now have you some matches? Don't say you haven't, for goodness' sake! I quite forgot that it would be dark."

"I've got plenty of matches, all right," Lionel Cutts assured her, drawing a box from his pocket. "Suppose anyone sees us hanging around here, though."

"That's all right," she answered briskly. "I left the note in the letterbox this morning and I've come for an answer. Just strike a match and look in at the window. I want you to see it just as I did."

It was a dark night, but windless. The match, when once kindled, burned steadily. The young man held it close to the window and peered into a plainly-furnished but comfortable little dining-room. At first he could distinguish nothing except a white cloth on the table. By degrees, however, he saw the other things. The cloth was laid for a meal which had apparently been hastily abandoned. An empty decanter lay upon its side and across the tablecloth was a dark stream of red wine. A glass by the side of the vacant place was still half filled. There was a barely touched cutlet on the plate, and a napkin thrown in a heap on a vegetable dish. A chair lay on its side where the diner had been sitting. The cloth had been dragged a little askew, and, staring at them with eyes like pinpricks of fire, a tail lifted straight into the air, was a tortoise-shell cat. It was mewing loudly and scratching the floor.

"What do you make of that?" the girl whispered. "It's just as it was this morning."

"Some one's done a skiddoo in a hurry," Mr. Cutts observed, lighting another match. "I wonder," he added, his practical mind for a moment triumphing, "why that cat hasn't eaten the cutlet."

The cat's red tongue shot out as it moved slowly toward them. It was at this precise moment that fear entered into the souls of both Lionel Cutts and Nancy Grey. It came from some hidden source and for some unexplained reason, but it seized a sure hold of them.

The scene upon which the young man had glanced with the idlest curiosity, became suddenly invested with a dim and creeping horror. There was something around them, something near, which was terrifying. He struggled against it bravely but his throat became dry and his knees began to shake. Then his companion spoke to him.

"Looks odd, doesn't it?" she faltered. "It was just like that this morning. I've been making believe about it all day. One might fancy—almost anything."

"Almost anything," he echoed, lighting another match with trembling fingers. "Isn't there a servant or anyone in the house?"

"Got one coming to-morrow, he told Father," she replied. "He seemed rather proud of being able to do everything for himself just for a day or two—said he was an old campaigner. He must have gone away in a hurry. Don't let's stop any longer."

An immense relief seized upon the soul of Lionel Cutts at his companion's suggestion. Yet he remained for a moment motionless. Just inside the room, the blazing eyes of the cat seemed to grow larger and larger.

"Devil take that cat," he muttered.

"Let's go," the girl begged, tugging at his arm and utterly heedless of his lapse. "We'll make up stories about this on the way home."

But Lionel Cutts, although his knees shook, knew quite well that the moment for flight had passed.

"There may be—a real story," he answered. "That cat is crying for help. Let's look in the other down-stairs room."

She caught him convulsively by the arm.

"It's silly," she faltered, "but I don't want to. I'm afraid! I want to get away, back to the lights. I want to run."

"So do I, like the deuce!" he groaned. "But we can't do it. Come along."

He led the way fearfully but doggedly. On the other side of the front door was another room, corresponding in size with the one into which they had been looking. They stole up to it on tiptoe. Cutts struck a match, held it down for a moment until the flame burned clearly—then up. Its light was sufficient. They saw in.

The girl tried to shriek, but her voice broke piteously. As for her companion, a curious thing happened. The fear of a few seconds ago fell away from him. He found his brain working, his muscles tingling for action. How best to help? For help seemed sorely needed.

On his side near the middle of the room, bound hand and foot with cruel cords, lay an elderly gentleman. His face was ghastly white; the veins were standing out on his forehead; there were specks of blood on his lips. His eyes were protruding—their stare was almost like the stare of the dead.

A few feet away from him, a man was on his knees before a small safe. His arms were clasped on the top of his head; he was swaying backwards and forwards, muttering to himself—and he was as black as jet.

"It's the elephant-rider from the circus!" Miss Grey faltered.

The young man's plan of campaign was already fixed. He had tried the window and found it fast. Suddenly he rained a hurricane of blows upon the panes with his ash stick. He found a place free of broken glass, placed his hand firmly upon it, and with a skill acquired from practicing over counters in his spare moments, he vaulted into the room of tragedy.

"What's going on here?" he cried.

There was no reply. The man who lay upon the floor made weak but ineffectual efforts to expel the clumsily-fashioned gag from his mouth. The elephant-rider had risen, without undue haste, to his feet. He came slowly across the room. He walked with a curious noiselessness. The veneer of civilization acquired with his European clothes, seemed to have fallen away from him. There was a wildness about his eyes, a threat in his very silence, alike terrifying. Lionel Cutts was miserably conscious of an immense inferiority of size and muscle. He gripped his ash stick firmly but he felt like a pigmy defying a giant.

"What is the meaning of this?" he demanded, his voice weakening.

There was no answer. The elephant-rider leaned forward. Cutts struck at him fiercely, but though the blow fell upon his head, the African never winced. With a sudden movement he seized Cutts in his arms. The two swayed backwards and forwards in an uneven struggle. Peering at them through the dim light, the girl, who had followed her escort into the room, began to scream. The African's long fingers had closed upon the young man's throat. Very slowly he began to strangle him.

Cutts, almost from the first, was in desperate straits. He was in the hands of a man of twice his physical strength, a man, too, who seemed fired with a homicidal fury. Cutts felt the cruel fingers burning at his throat, the hideous choking, the beginning of darkness.

The girl rushed towards them. Suddenly she paused. The bound man upon the floor was trying to make her understand something. He was looking toward his pockets. She dropped on her knees by his side. When she stood up, for the first time in her life she held a revolver. She looked at it and felt for the trigger. The Colonel nodded eagerly.

Once more she hastened across the room.

Cutts had become limp now. The African held him in his arms—seemed about to dash him upon the floor. Her hand shook. There was a red fire dancing before her eyes. She dared not aim. She pressed the revolver suddenly against the body of the African and pulled the trigger desperately— once, twice, three times. Then she ran away, shrieking and wringing her hands.

The room was full of smoke, hideous with the cries of the wounded man. Cutts sat on the floor, leaning against the wall, slowly recovering his breath. His face was black and his eyes staring.

"My God!" he sobbed. "My God!"

It was the girl's turn now; and her courage, too, arrived at this hour of trial in the midst of their adventure. She first of all lighted a candle, and then, with a knife from the dining-room, she cut the cords from the bound man, held wine to his lips and passed it on to Lionel Cutts. All the time the elephant-rider lay groaning upon the floor, his breathing becoming faint. He had rolled at first from side to side. Now he was almost still.

"Do you think I have killed him?" the girl moaned.

"Mighty good job if you have!" the Colonel exclaimed. "Thank heavens for your pluck, little girl! The brute! He's kept me here for nearly twenty-four hours, waiting for me to give him the word to unlock that safe."

"What is it? Jewels?" Lionel Cutts asked, as he staggered to his feet.

The Colonel drew a long breath. Then he groped his way across the room and with shaking fingers adjusted the lock and opened the door of the safe. Upon the iron shelf was a small black image, and around its neck, hanging from a thread of gold wire, a single pearl.

"I brought it back from a temple in Central Africa," he explained. "They told me there'd be trouble but I never dreamed they'd reach me here."

They all looked at the image, which seemed to be fashioned of some jet-black metal. The body was the body of a woman, the face hideous yet fascinating.

"Some day I'll tell you the story," the Colonel promised. "Just at present I've had enough of the thing."

He closed up the safe.

"I think," Cutts remarked, picking up his hat, "that we'll be going."

The Colonel nodded.

"Can't talk to you to-night," he groaned. "Call at the police-station, will you, and tell them about this fellow. I'm going to lie down."

They stole out of the house. They held one another tightly all the way down the half-lighted road. The horror of the night seemed to have afflicted them with a sort of mental paralysis. They scarcely spoke.

They came out into the lights. He drew a great breath of relief. The rattle of the electric car sounded like music.

"We don't need to make-believe about to-night!" he muttered.

A month later, on the occasion of Lionel Cutts' next journey to Norwich, Miss Nancy Grey and he dined with Colonel Ransome at the Grand Hotel. They had all become normal again, but the horror of that night had left behind it a certain effect. It was a very pleasant dinner and the Colonel talked to them for some time of his wanderings in Africa and his many remarkable adventures there. Finally, towards the close of the evening, he touched upon the one subject which up till then they had managed to avoid.

"I've presented that idol to the British Museum," he said, "and I've sold the pearl. Deuced valuable it was, too! The first jeweler I showed it to gave me a thousand pounds for it. And now, you two young people," he went on. "I'd like to tell you both what I am going to do with that thousand pounds."

Miss Grey, who was really an exceedingly practical young woman, nodded with an air of keen interest.

"I've invested it, for the present," the Colonel continued, "and it's going to be handed over as a dowry to the first young lady of my acquaintance of whose matrimonial plans I approve. Don't happen to know of anyone, do you, Miss Nancy?"

She sat, for a moment, quite still. There was a shade of pink in her cheeks. Mr. Lionel Cutts coughed.

"We thought sometime next autumn, sir," he remarked. "I am to have a small share in the business then."

"Congratulate you both!" the Colonel declared heartily. "It's just the answer I was hoping for. The money's ready any time."

And Mr. Baggs Was Only Twenty-three!

Mr. Harry Baggs came to an abrupt standstill before the closed gate, watched the train disappearing along the side of the platform and swore. The ticket collector listened to him with interest.

"I could have caught that on my head," Mr. Baggs declared vehemently.

"More than you will do on your feet, anyway," the ticket collector retorted pleasantly. "Our business is to see you foolhardy young gents don't go risking your lives in that way."

Mr. Baggs stared hard at him. The ticket collector was a large and powerful man, clad in the uniform of authority. Mr. Baggs, though dapper, was inclined to be undersized. These facts may have weight with him as he turned slowly on his heel.

"You're too officious by half, my good fellow," he remarked. "I shall get the money for my ticket back and report you at the same time."

The official, who was having a slack time, shook at the knees in well-simulated terror. Mr. Baggs, after a somewhat heated colloquy with the clerk in the ticket-office, received back the money for his ticket and left the station. He had an evening to spare upon his hands, an immense capacity for adventure, four and nine-pence halfpenny and three-quarters of a packet of cigarettes in his pocket. London, with all its possibilities and all its limitations, lay stretched out before him. He strolled nonchalantly out of the station, hesitated for a few moments at the corner of the street, and finally crossed the road and entered a very attractive-looking motion-picture theater.

For the first few minutes after his arrival, Mr. Baggs gave himself up to an appreciation of the performance. Then the young woman by his side dropped her program, and Mr. Baggs, after one glance into her face as he restored it, found himself fully occupied in the task of establishing sociable relations with her.

"You'll excuse my taking notice of you, miss," he whispered during a temporary interval. "Not my custom at all. Seeing you there a little lonely, though, and being that way myself, I couldn't resist it."

His neighbor smiled down at him. She was taller than Baggs and she had an air with her which puzzled him.

"Haven't you a young lady?" she inquired.

Mr. Baggs coughed. The inquiry was a little direct but he was a truthful person.

"In a sort of way," he admitted airily. "There is a young lady down at Thornton Heath, I take out sometimes. I was going down there to-night but missed my train. But there's nothing definite," he went on hastily. "A man needs to look around well, nowadays, before he settles down."

His new friend smiled delightfully.

"You must be quite young, too," she remarked.

"I am twenty-three," Mr. Baggs confessed, straightening his tie. "How old might you be?"

"I am twenty-two."

"And your name?"

"My name is Ruth."

Mr. Baggs ventured to steal a sideway glance. More than ever he was impressed with something undefinable but mysterious in his neighbor's appearance. She was probably a lady's-maid, he decided.

"In service?" he inquired diffidently.

She hesitated.

"Well, I suppose so," she admitted.

Mr. Baggs promptly decided that his first surmise had been correct. Confidential lady's-maid beyond doubt. He had come to various other decisions, too, and when at last the young woman murmured something about its being time to go, he rose promptly.

"You'll let me see you home?" he begged.

"If it isn't troubling you," she assented. "I have a sister here somewhere, though."

Mr. Baggs was a little disappointed, but he made the best of it, the more so as he discovered, when the sister was introduced, that she too possessed that nameless air of distinction which he decided could be possessed by nothing less than a lady's-maid. Mr. Baggs, usually at no loss for light conversation and chaff, felt a little subdued as he stepped out on the broad pavement of the Buckingham Palace Road. The jovial invitation which as a rule rose readily enough to his lips, came with almost shamefaced diffidence.

"You young ladies care about a glass of wine, eh, or something?" he inquired. "We can find a quiet little place somewhere near."

They distinctly hesitated and he felt emboldened by Ruth's tone of regret.

"I am so sorry," she explained, "but really they are so strict with us at the house where we live. If you like, you can come in and have something with us when we get home."

"Very good of you, I'm sure, if it's allowed," Mr. Baggs acquiesced.

They walked a very short distance and paused before one of the largest houses in a very important square. Baggs politely held open the gate of the area while the two girls glanced a little nervously around.

"You come last," Ruth whispered, "and don't make any noise."

"Don't want to get you into any trouble," Mr. Baggs remarked gallantly. "If you'd rather—"

"Come along," Ruth ordered peremptorily.

They passed through the door, which Ruth opened by merely turning the handle, along a stone passage, past a kitchen in which Mr. Baggs was much impressed by the sight of a French chef in white linen clothes, and finally into a moderately sized sitting-room, in which an elderly woman was seated, reading a newspaper. She rose at once at their entrance, which Mr. Baggs thought was very kind of her.

"My dear—"

"Please, Mrs. Green," Ruth began breathlessly, "may we have just a little supper? And this is a great friend of ours whom we haven't met for a long time. Mr. Baggs—Mrs. Green, the housekeeper here. You don't mind, do you, Mrs. Green?"

Mrs. Green looked the picture of puzzled perplexity. Ruth, however, was hanging on to her arm.

"If I am in the way, ladies," Mr. Baggs insisted, "just a word to me's enough. I have brought you home safely, and that's reward enough for any man," he added, with a little bow, and a pleasing sense of having said the right thing.

"Be a dear, Greenie," Ruth's sister begged.

"We'll get the supper ourselves, if you like," Ruth added.

"I couldn't think of such a thing," Mrs. Green protested.

"A parlor-maid has been known to set a table before now," Ruth's sister declared flippantly. "However!"

Mrs. Green hurried out. Ruth produced a gold cigarette case, at which Mr. Baggs stared with bulging eyes.

"Have one?" she offered. "Oh! you are looking at my case," she added, in momentary embarrassment. "That belongs to my young lady. She doesn't mind how many of her things I use."

Baggs accepted the cigarette and an easy-chair. Ruth took off her hat and hung it up behind the door. Her sister, whose name it transpired was Christabel, followed her example. Mr. Baggs felt their eyes regarding him a little critically. Their heads drew together.

"More than you could do to find one at all," Ruth retorted, in answer to something which sounded like a whispered criticism from her sister. "I think he's a duck."

They drew their chairs up to the fire. Presently a neatly dressed little maid came in and laid the cloth. She stared so much at this obviously unexpected visitor that twice she nearly dropped the things which she was carrying. Mr. Baggs' interest was almost painfully divided between the conversation of his two hostesses and the extraordinary liberality of the feast which was being placed upon the table.

"Seem to treat you here like one of the family," he remarked, his eyes resting upon a jar of *pâté de foie gras.*

"Oh, we have what we like," Ruth assented airily.

"Both kind of family treasures, I suppose, eh?"

"I honestly don't think they could do without us," Christabel acknowledged.

"What might your master's name be, now?"

Ruth hesitated.

"The Earl of Cullerden," her sister replied. "No one ever sees anything of him, though. He is abroad or in the country most of the time."

"Any family?"

"One or two girls," Ruth told him, throwing herself back in her chair and lazily watching the preparation of the repast. "Quite enough to keep us busy."

"The old lady much of a tartar?"

They both laughed, as he thought, unreasonably.

"You'd think so if she were to find her way down here now!" Christabel observed.

"No chance of it, I hope?" Mr. Baggs asked uneasily.

"Not the slightest," they both assured him. "She is at a dinner-party, and bridge afterwards. Won't be home till twelve."

"You have to sit up and look after her, I suppose?" Mr. Baggs cunningly suggested, sure at last of ascertaining the truth as regards the position in the household of his inamorata.

"How clever of you to guess!" Ruth exclaimed, with a grimace. "Yes, I have to put the old thing to bed. Now if you're ready, Mr. Baggs, we'll have something to eat."

They all sat down. Mr. Baggs tasted many dainties to which he was unaccustomed, and waited upon his two companions, whom he entertained with a constant fire of small-talk.

"I tell you what, young ladies," he remarked, glancing around the table, "I've had one or two friends in service, and been entertained a few times, but I have never been anywhere where they treated the young ladies like this. Wine, too!"

"We always insist upon it," Christabel declared, "wherever we go."

"Tell us, Mr. Baggs," Ruth asked, "if it isn't a delicate question. Most of our friends, of course, are—in service, too, in a kind of way. What is your profession?"

Mr. Baggs coughed.

"Well," he said meditatively, "it's rather hard to give an exact name to my job. I'm a motor-engineer."

"How interesting!" Ruth murmured. "Are you in a good place now?"

Mr. Baggs leaned a little across the table. His cheeks were a little flushed, and his tie had risen above the protecting stud at the back of his collar.

"I am doing very nicely indeed," he announced impressively, "so nicely that if a young lady and I were to what you might call get on together, and both be willing, there wouldn't be any real reason why we should wait longer than, say, a couple of months at the outside, just to make a few little arrangements. Matrimony," Mr. Baggs went on, "isn't one of those things one should hurry about, but if you are lucky enough to drop across just what you're looking for—it isn't toothache, is it, miss?" he broke off.

Ruth's head had disappeared between her hands, and her shoulders were shaking. She looked up, however, a moment later. There were certainly tears in her eyes.

"Oh, Mr. Baggs, you are so funny!" she exclaimed. "I love the way you put things."

"There's no beating about the bush with me," he admitted.

"But what about the young lady down at Thornton Heath?" Ruth murmured coyly.

"That's neither here nor there," Mr. Baggs asserted, helping himself to the remainder of the wine, after having gallantly proffered the bottle to his companions. "She may have had hopes—a good many of 'em have had—and I'm not denying that in a sort of way I've been fond of her, but as I said before, I've not committed myself, and to tell you the honest truth," Mr. Baggs went on, "I am just at the present moment feeling exceedingly glad that I haven't. And here's to what I am hoping for," he concluded, finishing off his glass of wine.

There was a discreet tap at the door. Ruth hastened there and was engaged for a moment or two in a whispered conversation with the housekeeper. Presently she returned.

"I am so sorry, Mr. Baggs," she announced, with a little sigh, "but I think perhaps you had better go now. Mr. Henderson—that's the butler, you know—is expected in from his bridge club shortly, and he is very irritable about strangers."

Mr. Baggs rose regretfully to his feet.

"I quite understand," he said. "I'll be toddling."

He took up his hat and gloves and bamboo cane. Then he coughed. He was not, as a rule, backward in such suggestions, but Ruth's pleasantly outstretched hand was a little uncompromising. He advanced his arm gallantly toward her waist.

"You won't object? Just a—"

The young woman glided gracefully beyond his reach. She shook her head at him.

"Mr. Baggs," she sighed. "I was afraid, from the first moment I saw you, that you were a Lothario."

"A what?"

"A flirt," Ruth declared severely.

"Not at this present moment, I assure you," Mr. Baggs insisted. "There are times when a fellow feels inclined to play about a bit, and there are times," he added, summoning up his courage and approaching a little nearer, "when he is in deadly earnest. Now, if your sister would just—"

Ruth became unapproachable.

"You must wait a little, Mr. Baggs," she said softly, looking at him in a way which utterly completed his subjugation. "This is only our first meeting, you know."

"The second," Mr. Baggs pronounced, "is in your hands. There's a little kind of a hop," he went on diffidently, "every Tuesday night, quite select, although perhaps not what you may be accustomed to, but if you'd favor me with your company, you and your sister," he added, with a little bow, "—there's another young fellow as I know of would be very glad of the opportunity of doing the civil by her—and you and me might have a little more conversation, Miss Ruth."

"It sounds delightful," Ruth confessed.

"I shall call for you, then, to-morrow evening at eight-thirty sharp. Evening dress is optional," Mr. Baggs went on. "I wear it myself, but it is a matter of taste."

"We'll do our best," Ruth promised. "By-the-by, if you are a motor-engineer, haven't you a car? Couldn't you take us for a ride some time? The worst of service is that it's so confining."

Mr. Baggs tried to look delighted.

"Nothing would give me greater pleasure," he declared. "I'm rather full up, though, for the next few days. You wouldn't care for a spin quite early in the morning, would you?"

"We should love it," Ruth murmured.

"Half-past seven too early?"

"Not a second."

"Corner of the square at half-past seven to-morrow morning," Mr. Baggs arranged promptly. "We'll have a turn round, anyway. Good night, young ladies both, and many thanks for the delightful evening—and meal," Mr.

Baggs added, with a glance at the table.

"You won't forget to-morrow morning, Mr. Baggs?" Ruth asked, smiling.

"Not on your life!" was the prompt reply.

Mr. Baggs was not likely to forget the following morning.

"What the devil have you been doing to the car?" his new employer demanded, stepping back and examining it critically through his eyeglass.

"Car, my lord? Nothing at all, my lord," Baggs replied, with sinking heart.

"Where's all this mud come from, then?" Lord Robert inquired, pointing with his cane to the splashboard.

"Roads just been watered, my lord."

"Dash it all, it's only five minutes' spin from the garage! Sure you haven't been joy-riding, eh?"

"Certain, my lord. I took her out a little way through the Park to see what was wrong—one of the cylinders was missing. She's quite all right now, my lord."

Baggs' employer looked a little doubtful but said no more. He took the wheel and drove, to Baggs' secret horror, to the very house in the great square which had become for him a home of romance.

"Go and ring the bell," Lord Robert ordered, "and see if the young ladies are down."

Baggs obeyed with sinking heart. The door was opened by a stolid-looking young footman, however, and there were no signs of any women servants about.

"Your young ladies down?" Baggs inquired, in friendly fashion.

"Whom might you be inquiring for?" was the dignified reply.

"Lord Robert Matlaske," Baggs explained, with a jerk of the head. "Him in my car out there."

The footman condescended to glance outside.

"You can tell his lordship he may come in," he said. "The young ladies are in the morning room."

Baggs delivered his message and sat in agony in the car for a quarter of an hour. He became a little less perturbed when he reflected that the rooms which he had visited last night were chiefly at the back of the house. Lord Robert came out at last and Baggs gave a little jump as he heard what seemed to him to be a familiar voice in the hall.

"So sorry, Bobbie, but we had a lovely spin before breakfast this morning. You must try us again another time."

The young man came down the steps and took his place once more in the car. Baggs was uncertain whether he was standing on his head or his heels. Then, as they glided off, he remembered the extraordinary assimilation, which no doubt extended also to the voice, going on all the time between young ladies of position and their confidential hand-maidens.

"Gave me quite a turn, though," he admitted to himself a little later on.

"Take the car back and wait for orders, Baggs," his employer directed. "The young ladies can't come out this morning."

"Shall you be requiring me to-night, sir?" Baggs asked, with his heart in his mouth.

His lordship shook his head.

"No! You can tell Charles to bring me the electric round at seven o'-clock."

Baggs heaved a sigh of relief and spent most of the rest of the day indulging in pleasurable anticipations, which for once were entirely gratified. It was quite the proudest moment of his life when at a little before nine o'-clock he entered the long dancing hall of the Spinner Street Dancing Academy, with Ruth and her sister.

"There's nothing to speak of in the way of ceremony here," he explained to them confidentially, "but don't you dance with anyone you don't fancy the looks of. My pal will look after you, Miss Christabel, and you'll find me pretty hard to get rid of," he whispered to Ruth. "Here you are, Freddy," he called out to a young man who was approaching them a little sheepishly. "Want to introduce my pal, young ladies—Mr. Frederick Bolster—Miss Ruth and Miss Christabel, other name not signifying. Now Freddy, if you'll look after Miss Christabel a bit, we'll have a turn. You'll excuse Freddy not being in evening dress? He's at a shipping house in the city where they keep 'em pretty late. Here we go, then, Miss Ruth. You don't mind a hop, now and then? Seems to give a bit of life to the waltz, I always think."

"I adore it," Ruth assented. "Come on."

The evening was an immense success. Baggs was pestered with inquiries concerning his two friends, whose costume and looks met with universal approval, but he shook his head portentously in reply to all demands for an introduction.

"Young ladies out on the quiet," he confided. "Don't want to make any acquaintances except with Freddy and myself."

"And a little bit of all right they are!" Freddy remarked, mopping his brow. "Licks me when you picked 'em up, Harry. You do have the luck, and no mistake."

"It isn't altogether luck," Mr. Baggs pointed out. "It's just letting them see at once you know how to behave like a gentleman. Come on, old fellow; they'll be missing us."

The only blot on an otherwise perfect evening, so far as Mr. Baggs and his friend were concerned, was that their young lady companions insisted upon only one taxi for the return home, and begged them not to dismount for fear of causing jealousy in the servants' quarters. That they had enjoyed themselves, however, was beyond doubt. Ruth lay back in her corner and laughed till the tears came into her eyes, and her sister was almost light-hearted. Just as they were preparing to descend, Ruth leaned forward.

"You must promise me one thing," she insisted. "The old lady is letting us have a servants' ball on Thursday. You must both come, if you please, at ten o'clock."

"No fear of us forgetting that," Baggs declared heartily.

"Not likely!"

"Wouldn't you care," Ruth asked, glancing at Mr. Baggs with a queer little smile upon her lips, "to bring your young lady?"

"Thank you," Mr. Baggs replied boldly, although for a moment a pathetic little vision drifted before his eyes, "you're all the young lady I want!"

She slapped his hand and laughed once more.

"Don't be silly! I hope I am, but still, you do owe her a good turn, you know. There'll be heaps of young fellows here, and we're really short of girls. You give me her name and address and I'll send her a card."

"Mightn't be altogether pleasant for me," Mr. Baggs grumbled.

"Booby!" Ruth exclaimed derisively. "I'll take care of you."

Baggs handed her an envelope and she got out, waving her hand. The two young men watched the girls disappear.

"Dash it all. I feel like a prince!" Baggs declared, leaning back in his seat. "Savoy, chauffeur!"

"Don't be an ass!" Freddy protested. "You drive to the corner of the square and put us down there, driver. I know where we can get a quiet bite to eat, only a few yards away."

"Righto!" Mr. Baggs acquiesced sentimentally. "Seems a bit thick, I suppose, driving about in taxies, but when a chap's feeling like I am, Freddy—"

"Oh, chuck it!" his friend protested. "Do you happen to have noticed the color of Chris' eyes?"

A little later than the appointed hour on Thursday evening, Mr. Harry Baggs and Mr. Frederick Bolster, arm-in-arm, approached the house in Belgrave Square. They wore tweed caps and carried brown paper parcels, containing their dancing pumps, under their arms. As they reached the front door they stopped, a little aghast. The striped canvas awning was up, stretching from the front door to the edge of the curbstone. The area was dark and lifeless.

"Doing it slap up, for a servants' ball," Mr. Bolster remarked nervously.

"Thought a lot of in the family, Ruth is," Mr. Baggs replied, with an attempt at confidence. "Come on."

Each clutching his parcel, they strode up the druggeted way, past a policeman and several footmen. Their arrival was taken, apparently, quite as a matter of course, and a beneficent person in somber black indicated the way to the gentlemen's cloakroom. The sight of its contents inspired Mr. Baggs with a moment's irresolution. Everywhere were neat little mounds of black overcoats with silk linings, and either silk hats or opera hats.

"There aren't two dances on here, by any chance, are there?" he inquired a little anxiously.

The cloakroom attendant shook his head, and the major domo, who had followed them in, smiled reassuringly.

"It's quite all right, gentlemen," he said. "You are expected. This way, if you please."

Mr. Baggs took a final look at himself in the mirror and on the whole was satisfied. The little curl to the left of his parting was carefully arranged with becoming negligence. His white tie, which had only done duty once before, showed some tendency to depart from the exact center, but its peregrinations were atoned for by the fact that it displayed a collar stud which professed to have a small diamond in the center. Scarcely more than an inch of his lilac-bordered handkerchief was showing, and his white waistcoat, although unusually stiff, was in other respects a complete success. Nevertheless, when he stepped into the ballroom his confidence for a moment oozed away. He was conscious of a sudden inclination to retreat, and he felt a vigorous and sympathetic tug from Frederick at his coattails. Before he could speak, however, Ruth, who had been dancing, came suddenly up to him with the most charming of smiles.

"How dare you come so late, Mr. Baggs! Dance with me at once, please. My sister is looking for your friend. Come!"

Mr. Baggs set his teeth, but it needed all his courage to place his hand reverently around the waist of this white-satin-clad apparition. In a moment or two they were dancing, and as he really danced quite well, and his partner wonderfully, he soon lost his nervousness.

"If this is a servants' dance—" he muttered to her.

She laughed softly.

"I've all sorts of things to confess presently, Mr. Baggs," she whispered.

They danced to the last bar of the music. Then she rested her fingers upon his arm. A young man who was passing accosted them.

"Lady Ruth," he protested, "do you know that was my dance? I—"

He stopped short. Baggs felt for a moment that he was sinking through the ground. It was his employer who was surveying him, his expression one of blank amazement.

"God bless my soul!" Lord Robert gasped. "Why, it's Baggs!"

"You know Mr. Baggs?" Lady Ruth murmured sweetly.

"Hang it all!" the young man exclaimed. "Know Mr. Baggs? Well—er—

yes!—well. I suppose I do know you, don't I, Baggs?"

"Certainly, my lord," Baggs replied, a little dizzy.

A third person suddenly intervened. He was an elderly gentleman who smiled very pleasantly at Baggs and drew him to one side.

"My daughter has forgotten to introduce us," he said, "but you and I are going to have a glass of wine together, Mr. Baggs. Christabel, bring Mr.—Mr. Bolster, isn't it?—here," he added, as Christabel and her partner approached. "Mr. Bolster, I am very pleased to meet you. I am Lord Cullerden. We are going to take a glass of wine together. Robert, won't you join us?"

"Delighted, sir," Lord Robert murmured.

The four passed through an open door into a room where many bottles of champagne were set out at a long buffet. Lord Cullerden led the way to a small table, and at a sign from him a footman brought some champagne and four glasses. Mr. Baggs sat on the extreme edge of his chair and secretly pinched himself.

"Mr. Baggs," Lord Cullerden proceeded. "I really feel that I owe you an apology. I have—some people say for my sins—two daughters of whom I am very fond and very proud, but who are, alas! notorious amongst their friends in London for their wild escapades, sometimes conducted, I am sorry to say, without reference to the feelings of others. My daughter Ruth was foolish enough to make a bet with Lord Robert here that she would go to a picture show, or some other place of entertainment, unattended, passing herself off as her own lady's-maid, make acquaintance with some young man to whom she should not be introduced, bring him to her dance to-night and waltz with him. You, Mr. Baggs, I regret to say, are the victim of my daughter's foolish propensity for joking, and you, Mr. Bolster, of Lady Christabel's imitative faculties."

Mr. Baggs sat quite still for a moment. The world seemed falling away around him.

"Then Ruth," he said slowly, "doesn't exist at all? She is Lady Ruth—your daughter?"

"That is so," Lord Cullerden admitted. "It was a foolish trick of hers, but she was fortunate in having met some one like yourself, Mr. Baggs, whom we are pleased to see here to-night. Now finish up your wine and we will go back to the ballroom."

Mr. Baggs and his friend exchanged covert glances. The former rose slowly to his feet.

"I think, sir, if you'll excuse me," he began.

"Don't go on my account, Baggs," Lord Robert intervened pleasantly.

"You know one another?" Lord Cullerden remarked.

"Mr. Baggs does me the honor to be my chauffeur."

"Capital!" Lord Cullerden exclaimed. "What an interesting coincidence!"

Lady Ruth came gliding up to the four men.

"Father, have you quite finished with Mr. Baggs?" she asked. "If so, I want him."

"Quite, you outrageous young woman!" Lord Cullerden said. "I have done my best to apologize for you. You had better see what you can do."

"I have something better than an apology for him," Lady Ruth declared. "Come along, Mr. Baggs."

She laid her fingers once more upon his arm and led him across the ball-room, down the corridor, and along a familiar passage to the little sitting-room. She pushed open the door.

"There," she said. "I have brought you to see your partner for the next dance."

Baggs gave a little exclamation. Lady Ruth had disappeared, closing the door behind her.... Mary rose slowly to her feet. She was wearing a very pretty gown, which Baggs did not recognize in the least, and there was a very becoming flush upon her cheeks. Her eyes were fixed upon him anxiously.

"You are not cross, Harry?" she asked, a little tremulously. "The young lady came down to Thornton Heath this morning. She has made me leave my place. I am to have a position as sewing-maid here. And I think she wants—she wants—"

Baggs took her into his arms. It was astonishing how easily he had stepped out of fairyland.

"I want the same thing, dear," he said.

Autobiographical Writings

My Books and Myself

(from the *New York Times Book Review*, February 26, 1922)

Large numbers of people have noted the fact that in certain of my earlier novels I prophesied wars and world events that actually did come to pass. In *The Mysterious Mr. Sabin* I pictured the South African Boer War seven years before it occurred. In *The Mischief Maker*, *The Great Secret* and *The Maker of History* I based plots upon the German menace and the great war that actually did occur. And in my new novel, *The Great Prince Shan* I have tried to picture the consequences that would result if Great Britain abolished her international secret service, her army and navy, and relied on some form of a League of Nations solely for protection and peace. First of all, it must be understood that what I write is done absolutely from the standpoint of fiction. But I try to put more into the books than romance. Plausibility is one of the things I aim at. Indeed, I think that no novel can stand sturdily upon its own legs unless it possesses sufficient plausibility to make the theme possible in actual life.

The Great Prince Shan will be taken in some quarters as an attack on an association of nations. It is, so far as I am concerned. It is not in broad agreements to disarm that universal accord will be secured. If I were asked for my idea of the finest thing that could happen to promote world peace I should say a treaty of offense and defense between the United States and Great Britain, with France possibly as a third member. The Yellow Peril is much in the air at present but, although my Prince Shan is an example of the Oriental who possesses unlimited power, I hardly think that the Occident has much to fear from the East. Even my Prince declares, "Europe for the Europeans, Asia for us."

I'm afraid that I cannot lay any claim to being an actual prophet of world events. I don't go into trances and neither do I gaze into a crystal and read the future. But I do try to keep abreast of contemporary events and put two and two together. If there is "writing on the wall" I try to see it. I was not the only one who prophesied war with Germany. The signs were there for all to read who took the trouble.

The war has, of course, been a great hindrance as well as a great stimulus to the writer of imaginative fiction. After having written some fourteen novels foretelling exactly what has happened and preaching national service, the actual falling of the thunderbolt was none the less stupefying. I was in Florence in the early Summer of 1914, and what I heard in political circles there brought me home just in time to fetch my daughter from boarding school in Brussels and reach London before the fateful 4th of August. I remember in those first few months I was inclined to take almost seriously the badinage of my friends, who opined that now war with Germany had actually come to pass, there would be nothing left for me to write about. That, however, was only in the first few clouded weeks. Now that the cataclysm is over, although the whole world is trembling with the shock of it, the stage is being set for even more tragic happenings. So long as the world lasts, its secret international history will continue to engage the full activities of the diplomatist and suggest the most fascinating of all material to the writer of fiction. *The Great Prince Shan*, for instance, opens a field for me that I may explore again and again. Future wars will be bound to come. New alliances of nations will fight each other both in battle and in secret diplomatic conspiracies.

It will be noticed that in the majority of my novels I display considerable familiarity with foreign capitals, but, I am sorry to say that outside of Europe, I have never been a great traveller. I have visited more or less frequently most European countries, and I have been to the United States a dozen times, but so far as regards actual influences upon my work, I would be perfectly content to spend the rest of my days in London. It is no gift of mine to impart reality into scenes and events taking place in a country in which I have not actually lived. Half a dozen thoroughfares and squares in London, a handful of restaurants, the people whom one meets in a single morning, are quite sufficient for the production of more and greater stories than I shall ever write. The real centres of interest in the world seem to me to be the places where human beings are gathered together more closely, because in such places the great struggle for existence, whatever shape it may take, must inevitably develop the whole capacity of man and strip him bare to the looker-on, even to nakedness. So the cities for me.

It is in these great cities, too, that men meet and mingle who shape the destinies of nations. There is no more thrilling subject than the activities of these men. The romance of secret diplomacy has enthralled me for years; I have tried to reason out the desires and ambitions of various nations through these secretive individuals. In my novels I have had no particular advance knowledge of world affairs. I have reasoned to myself, "This nation is aiming toward this," and "That nation is aiming toward that;" then I have invited my puppets representing these conflicting ambitions and set them in action. If I have frequently reached conclusions that later developments in the real world have established as true it is because I have reasoned in a logical manner and not through any supernatural insight. After all, the roadways that great nations desire to travel are plain enough.

It was the story first of all that appealed to me and not any burning desire to express political convictions and lay bare great conspiracies. I was 18 years old when my first short story was published, and only 20 when my first novel appeared. I have therefore had more than thirty-five years of story writing, and the first thing which it occurs to me to say about it is that I do not think there can be another profession in the world which maintains its hold upon its disciples to such an extraordinary extent. I do not know how else to account for the fact that at 55 years of age I sit down to commence a new story with exactly the same thrill as at 20. The love of games, sport, of sea and mountains, the call of strange cities, wonderful pictures and unusual people, however dear they may still remain to one, lose something of their first and vital freshness with the passing of the years. Not so the sight of that blank sheet of paper, waiting for the thoughts and pictures which crowd their way into the brain. For every story has about it something new, every slowly unwinding skein of fancy leads along some untrodden paths into virgin fields. The lure of creation never loses its hold. Personally, I cannot account for the fact. Perhaps it springs from the inextinguishable hope that one day there will be born the most wonderful idea that has ever found its way into the brain of a writer of fiction, an idea, dim glimmerings of which have passed through the mind when one is half awake and half dreaming. Every imaginative writer knows those will-o'-the-wisps. With the morning their light has gone, but they do their good work—they keep hope alive.

The measure of success which my stories have attained enables me to write them in the manner I like best. I live in the country, with excellent golf links near at hand. I have no system of work, but, generally speaking, half my time is devoted to actual writing and the other half is divided between exercise and sport, visits to London and travel. My work itself is accomplished with the aid of a secretary, to whom I dictate my stories as they unfold themselves in my mind, in Summer out-of-doors into a shorthand notebook, and in Winter in my study onto a typewriter. Many a time, earlier in life, when I used to write my stories with my own hand, I have found that my ideas would come so much faster than my fingers could work that I have prayed for some more speedy method of transmission. My present method is not only an immense relief to me, but it enables me to turn out far more work than would be possible by any other means.

To end these personal matters where I should have begun, I may say that I was born in London in 1866, married in the United States thirty years ago, and have one daughter. My chief interests outside my work are the theatres, travel, sports and games of all sorts. I enjoy my country life and my club life in London, and the thing I like better than anything else in the world (need it be stated again?) is writing stories.

No, after all, I am not a prophet. I try to be, first of all, a teller of tales, of the sort that will hold the interest of every adventurously minded man and woman, and whether I have succeeded or failed rests entirely with that public which has greeted me so sympathetically for thirty-five years. To them I send my greetings and into their hands I deliver *The Great Prince Shan*, with the warning not to walk—head in the air—through the rocky path of modern intrigue. It is so easy to stumble upon unexpected bayonets.

Address to the Boys of Wyggeston School

(delivered at Wyggeston School, July 27, 1926)

Some forty-three years ago, upon a similar occasion to this, I remember sitting on the end of the balcony in the Temperance Hall, hugging a square of cardboard which represented my sole share in the day's spoils, and hoping fervently that on this, the first day of the holidays, the old jossers upon the platform would get through their speechmaking quickly so that I could get up to the cricket nets before tea. Notwithstanding the bridge of time, my sympathies remain with my modern prototypes, and I can assure them that in a very few minutes—so far as I am concerned—they will be free.

A great writer has told us that the obvious speech and sentiment can always be redeemed by intense sincerity, and therefore I do not hesitate to tell you, simply and from the bottom of my heart, how proud it makes me to be among the first Old Boys of the Wyggeston School to distribute these prizes. I am forced to admit what those of you who have delved into the records of the School doubtless already know, that in the matter of studies and prize-winning, I was not a brilliant success. I managed to make my way into the Sixth Form, and hang on there, but my last three terms were, I regret to say, periods of extremely strained relations between myself and my mathematics master. I remember his taking me on one side a few days before I left, and asking me quite earnestly what I was going to do in life. I told him that I thought my father wished me to go into his business.

"I am very glad to hear," he said, with perfect sincerity, "that you have business to go into, for I am perfectly certain I can think of no walk of life in which you could ever make your own living."

This little aside is for the encouragement of all you others whom I have not had the pleasure of welcoming upon the platform this afternoon.

So you see I have admitted frankly that I was not a highly intelligent lad, but I was at least a hard-working one in ways which few people were aware, and I never remember a more astonished man than Canon Went when, barely a year after I left school, I presented myself in his study with a huge brown paper parcel under my arm, containing some hundreds of pages of manuscript and, as I confessed with some trepidation, a novel!

Whatever surprise Canon West may have felt, he tactfully concealed, and promised to read and give me his opinion upon my effort. I gave him, I think, to understand at the time, that I was content to accept his judgment as final, that if he could see no signs of merit in my outpourings, I would abandon all hopes of story-writing as a profession. In three weeks' time I made my reappearance. Not to be to prolix, Canon Went, although he must have been more conscious than he told me of the many defects of my story, still found certain redeeming qualities there. In a word, he encouraged me to persevere. I departed with my brown paper parcel under my arm, determined that I would persevere, and I have just finished my hundredth novel, and I have written altogether, since those days, some five hundred or so of short stories and articles, which have appeared in magazines and newspapers all over the world. The point which I have come over here to tell you, however, is that, but for the kindly and tactful manner in which I was treated by Canon Went at that time, I should probably—being rather a sensitive lad—have chucked the whole business, and you would have your money invested in paper mills would be receiving small dividends.

One word I have to add whilst on this subject: I have always looked upon Canon Went as being to a certain extent the sponsor of my literary career—if I may be allowed to use so grandiloquent a phrase—and I look upon it as largely owing to his influence that I have gone on through life as I commenced in my younger days, by writing stories of adventure—melodramatic, if you will, in those unbridled times, without humour, perhaps, until humour came—but still books which you lads may read and pass on to your sisters. That debt, too, and I feel it a very great one, I acknowledge in large measure to Canon Went.

I come back, ladies and gentlemen, to a city—a town in my days—changed almost beyond recognition, and I like to think—as I know to be the case—that a great deal of the progress of this place has been due to the wonderful education which has been provided for its citizens, superintended for such an amazing number of years by Canon Went. A life's work, ladies and gentlemen, of which any man in the world might be justly proud. In my days as a schoolboy here, the Wyggeston School, admirable alike in its aims and methods, lacked the great gift of tradition. Tradition is a curious thing. At the Eton and Harrow match this season, I happened to be talking to a dignitary connected with one of these schools, and I ventured upon a remark—bearing in mind the fact that the great majority of the matches had been drawn, and that interest in the result was nearly all over long before the match was concluded—that it was a pity, as it was a two days' match, that the result could not be decided upon the first innings when it was unable to be played out. My acquaintance looked at me reprovingly, and answered me in two words—"Tradition forbids." Well, to my mind, that is the wrong sort of tradition. The tradition worth having is the tradition of progress—the tradition which Old Wyggestonians have established in every quarter of the world, and in the Universities of their own country—the tradition of brilliant scholarship, Empire building, and good and effective work. I have come across Old Wyggestonians in every quarter of the world—in the tomb of Tutankhamen, in New York, enjoying the sunshine of the Riviera, and my last meeting with one—a successful soldier on his way home from India—was on the steamer which brought me back to keep my engagement with you. But, ladies and gentlemen, proud though I think the Wyggeston School should be of its now established traditions, I think that there is nobody of whom it should be prouder than of those citizens who have remained at home, and who have brought their native town to so great a state of prosperity.

Ladies and gentlemen, my first words were addressed to the most important portion of this assembly—the lads—and so shall be my last. I can offer them little of advice, because nearly everything which can be said to the young has been said so much more eloquently, but I will tell them, if they care to hear, two things which I think are amongst the greatest essentials to success in life. The first is concentration—the steady absorbed progress towards the goal which you have set for yourself; the second, not I think so widely recognised, is the capacity to appreciate a certain amount of solitude, a determination not to get too much entangled with the outside life, which these days presses so closely upon one, a capacity to keep zealously to yourself and for yourself, if it be only an hour each day, to live a little with your thoughts instead of all the time in the society of friends, however entertaining and stimulating they may be. One has to learn in this world to be able to stand by oneself, and those of you who can do this, and yet resist the vice of selfishness, who can keep a kindly outlook upon the doings of their neighbours and yet press fervently onwards along their own appointed path are those who will meet with success. We should never forget that life—I talk to you now merely from the secular standpoint—should be a gracious and joyous thing, and not an effort of drudgery.

And now to end on a purely practical note, as some slight measure of return for the benefits I received from the School in the person of my dear friend Canon Went, I make you lads this offer. If any of you on leaving School—take my advice, and don't commence before you do leave—have any idea of taking up a journalistic or literary career, and needs advice at any time upon its practical details—apply to me as an Old Wyggestonian, and I will give you such advice as I can. I may not be the best judge in the world of your possible literary productions, but experience has at least taught me whether there is a marketable value to the manuscripts which I have had sent to me to read. Don't send me too many, send them typewritten, and if my advice doesn't happen to please you, please remember that it will at least be honest.

And now, ladies and gentlemen, there remains nothing more for me to say, except thank you, sir, for the opportunity you have given me, after a life of some vicissitudes, of reviving old associations here, and you, ladies and gentlemen, for your kind reception.

A Collector's Catalog of Oppenheim Works

by Daniel Paul Morrison

The collecting gene: you either have it or you don't. But please don't confuse collecting with hoarding.

Hoarders, the diseased cousins of collectors, have enjoyed some recent fame thanks to reality television. As we've seen, those tortured souls are compelled to acquire and are loath to relinquish. They gather more and more stuff—whatever they can get their hands on—heaping up an ever-growing, disordered pile.

But a pile is no collection.

Because while a hoarder accumulates, a collector cultivates.

Like a nurseryman, the collector plans his garden of delights. He lays out the rows and pulls the weeds. And while he treasures rare fruits and showy flowers, he's quick to thin and prune whatever distracts.

Gardens and collections are more than the sum of their parts. Their caretakers want to understand how the components relate one to another. They are fascinated by the patterns that emerge and the underlying order that is revealed only when all the members of a given genus are assembled.

Typically, a collector begins his collection innocently enough. A single novelty crosses his path, catches his attention, and prompts the question: "I wonder if there are more like that one?"

My Oppenheim collection, perhaps the largest in the world, began with a chance encounter with *Mr. Grex of Monte Carlo.* I picked up a tattered copy in a second-hand store and was captivated by the story. I knew I wanted to read another Oppenheim. And pretty soon, I realized there were lots of Oppenheims and they were rather inexpensive. Perfect fodder for a collection!

At some point, a serious collector begins to develop a catalog of his collection. As Thomas Carlyle, the nineteenth-century Calvinist scourge noted, "A library is not worth anything without a catalog."

And so that's what you have here. This is the third edition of my Oppenheim bibliography. The first was published by Stark House Press in 2004 in *Secrets and Sovereigns: The Uncollected Stories of E. Phillips Oppenheim.* That was followed up in 2009 by a revised bibliography in *The Amazing Judgment/Mr. Laxworthy's Adventures.*

And here we have a third, yet again improved, catalog of the creative output of E. Phillips Oppenheim. This time around, I have added a list of 45 motion pictures written by Oppenheim. I wonder if any other author has had so many films based upon his work.

Items included. From *Expiation* in 1887 to *The Oppenheim Secret Service Omnibus Number One* in 1946, this catalog attempts to gather all the English-language books and films published or released during Oppenheim's lifetime. With the sole exception of a recently-discovered Canadian edition of *The Amazing Judgment,* I have included only first editions from the United Kingdom and the United States.

Sources of information. The foundation of this bibliography is my 500+ volume collection of Oppenheims as well as the 100+ volume collection of Oppenheims at the Firestone Library of Princeton University. Every piece of information gathered from those Oppenheim volumes has been compared with information in six important catalogs: *The English Catalogue* (EC), *The American Catalog* (AC), the *Cumulative Book Index* (CBI), the *National Union Catalog, Pre-1956 Imprints* (NUC), the *British Museum General Catalogue of Printed Books* (BM), and the Online Computer Library Center's WorldCat (OCLC). The EC, AC and CBI are compiled from information provided to the editors by publishers regarding books they have published. The massive 754-volume NUC is a compilation of the entire card catalog of the Library of Congress along with catalogs of a number of other American libraries. The British Museum is the UK equivalent of the Library of Congress, and thus the BM is similar to the NUC. The OCLC is a union catalog of more than 52 million items at more than 9,000 libraries worldwide. It is the twenty-first century digital online version of the NUC.

In cases of conflict between the catalogs and the first editions, this bibliography follows the first editions, recording any differences in the footnotes. For example, *The American Catalog* lists a November 1909 Little, Brown publication date of *Jeanne of the Marshes,* while the first edition bears the date October 1909; this bibliography uses the October 1909 date.

Ellen Wellman and Wray D. Brown (WB) provide important information in their article "Collecting E. Phillips Oppenheim" which appeared in the Summer 1983 issue of *The Private Library.* In compiling this bibliography, I have also consulted the useful list published in Lesley Henderson's *Twentieth Century Crime and Mystery Writers* (CMW). A longish biographical article, bibliography and price list devoted to Oppenheim were published by Graham Andrews (GA) in the March 2007 issue of *Book and Magazine Collectors.*

The article seems largely dependent on Robert Standish's 1957 *The Prince of Storytellers: The Life of E. Phillips Oppenheim* and my 2004 *Secrets and Sovereigns: The Unpublished Stories of E. Phillips Oppenheim*. The price list is flawed—the unfindable *The Amazing Judgment* is listed at the same price as the much more easily found *A Monk of Cruta*.

I use the abbreviation LB to refer to the list of titles published in the back pages of the Little, Brown first edition of *The Man Who Changed His Plea*. The LB list indicates the year of the first publication of a work in book form.

Pirate and Phantom Titles. Not all the books listed in this catalog were published with Oppenheim's knowledge or permission. Those unauthorized books are called "pirate" editions. Just as the People's Republic of China regularly ignores copyright and trademark in our time, the United States was an intellectual property scofflaw in the late nineteenth and early twentieth century. Pirated editions can be distinguished by the fact they do not appear in the LB directory or other catalogs of Oppenheim titles listed in the front of other legitimate Oppenheim books.

While pirated books can exist on your shelf but are missing from the book lists, phantom titles present just the opposite problem: these are books that appear on the book lists, but have never been seen on a shelf.

There are a number of titles which are mentioned in various lists of titles and catalogs, but have never been seen in book form. The best guess about these phantom titles is that they were proposed titles of books soon to come out which either did not come out or had their titles changed. Oppenheim, keep in mind, was a writing machine. Some years he produced five books.

Future Oppenheim Catalogs. Since the publication of the first version of this catalog back in 2004, Oppenheim collectors from around the world have written to me care of Stark House Press with additional bibliographical information. Those tidbits all have been included in this present catalog. In this internet age, we call that "crowdsourcing," and it really is a terrific boon to the endless job of a bibliographer. So please continue to write in with your suggestions!

Novels and Story Collections

Expiation: A Novel of England and our Canadian Dominion. London, J. & R. Maxwell, 1887.

The Peer and the Woman. London, Ward Lock, May 1895; New York, J. A. Taylor, 1892.[1]

A Monk of Cruta. London, Ward Lock, Dec. 1894; New York, Neely, 1894; as *The Tragedy of Andrea,* New York, J. S. Ogilvie, Sept. 1906.[2]

A Daughter of the Marionis. London, Ward and Downey, Sept. 1895; Boston, Little Brown, Sept. 1910; as *To Win the Love He Sought,* New York, D. W. Newton, 1910.[3]

The Modern Prometheus. London, Unwin, Feb. 1896; New York, Neely, 1897.[4]

The World's Great Snare. London, Ward and Downey, 1896; Philadelphia, Lippincott, 1896.[5]

The Mystery of Mr. Bernard Brown. London, Bentley, March 1896; Boston, Little Brown, Sept. 1910; as *The New Tenant,* New York, D. W. Newton, 1910;[3] as *His Father's Crime,* New York, Street and Smith, April 1929.[6]

The Wooing of Fortune. London, Ward and Downey, July 1896.[7]

False Evidence. London, Ward Lock, Dec. 1896; New York, Ward Lock, 1897.

The Postmaster of Market Deighton. London, George Routledge, Sept. 1897.

The Amazing Judgment. London, Downey, Nov. 1897; Toronto, Copp Clark, 1904.[8]

A Daughter of Astrea. Bristol, Arrowsmith, Feb. 1898; New York, D. W. Newton, 1910(?).[9]

As a Man Lives. London, Ward Lock, May 1898; Boston, Little Brown, Dec. 1908; as *The Yellow House,* New York, C. H. Doscher, Dec. 1908.

Mysterious Mr. Sabin. London, Ward Lock, Oct. 1898; Boston, Little Brown, Feb. 1905.

Mr. Marx's Secret. London, Simpkin Marshall, April 1899; Boston, Little Brown, Jan. 1916.[10]

The Man and His Kingdom. London, Ward Lock, April 1899; Philadelphia, Lippincott, 1900.[11]

A Millionaire of Yesterday. London, Ward Lock, July 1900; Philadelphia, Lippincott, July 1900.[12]

The Survivor. London, Ward Lock, Feb. 1901; New York, Brentano's, Dec. 1901.

A Master of Men. London, Methuen, Sept. 1901; as *Enoch Strone,* New York, Dillingham, March 1902.

The Great Awakening. London, Ward Lock, June 1902; as *A Sleeping Memory,* New York, Dillingham, Oct. 1902.[13]

The Traitors. London, Ward Lock, Oct. 1902; New York, Dodd Mead, March 1903.

A Prince of Sinners. London, Ward Lock, March 1903; Boston, Little Brown, May 1903.[14]

The Yellow Crayon. New York, Dodd Mead, Sept. 1903; London, Ward Lock, Oct. 1903.

Anna the Adventuress. London, Ward Lock, March 1904; Boston, Little Brown, May 1904.

The Betrayal. New York, Dodd Mead, Oct. 1904; London, Ward Lock, Aug. 1907.[15]

The Master Mummer. London, Ward Lock, April 1905; Boston, Little Brown, May 1905.

A Maker of History. London, Ward Lock, Oct. 1905; Boston, Little Brown, Jan. 1906.

Mr. Wingrave, Millionaire. London, Ward Lock, March 1906; as *The Malefactor*, Boston, Little Brown, Jan. 1907.

A Lost Leader. London, Ward Lock, Sept. 1906; Boston, Little Brown, Aug. 1907.

The Secret. London, Ward Lock, March 1907; as *The Great Secret*, Boston, Little Brown, Jan. 1908.[16]

The Conspirators. London, Ward Lock Sept. 1907; as *The Avenger,* Boston, Little Brown, May 1908.

The Missioner. London, Ward Lock, April 1908; Boston, Little Brown, Jan. 1909.

The Governors. London, Ward Lock, Sept. 1908; Boston, Little Brown, June 1909.

The Ghosts of Society. (Anthony Partridge) London, Hodder and Stoughton, Sept. 1908; as *The Distributors*, New York, McClure, Nov. 1908.

The Long Arm of Mannister.[†] Boston, Little Brown, Oct. 1908; as *The Long Arm*, London, Ward Lock, Jan. 1909.

Jeanne of the Marshes. London, Ward Lock, May 1909; Boston, Little Brown, Oct. 1909.[17]

The Kingdom of Earth. (as by Anthony Partridge) Boston, Little Brown, May 1909; London, Mills and Boon, Aug. 1909; as *The Black Watcher*, as by E. Phillips Oppenheim, London, Hodder and Stoughton, Sept. 1912.

Passers-By. (as by Anthony Partridge) Boston, Little Brown, Jan. 1910; London, Ward Lock, Feb. 1911; as by E. Phillips Oppenheim, London, Lloyd's, March 1918.

The Illustrious Prince. London, Hodder and Stoughton, April 1910; Boston, Little Brown, May 1910.

The Missing Delora. London, Methuen, Sept. 1910; as *The Lost Ambassador, or, The Search for the Missing Delora*, Boston, Little Brown, Sept. 1910.[18]

Berenice. London, Ward Lock, 1910; Boston, Little Brown, Jan. 1911.[19]

The Golden Web (Anthony Partridge) Boston, Little Brown, Jan. 1911; as E.

Phillips Oppenheim, London, Lloyd's, Nov. 1918; as *The Plunderers*, as E. Phillips Oppenheim, London, Hodder and Stoughton, March 1912.

The Falling Star. London, Hodder and Stoughton, Feb. 1911; as *The Moving Finger*, Boston, Little Brown, May 1911.

Havoc. Boston, Little Brown, Oct. 1911; London, Hodder and Stoughton, Jan. 1912.

The Double Four.[†] London, Cassell, 1911; combined with *Peter Ruff* and published in US as *Peter Ruff and the Double Four*, Boston, Little Brown, Jan. 1912.[20]

For the Queen.[†] London, Ward Lock, Feb. 1912; Boston, Little Brown, June 1913.

Peter Ruff.[†] London, Hodder and Stoughton, April 1912; as *The Adventures of Peter Ruff*, London, Hodder and Stoughton, Aug. 1916; combined with *The Double Four* and published in US as *Peter Ruff and the Double Four*, Boston, Little Brown, Jan. 1912.

Those Other Days.[†] London, Ward Lock, July 1912; Boston, Little Brown, June 1913.

The Court of St. Simon. (as by Anthony Partridge) Boston, Little Brown, Aug. 1912; as *Seeing Life*, as by E. Phillips Oppenheim, London, Lloyds, 1919.[21]

The Lighted Way. Boston, Little Brown, May 1912; London, Hodder and Stoughton, Sept. 1912.

The Tempting of Tavernake. Boston, Little Brown, Oct. 1912; as *The Temptation of Tavernake*, London, Hodder and Stoughton, April 1913.

The Mischief-Maker. Boston, Little Brown, March 1913; London, Hodder and Stoughton, Aug. 1913.

Mr. Laxworthy's Adventures.[†] London, Cassell, May 1913.[22]

The Double Life of Mr. Alfred Burton. Boston, Little Brown, Aug. 1913; London, Methuen, Sept. 1914.[23]

A People's Man. Boston, Little Brown, Jan. 1914; London, Methuen, Jan. 1915.

The Way of These Women. London, Methuen, Feb. 1914; Boston, Little Brown, Sept. 1915.

The Amazing Partnership.[†] London, Cassell, Feb. 1914.[24]

The Vanished Messenger. Boston, Little Brown, Aug. 1914; London, Methuen, Feb. 1916.

Mr. Grex of Monte Carlo. Boston, Little Brown, Jan. 1915; London, Methuen, Sept. 1915.

The Double Traitor. Boston, Little Brown, May 1915; London, Hodder and Stoughton, March 1918.

The Game of Liberty.[†] London, Cassell, June 1915; as *The Amiable Charlatan*, Boston, Little Brown, April 1916.

The Black Box. New York, Grosset and Dunlap, 1915; London, Hodder and Stoughton, Feb. 1917.

Mysteries of the Riviera.[†] London, Cassell, June 1916.

The Kingdom of the Blind. Boston, Little Brown, Oct. 1916; London, Hodder and Stoughton, July 1917.

The Hillman. Boston, Little Brown, Jan. 1917; London, Methuen, Feb. 1917.

The Cinema Murder. Boston, Little Brown, June 1917; as *The Other Romilly*, London, Hodder and Stoughton, July 1918.

The Pawns Count. Boston, Little Brown, March 1918; London, Hodder and Stoughton, Nov. 1918.

The Zeppelin's Passenger. Boston, Little Brown, Sept. 1918; as *Mr. Lessingham Goes Home*, London, Hodder and Stoughton, April 1919.

The Wicked Marquis. London, Hodder and Stoughton, July 1919; Boston, Little Brown, 1919.[25]

The Box with Broken Seals, Boston, Little Brown, Oct. 1919; as *The Strange Case of Mr. Jocelyn Thew*, London, Hodder and Stoughton, Jan. 1920.[26]

The Curious Quest. Boston, Little Brown, 1919; as *The Amazing Quest of Mr. Ernest Bliss*, London, Hodder and Stoughton, Jan. 1924.[27]

The Great Impersonation. Boston, Little Brown, Jan. 1920; London, Hodder and Stoughton, Oct. 1920.

Aaron Rodd, Diviner.[†] London, Hodder and Stoughton, May 1920.[28]

Ambrose Lavendale, Diplomat.[†] London, Hodder and Stoughton, May 1920.

The Honourable Algernon Knox, Detective.[†] London, Hodder and Stoughton, May 1920.

The Devil's Paw. Boston, Little Brown, Sept. 1920; London, Hodder and Stoughton, May 1921.

Jacob's Ladder. Boston, Little Brown, Feb. 1921; London, Hodder and Stoughton, Aug. 1921.

The Profiteers. Boston, Little Brown, June 1921; London, Hodder and Stoughton, Jan. 1922.

Nobody's Man. Boston, Little Brown, Nov. 1921; London, Hodder and Stoughton, Nov. 1922.

The Great Prince Shan. Boston, Little Brown, March 1922; London, Hodder and Stoughton, Aug. 1922.

The Evil Shepherd. Boston, Little Brown, Sept. 1922; London, Hodder and Stoughton, March 1923.

The Seven Conundrums.[†] Boston, Little Brown, Feb. 1923; London, Hodder and Stoughton, Feb. 1924.

The Mystery Road. Boston, Little Brown, May 1923; London, Hodder and Stoughton, Feb. 1924.

The Inevitable Millionaires. London, Hodder and Stoughton, Oct. 1923; Boston, Little Brown, Jan. 1925.

Michael's Evil Deeds.[†] Boston, Little Brown, Nov. 1923; London, Hodder and Stoughton, April 1924.

The Wrath to Come. Boston, Little Brown, April 1924; London, Hodder and Stoughton, April 1925.

The Passionate Quest. London, Hodder and Stoughton, July 1924; Boston, Little Brown, Oct. 1924.

The Terrible Hobby of Sir Joseph Londe, Bart.[†] London, Hodder and Stoughton, Oct. 1924; Boston, Little Brown, Jan. 1927.

Stolen Idols. London, Hodder and Stoughton, July 1925; Boston, Little Brown, May 1925.

The Adventures of Mr. Joseph P. Cray.[†] London, Hodder and Stoughton, Aug. 1925; Boston, Little Brown, 1927.

Gabriel Samara. London, Hodder and Stoughton, Oct. 1925; as *Gabriel Samara, Peacemaker*, Boston, Little Brown, Oct. 1925.

The Golden Beast. Boston, Little Brown, Feb. 1926; London, Hodder and Stoughton, May 1926.

The Little Gentleman from Okehampstead.[†] London, Hodder and Stoughton, Feb. 1926.

Prodigals of Monte Carlo. Boston, Little Brown, June 1926; London, Hodder and Stoughton, Aug. 1926.

Harvey Garrard's Crime. Boston, Little Brown, Oct. 1926; London, Hodder and Stoughton, Feb. 1927.

Madame.[†] London, Hodder and Stoughton, Jan. 1927; as *Madame and Her Twelve Virgins*, Boston, Little Brown, Jan. 1927.

The Channay Syndicate.[†] London, Hodder and Stoughton, Jan. 1927; Boston, Little Brown, Jan. 1927.

Mr. Billingham, the Marquis and Madelon.[†] London, Hodder and Stoughton, March 1927; Boston, Little Brown, May 1929.

Nicholas Goade, Detective.[†] London, Hodder and Stoughton, April 1927; Boston, Little Brown, Nov. 1929.

The Interloper. Boston, Little Brown, April 1927; as *The Ex-Duke*, London, Hodder and Stoughton, Aug. 1927.[29]

Miss Brown of X.Y.O. Boston, Little Brown, Aug. 1927; London, Hodder and Stoughton, Oct. 1927.

The Light Beyond. London, Hodder and Stoughton, Jan. 1928; Boston, Little Brown, Jan. 1928.

The Exploits of Pudgy Pete & Co.[†] London, Hodder and Stoughton, March 1928.

The Fortunate Wayfarer. Boston, Little Brown, May 1928; London, Hodder and Stoughton, Sept. 1928.

Chronicles of Melhampton.[†] London, Hodder and Stoughton, July 1928.

Matorni's Vineyard. Boston, Little Brown, Oct. 1928; London, Hodder and Stoughton, Feb. 1929.

The Treasure House of Martin Hews. Boston, Little Brown, Jan. 1929; London, Hodder and Stoughton, June 1929.

Jennerton & Co.[†] London, Hodder and Stoughton, Jan. 1929.

The Human Chase.[†] London, Hodder and Stoughton, April 1929.

The Glenlitten Murder. Boston, Little Brown, Aug. 1929; London, Hodder and Stoughton, Oct. 1929.

What Happened to Forester.[†] London, Hodder and Stoughton, Dec. 1929; Boston, Little Brown, May 1930.

Blackman's Wood. Story included with Agatha Christie's *The Under Dog* in *Two Thrillers,* London, Readers Library, 1929.

The Million Pound Deposit. Boston, Little Brown, Jan. 1930; London, Hodder and Stoughton, March 1930.

Slane's Long Shots.[†] London, Hodder and Stoughton, July 1930; Boston, Little Brown, Nov. 1930.

The Lion and the Lamb. London, Hodder and Stoughton, Aug. 1930; Boston, Little Brown, Aug. 1930.

E. Phillips Oppenheim: The Prince of Storytellers Tells His Own Story. Boston, Little Brown, 1930(?).[30]

Up the Ladder of Gold. London, Hodder and Stoughton, Jan. 1931; Boston, Little Brown, Jan. 1931.

Inspector Dickins Retires.[†] London, Hodder and Stoughton, Feb. 1931; as *Gangsters' Glory,* Boston, Little Brown, Nov. 1931.

Simple Peter Cradd. London, Hodder and Stoughton, July 1931; Boston, Little Brown, July 1931.

Sinners Beware.[†] London, Hodder and Stoughton, Oct. 1931; Boston, Little Brown, April 1932.

Moran Chambers Smiled. London, Hodder and Stoughton, Jan. 1932; as *The Man from Sing Sing,* Boston, Little Brown, Jan. 1932.

The Ostrekoff Jewels. London, Hodder and Stoughton, Aug. 1932; Boston, Little Brown, Oct. 1932.

Crooks in the Sunshine.[†] London, Hodder and Stoughton, Sept. 1932; Boston, Little Brown, 1933.

Murder at Monte Carlo. Boston, Little Brown, Jan. 1933; London, Hodder and Stoughton, June 1933.

Jeremiah and the Princess. London, Hodder and Stoughton, Jan. 1933; Boston, Little Brown, July 1933.

The Ex-Detective.[†] London, Hodder and Stoughton, Sept. 1933; Boston, Little Brown, Nov. 1933.

The Gallows of Chance. London, Hodder and Stoughton, Jan. 1934; Boston, Little Brown, Jan. 1934.

The Man Without Nerves. Little Brown, May 1934; as *The Bank Manager,* London, Hodder and Stoughton, June 1934.

The Strange Borders of Palace Crescent. Boston, Little Brown, Sept. 1934; London, Hodder and Stoughton, Jan. 1935.

The Spy Paramount. Boston, Little Brown, Jan. 1935; London, Hodder and Stoughton, July 1935.[31]

General Besserley's Puzzle Box.[†] London, Hodder and Stoughton, May 1935; Boston, Little Brown, May 1935.

The Battle of Basinghall Street. Boston, Little Brown, Sept. 1935; London, Hodder and Stoughton, Nov. 1935.

Advice, Limited.[†] London, Hodder and Stoughton, Sept. 1935; Boston, Little Brown, May 1936.[32]

Floating Peril. Boston, Little Brown, Jan. 1936; as *The Bird of Paradise,* London, Hodder and Stoughton, March 1936.

Ask Miss Mott.[†] London, Hodder and Stoughton, May 1936; Boston, Little Brown, May 1937.

The Magnificent Hoax. Boston, Little Brown, July 1936; as *Judy of Bunter's Buildings,* London, Hodder and Stoughton, Sept, 1936.

The Dumb Gods Speak. Boston, Little Brown, Jan. 1937; London, Hodder and Stoughton, Feb. 1937.

Envoy Extraordinary. London, Hodder and Stoughton, July 1937; Boston, Little Brown, July 1937.

Curious Happenings to the Rooke Legatees.[†] London, Hodder and Stoughton, Oct. 1937; Boston, Little Brown, March 1938.

The Mayor on Horseback. Boston, Little Brown, Nov. 1937.

The Colossus of Arcadia. London, Hodder and Stoughton, Jan. 1938; Boston, Little Brown, June 1938.

A Pulpit in the Grill Room.[†] London, Hodder and Stoughton, June 1938; Boston, Little Brown, March 1939.

The Spymaster. Boston, Little Brown, Nov. 1938; London, Hodder and Stoughton, Jan. 1939.

And Still I Cheat the Gallows.[†] London, Hodder and Stoughton, Nov. 1938.[33]

Sir Adam Disappeared. Boston, Little Brown, May 1939; London, Hodder and Stoughton, Sept. 1939.

General Besserley's Second Puzzle Box.[†] London, Hodder and Stoughton, July 1939; Boston, Little Brown, Feb. 1940.

Exit a Dictator. Boston, Little Brown, Aug. 1939; London, Hodder and Stoughton, Nov. 1939.

The Strangers' Gate. Boston, Little Brown, Nov. 1939; London, Hodder and Stoughton, Feb. 1940.

The Milan Grill Room: Further Adventures of Louis, the Manager, and Major Lyson, the Raconteur.[†] London, Hodder and Stoughton, Jan. 1940; Boston, Little Brown, 1941.

The Grassleyes Mystery. London, Hodder and Stoughton, July 1940; Boston, Little Brown, July 1940.

Last Train Out. Boston, Little Brown, Nov. 1940; London, Hodder Stoughton, Feb. 1941.

The Shy Plutocrat. Boston, Little Brown, July 1941; London, Hodder and Stoughton, Nov. 1941.

The Man Who Changed His Plea. London, Hodder and Stoughton, March 1942; Boston, Little Brown, April 1942.

Mr. Mirakel. London, Hodder and Stoughton, June 1943; Boston, Little Brown, Oct. 1943.

Burglars Must Dine. London, Todd Publishing Co., 1943.[34]

The Great Bear. London, Todd Publishing Co., 1943.[35]

The Man Who Thought He Was a Pauper. London, Todd Publishing Co., 1943.[36]

The Hour of Reckoning and The Mayor of Ballydaghan. London, Todd Publishing Co. 1944.[37]

Plays[38]

The Money-Spider. (produced 1908).

The King's Cup. [co-written with H. Dennis Bradley] London and New York, Samuel French, 1913. (produced 1909).

The Gilded Key. (produced 1910).

The Eclipse. [co-written with Fred Thompson] (produced at Garrick Theatre, London, 1919).

Omnibus Volumes

The Oppenheim Omnibus: Forty-One Stories by E. P. O. London, Hodder and Stoughton, March 1931.

The Oppenheim Omnibus: Clowns and Criminals. Boston, Little Brown, April 1931. Contains: *Michael's Evil Deeds; Peter Ruff and the Double Four; Recalled by the Double Four;* and *Jennerton & Co.*[39]

Shudders and Thrills: The Second Oppenheim Omnibus. Boston, Little Brown, July 1932. Contains: *The Evil Shepherd; Ghosts of Society; The Amazing Partnership; The Channay Syndicate;* and *The Human Chase.*

The Secret Service Omnibus: Five Full Length Novels of International Intrigue. London, Hodder and Stoughton, Sept. 1932. Contains: *Miss Brown of X.Y.O.; The Wrath to Come; Matorni's Vineyard; The Great Impersonation;* and *Gabriel Samara.*

Spies and Intrigues: The Oppenheim Secret Service Omnibus. Boston, Little Brown, Oct. 1936. Contains: *The Wrath to Come; The Great Impersonation; Gabriel Samara, Peacemaker;* and *Mr. Billingham, the Marquis and Madelon.*[40]

The Oppenheim Secret Service Omnibus Number One. Boston, Little Brown, May 1946. Contains: *Mysterious Mr. Sabin; A Maker of History;* and *The Illustrious Prince.*

Autobiographical

My Books and Myself. Boston, Little Brown, 1922.[41]

The Quest for Winter Sunshine. [travel] London, Methuen, Nov. 1926; Boston, Little Brown, Jan. 1927.[42]

The Pool of Memory. London, Hodder and Stoughton, Nov. 1941; Boston, Little Brown, Feb. 1942.[43]

Collection edited by Oppenheim

Many Mysteries. Selected by E. Phillips Oppenheim. London, Rich & Cowan, May 1933.

Collections containing works by Oppenheim[44]

My Religion, London, Hutchinson, 1925; New York, Appleton, 1926. Contains an untitled essay by Oppenheim regarding his religious beliefs.

What I Think: A Symposium on Books and Other Things by Famous Writers of To-Day, (ed. H. Greenhough Smith). London, George Newnes, 1927. Oppenheim contributes an essay.

The World's One Hundred Best Short Stories [in Ten Volumes]: Volume Three: Mystery, (ed. Grant Overton). New York, Funk & Wagnalls, 1927. Contains "The Bamboozling of Mr. Gascoigne" from *Mr. Billingham, the Marquis and Madelon.*

World's Great Detective Stories. New York, Walter J. Black, 1928. Contains "Mr. Vincent Cawdor, Commission Agent" from *Peter Ruff and the Double-Four.*

Baffling Detective Stories by Masters of Mystery. New York, Walter J. Black, 1928. Contains "Mr. Vincent Cawdor, Commission Agent" from *Peter Ruff and the Double-Four.* This volume is a reduced version of *World's Greatest Detective Stories.*

Two New Crime Stories. London, Readers Library, 1929; as *Two Thrillers,* London, Daily Express Fiction Library, n.d. Contains *Blackman's Wood* along with Agatha Christie's *The Under Dog.*

The Best English Detective Stories: First Series, (ed. Father Ronald Knox and H. Harrington). New York, Horace Liveright, 1929. Contains "Blackman's Wood" which first appeared in *Two New Crime Stories.*

My Best Detective Story. London, Faber and Faber, 1931. Contains "The Thirteenth Card" from *Slane's Long Shots.*

Best Detective Stories: First Series, (eds. Father Ronald Knox and H. Harrington). London, Faber and Faber, September 1933. Contains "Blackman's Wood" which first appeared in *Two New Crime Stories.* This volume is a reprint of *The Best English Detective Stories: First Series.*

A Century of Spy Stories, (ed. Dennis Wheatley). London, Hutchinson, 1935. Contains "The Phantom Fleet" from *General Besserley's Puzzle Box.*

The Great Book of Thrillers, (ed. H. Douglas Thomson). London, Odhams Press Ltd., 1935. Contains "The Café of Terror" from *Mr. Billingham, the Marquis and Madelon.*

My Best Thriller: A Collection of Stories Chosen by Their Own Authors. London, Faber and Faber, 1937. Contains "The Table Under the Tree" from *Crooks in Sunshine.*

Century of Thrillers: Volume I. New York, President Press, 1937. Contains "The Great Bear" from *Jennerton & Co.*

The Mystery and the Detective: A Collection of Stories (ed. Blanche Colton Williams). New York, Appleton-Century, 1938. Contains "Christian, the Concierge" from *Mr. Billingham, the Marquis and Madelon.*

The Second Century of Detective Stories, (ed. E. C. Bentley). London, Hutchinson, 1938. Contains "The Thirteenth Card" from *Slane's Long Shots.*

My Best Adventure Story. London, Faber and Faber, 1939. Contains "Neap-Tide Madness" from *Slane's Long Shots.*

Beware After Dark! The World's Most Stupendous Tales of Mystery, Horror, Thrills and Terror, (ed. T. Everett Harré). New York, Emerson Books, 1942. Contains "Two Spinsters" from *Nicholas Goade, Detective.*

Wag's Hand-Book: Three Hundred Jokes (by E. R. Skeels). London, Werner Laurie, 1942. Oppenheim contributes the introduction.

Three Famous Spy Novels, (ed. Bennett A. Cerf). New York, Random House, 1942. Contains *The Great Impersonation.*

World's Greatest Detective Stories, The, (ed. Howard Spring). London, Daily Express Publications, 1934. Contains "Seven Boxes of Gold" from *Michael's Evil Deeds.*

The Avon Book of Modern Short Stories. Toronto, New Avon Library, 1943. Contains "The Gambler's Road," a story which never appeared in an Oppenheim volume.

World's Great Spy Stories, (ed. Vincent Starrett). Cleveland, World Publishing Company, September 1944. Contains "The Little Lady from Servia" from *Peter Ruff and the Double-Four.*

Films written by Oppenheim

The Floor Above [The Tragedy of Charlecot Mansions, ss]. B/W silent. Director: James Kirkwood. April 1914. Continental Film Features Corporation.

The Black Box. B/W silent, serial. Director: Otis Turner. March 8, 1915. Universal Film Manufacturing Company. 195 minutes total.[45]

Mr. Grex of Monte Carlo. B/W silent. Director: Frank Reicher. December 2, 1915. Jesse L. Lasky Feature Play Company.

The World's Great Snare. B/W silent. Director: Joseph Kaufman. June 25, 1916. Famous Players Film Company. 50 minutes.

Under Suspicion [The Game of Liberty]. B/W silent. Director: George Loane Tucker. October 2, 1916. London Film Productions.

A Master of Men. B/W silent. Director: Wilfred Noy. 1917. Harma Photoplays.

The Silent Master [The Court of St. Simon]. B/W silent. Director: Léonce Perret. June 1917. Robert Warwick Film.

A Sleeping Memory. B/W silent. Director: George D. Baker. October 15, 1917. Metro Pictures Corporation.

In the Balance [The Hillman]. B/W silent. Director: Paul Scardon. December 17, 1917. Vitagraph Company of America.

The Test of Honor [The Malefactor]. B/W silent. Director: John S. Robertson. April 6, 1919. Famous Players-Lasky Corporation. 50 minutes.[46]

The Double Life of Mr. Alfred Burton. B/W silent. Director: Arthur Rooke. July 1919. Lucky Cat.

The Illustrious Prince. B/W silent. Director: William Worthington. November 2, 1919. Haworth Pictures Corporation. 50 minutes.

The Long Arm of Mannister. B/W silent. Director: Bertram Bracken. November 16, 1919. National Film Corporation of America.

The Cinema Murder. B/W silent. Director: George D. Baker. December 15, 1919. Cosmopolitan Productions.[47]

The Amazing Quest of Mr. Ernest Bliss. B/W silent. Director: Henry Edward. 1920. Hepworth.

The Golden Web. B/W silent. Director: Geoffrey H. Malins. Garrick Pictures. 1920.

Anna the Adventuress. B/W silent. Director: Cecil M. Hepworth. February 1, 1920. Hepworth.

The Amazing Partnership. B/W silent. Director: George Ridgwell. 1921. Stoll Picture Productions.

The Mystery of Bernard Brown. B/W silent. Director: Sinclair Hill. 1921. Stoll Picture Productions.

The Mystery Road. B/W silent. Director: Paul Powell. July 10, 1921. Famous Players-Lasky Corporation. 50 minutes.

Behind Masks [Jeanne of the Marshes]. B/W silent. Director: Frank Reicher. July 25, 1921. Famous Players-Lasky Corporation.

Dangerous Lies. B/W silent. Director: Paul Powell. September 18, 1921. Famous Players-Lasky Corporation. 60 minutes.

Pilgrims of the Night [Passers-by]. B/W silent. Director: Edward Sloman. September 26, 1921. J.L. Frothingham Productions. 60 minutes.

The Great Impersonation. B/W silent. Director: George Melford. October 9, 1921. Famous Players-Lasky Corporation. 70 minutes.

False Evidence. B/W silent. Director: Harold M. Shaw. 1922. Stoll Picture Productions.

Expiation. B/W silent. Director: Sinclair Hill. 1922.

A Lost Leader. 1922.[48]

The Missioner. 1922.[49]

The Conspirators. B/W silent. Director: Sinclair Hill. May 31, 1924.

The Great Prince Shan. B/W silent. Director: A. E. Coleby. 1924. Stoll Picture Productions.

The Hillman. 1924.[50]

The Golden Web. B/W silent. Director: Walter Lang. September 1, 1926. Gotham Productions. 64 minutes.

Monte Carlo [The Prodigals of Monte Carlo]. B/W silent. Director: Louis Mercanton. February 22, 1926. Phocea Film.

The Passionate Quest. B/W silent. Director: J. Stuart Blackton. July 10, 1926. Warner Brothers Pictures. 70 minutes.

The Prince of Tempters [The Ex-Duke]. B/W silent. Director: Lothar Mendes. October 17, 1926. Robert Kane Productions (1926). 80 minutes.

Millionaires [The Inevitable Millionaires]. B/W silent. Director: Herman C. Raymaker. October 1, 1926. Warner Brothers Pictures. 70 minutes.

Sisters of Eve [The Temptation of Tavernake]. B/W silent. Director: Scott Pembroke. September, 1928. Trem Carr Pictures. 60 minutes.

The Lion and the Lamb. B/W mono. Director: George B. Seitz. January 1, 1931. Columbia Pictures Corporation. 75 minutes.

Behind the Masks [Jeanne of the Marshes]. B/W mono. 1931.[51]

Midnight Club [ss]. B/W mono. Directors: Alexander Hall and George Somnes. July 29, 1933. Paramount Pictures. 64 minutes.[52]

Monte Carlo Nights [Numbers of Death, ss]. B/W mono. Director: William Nigh. May 20, 1934. Paul Malvern Productions. 62 minutes.

The Great Impersonation. B/W mono. Director: Alan Crosland. December 9, 1935. Universal Pictures. 68 minutes.

The Amazing Adventure [The Amazing Quest of Ernest Bliss]. B/W mono. Director: Alfred Zeisler. February 27, 1936. Garrett-Klement Pictures. 80 minutes.

Strange Boarders [The Strange Boarders of Palace Crescent]. B/W mono. Director: Herbert Mason. August 1, 1938. Gainsborough Pictures. 74 minutes.

The Great Impersonation. B/W mono. Director: John Rawlins. December 18, 1942. Universal Pictures. 70 minutes.

Biographical and critical works

Overton, Grant. *Cargoes for Crusoes.* Boston, Little Brown, September 1924. Contains a chapter-length literary and biographical appreciation of Oppenheim.

One Hundred Years of Publishing: 1837-1937. Boston, Little Brown, February 1937. This history of the Little, Brown and Company publishers contains a portrait of Oppenheim and a discussion of his relationship with the publishing house.

Standish, Robert. *The Prince of Storytellers: The Life of E. Phillips Oppenheim.* London, Peter Davies, 1957. This is the only book-length biography of Oppenheim.

Adcock, A. St. John. *Gods of Modern Grub Street: Impressions of Contemporary Authors.* New York, Frederick A. Stokes Company, 1923. Profiles and portraits of 32 popular authors, including Oppenheim.

Oppenheim, E. Phillips. "Memoirs of a Mystery Man." In *Maclean's,* December 15, 1935. Oppy tells his own story.

Phantom Titles[53]
A Woman's Blindness
The Lesser Sin
The Vindicator

[†] Short story collection

Footnotes

[1] Taylor edition a paperback and is No. 4 of the Mayflower Library series. It bears an 1892 copyright date but no publication date given. LB indicates that first publication of *The Peer and the Woman* is 1895.

[2] First UK edition of *A Monk of Cruta* was in *Beeton's Christmas Annual*. Many catalogs indicate that *The Tragedy of Andrea* as an alternate title of *A Monk of Cruta*. LB, however, lists it as an entirely separate book. I have not seen a copy of *The Tragedy of Andrea* so I cannot confirm either claim.

[3] *The Yellow House*, *The New Tenant*, and *To Win the Love He Sought* are three pirate titles first published by C. H. Doscher & Co. AC lists Dec. 5, 1908 Doscher publication of *The Yellow House*. Doscher editions of *The New Tenant* and *To Win the Love He Sought* do not appear in AC or CBI, however Donald W. Newton editions of *The New Tenant* and *To Win the Love He Sought* list a 1910 Doscher copyright date. The Newton editions also do not appear in AC or CBI. Subsequently, P. F. Collier & Sons, New York, published a three-volume set containing: vol. 1) *The Yellow House* and an abridged version of *Master of Men*; vol. 2) *The New Tenant* and an abridged version of *A Daughter of Astrea*; and vol. 3) *To Win the Love He Lost* and an abridged version of *The Great Awakening*. CBI lists a Feb. 1915 publication for the three-volume set. This set has gone through at least three separate editions.

[4] Neely edition not listed in AC; Neely edition has 1897 copyright date, but no publication information.

[5] AC lists Lippincott edition; EC does not list 1896 Ward and Downey edition, it appears, however, in Yale University Library catalog. LB lists 1900 as the date of publication.

[6] Title does not appear in NUC, but is listed as to be published March 1929 by Street & Smith, in *The Great Awakening*, (No. 110 The Adventure Library), Street & Smith Corp., New York.

[7] WB notes: "In 1896 the first rare title was presumably published, since it is listed in the English Catalogue of Books for 1890-1897 as *Wooing of Fortune*, 8vo, 304 pp. 8s., Ward and Downey. Some of the *aficionados* do not think that it was ever published but probably rewritten and published under another title. Mr. Nicholas Davies, the English publisher, recently deceased, was the foremost Oppenheim collector and had never heard of a copy."

[8] According to WB, "the King or Queen of hard-to-find Oppenheims is *The Amazing Judgment* (Downey & Co., 1897). There is a copy in the British Museum and a copy appears for sale about every ten years." A copy was

offered for slightly more than US$1,500 in October 2013 by A Book For All Reasons, a dealer in England. OCLC lists six libraries (up from three in 2009) holding copies of this book: Kent State University, University of Missouri at St. Louis, National Library of Scotland, The British Library, Cambridge University Library and the European Register of Microform and Digital Masters (EROMM). The copy at the University of Missouri is a photocopy and the EROMM copy is microform, leaving perhaps four copies in public libraries. The Copp Clark edition, previously uncataloged, came to light as a result of the publication by *The Amazing Judgment/Mr. Laxworthy's Adventures* by Stark House Press in 2009.

[9] AC does not list 1910 Newton edition; it does appear in NUC.

[10] CMW lists 1899 Street and Smith edition, but there is no such listing in AC, OCLC or NUC. CBI lists US first as 1916 Little, Brown.

[11] Little, Brown edition lists first as March 1906.

[12] CMW lists 1899 publication date for Lippincott edition; AC lists 1900 Lippincott publication date with 1899 copyright date.

[13] Dillingham edition lists Oct. 1902 publication date, while AC lists Nov. 1902.

[14] Little, Brown edition lists May 1903 publication date, while AC lists June 1903.

[15] First EC listing is Ward Lock, August 1907; BM lists Ward Lock, 1904, likely a reference to copyright date rather than publication date. AC lists Dodd, October 1, 1904.

[16] LB lists 1908 date of first publication of *The Secret*. AC, however, indicates first publication was by Ward Lock in March 1907.

[17] Little, Brown edition lists Oct. 1909 publication date, while AC lists Nov. 1909.

[18] Little, Brown edition lists Sept. 1910 publication date, while AC lists Oct. 1910.

[19] CMW lists 1907 Little, Brown edition. Little, Brown first edition is Jan. 1911, copyright date is 1907. First listing in EC is Sept. 1911 for a cheap edition, however the Ward Lock first edition bears the date 1910, with no month indicated. Additionally, LB lists first as 1907.

[20] CMW lists 1911 Cassell edition. Earliest EC listing is July 1913 for a popular edition, however there are multiple OCLC listings for a 1911 Cassell edition.

[21] *Seeing Life* listed in BM, but not in EC or NUC.

[22] There may be an alternate title for *Mr. Laxworthy's Adventure*. The Library of Congress catalog lists *The Peculiar Gifts of Mr. John T. Laxworthy* (New York, n.p., 1911) but notes that its copy is missing. This alternate title is not listed in OCLC or the NUC. The twelve Laxworthy stories were serialized under this title in *Popular Magazine* from May 15, 1912 through No-

vember 1, 1912. *Popular Magazine* was a cheap, story magazine and generally not the first-run publisher of serialized stories. It is likely *The Peculiar Gifts of Mr. John T. Laxworthy* appeared earlier in another magazine or newspaper. The LOC item might be a fan-assembled chapbook of clippings. I have such a chapbook containing the whole of *Miss brown of X. Y. O.* assembled from newspaper clippings.

[23] LB lists first as 1913.

[24] Cassell edition bears Feb. 1914 publication date, while EC lists March 1914.

[25] Little, Brown edition does not list month of publication.

[26] EC lists publication date for *The Strange Case of Jocelyn Thew* as January 1920 while the book's title page carries a 1919 date.

[27] OCLC has multiple listings of *The Amazing Quest of Mr. Ernest Bliss* with a 1922 publication date. CMW also lists this date. EC, however, first lists this title with the date Jan. 1924. The Little, Brown edition does not list month of publication.

[28] CMW lists a 1927 Little, Brown edition of *Aaron Rodd, Diviner*, but OCLC and NUC do not list a Little, Brown edition.

[29] CMW mistakenly lists the Little, Brown publication date as 1926. The copyright date of this work is, however, 1926.

[30] This is a 13-page pamphlet.

[31] LB lists 1934 publication date, however, the Little, Brown first edition of *The Spy Paramount* bears a January 1935 publication date.

[32] LB lists 1936 publication date; EC indicates Hodder and Stoughton edition was published September 1935.

[33] LB lists 1939 publication date; EC lists Feb. 1939 publication date; Hodder and Stoughton first edition, however, bears a Nov. 1938 date.

[34] BM claims that this title is 16-page pulp edition of a story from *Ask Miss Mott*. There is, however, no story named "Burglars Must Dine" in *Ask Miss Mott*. Reprinted in 1945 by Vallancey Press of London. Listed in BM.

[35] Title is 16-page pulp edition of a story from *Jennerton & Co.* Reprinted in 1945 by Vallancey Press of London. Listed in BM.

[36] Title is 16-page pulp edition of a story from *General Besserley's Puzzle Box*. Listed in BM.

[37] Title is a 16-page pulp edition of two stories from *A Pulpit in the Grill Room*. Listed in BM. AG claims this title appeared in 1943.

[38] Oppenheim's plays are not listed in AC, EC, NUC, BM or OCLC. I have a copy of *The King's Cup*, but have never seen scripts of the other plays.

[39] The 20 stories listed in this omnibus as the contents *Peter Ruff and the Double-Four* and *Recalled by the Double-Four* are, in fact, equivalent to 21 stories contained in the Little, Brown edition of *Peter Ruff and the Double-Four*. The Little, Brown volume is divided into Book One, containing 10

stories, and Book Two, containing 11 stories. There has never been a book published with the title *Recalled by the Double-Four*. In the *Omnibus* edition, the first two stories of the Little, Brown edition's Book Two are combined to form a single story, thus accounting for the reduction of 21 stories to 20.

[40] EC lists Oct. 1932 publication date; Hodder and Stoughton first edition carries Sept. 1932 publication date.

[41] Pamphlet reprint of an article from *The New York Times Book Review*.

[42] LB lists 1927 publication date; EC lists Nov. 1926 publication of Methuen edition.

[43] EC lists publication date for the Hodder and Stoughton edition as Dec. 1941 while the book itself carries Nov. 1941 publication date.

[44] I have included only those volumes published during Oppenheim's life.

[45] This was a 15-episode serial.

[46] This film, which starred John Barrymore and Constance Binney, is believed to be lost.

[47] This film is believed to be lost.

[48] This title appears in a Wikipedia article, but not in the IMDb index.

[49] This title appears in a Wikipedia article, but not in the IMDb index.

[50] This title appears in a Wikipedia article, but not in the IMDb index.

[51] This title appears in a Wikipedia article, but not in the IMDb index.

[52] I know of no short story or novel by Oppenheim which corresponds to this film. An internet search using Oppenheim's name matched with the names of characters from the film – Colin Grant, Nick Mason, Iris Whitney – turns up no mentions of a book or short story. Thus, it is possible that this film was written by Oppenheim without being adapted from an existing Oppenheim work.

[53] There are a number of titles that appear on various lists that have not been located by even the most advanced Oppenheim collectors. It seems that publishers announced the titles before the books were actually published and subsequently published the books under a different title.

WB writes: "*A Woman's Blindness* is in a panel listing in *Mr. Marx's Secret (Sheffield Weekly Telegraph*, 1899) though no one has found a copy of it. So, too, *The Lesser Sin* is included in a list of Oppenheims in *The Honourable Algernon Knox, Detective* (Hodder & Stoughton, 1920). If *Lesser Sin* was published, where is it now? The Library of Congress had a card for *The Vindicator* but removed it after it was unable to find the book. We think that it was a reprint of *The Avenger* (Little, Brown & Co., 1908)."

Acknowledgments

The Modern Prometheus
London and New York, F.
Tennyson Neely, 1897.

Gambler's Choice
Cosmopolitan, pp. 32-37, 108-112.
(December 1928)

A Fool and His Money
Cosmopolitan, pp. 76-79, 114.
(January 1929)

The Master Cheat of Monte Carlo
Cosmopolitan, pp. 94-100.
(February 1929)

One Night in Nice
Cosmopolitan, pp. 92-98.
(March 1929)

The Big Winner
Cosmopolitan, pp. 100-106.
(April 1929)

The Gambler's Road
Cosmopolitan, pp. 100-106.
(May 1929)

Darton's Great Picture
The Sketch, pp. 439-440.
(April 1, 1896)

The Reformation of Circe
The Sketch, pp. 389-390.
(September 30, 1903)

The Little Grey Lady
Windsor Magazine, pp. 286-292.
(January 1905)

The Two Ambassadors
Windsor Magazine, pp. 535-541.
(March 1905)

The Lord of Crersa
*Boston Daily Globe Sunday
Magazine*, p. 13.
(December 9, 1906)

One Shall be Taken
*Boston Daily Globe Sunday
Magazine*, p. 13.
(December 16, 1906)

A Strange Conspiracy
Boston Globe Sunday Magazine, p.
13.
(January 27, 1907)

The Girl from Manchester
The Strand Magazine, pp. 308-320.
(March 1912)

The Storming of Eve
Good Housekeeping Magazine, pp.
445-453.
(October 1912)

The Road to Liberty
The Strand Magazine, pp. 156-165.
(August 1913)

A Lesson for Mr. Cutts
Redbook Magazine, pp. 678-685.
(August 1914)

And Mr. Baggs was only Twenty-
Three!
Redbook Magazine, pp. 1087-1096.
(April 1916)

My Books and Myself
New York Times Review of Books
(February 26, 1922)

Address to the Boys of Wyggeston
School
(July 27, 1926)

www.ingramcontent.com/pod-product-compliance
Lightning Source LLC
Chambersburg PA
CBHW071723190726
48292CB00003B/579